Copper Sky

Milana Marsenich

Published by Open Books

Copyright © 2017 by Milana Marsenich

Cover image by Murray Foubister

Learn more about the artist at www.flickr.com/photos/mfoubister/

ISBN-10: 0998427462/ISBN-13: 978-0998427461

To those who have passed on, especially my parents,
Milan and Frances Marsenich, for their absolute love,
and my brother, Mark Marsenich, for his courage
and all the gifts that he left with us.

1895
THE WHITE DOG

On the edge of his last dust-filled breath, an old-time miner says that he can forget he has a body attached to the earth. He can drop it somewhere safe and let his spirit soar, like an eagle or an escaped parakeet, flapping away from the poisonous gases, above the Copper Camp. He can look down on the town from the rock outcropping of the East Ridge. The hill is littered with dozens of black metal head frames. Within walking distance, rows of meager houses tuck into each other like honeycomb. They are houses where pasties, polenta, povetica, calzones, and spring rolls bake.

The houses line up next to the Best Brothel in Town and the Polly May Home for Kids. Two fighters rush through the snow for the big match. An armless, toeless man wobbles toward a gin house. In a tiny hovel, a group of Slavs corner up in front of a warm coal stove and pray for a church, the onion-domed type, with an iconostas and a parish hall. At night, under the sweet oppression of smoke residue and smelting dust, the lights of Butte sparkle and shine, more beautiful than the parade's last glitter.

When morning arrives, a vagrant white dog rises for his usual haunts in the sanguine dawn. He wanders through the crimson town, past pawnshops and dress stores, down a snow covered hill, toward the Polly May, where the woman washes the ghostly wet sleep from her cheeks. She wakes early often and he always stops here first. He rubs his head into her palm and licks the dried salt from the back of her hands.

They start their days together this way, before the children return from their fairy dreams and the morning lights blink on. The woman carves a biscuit and spreads it in a pan. The white dog sits still as skinned fur while she drizzles bacon grease onto the slices.

When the children arrive in the kitchen the dog licks their hands, nuzzles his nose into their nightshirts, and carefully leans his weight against theirs. Two little girls come to him before breakfast. They look just like each other, except that one has dark black hair and the other light brown and, under the same light, their eyes shine differently, and one, the dark haired girl, looks off in an odd direction. The look-alike girls are not tall yet and their heads barely reach above his own. The dark girl ruffs up his fur; the light one hugs him.

"Kaly, Anne Marie, wash up for breakfast," the woman tells the girls.

Mornings at the big house are quiet, after the woman's bad dreams, before the sun glares and the noise begins. It is the town's safest hour.

Later, the white dog trots to the Copper Tavern and the Goldmine Cafe for steak bones and stale muffins. Throughout the day he roams, sniffing the men and women who pass him with outstretched hands, or licking the children who paw his ears with colorful mittens. They smell like popcorn or dirt or dried whiskey. Many ignore him, striding quickly with their heads down.

It isn't until darkness slides over this winter day in the Copper Camp of Butte, Montana, that the white dog recedes into the shadows. Late in the night, he hears hissing and crackling near the warehouses on East Platinum Street. Flames blaze the icy streets and snow reflects red like the dawn. Soon the wail of sirens cuts into the dog's ears, and fire wagons and teams of horses charge past him. Men and women run toward the fire. The dog haunches backward, away from the displaced night, a wild lonely sound escaping his throat.

The dog doesn't get far when the woman's hand touches his neck. A line of children, attached to her other hand, snake up the road toward the fire's glow. A tall copper-haired boy, at the snake's head, pulls them closer and closer to the flame. The look-alike girls move nearer the white dog and, as though roped by their delighted cries, the dog follows.

People push toward the burning warehouse like a theater crowd. The wind blows the fire into a nearby hardware building, a building where several boxes of dynamite hide. Something pops and explodes. The dog backs away from the fire. When the woman and children don't move, he wags himself over to them. He grabs the mitten of the little girl with the dark hair and pulls. The snake of children and the woman hold fast, their gazes lashed to the flames.

The fire expands abruptly and another explosion jolts the crowd. It tears at the dog's ears. He tugs harder on the girl's mitten. The woman shrieks like the fire wagons and slips backward into the soot-covered snow. The dog lets go of the girl, runs to the woman, and sinks his teeth into her coat sleeve, trying to pull her up from the frozen ground. The sleeve comes apart in his mouth and falls like dried leaves. He sinks his teeth into the sleeve a second time, near her shoulder. When the tall copper-haired boy swings a stick at the dog, the stick drives the dog back again and again, until he can't reach the woman or the girls.

The dog withdraws into the shadows, away from the

blows. He runs his tongue across his mouth where the stick crashed against his teeth and shrinks away from the sweltering heat of the burning buildings. The boy helps the woman and the children cross the street, away from the fire.

When the fire reaches the bulk of the dynamite the final explosion rips a hole in the night. Much of the crowd disappears and for a brief moment the sky rains blood, speckling the snow and the dog's white paws with flesh. Several fingers and a foot drop beside him, silent as the mountain or a tree rustling in a brief wind.

Across the street, the look-alike girls stand with their heads tilted in his direction. The two girls stand between the woman and the boy with the stick. The light-haired girl puts her hand up, palm out, and rocks it back and forth, waving at him. The dark girl stands like stone, one hand clasping her mouth, the other hand holding her head, as if to stop a pain. Beside her in the snow lies a disembodied arm. Smoke soon fills the gap of street between the dog and the girls. The look-alike girls, the woman, and the tall copper-haired boy disappear into the fragmented night, like the wild ghostly crowd.

WINTER 1917
1
THE OLD HOUSE

Kaly Shane stood across the street from the Polly May, holding the hem of her red satin dress above the snow, and watched the old house where Miss Anderson cared for orphaned children. God knew Butte had enough of them. Constant mine disasters snatched fathers, and tuberculosis or rampant flus took young mothers down the glory road every day. Miss Anderson harnessed the motherless children, every last one that the house would hold, and tried to keep them safe.

Kaly knew. She grew up in the Polly May. Grew up. Grew scared. Grew wild. Joined the working girls in the red light district and fostered bad luck. As every working girl had a bad habit, Kaly had hers. She ran from love, and it had been no easy feat since finding herself pregnant. On this cold winter day she rehearsed the words she'd say to Miss Anderson: Will you raise this child? A child born where luck rises up out of the ground in shimmering copper will need one good parent. Will you be hers?

Across the street, two wide-eyed windows looked out

from the second floor dormer of the Polly May. The roof of the dormer peaked between two chimneys on either side of the house. Decorative ironwork tiptoed across the roof, from one stack of bricks to the other. The porch below separated two bay windows. An open slat fence, turning gray in the falling snow, protected the house like an old friend.

Beth, Kaly's best friend, said that the houses in Butte were filled with ghosts. The wise ones chose a house with plenty of rooms and windows that opened. A good ghost could feel nearly alive on a moonless night, with the wind blowing curtains through an open window. A good ghost could move freely on that wind from room to room, lodging among the more substantial boarders.

Kaly had her own ghosts and she thought of them as she crossed the street to the Polly May. Tommy, Bert Brown, her lovely sister, Anne Marie, a cold winter day when they were ten. Icy flakes landed in her eyelashes. She melted them by breathing deeply, warming the air in her aching lungs, like she had done as a child, and blowing the warmed air up one side of her face and then the other, toward her brown curls. The old rhythm calmed her.

Brick surrounded the carved wooden door of her old home. Past the building and further up the northern slope, she saw the neighborhood houses. Beyond their roofs the head frames of the Speculator and Granite Mountain mines loomed over the city. The mine whistles blew, announcing the noon hour. A stray dog howled. The snowstorm had already layered the porch with a full foot of white fluff and Kaly turned toward the Flats and sat down in the cushion of it. She pulled the warm wool coat under her like a blanket.

She'd spent her life tripping from one trouble to the next and now, with her belly swelling toward the inevitable, and her lungs buzzing with fever, she counted her hours in time to the siren sound of the mining whistles. The burrowed tunnels produced a robust supply of copper for bullets for the war. When she was young, Kaly memorized the names of several of the copper mines as a chant to calm herself.

Wake Up Jim, Neversweat, Mountain Con, Orphan Girl.

She knew men who worked and died in all of them. They were her best customers, mostly drunk on whiskey, tired from a shift, occasionally jovial or kind. Kaly managed them all with a professional distance. Lately, though, something like love or anger, a sense of betrayal or grief, burst through without warning and she'd find herself crying in some John's arms. Later she'd be bitter or sullen, feeling like someone had slipped her a mickey.

The funny thing was that her business thrived. The men seemed to enjoy comforting her as much as having sex, sometimes more. They brushed the hair out of her face and apologized. One man left two dollars on the nightstand and he hadn't even loosened his pants. He'd simply wet his palms on her tears, brushing the tiny droplets aside, a deep sigh pressing out from his lips. She'd felt her stomach twist and lurch into her throat that day, and the dreaded heat had sauntered up her belly, and her lungs hurt. She found herself running toward the Flats just to be alone, her gaze fixed on the beautiful snow-filled peaks of the Highland Mountains.

Kaly stood up and turned toward the door of the old house. Heat swept up her back and played at her stomach, causing it to twist and turn. The heat spread a bitter taste up her throat and into her mouth, the pure wave of it heightening the heaviness in her breasts. She climbed the stairs, expending a mountainous effort to reach the metal knob at the grand entrance. She picked the metal knob up and dropped it down, knocking on the wooden door of her youth.

The winter that she and Anne Marie turned ten, five years after the warehouse fire, the Rocky Mountains brought twenty inches of snow in four hours. The two girls emptied their dresser drawers, piling on leggings, undershirts, blouses and sweaters, making it impossible to bend their arms.

"Kay, will you help me?" Anne Marie moaned from under the deluge of clothes, swiping the air beyond her chest. "I can't reach my buttons."

Kaly pushed her arms straight in front of her, pressed them together like scissors and fastened Anne Marie's coat. "Now me, my turn," she said.

Anne Marie smiled and waddled a few steps away. "First," she said, "say the magic word."

Kaly thought about it. "Mother?"

Anne Marie squished up her nose. "No. Try again."

"Blanket?"

"Not that one."

"Food."

"More magic than that."

"Come on, Annie. Button my coat for me. I feel like a winter whale."

"Winter. That's it. Winter." Anne Marie clapped and scissored her arms in the same way that Kaly had.

Together they walked past Bert Brown, lurking in the hallway, and stepped outside into the burning cold. Icicles formed on their upper lips. Kaly felt her heart beat fast. Her face tingled with frozen warmth and her arms felt strong. Tree branches lifted up, sharp and bright, cradling the welcomed snow, offering passage to the secret world behind their trunks. Kaly and Anne Marie walked into that secret world. They stepped off of a frazzled edge, crisp white innocents, and disappeared into the frail deep snow.

Kaly shoved the memory off. Right now she needed to decide what to do about the baby. The door opened and Coral Anderson stood in its abandoned frame. Her hazel eyes widened. Her dark hair had turned perfectly white. The white curls hung in neat terraces away from her face. Her ruddy face drooped tiredly, as if it had gathered a certain unwelcome wisdom.

"The voiceless girl has returned to her queendom,"

Miss Anderson said.

Kaly shuddered. "You're angry still."

"What would I have to be mad about? I spent years asking you about that day. All I got was crumbs. And only when you wanted something."

Kaly looked at the sky and then at her feet. "I was ten years old. I had no say in what happened then. I'm hoping to make peace between us."

"Was it too much to ask for a brief visit, or a letter even? No one expected you to stand in and fill Annie's place. We expected you to cry, ask questions. But you didn't cry. You said nothing. And then you left without a goodbye."

"I need your help now," Kaly said.

"Of course." Miss Anderson looked beyond Kaly, toward the flats. "I did what I could in those years and you shunned me like a consumptive on his last breath. I hear from others you chatter up a storm all over town."

A burst of giggles trickled down the hall. "Go wash up for a snack," Miss Anderson said to a small group of children just beyond the entryway. "I don't know how I could possibly help you. Nor what good it would do. You're living a dangerous life. A dangerous life is a short life."

Kaly looked at the room in front of her. A red Oriental carpet covered the dark mahogany floor. A wrought iron bench sat across from a closet lined with small coats and tiny snow boots. Photos of young children hung on the wall above the bench. Roughly one third of the photos had tiny golden crosses painted in the lower left-hand corners, indicating the child's death. Miss Anderson always said she did the best she could and some children were just luckier than others. Beth would say that the unlucky ones crowded the second floor dormer.

Kaly located Anne Marie's picture on the wall. She saw the small curves in her cheeks, the soft line of her nose, her deep brown eyes, bangs clipped perfectly across her eyebrows, a white stone cross at her neck, the tiny sparkle of gold in the photo's corner. Next to Anne Marie's picture was her own. She had soft green eyes, brown curly hair, a matching white cross hanging from her neck. She looked like a simpler, lighter version of Anne Marie.

Two photos down from Kaly's, Bert Brown's red hair had faded to tan. Further yet, he sat in Miss Anderson's lap, younger but no happier. Next to Bert's young picture, Tommy Monroe stared out at her, his dark hair combed off of his forehead, a shadow falling across one half of his face.

Kaly's skin burned. She felt a tingling in her cheeks and her eyes watered. She ran her fingers through her hair, messing the curls. She had no business being here, asking Miss Anderson for help. The time for help was gone and she should go too. Being here wouldn't bring her lovely sister back, wouldn't tell Tommy he'd be a father soon, would not wash the black out of Bert's icy smile.

"I shouldn't have bothered you," she said.

"You've been more bother than any other child that came through these doors. Others acted worse. But I didn't expect anything from them." Miss Anderson's voice softened. "Give me your coat. We'll try this again."

She hung Kaly's coat on a hook in the hallway closet. She paused briefly, then turned and hurried into the kitchen, her gray skirt flying up and behind her as if caught in its own windstorm.

Kaly lowered herself slowly onto the wrought iron bench. From the entryway she heard the familiar moan of the bathroom pipes and the wood in the kitchen stove cracking. She heard the creaking stairs where some child sat drawing. The muffled cry of another child came from one of the lower rooms. Kaly had learned to pay attention in these rooms, learned to distinguish a cry of anger from a cry of fear, learned the baleful sounds of loneliness and that of bad company. She unlaced her boots and placed them in line where they towered over the tiny snow boots.

"Julian, fix some cheese and bread. The Polly May has a guest. And we do our best to treat guests, even the most unexpected ones, with manners."

Kaly laughed, thinking Miss Anderson must have just downed a glass of gin. She heard the age in Miss Anderson's voice and realized that she must've been very young when she first took Kaly and her sister in as infants.

Miss Anderson had named the Old House after the aunt who raised her and who, on her death-bed, left both the house and a small inheritance to her. Kaly asked one time why her own mother didn't raise her. Miss Anderson sent Kaly out to collect dropped coal from train cars. It was a long walk and the coal heavy and Kaly never asked about Miss Anderson's mother again.

"I need to speak with you alone," Kaly said from the hallway.

"Wonderful. Come back in another ten years. Julian. Let George help. George. Stop being bossy." Miss Anderson's voice sprung out from the kitchen, where the two boys fought over who would slice the cheese and bread.

Kaly arrived in the kitchen as the larger boy leered at the smaller one. Dirty dishes filled the sink. A hearty bottle of gin stood alone on the counter.

"Stop looking so smug, Julian," Miss Anderson said. The leer quickly transferred to George's face. "Contain yourself, George. You didn't win the World Series."

George flushed red. He turned and glared at Kaly. Dark brown hair fell into his eyes and he reminded her of Tommy Monroe. A girl, about six years old, huddled in the kitchen corner. Kaly had sat huddled in that very corner watching Tommy and Bert Brown fight over a meat cleaver.

Julian waved the knife in front of George who immediately lunged into Julian, grabbing for the knife. Miss Anderson dove between the boys and restrained George in a bear hug.

"Enough," Miss Anderson said. George flailed in her grip. She twisted him and pasted his back to her front. He kicked at her and she pulled him to the floor. He flung his head back, nearly cracking his skull on her dentures. She dropped her shoulder into the back of his head and pinned his chin to his chest. As if on some secret cue, George went limp in her arms. The girl in the corner made a break for the hallway.

"I wondered how long it would take you." At first Kaly thought that Miss Anderson spoke to George. "To come asking questions. It's the nightmares. You still have them, don't you?"

"I need your help," Kaly said again. The reluctant words climbed up over the cliffs in her throat. She remembered how she favored her silence, how good it was to stone up her mouth and turn her voice inward and downward, so that only she could feel its soft quiver.

"Go to Tommy. He might console you. He'll help," Miss Anderson said when she set George free. "He's the one who can answer questions about that day. He may not remember everything, but enough to put your dreams to rest."

"Tommy?" She sat down at the kitchen table. "He went to The Montana State Reform School because of Annie."

"Yes, as I recall because you blamed him for Annie's death."

"He won't like me bringing it up."

"He won't mind. He didn't fair that badly. Talk to him. You can't run forever. Look at your life. Entertaining men for what, a few dollars."

"Will you help me or not?"

The woman tossed her head impatiently. "How convenient for you to just forget it all. No sister, no death, no pain. So long as you realize you're dying too. Just a slower death."

Kaly narrowed her eyes. "If you would've been watching us that day instead of drinking, Annie would be here now."

"First you blame Tommy and now me. Who is really to blame? You should look into your own heart. Do you think keeping it all locked up inside helps?"

"I need help with something else," Kaly murmured. She knew Miss Anderson was right. It wasn't Miss Anderson's fault that Annie died. A sudden pain flared in her head. Her left eye twitched. It wasn't Miss Anderson's fault. It was Kaly's. She should've protected her sister.

Her head was spinning from the boys' fight and the smoky room. The smell reminded her of that day when they returned from the warehouse fire, when she and Anne Marie were five. Before Tommy came to live with them. Before things changed.

When they got home from the fire, Anne Marie had a distant look in her eyes. Miss Anderson had put her to bed, explaining that Anne Marie had been pelted by splintered wood from the explosion. But Kaly knew that it wasn't wood that had hit her sister. She'd seen what had flown into Anne Marie, and she'd looked away, into the crowd, where people ran in every direction. When Kaly looked back, she saw the woman's arm on the ground, still covered by a lacey sleeve, a silver bracelet circling the wrist, the index finger pointing toward the fire.

Now, all these years later, Kaly sat gazing out the kitchen window at the snowy back yard. Once more she felt the old urge to walk into that blue wave of snow, to bury herself under feathered flakes, to lie as still as a fallen bird, to be pulled into a silky white world where the crocus bloom and Anne Marie lives, where a baby crawls to her mother's arms, and a happy Kaly picks up her child and carefully wipes the dirt from her mouth.

A wave of sadness washed over Kaly. She wanted a mother, if only for a moment. She wanted someone to hold her, to wash her face and braid her hair. She loosened her fists and dropped her shoulders. It was no good. Why hope? Why should she remember the fire, or even her sister's fatal day five years later? Miss Anderson wouldn't be there to catch her when she fell. No one had ever been there when she needed them.

But self-pity hadn't exactly been a friend either.

Kaly fixed her green eyes on the door and pressed her red dress against her thighs. Her brown curls had straightened with the snow and she felt the moist hairs on her cheeks. The sweltering heat of the Polly May did nothing to soften the confused desire in her heart: *She* could raise the child.

No. She was a whore and—half the town would agree on this—she had no business raising a child. She had to ask Miss Anderson to do it.

"I have a secret," she told the matron.

"Pray tell then. I'm all ears."

"I'm pregnant. I'd like you to take the baby when she's born."

"Ninety thousand people in town and you choose me." Miss Anderson sipped her tea. "Why me?"

"It was a mistake coming here today."

"The father?"

Kaly shook her head, her brown hair brushing her ears. Her stomach turned again and she bit her lip to control the sick feeling. She glanced toward the pictures that hid in the hallway, as if able to see them through the wall. As if she could see Tommy's grin. Tommy's earnest eyes. She could have told Miss Anderson that it was his child, but not here, not now—she suddenly understood—not before she told Tommy.

He'd moved into the big house the day after the warehouse fire. Both of his parents had been killed in the explosions. He was nine and had immediately zeroed in on Anne Marie, gluing himself to her side as if he were her twin instead of Kaly. That first day, with strangers in the halls and the bitter stench of burned flesh still wafting down from the hill, Tommy had lured five-year-old Anne Marie into his room with card games and magic tricks.

Kaly heard their laughter behind the door and knocked hard.

Suddenly the room became very quiet.

She knocked again.

A giggle rose and was stifled.

Bert Brown sat on the steps shuffling a deck of cards into his large palms. He shook his head and smirked.

Kaly ignored him and focused on her sister and Tommy Monroe.

She pleaded with them to let her in. "You're not allowed behind closed doors," she'd reminded them.

When no one answered, Kaly did the unthinkable. She told on her sister. Both of them got a whipping and Anne Marie spent the night in their room without dinner. Kaly snuck a muffin into her pocket and brought it to her sister before bedtime, but Anne Marie wouldn't look at her. In the morning the muffin sat untouched on the nightstand.

Miss Anderson followed Kaly's glance toward the photos. She lifted her eyebrows. A smile almost crossed her lips. "Bert?"

Kaly shook her head no.

"Must be Tommy then. Are you sure you're expecting?"

"I know."

"Does he know?"

Kaly bit her lip hard and said nothing.

"You need to see a doctor."

Exhaustion overcame her. She wanted to curl up in her old bed at the top of the stairs and just sleep. She wanted something, one thing, anything, to be easy.

As if to deny her, George darted from the sink and stabbed at Julian with the bread knife, catching him in the shoulder with the serrated edge. He pulled it back as if to stab again.

Miss Anderson, quick on her feet, blocked the thrust and pinned him in another hold. Blood drenched Julian's shirtsleeve. Something like surprise and satisfaction crossed his face just before he screamed and bursts into sobs.

The heat rose in Kaly again, searing her belly and throat. She raced for the bathroom.

Memories flooded her. She and Anne Marie had gotten separated in the storm. Kaly had lost her way in the snow. When she finally made it back to the big house, Anne Marie lay motionless in the snow, her dark hair fanned across the drift, her blue hands clenched to her chest. Her eyes stared and looked nowhere at the same time. Tommy leaned over her, his dark hair falling across his forehead, his trousers frozen tunnels for his legs, an astonished look in his eyes.

Kaly had shaken Anne Marie to wake her up. She knew she had to get her sister into bed. Miss Anderson would warm some broth for her.

"Come on, Annie," Kaly begged. "Come on. Quit playing around! It's winter! Winter," she said, trying the magic word, trying to lift her sister, falling forward with the weight.

When she couldn't wake her, Kaly lunged into Tommy, flailing her padded useless arms at him, until he pinned her in a hold similar to the one that Coral Anderson had just used to restrain George.

"You wait here," Tommy said when she'd calmed down. "I'll get Miss Anderson."

Kaly had waited, willing Anne Marie to get up and walk inside. Willing her sister with all her might, to finish the dishes, or empty the garbage, or make one more yarn doll.

But Anne Marie didn't get up. Didn't blink or yawn or pull away. She didn't move.

Kaly'd felt herself falling into a dark endless pit. She searched the vast black chasm for her sister. The empty air crushed her chest, and she couldn't breathe. Fear singed her legs and arms, severed her head from her torso. Just before she disintegrated, she reached out for help and caught, not Miss Anderson's hand, but Tommy Monroe's, and for the first time, allowed herself to be hauled up into the arms of wrong company.

Wake Up Jim, Neversweat, Mountain Con, Orphan Girl, Orphan Girl.

Anne Marie wasn't the only dead one. Another girl had died at the Polly May. An older child—Kaly never knew who—wrestled the girl to the ground, smothering the child in cold daylight. Other youngsters had been stabbed by knives and sticks. Cheeks had been cut wide open by rocks flung hard from a four-year-old's hand.

No matter how Miss Anderson tried, she couldn't protect the children. They were too far gone, too wounded. There was too little of her to pass around, so the children learned to count only on themselves.

Kaly emerged from the bathroom.

Coral Anderson thrust George into her arms. In a motion Kaly fell with the boy to the floor and locked him in her grip, the resistance gone out of him. She looked at Julian. His chin was lax. The flat edge of his face betrayed nothing. His shirt was soaked in blood.

"Stop feeling sorry for him. They're all liars and thieves," Miss Anderson said, as she disappeared into the bathroom with Julian.

Holding George, who was quiet now, was like holding a snowflake. Light, invisible and then gone, like the ghosts tucked into the second floor dormer, both haunted and haunting. He eased into her, resting his back against her chest.

She sat completely still, afraid to move. She imagined George one day, maybe a year or two from now, taking a knife, or a pillow, or an open palm and hurting the child that grew in her belly. Demanding that someone look, listen. Demanding that someone love him.

She pulled him close and held him tight and thought of her own mother. The thought hurt all over, like when the flu first sets in or when the whiskey is bad. Where was her mother? Where had she been when her girls needed protection and comfort?

Miss Anderson returned and sent the boys outside. They wore coats and hats. Julian wore gloves but George played bare-fisted.

"I'll help you," Miss Anderson said, pulling a hairpin from her curls and repositioning it. A practiced tick to regain composure. "You can have your old room back and help me with the kids. Raise the child here. Much safer than the cribs."

"I have no money."

"I'll watch the child while you work."

"Work?" Kaly lifted an eyebrow.

Miss Anderson shook her head. "A child's mother has no place on the street."

Kaly laughed a short, cynical laugh. She palmed the white stone cross at her throat. The necklace hung on a worn leather lace. Their mother had given the matching crosses to Kaly and Anne Marie when she left them as infants in Miss Anderson's care. Her good-bye. "A mother. What happened to our mother? Our parents? Where are they?"

"I'm your parent."

"No, my real mother. Who was she?"

"It's no good. Let sleeping dogs lie."

"Is she alive?"

Miss Anderson shook her head. "My home for you and your child. That's it."

The mine whistle sounded again, followed by a dog's long howl. But this time it was several whistles together, indicating an accident. Kaly straightened, wondering what had happened. A landslide? A fire? How many deaths? She would find out who'd died later, when she joined the girls on the line. The day shift would finish in a few hours and the taverns would bustle with miners. Dinners would be pulled from ovens. People would talk about the loss and be glad if it wasn't one of their own.

The young girl, who'd fled earlier, peered through the

kitchen door, her hair in tangles. Miss Anderson waved the girl in. She sat at the table and pulled the girl toward her affectionately.

Kaly had no memories of the matron ever showing affection like that to her or Annie—or to any of them. Maybe Miss Anderson had changed and the Polly May was a better place now.

"Can I have some cheese and bread?" the girl asked, running dirty fingers across the white cuff of Miss Anderson's ironed sleeve.

"Sure sweetheart." The woman popped a bit of cheese into the girl's mouth. Miss Anderson remained cool as the frosted windows as she fed the girl, as if she was an old pro at holding children. As if she hadn't slapped a dozen dirty little hands away from her stiff blouses.

Through the kitchen window, Kaly watched Julian toss a snowball with his uninjured arm. George ducked, laughed, and fell into the white powder. He rolled over and over, right onto the paws of a gray wolf-like dog that was curled at the edge of the yard. Kaly saw it in slow motion, as if in a dream: the great knife-like teeth sinking into George's shoulder; the red blood soaking his coat the same way blood had soaked Julian's shirt sleeve, a mining town debt paid, justice served.

But the dog didn't bite George's shoulder. Instead the big dog rolled with the boy, jumped out of the deep snow, and flew into the air. The animal landed with his legs stretched out in front of him, hind end in the air and large tail wagging. He licked George's laughing face.

George playfully caught the dog's ears in his palms. He pulled the dog close, nuzzled his forehead against the thick fur. Then they were up and running again, both boys, with the wolf dog chasing them, shifting this way and that, rolling in the snow, landing on their feet only to trip and stand again and again. They raced across the very land where Kaly had found Anne Marie frozen. Kaly saw her sister in the golden sun flickering in the branches above them.

"Move in here," Miss Anderson was saying. "You know what it's like to grow up without a mother. You can do what your own mother couldn't. It just takes a little courage."

Kaly shook her head. No. She would not move in. She would not be what her own parents weren't. Kind. Loving. There. She put on her coat and boots and left. Outside, the odd beauty of her town—with its massive head frames and dusty sky—crushed down on her, igniting the ache in her lungs, just above the baby's tiny heart.

2
THE SILVER BOW BAKERY

Marika Lailich put her ear to the door of the washroom. Something was wrong. Papa was dying. This much she knew but her parents didn't talk about Papa's consumption. Their conversation centered on a less tragic and more loathsome subject. They wanted her to marry Michael Jovich, a man she had never met. They wanted her to marry a man she only knew by sight and, as she recalled, the sight was not too pretty.

"Is he kind?" Mama asked.

"He's a strong thinker, a good union man," Papa said. "He works hard for the miners. Without people like him, the Speculator would be as treacherous as the other mines."

"It's dangerous work then," Mama said.

Marika stood in the main room of their small house. Her parents had shut the rough wooden door to the washroom for a reason, but that didn't stop her from eavesdropping. The fire in the wood stove roared and cracked and the heat roasted her back and steamed the room. Marika wiped her forehead with the palm of her hand. She pushed her long black hair away from her face.

Feeling dizzy from the heat and the idea of marriage, her mind raged.

Why didn't Mama stop Papa?

She was brave enough. She had dark brown eyes, sharp cheekbones and strong arms. Even behind the thick wood, Marika—who was the spitting image of her mother—heard her mother's strength as she scrubbed the clothes on the washboard.

"He's dedicated, if that's what you mean," Papa said.

"Stojan. Look at me." Marika heard Mama's hands go quiet. "Will he be good to our Marika? Will he take care of her?"

"He's a good man, Milla. He comes from a good family."

"If you think it best, talk to his father."

Papa coughed and hacked. Marika could hear the mucus in his throat. After that she heard nothing but the sound of water dripping down the washboard, and the pounding of her own heart.

Marko entered through the front door carrying an armload of wood. "What are you doing?" He asked.

"Papa wants to marry me off," Marika whispered to her brother.

"Papa means well. With his sickness he just can't work enough to support us any more." Marko dropped the wood in a metal box near the stove. He wore bib overalls and a winter coat. His black bushy hair framed his face, like Papa's.

"It's wrong to even talk about marrying me off, without asking what I think, what I feel." Although she wanted to scream she kept her voice low. "I'm seventeen. He should talk to me."

"You shouldn't be so surprised," Marko said, feeding the fire.

"Stop. It's hot enough in here."

"You know he always does what he thinks is best."

"This is the mining frontier. Women have rights! Just

last week Grace Hedges won a contested divorce from Henry. And he's a shift boss at the Gray Rock."

"You don't understand Papa."

"No, brother, Papa doesn't understand me," she said. "He doesn't want to. The consumption affects his lungs not his brain."

"Just meet Michael. For Papa."

"No."

But Marko was right. Marika should meet Michael for Papa. Papa was right too. She should be a good daughter and do as he said. She'd been raised to do as Papa said, even when he taught her to think for herself.

A thought hit her and her stomach dropped. "Wait a minute, Marko. How did you know he wants me to marry Michael?"

"I don't know. Lucky guess."

"He told you. He talked to your about it!" She was furious. Her life and she was the last to know. In fact, Papa hadn't even talked to her about it yet!

Marika felt sick and had to get out of that heat. It was all too much. She gathered her long hair into a tight bun at the back of her neck and secured it neatly under a flowered scarf.

She pulled the heavy blue curtain aside to reveal four sleeping cots. Behind the curtain she put leggings on under her simple brown skirt. The heavy cotton draped down to her ankles. The boots she wore were one size too large for her. She hoped she'd grow into them.

Rummaging through a large trunk, she moved her medicine bag and found the shawl Baba, her grandmother, had crocheted as a gift before they left Montenegro. She cocooned it tightly around her shoulders and the warmth of it felt good. At least she could still count on Baba, even if she was thousands of miles away in another country. Baba would understand her.

Her grandmother was a healer in their small mountain village. Before Marika left the Balkans, Baba taught her a love for medicinal plants and caring for the ill. Baba taught her to pray for the sick, to hold the image of their healthy bones in her mind as she ministered their diseases with milk thistle and frankincense.

Baba taught her that the lungs hold grief, the liver anger and the bladder fear. She taught Marika to read the body as well as the medical books, to look at the person's eyes and tongue, to feel the pulse in their wrists and to check their breath. Even as a young girl Marika understood that passion heals.

"Go to school, learn all you can," Baba had told her under the shadow of Dumitor on their way to market one morning. "Study hard, but always remember it's love that ignites the cure."

If Marika married this union man she would never have the chance to study western medicine. The union was all consuming. The fight against the Company strained a man's senses and he forgot to laugh.

She had seen it in her own family, seen it with Mama and Papa. Mama was generous and even excited about Papa's union work. She often scrimped on family meals, just to purchase and roast a lamb for the union organizers. The organizers talked long and hard through the night only to have their ideals shot down in broad daylight by the threat of losing their rustling cards.

Marika did not have the courage that Mama had. And she certainly didn't have a heart as big as Mama's. There was no room in her heart for Mr. Jovich. Marika wanted nothing to do with him, nor his unions. She had no intention of giving up her dreams, not to feed the Company fodder, which oppressed the men and fueled the mines.

Even the names of the mines disturbed her, especially the ones named for wives and sweethearts. *The Emma. The Nettie. The Little Minah.* They were likely the names of women and daughters living cramped together in some rooming house off Dakota Street, wives and daughters left behind by men caught in a dead end of a poisoned drift. Men who simply failed to come home one night.

No. She had no room in her heart for marriage. Still, Papa didn't ask for that much. She should consider his request. Her stomach turned and her head ached, making her feel weak and pathetic. But Papa knew the dangers.

His own brother died in a mining accident in Butte. Certain that his brother had been tossed into a pauper's grave, Papa saved for the family's fare to America. He wanted to recover Uncle Vuko's remains and give him a proper burial. When they arrived in America, Papa found that Uncle Vuko had already been properly buried, in the Slavic part of the cemetery, with a proper stone and an Orthodox blessing.

Marika stole a last glance at the washroom where her mother and father conspired. She threw a warning look at Marko, blessed herself, and kissed the icon on the east wall.

Outside, in the fresh snow on South Idaho, she walked up the hill toward Park Street. The sun sparkled on the East Ridge. She imagined the beautiful evergreens, their branches heavy with snow, and large boulders covered in shiny winter blankets. She looked from the East Ridge to Homestake Pass. In the spring she'd see loons on the nearby lakes. Here in the town, though, the natural world died. The smelter blackened the sky and the ground, making the land a barren place.

Before the turn of the century, the mining fumes in Butte had singed the air so badly that businesses turned their lights on during the day and the trolley cars sounded their horns before turning a corner.

When most of the smelting moved to Anaconda, the air remained tinted, mostly noticeable at twilight when the sun turned the sky a brilliant array of crimson, pink and orange. Later the moon would shine golden red through the vaporized veil.

The sour smell of sulfur and arsenic quickly reached

her nose. She had heard stories about cows from nearby Anaconda raised on arsenic-laced grass. They grew fine and produced a sweet meat, unless they were sold and turned out to purer pastures. Addicted to the arsenic, the cows needed it to live; without it they died.

Marika lifted her skirt to keep it from getting crusted with snow. An automobile followed a horse and buggy up the hill. The auto slid in the snow and struggled to gain purchase. Behind her she heard footsteps and turned to see Marko following her, an Irish cap tipped forward and down toward his nose.

"Papa will pitch a fit when he sees you in that cap."

"You shouldn't smash your chickens before they hatch," Marko said.

"I've nothing to say to the man."

"Michael Jovich might not be as bad as you think."

"What would you know? You're just a boy. Go play with some bricks."

"I'm only two years younger than you. And I'm man enough to have a job."

"As a nipper."

"It still gets me a bigger piece of ham on holidays."

"You think I'm being selfish, don't you. Papa's sick, his lungs fill with black mucus. Don't you think I know that? I hear him coughing at night."

"You're so clever you can hold both ends of the conversation."

"Do you know Michael?"

"Not well. He seems nice."

"Nice."

She and Marko squeezed between a group of boys and men trudging toward the mines. The sun reflected off the snow, shining in Marika's eyes. Soon the buildings closed in on her and the blue sky leered at the crowded street. She felt suddenly afraid and confused. Maybe she was being selfish. Again, she thought: I should do as Papa says.

"Think of Mama and Papa," her brother was saying.

"Their marriage was decided before Mama was even born, and look at how they laugh. Back home a girl simply accepts the man her parents choose for her. It works for others."

She felt torn. "So, you do think I'm a spoiled child."

"Just think about it," Marko said. "It won't hurt to meet him."

Marika didn't want to think about it. She didn't want to meet Michael Jovich. And she didn't want to disappoint Papa. She longed for her own life, a life of medicine and healing. There was no way she could do both: keep Papa happy and follow her heart.

But then that was selfish. Following one's own heart when people died everyday and so many needed help. When Papa was dying. When Papa needed help. What was wrong with her that she didn't consider Papa's condition?

And, honestly, what would be wrong with marriage? It could be comfortable, and a sure means of support. Mama said having children was life's greatest blessing.

Marika reached Park Street and stepped onto the boardwalk. Even though the Butte hills had toned her muscles over the last six years, her legs burned from the climb. The winter air felt good against her cheeks, which had to be bright red from the cold. She remembered when Baba would splash cold water from the Black Creek on her wrinkled face. It tightened the skin around her cheekbones and made her look young again.

At the center of town, women and children flowed in and out of the shops. The children burst through the doors with new toys or a bag of marbles or groceries. Tired miners stumbled out of the bars, toward home or another bar, the mixed smell of sweat and whiskey trailing them. Pretty women in shiny red and purple dresses, who lived from the wages of the off-shift workers, stood bundled up on street corners. Their dresses dropped in folds to their ankles or flared out like brightly colored balloons. Some of the dresses were faded and worn, the hems frayed and stained the color of dirt.

"There's a hierarchy to prostitutes," Marko said. He blew frosted air up under his hat, stuffed his hands in his pockets and hunched his shoulders up near his ears as if to ward off the cold.

"Do you ever stop being a know-it-all?" Marika asked.

"The women with the prettiest, cleanest, fanciest dresses, the dresses with laced or beaded collars," he said, "work for the madams in the parlor houses."

"Work for the madams in the parlor houses," she mimicked.

"A less elaborate dress, made of bright satin or silk in plain designs, like that woman right there," he said, his chin pointing to a woman in a pink satin dress with a matching satin coat, "indicate women who live and work in the brothels. When the dresses are simple and frayed, the women usually work for themselves and live in one of the cribs."

"The small rooms attached to each other, each of them barely large enough for a bed and stove," Marika said in a professorial tone. "You ought to write a book."

"The street women are poorly dressed and often have no home. They sleep in abandoned tunnels or huddle together under broken carriages. They survive on kindness or violence."

"Whichever pays. Look Marko, I'm not trying to be mean, but I have some thinking to do and I really don't want my little brother tagging along right now. So can you be like the gold and vanish?"

"Fine." He sat on a snow-dusted bench in front of the drug store. "I tried. You are now officially on your own."

Marika turned sideways to slide past two women and recognized one of them. Kaly Shane wore a pale red dress with a tear in the hem but her friend wore a stiff blue satin dress that looked brand new. By Marko's discourse, they were an unlikely pair. The women smiled at Marika. Kaly coughed and dropped her head. She looked weak with a paltry tone to her skin. She should be in bed resting, Marika said to herself.

"Market is no place for the sick," Baba had told her.

"Hello," Marika said, stopping quickly, her feet skidding in the snow. "Are you OK?" she asked. "You don't look well. I can help you if something's wrong." She said the words she most wanted others to know: she could help.

"I'll keep that in mind," Kaly replied and smiled like they were old friends.

"Where are you going?"

"We're heading for the Copper Tavern for afternoon tea."

Marika didn't believe they'd be drinking tea there, but it caught her curiosity. "Can I go with you?"

Kaly shook her head. "It's no place for you. Your father would not be happy if you followed us into a bar. You run your errands and go home to your family where you belong."

It was true. Papa would flip if she went into a bar. He'd flip about Marika talking to prostitutes. He had two sets of rules, his and hers. Papa would talk to whomever he pleased. That kind of stubbornness and self-assured attitude was part of his nature. But he didn't want her following in his footsteps.

She could tell him that she knew things, medical things that could keep people healthy, that talking with them could help them. She could help people. But Papa wouldn't listen to her.

They waited on a crowded corner while a horse-drawn carriage crossed Park Street. Two young boys were curled up like snails, hanging onto the carriage's back railing. Probably sneaking a ride to the Flats. She watched as they descended the steep hill toward the town's edge.

"I know them," Kaly said, pointing to the boys. "Julian and George. They live at the Polly May, where I grew up."

"An orphanage?" Marika asked.

"Something like that. Good boys, but fighters."

"They'd have to be," said the woman with Kaly. She seemed impatient and ready to go, her hands pulled in her coat sleeves, shivering against the cold.

"Marika, this is Beth. Beth, Marika," Kaly introduced them. "Marika is the girl I told you about who looks like my sister." Kaly was looking at Marika with soft hazel eyes. "You're the spitting image of her. How old are you?"

"Seventeen."

"Close enough."

"Pleased to meet you," Beth said. "Kaly, let's go."

Kaly nodded and they walked up the street toward the tavern.

Marika looked out across the town to the snowy slopes of the Rocky Mountains—the beautiful, treacherous mountains they'd crossed by train coming to Butte six years ago.

She was eleven years old at the time and in love with her grandmother. It broke Marika's heart to leave Baba behind in the Black Mountains. She begged her *baba* to come with them. But Baba had said she was too old to travel, and people needed her.

Cheered up by the bustle of town and the chattering street corners, Marika wondered what Mama and Papa thought when they emerged from the washroom to tell her about Micael Jovich. She could see Papa's hand held out at his chest, his mouth opened to speak, beginning his lecture to the thick hot air. Ha, she thought.

But it was a small victory.

So far, she had managed to remain inconspicuous in the world of suitors. On union nights she disappeared into the washroom to do the evening dishes. Most days she wore dark, shapeless skirts and pulled her scarf just so, to hide her face. When men were around she kept her opinions and her smile to herself.

It wasn't that she didn't like men. She'd had crushes on boys in Montenegro and in America. Just last month, she'd had a crush on Dan McClane. She saw him helping a young girl who had tripped and fallen in the snow outside his mother's bakery. His hazel eyes had sparkled as he tenderly lifted the girl to her feet. He kindly asked if she was alright, and Marika could tell he really wanted to know.

Since he hadn't noticed Marika watching him, she was relieved to have put it behind her, skating easily out of that near romance.

"Hey! They got the best damned Irish band in there," a man yelled, pointing to the Silver Bow Bakery. "You wanna dance, ma'am?" She heard the faint music coming from inside. She had never danced in America; it seemed too bold, too wild. Perhaps it was just what she needed. She began to accept his offer when a short woman with long stringy hair reached out a stubby hand to him.

He looked at Marika and then at the short woman. "Damn the rotten luck," he said, and disappeared into the bakery with the woman.

Marika unpinned her hair, pulled the flowered scarf off her head, and tied it around her wrist. Her pitch-black hair fell straight below her shoulders, nearly reaching her breasts. She flipped it behind her ears and exposed the flush in her cheeks as she walked toward the bakery. She dropped the shawl to her waist and tied a knot at her hip.

If I am doomed to marriage, she thought—knowing the impossibility of denying Papa—let me enjoy myself now.

She walked into the Silver Bow Bakery and stopped short, waiting for her eyes to adjust to the dim light. Probably it was that motion and the wide smile on her face that caught the attention of the young man at the end of the counter. He waved his hard-hat toward the leather stool, motioning for her to sit. Marika felt her heart slip and accepted the invitation from Dan McClane.

He wore rough coveralls the color of copper-stripped earth, and a canvas work jacket. In the low light she studied his green eyes, his brown hair and the shine of his skin. He stood nearly six feet tall and carried himself well, his slender back straight and strong still, not yet broken down by the hard work of mining.

She smelled fresh bread and cookies baking. A large pot of soup rested on top of the stove. Pasties, Irish meat pies, lined the back cooler. On a shelf above the cooler, tea plates sat in a row. Someone had painted the plates with elaborate pictures of doves, crosses and flowers. Two yarn dolls lounged next to the tea plates.

The booths were filled with customers, their faces dancing like storytellers. The babble of the crowd mixed together into one loud hum. Someone near the back, where the band played, was smoking a cigar. Its sweet scent reminded her of Papa.

Dan motioned to a woman behind the counter and she stepped over to take Marika's order. The woman looked a lot like an older version of Kaly Shane, with the light brown hair and the same soft hazel eyes.

"So you've met my son, Danny," she said.

"Dan," he corrected. "My mother, Tara McClane."

"Nice to meet you," Marika said. They both had eyes like Kaly's, in the same hue and soft slant, making it the day for hazel eyes. Both Dan and his mother had strong jaw lines and slender builds. No question that they were related. Marika ordered coffee for herself and a loaf of soda bread to take home to her family.

Mrs. McClane returned with coffee. "Danny works at the Orphan Girl," she said.

"My father and brother used to work there. Now they work at the Speculator. Marko is too young to be anything but a nipper. But he's glad for the work."

"The Speculator's a huge operation, with nearly 500 men working each shift," Dan said.

"Papa seems to have a voice there. He's insisting on fair wages and safe working conditions."

"He must be making some headway. They're getting

pretty strict about safety."

"Oh yeah, Papa always gets his way."

"I'm with him. I'd like to quit the Orphan Girl and get on at the Speculator."

Marika couldn't decide whether to respect a man who agreed with her father, or walk away from him. She knew one thing: Papa would never approve of her talking to Dan McClane. The Irish were fine workers and strong supporters of the unions, but they were not people his daughter should know.

"My husband knew your father," Mrs. McClane said, staring at Marika. "They worked together at the Leonard."

Marika lowered her eyes and rubbed her earlobe as though it itched. She felt her skin tingle and tighten. Shortly after they arrived in America her father worked at the Leonard Mine. One unfortunate evening the cage went out of control with a group of men on board. The cage fell to the sump. All five men on the lower level were crushed and died. Daniel McClane had been one of those men. She'd heard the story. Moments before the cage crashed to the bottom of the shaft, Papa had walked off it. Papa was lucky. Such luck, he'd said, was a terrible curse.

"I'm sorry about your husband," Marika said. Dan's father had died. She still had her father. She should be grateful.

"After the accident," Dan said, "your father brought us half a sheep. He brought plenty of ice every week for a year. Once a month he cut and stacked our wood. I'll never forget your father's kindness."

Marika remembered. They had just arrived from Montenegro, their cupboards empty. Papa worked double shifts at the mines and took his time coming home. Mama wanted to know where all the money was going and accused Papa of gambling, a habit Papa loved from his youth. Did she know that he had bought food for Mrs. McClane?

"Even now, sometimes, I find a bag of wheat on our

doorstep. Your father is a good man." Mrs. McClane smiled.

Their words hit Marika hard, like pelting rocks.

Mama and Papa fought every day that year, yelling and throwing things like the coffeepot or a breakfast tin. Marika and Marko had hid in the washroom, passing the time by playing "rock, paper, scissors." At first Marika didn't like the game. The winner slapped the loser hard on the wrist with two fingers made wet with saliva. But as time went on and the fighting didn't stop, she took solace in both the giving and taking of pain and in the red welts, like rolling hills, on their wrists. Her parents' voices had beat like drums, a rhythm with which Marika and Marko kept time. Rock, paper, scissors. Rock, paper, scissors. Rock. Paper. Scissors.

"Come on, let's dance." Dan grabbed her by the hand.

On the polished linoleum floor he taught her an Irish jig called "The Siege of Ennis." Marika understood a celebration of battles. As a girl in Montenegro she had joined in the many village *kolos* and danced to songs about the great battle of Kosovo.

As Dan taught her the steps, she lifted her feet and pointed her toes, moving forward and back and stepping side to side. She concentrated, but felt clumsy and forgetful. Marika finally caught on to the order of steps and moved her feet faster and faster, with confidence. She danced in unison with Dan and the others on the floor, and felt a strong, quick sense of belonging.

Dan caught her and swung her around.

Her breath paused in her throat and her spine shivered. She'd never been this close to a man who was not a relative. Only a month before, Dan had been a complete stranger. But now, in his arms, she nearly forgot about the conversation between her parents about Michael Jovich. She nearly forgot about Papa's strange loyalty to Tara McClane and the fact that Dan worked in the mines.

When the swing ended he let her go, but held her with

his beautiful green eyes, his strong jaw and the soft tilt of his head, inviting her to stay close. She was a young girl again, in the mountains of Montenegro, dancing with her father and uncles. She could see the campfires, hear the hoot owls in the trees. She felt light again, as she had at that time, before they moved to America, before she left her *baba* and the wars began again, before the glory of the circle dances faded.

Still giggling to herself when she sat back down, she noticed the bakery with new clarity, as if the dancing had sharpened her senses. A package of soda bread sat near her coffee cup. Mrs. McClane leaned against the back bar, near the brightly colored plates and yarn dolls, her lips crooked into a half smile, arms folded across her chest. She looked like she was cherishing a secret. The booths were mostly empty now, and dusk was settling on the town.

She needed to go home. They would be waiting for her. Marika paid for her coffee and the soda bread with money from Mama's grocery fund and walked out into the fading light. Dan followed her.

"Meet me at the Columbia Gardens next week," he said as he caught her arm.

"You're crazy. In the middle of winter?" She laughed, feeling wonderful and free with his fingers hooked in her shawl. "They won't be open."

"That's the best time, when the gardens are quiet," he said.

"I better not." She smiled.

"At the ice rink then?"

"I don't know. Papa's sick. I'm needed around the house."

"How about May, when the Gardens open?"

"That's a long way off."

"Saturday at one o'clock on the corner of Park and Main, opening weekend. We'll take the trolley car up and make an afternoon of it."

"You're standing out here without a coat on. You'll

catch cold."

"Opening weekend," he said.

Marika thought about her first visit to the Gardens, not long after arriving in Butte from Montenegro. She didn't speak English yet and was lonely for new friends. All day long she'd wandered the grounds, talking to the blooming lilac bushes, the tall pines, the pansy gardens. She loved the baby green smells mixed with the aromas of cotton candy and popcorn, and the excited, happy sounds coming from the midway.

She'd hoped she could get over her childhood fear of heights and ride the roller coaster and the electric airplanes. She'd imagined herself with new friends, once she learned their language, soaring together in the mountain air. Since that day she'd gone to the Columbia Gardens dozens of times with Marko, and by herself. She swooned at the thought of riding the trolley car with Dan.

On the other hand, the end of May was a world away. A lot could happen by then.

"At one o'clock on Saturday, opening weekend then, if I'm well and the sun shines and Papa doesn't have too many chores for me to do, I'll be there," she told him, leaving herself plenty of outs.

On the way home she again noticed the sour, stifling stink of sulfur and arsenic in the air. She thought about Dan's face as he taught her "The Siege of Ennis," his hand on her shawl, and his long fingers tapping in time with the music.

Papa would never allow her to spend time with Dan McClane. Why should Papa forbid it though? He'd supplied Dan's mother with food and ice for an entire year—and still brought her food from time to time. If Papa could care about Dan's family, Marika could care about Dan. Plus, Dan was a union man, something Papa respected.

At the moment she didn't even care that Dan was a miner. Perhaps, the arsenic thick air had also poisoned her.

But if Mama and Papa were serious, and she was to be married off, perhaps Papa would let her choose the person she'd marry.

Papa considered himself a reasonable man. She would talk to him, convince him that they lived in America now, and times have changed.

Of course, Papa would never agree.

She walked down Idaho Street, as the sun went down and a copper hue crossed the land, resolved to fight Papa on this. As she passed the iron fence of the Orthodox Church she heard a woman scream. The cry quickly turned to a bone-chilling silence, sharp as a knife cutting across the town. The hair on Marika's arms and neck stood up, an icy pain crossing her stomach, collapsing her throat.

A tall, angular man with long stringy hair and strong shoulders, hands gripping a shiny object, staggered away from the far side of the church. A cold wind stung Marika's face, paralyzing her with fear, a fear that lodged firmly in her chest and stole her breath. Go, she told herself, and forced one foot forward, and then the next. A small, thin woman lay slumped over on the ground, still as the winter sky.

Marika went to her. "Are you ok?"

When the woman didn't answer, Marika was suddenly in the medical tent again in Montenegro with her grandmother where a man had just died. She shook off the image and touched the woman gently on the shoulder. The woman's green dress was soiled and worn. She wore a light sweater over the dress, a sad guard against the cold. Worry lined her pale forehead. An old scar stretched passed her ear and down the thin line of her neck.

"Excuse me please," Marika said, and felt for a pulse, feeling nothing, not even the last shimmer of life.

Removing the shawl that Baba had crocheted for her, Marika laid it over the woman, covering her from the cruel night. The sun disappeared behind the leather brown hills, turning the copper sky the color of wilted rhubarb.

3
HOPEFUL MALADIES

Kaly's stomach churned as she sat in a booth at the Copper Tavern, too weak to move. Morning sickness had slapped her in its grip and the day was ruined. She felt heavy and dull, her belly and chest filled with an oppressive heat. She held her breath against the sour smell of two noon drinkers arguing about the war. The room swooned around her as she pushed her light brown curls behind her ears and patted the red satin dress against her thighs. She willed herself to get up and walk. Standing should be simple enough. But this afternoon, the sickness paralyzed her.

"Would you like a drink? The guys want to buy you a drink." Big Joe, the bartender, wiped her table with a dirty rag and left the table wet.

Kaly turned her palms up in her lap and focused on the smooth skin over his cheekbones. The angles in his face were just right, his eyes hazel green like her own. For all she knew, Big Joe was her father. But probably not. He'd have claimed her by now. She curled her painted lips into a half smile. "I do," she said. "But I don't."

"I can't do both. You have to decide."

Behind Big Joe, Bert Brown was nodding in her direction. His mining clothes lay in a bundle on the bar beside his beer. His long red hair stuck out from his cap, his steel blue eyes glaring at her. She shook off his icy look and coughed, her lungs rough and hurting. A pang of memory barged through, and she pushed it back.

"Tell him to spend his money on the shoe shine kids or the paper boy. I've got no use for that man."

"Not so quick." Beth slipped into the seat across from Kaly. She unbuttoned her wool coat and dropped her scarf on the wooden bench. Her dark hair swept to her chin in a sharp angle. "Since she's in the family way, I'll take her whiskey."

Kaly glared at Beth.

Big Joe put three fingers over his lips. "I speak no evil," he said. "You want a glass of soda, Miss Shane?"

"Please," Kaly said. "But we'll pay for our own."

"Not me, I'll take the man's drink," Beth said, waving at Bert. "What do you have against him? He's one of the top fighters in town. He's good business and he took good care of Lacy Blue."

"Until last night when she got beat up and left dead."

"I heard. I guess that Slavic girl found her over by the Orthodox Church. If you got to die, might as well die close to a church."

"She didn't just die. She was killed. Bert didn't do her much good."

Kaly felt the danger—like a traveling mist—fill the room. A horrible shadow stood over her, descended and flooded her body, pulling her gaze toward the bar. Bert Brown was staring at her.

"That wasn't Bert's fault," Beth said. "She ducked out on him and probably picked up the wrong boy. They say the motive was robbery. Her beaded purse was missing."

Kaly shivered, fighting against the dark formless threat that tried to suck the air out of her. She didn't want to think about Lacey Blue and who killed her. She didn't want to think about Bert's icy look. She couldn't afford to think about any of it.

"She made it herself," Beth was saying, "you know, the purse, blue beads for sad days and silver for bright days. Guess what color it mostly was."

"That's a tough one. Blue?"

"I'd like to get my hands on that purse," Beth said. "Not for its sadness, for its beauty. Lacy was in the wrong place at the wrong time. Could happen to any of us. You have to be careful." Beth fingered the scar on her own face. "I bet a guy like Bert can keep a girl safe."

Big Joe delivered the drinks and walked away, whistling.

"You going to live at Miss Anderson's?" Beth asked.

Kaly shrugged her shoulders. "I want the baby to have a good life, something different than mine. "

"Come live with me at Miss Lottie's. She's a good Madam. You'll be safe and the rest will be easy." Beth turned, raised her glass to Bert, and sipped her whisky.

Kaly pulled her coat tight. "No, thanks. I don't trust Miss Lottie."

"What does trust have to do with anything?"

Kaly shrugged and stood up. "I have to go home. Meet me later?"

"Not tonight," Beth said, looking at Bert. "Tomorrow or the next day, whenever I get free from the brothel. Staying at the cribs is dangerous. Talk with Miss Lottie. Please. It's your only chance for safety."

"Two bad choices, the story of my life," Kaly said, turning on her heels and exiting the tavern.

At home the winter sun shone through the window onto a tiny pot of snow lilies. Kaly picked a bouquet and wrapped the stems in a dry handkerchief to protect them. The flowers made her long for spring. Women came out of their tiny hovels in the spring, just to watch the snow melt. The Red Light District filled with laughter and celebration for each girl who'd made it through the winter. The women fawned over each other's healed scars. They compared notes, sorting the dangerous men from the prosperous ones. Kaly tucked her own notes into the hidden pocket of her red satin dress and left to find Tommy.

She waved to the women and girls sitting in their Mercury Street windows. Three tiny children in snow boots dodged her as they chased each other down the boardwalk. Kaly inhaled the scent of baking cookies that wafted out from an open crib window. A girl sang a back street ballad and Kaly quietly joined in.

We'll show them our goods, they'll show us their money, we'll take them for good, but don't call us honey.

On the corner, two drink runners looked up at her, waiting for an order and a two-bit tip. The teens pulled their caps forward and tilted their chins into their collars, ready to make a beeline to the nearest saloon.

She pulled her coat tight, warding off the cool winter air and a sudden sprinkling of rain. Her boots sloshed through the melting snow as she made her way uptown, to a back alley and the door to Tommy's gym. A cautious wind pushed her down the alley, the light rain pelting her back with a satisfied rhythm.

The gym was dimly lit, with no windows, and smelled like old wine barrels and swamping dust. Three heavy bags lounged next to a speed bag at the end of the wooden floor.

The salty air of the room hung heavy at Kaly's chest. The feeling threatened to crawl up her throat and squeeze her windpipe. A dreaded heat rippled across her belly. She pushed her hands deep into her pockets. It felt wrong, being here like this, in need, and not knowing how to ask for help.

Tommy's chest and arms were strong and muscular, with good shoulders. Years of training had made him quick, agile, a man who left the air singing when he walked through a room.

He pulled off his unlaced gloves, his face overheated, bright, and feverish. Sweat pasted his dark hair to his forehead. He smiled at her, his sharp brown eyes curious, an eyebrow raised. Hooking a towel from the ring rope, he wiped the sweat from his bare chest and pulled on a gray jersey.

"It's my lucky day," he said and smiled again, a smile that went right to heart and made her weak. She looked down, not wanting to see the question in his eyes. One glimpse of those eyes and she'd lose her resolve. She ran her hand through her side curls and checked the bun at the back of her neck, stifling the urge to run, to get far away from him. To get far away from anything like love.

"Luck. That's a good thing for a fighter," she said.

Tommy was a town favorite. Fast and clever in the ring, an up and coming champion. But he was better than a champion. He didn't just save his passion for the ring, or blow it on useless brawls, like some of the other fighters. Tommy used his passion to help people wherever he saw a real need.

Last week, at the Casino, four men from the coast had roughed up a working girl. They'd tossed her back and fourth like a sack of spuds, tearing her dress and trashing her hair, her lipstick smeared across the back of their hands. When the bouncer joined the attack, Tommy walked in to stop the assault.

He struck a lightning-quick blow to the bouncer's head, and pulled the girl away from the men. She went home with a handful of dollars for a new dress and the bouncer got fired. Word spread quickly on the line. By the end of the week, Tommy was a hero and the Casino deemed the safest tavern in town.

Tommy was good at helping people.

So why was she so afraid to ask him for help with the baby, his baby?

He sat on the edge of the ring and motioned for her to

join him.

A soft shake of the head and she declined. Heaviness washed over Kaly's pregnant belly again. Her body hurt and she was afraid to sit, afraid she'd never get up. She handed Tommy the snow lilies.

"Figured they'd brighten your day. I hear you and Bert have a fight planned."

"Yeah, Bert and I'll actually get paid for pounding on each other. In all the years he's been gone, I didn't miss him. Not once. He's earned a name for himself in Colorado and California."

"Boxing is dangerous. People get killed."

"People get killed doing lots of things. Three men died in that fire at the Little Minah last week. Across the way, another man was crushed by a loose timber."

"Did you know any of them?"

"Just the one under the timber, Ted Framer's brother. It's not just the mines though. Word in the Copper Tavern is that Lacy Blue was murdered. That girl, the one who lives at the end of the cribs in the Alley?"

She thought about it. Lots of girls lived in the cribs. "Pamela?"

"She's dying of Syphilis. She went crazy last night and set her bed on fire. Some of the girls and their men helped put it out."

Kaly nodded, then shook her head. Danger, like the town's shadowy haze, came from everywhere.

"Town's gone crazy," Tommy continued. "If I didn't know better, I'd say it's about to set fire to itself. If that happens, it'll take a miracle to cool it off. Fighting Bert Brown? That's nothing. I'm safe as can be in the ring with him."

Tommy had a strong jaw and rough, blunt features, the scarred face of a boxer, a man who safely found his way down dark streets. After his parents died, his mother's friends frequently visited him at the Polly May. The women who visited coddled Tommy and cooed over him.

His mother had been a midwife and so were her friends. They brought him herbal remedies during cold season and warm teas in the winter. Although none of them ever took him away from the Polly May, they all adored Tommy. Even in the early years, with Anne Marie at her side, Kaly'd been jealous. No adult had ever kissed Kaly's cheek or told her how clever she was. No one ever brought her candies or new mittens.

Then Anne Marie died and her world got a lot darker.

She wanted to be coddled and to coddle Tommy now, to make their worlds brighter. But Kaly had a restless, suspicious nature infused with dark habits. Avoiding love topped the list. Still, she wanted to trust Tommy, to tell him about the baby, to ask him for help. It would take courage. She almost felt it.

But courage and trust, the fickle fawns, didn't come easily to Kaly. Instead of telling Tommy about the baby, she wished him good luck in the boxing match with Bert.

"Look Kaly," he said, a tender look in his eyes. "I'm thinking we might have something, you and me."

"It's a nice thought Tommy, but I don't need your pity."

"It's not pity."

"What then?"

"Love."

"No offense, but look where your love got Annie." Kaly hated herself the second the words were out her mouth. In another life, in another world, she might have just let his kindness stand, or better yet, she might've graciously accepted his kindness and walked away full of joy. But this was not another world. In a way she didn't understand, even though she needed it, Tommy's kindness hurt her.

Tommy shook his head. Sweat poured down his cheeks. "I like boxing," he said, "it reminds me that I've been fighting my whole life. To live here is to fight. Just look at yourself. You think you put it all behind you, that you don't care. But you're a fighter. Everyday down there on Mercury Street, when the red lights come on, you're fighting."

"I need to go," she said, the heat heaving across her belly again and climbing up her chest. The room went so quiet that she could hear the wind soar down the alley, tossing litter toward the street. But she didn't leave. She stood still as a mountain. When she finally looked at Tommy, his brown eyes held an old grief, ripe and swollen with time, a festering wound that haunted him, marking each action for failure.

She saw the child he'd been and it hurt.

"Have you ever been in the wrong place at the wrong time?" he asked. "I loved Anne Marie. I had a bad feeling that day. I followed you two in case you needed help. The snow was thick and you disappeared. I found Anne Marie. I didn't kill her."

"You didn't protect her." Cold. How could she be so cold? She repulsed herself.

"No. I didn't protect her. Let me make up for it now."

"The time for that is gone." Kaly gave him a blank look. Tiredness overcame her and she wanted to lie down alone on one of the wall benches, just nap for a long time. She felt dizzy and light-headed. Her legs and back ached. A fever edged up her neck.

To counter her repulsion Kaly calculated her own worries, disregarding Tommy's plea. The girls in the Alley and on Mercury Street talked about pregnancy. They had strategies so they could work while the baby grew. Eat small meals all day long. Keep some soda bread near the vanity table. When feeling weak, pretend you're swooning over the man. Bite down hard on a fist when the smell turned bitter. Take the top to keep him from pressing against the bladder.

There were alley surgeons who performed procedures in dark rooms on dirty tables, bound to kill or maim a girl. Chemical and herbal strategies weren't much better, designed to stop the pregnancy but often failing. Things like black cohosh, pennyroyal, and tansy were often too weak to end the pregnancy. Desperate women used them anyway. The potions destroyed the fetus so that a half-developed child was born, incapable of growing up normal.

Some women even used solutions containing mercury or arsenic. These solutions poisoned the woman. Instead of children, the women gave birth to lifetimes of tremors, emotional instability, insomnia, and violent stomach pains. The solutions damaged the liver and kidneys, sometimes killing the women.

Tansy, a strongly scented herb, was easy to find and identify with its fern-like leaves and yellow button flowers. In large doses the oil caused convulsions, vomiting, and death. The lungs stopped working or the organs degenerated, and the women died slow rotten deaths. Some women took it laced with arsenic, stepping out of this world before the child ever stepped in.

Kaly understood that desperation. It seeped through her pores and hurt her eyes. The world would go on without her and her baby, just as it went on without Anne Marie. Dying was simple. Living was hard. Tommy was right. Under it all she was a fighter.

So, fight for this, she told herself. Ask for help.

"I'll help you, if you let me," he said, as if reading her mind.

"Just beat Bert in the fight, that's all." She looked at the ground, plagued by a terror that she might tell him the truth and he'd send her away.

"You don't have to live this way."

"Yes, I do," Kaly said and walked outside to the rancid air.

She picked up a handful of snow and pressed the icy coolness against her face. The snow melted and dripped down her chin. Her lungs throbbed. She pulled a handkerchief from her pocket and coughed into it. The fever swelled and a deep chill set in. The wolf dog trotted down the alley. He stopped, sat on his haunches, and whined.

"Come here, boy," she called. But the dog jumped up and chased after something Kaly couldn't see. Her eyes twitched. Her lips stiffened and stifled a cry. Clouds filled the sky. The beautiful bright sun hid somewhere far beyond them.

Slightly later, after Tommy closed the gym and insisted on walking Kaly home, the wind settled and a snowstorm dropped an eerie white veil in front of them. They hid in a stairwell at the edge of The Alley. In horror, they watched as soldiers flung crib doors wide open and left them to hang on their hinges. The men dragged women from their homes and trudged through the newly fallen snow, escorting the whores—and their children—screaming and crying, to the deportation wagons.

Five wooden wagons with their large spoke wheels lined the Alley. The horses pulling the wagons neighed and threw their heads, as they stepped out, carrying the women and their children away. Snow lit up their manes, turning them white as wonder.

More women and children came from the cribs, some of them quietly, their possessions in small bags tied to their sides and anything extra stuffed into their large pockets. A woman in a red scarf clutched her young child to her chest, cooing softly to the child and petting her hair. As an officer dragged a teenage girl through her doorway, she slammed her head into his chest. He slapped her across the face, turning one cheek bright red, shoved her into the street, and ransacked her crib.

With her eyes glued to the crib door, the girl climbed into one of the wagons, spitting obscenities at the officer. Her black hair drooped to her shoulders. She shivered in the light coat on her thin frame, her red fists clenched at her sides. When the girl turned and saw Kaly watching the fiasco, she put a finger to her lips and pointed to the signs nailed to the walls.

Squinting, Kaly strained to read one of the signs. When she read it her heart slammed against her ribcage, stealing her breath and giving it back in a beat. A low soft wail escaped her lips. The sign read: "All women inhabiting public houses of ill fame are to be put under complete ban."

"You're being kicked out of town," Tommy said.

His voice sounded edgy, fragile, filled with real worry. In that moment a strange need welled up in Kaly and she leaned into him. In the midst of the storm he smelled like the solid earth, like salt and good leather. She wanted—more than anything—for him to hold her close. She let the tiny animal of trust creep out from its dark cave inside of her. "I'm scared, Tommy," she whispered. "Without something good soon, I'm afraid of what might happen to us."

4
PROMISE

Marika sat on the rock wall across the street from her family's tiny house, hands shoved into the large pockets of her brown wool coat. The black velvet collar softly hugged her neck and she pushed her chin into it. Keeping her eyes tightly focused on Mama and Papa's door, she looked for movement and listened for the sounds of dinner: a pot banging down, a fork clanking against a plate, a full cup setting down hard on the wooden table. She crossed herself and willed her spirit across the street, through the door, inside the sweltering house to test the mood, while she sat at a safe distance.

She heard the whistle from a mine, a mess of stray dogs barking, the sound of a horse clopping cheerfully down the street, the shrill wind blasting at her ears. Her wild heart beat so loudly that she was certain Papa would hear it. Still, nothing rustled at her house.

The cold night bit at her feet, reminding her of how cold the woman had looked when she found her on the other side of the church. Finding the woman bruised up, alone, the life yanked out of her, had been terrible. The poor woman was killed just moments from where Marika had been walking. She should have heard something more, done something to stop her death. She ran to Papa and Papa got the police.

After she found the dead woman Papa did not want her out after dark. And yet, here she was, afraid of the night, afraid of the killer, afraid of Papa. It was dangerous and stupid to be out in the darkness. But before she went into their tiny home she just needed a few minutes to remember and dream, a few minutes to fill that growing hollow carved in her stomach from Papa's talk of marriage.

She wriggled her toes inside her boots to warm them. She pulled her hands from her pockets and rubbed them against her forearms. The friction hinted at the warmth she'd find inside of the house. The windows of Butte homes lit up, one or two at a time, until the hillside sparkled and seemed to say, "you, you're good."

The very thing she needed to hear, the very thing Papa had never said.

Tonight, it didn't matter.

Nothing could quell her memories.

On the way home from the day's errands, she'd danced across the ice and over the snowy hills, reliving the Siege of Ennis. She'd been reliving that dance for days now—ever since Dan taught it to her. One more time she replayed the steps of threes and sevens. He had held his hand on her waist. Stop there for a moment. Breathe. She let the warm feeling run down her torso into her legs. It was sweet. Dancing with Dan was sweet. It was the most wonderful thing she had ever felt.

A carriage rolled by, throwing snow from the prancing horses' hooves onto the sidewalk. Marika got up and bowed to the horses. She twirled. It hadn't taken her long to learn the dance. Now her feet moved with no thought, as if the steps had lived inside her all along. It was as if that one dance with Dan had awakened a slumbering version of herself.

Finding the dead woman had nearly sent that lively self back to the shadows. Now she felt that dancing inside of her again. She could dance wherever she was. Whether she was walking or talking or just breathing, she was dancing. It was delightful.

Surely Dan was remembering her, just as she was remembering him. She wondered what he felt when he imagined his palm on her waist. What image of her did he remember and think about? That warm feeling started again. She shivered, and it was not from the cold.

She twirled, dropping her head back over her shoulder to glance at the house. A dim light in a tiny window winked at her like a safety beacon, calming her fears, flashing the way home. She was a ship bouncing along on the dancing waves of the sea. The tiny light welcomed her, saying: here, you belong. Here, you are safe and warm, here you rest your tired feet until the wind sails under them and you go off dancing with your love.

Dan.

A dog barked again and she started, the hair rising on her arms like it had the night she'd found the dead woman staring out at the cold copper sky. She looked around for the killer, the fine memory of Dan halted, doom filling the night.

She was wrong. Dan probably didn't even like her. And Papa hadn't taught her to behave this way. Weekly church services united her with God, not a man. Not until she was married. And in Papa's mind never an Irishman. But then, how did she know? She hadn't even asked Papa about Dan.

The moon peeked out from behind a row of clouds, the clouds doing something funny to the night, spreading dark streaks across the poisoned air, sapping her courage. She crossed the street. She was late getting home. Papa would be mad. Mama would be disappointed. Marko would be, well, what ever suited him. They were probably eating dinner without her. Mama wouldn't hold it again like she had last week when she'd come home late from the Silver Bow Bakery, and panicked from finding the dead woman.

Nickel Annie, a local vagrant, stood at the top of the block huddled in her winter coat. The streetlight shone on the dull scarf over Annie's ears. Marika understood, now, the danger that followed the homeless woman. She sadly waved at her. Annie waved back, her fingers sticking out through the holes in her gloves. Then she tramped off toward the western edge of town.

"Annie," Marika said in a low voice. She chided herself for complaining. She had so much when others had so little. She vowed to be a good daughter, to follow the rules that Mama and Papa expected of her, to make Papa proud. Even as she thought this, the heavens grew heavy, sucking the air out of her lungs.

"Don't go," she wanted to tell Nickel Annie. "Stay. Dance with me."

It seemed that all the homeless women were Annies. Nickel Annie, Shoestring Annie, Bonnie Annie, Boxcar Annie, Red-light Annie. On a good night she could gather them up in a warm building with good soup and song, tend to their wounds, find them real homes, keep them safe. As if she could keep anyone safe, the image of the dead woman troubling her heart.

She glanced at the house again and moved slowly toward it. The light in the window appeared dimmer. When Marika opened the front door, the heat reached out to greet her. Candles burned on the table near her cot, peeking out from behind the half-open curtain that separated the sleeping area from the dining room. Above the oven in the main room, a low-watt light bulb swayed sadly from the ceiling.

Mama, Papa and Marko sat quietly, too quietly, around the empty dinner table. Papa's black eyes were glazed over, almost lost under his black bushy eyebrows, as he stared at something on the far wall. He lit his pipe and the sweet smoke rambled up to the ceiling, filling the two small rooms.

Marika could tell by the distant look on Papa's face that he knew she wouldn't like the news he was about to deliver. "What is it?" she asked. "Did someone die? Did America join the war?" Her eyes slipped from Papa to Marko.

Her brother ran a hand through his dark, curly hair. His face was scratched up and one of his hands wrapped in a bright white cloth. Guilt slipped its leash and surged full force into her chest, a frazzled gray animal that bore a hole right through her. While she'd been out dancing alone, there'd been an accident.

"What happened to you Marko?" Marika asked as she pushed the door closed behind her.

"It was nothing. A misfire of dynamite at the Speculator," he said.

"You're hurt."

"Just a few scrapes. Mama took care of it."

"Marika," her father said, "sit down." He stared at the far wall as if he was gazing into the high plains of Montenegro, her beloved *Cyrna Gora*, or deep into the mining tunnel where Uncle Vuko died.

"But Papa, I need to fix dinner." She pointed to the empty table. Her heart raced and bumped into her throat, strangling her breath. She'd put on water to cook potatoes and turnips. "You must be hungry." She looked at her mother. Whatever it was, Mama would make it better.

Milla Lailich, a handsome woman with sharp elegant features, wore a brown scarf that was embroidered with richly colored flowers. Her pale lavender dress fell softly to her ankles. Mama saved that dress for special occasions, like Marko's birthdays or a neighbor's wedding. If this was a celebration, why did they look so grim?

Her mother sat stiff-backed in a wooden chair that Marko had made, her face tilted toward Papa. She nodded for Marika to sit down as her father had commanded. They all focused on Marika. Strange. The girl was not usually the center of attention.

Marika pulled a chair out from the table, smoothed her skirt under her legs, and sat down. She slipped her coat off and hung it over the back of the chair, stalling for time, buying a few more minutes before some dreaded future opened up. Papa's sickness? Baba's death?

"Papa, I'm sorry I was out late. I broke the rules. I'll take my punishment. I'll stay home for a week, chop the wood, do Marko's chores..." She threw a feral glance at Marko.

Papa's eyes came into focus as he finally looked directly at her. "This isn't about your misbehavior. It's about your life," he told her. "Milosav Jovich came by today to ask for your hand in marriage to his son, Michael."

Although she'd been expecting it, the news slammed into her. Papa knew she didn't want to marry. She was too young and she had dreams. Good dreams.

"Neither Michael nor his father know me," she murmured.

"They know me," Papa said, "and Milosav knows our family."

"I've just finished school. Give me some time and I'll think about it."

"They are good people."

"I'm only seventeen."

Papa didn't answer. Marika followed his eyes to the embroidered tablecloth. Songbirds flew on the white cotton. A pair of robins flying side-by-side stared out at her. Baba had made one just like it for Marika. It was the tradition among the grandmothers back home to make gifts for some future wedding day. Marika had tucked hers safely away.

"I am needed here, to care for you. For Mama and Marko." Her face flushed and her hands felt hot. She looked at Marko's scratched up face. He was Papa's young double, large bushy eyebrows, dark—almost black—eyes, a tall, flat forehead, his nose narrow at the bridge, and full, puffy lips. He pulled at his thin mustache and gave her a helpless, I-told-you-so-how-can-I-help-you-now look.

"I have sent a letter to Baba requesting her blessing," Stojan said. "I asked that she attend, and that she keep you and Michael in her prayers during the short engagement period. The wedding will take place as soon as we receive her blessing."

"She can't come here. The village needs her. Why take what little solace our old friends have?" But Marika's words fell into a mile-deep chasm. Of course Baba would not come to America for the wedding. It was a formality, a very important tradition, to proceed only with her blessing, which she would undoubtedly give. Baba would think this was something good, something that Marika wanted. Even if she somehow sensed Marika's hesitancy, Baba would support Papa.

"She will, perhaps, make the long journey by boat and stay to live with us," Papa said. "Once you are married we will have more room."

How could he ignore the severity of his illness, making plans for a future he wouldn't live to see? He probably wouldn't live long enough for Baba to board a boat and cross the waters to America. Not with the consumption destroying his lungs. The consumption was like a giant rat that'd gathered twigs and made a home in his chest. Even the best doctors had no way to kick it out.

No one in the family talked about his sickness and, even in her worst self, she didn't have the heart to bring it up in this argument.

Still, the anger swelled in her. Marika felt the muscles in her face tighten. She clenched her hands against each other. Did they think they had only to say it and it was done? Without talking to her? They knew she dreaded the idea of marriage. Didn't Papa have any consideration for her desires? She didn't even know this Michael Jovich. But she promised to hate him. She would not respect a man who got a wife under the disguise of tradition, treating her like so much chattel.

Papa's betrayal brought tears to her eyes. Marika stiffened her face, struggling to compose herself. If she cried, Papa would tune her out, give no credence to what she said. She'd had too much experience with his cold silences to think anything different.

"Papa," she began, "you know I don't want this. I have only just begun to think that marriage might be a good idea." Her mind flitted to Dan McClane. "I'm not going to marry this Michael. I don't even know him. Surely you can't just dispose of me to the first asker."

Her father shot his dark eyes at her.

She felt the burn from those eyes.

He held himself perfectly still. Marika couldn't even hear the breath that he normally labored over. It was as if his lungs had cleared and grown healthy with his decision. She wanted to hold Papa's shoulders in her palms, the way large men do with young children who have misbehaved. Instead, she kept her hands folded politely in her lap.

"I don't mean to be disrespectful," she said, "I'm just asking that you listen to me."

Papa nodded his agreement.

"I don't want to marry. I want to continue my education, which you, yourself, have taught me to value." Marika chose her words carefully. "I have a dream, to study medicine, to become a doctor, here, in America. And if the time is right, to bring what I learn back home to the mountain villages.

"I've always wanted this. Baba taught me the medicinal uses of local herbs. She taught me to care for people. If I have both modern knowledge and the ancient ability to care deeply, people will heal and my life will be of purpose."

"You think your mother has no purpose? Are you and Marko not purpose enough for her? You think you're better than others. What makes you think you'll be admitted to a school of medicine? And who, pray tell, will pay for it?"

"You told me that America was the land of opportunity. You work in the mines and speak of fairness to miners. What about fairness to women, Papa? When we were children you told both of us to read, learn, and study. When I was eight years old, exploring the caves of Dumitor, you said I could climb as well as any boy. *You* taught me to shoot a gun!"

"Enough." Stojan Lailich stared through the cigar smoke. Marika saw a glint of water in his eyes. Smoke probably, but she hoped it was compassion. She took it as a good sign.

"Papa, please." She hesitated, her feet flat on the ground. "I do not want to marry a miner. I fear he will die and I will be left alone to care for our children. How will I be able to feed them if I am not educated enough to make a living wage? Women get paid less than a dollar a day. I can't feed my children on that."

Before Papa could speak, she turned toward her mother. "Mama, you don't agree, do you? Just last week Roberta Owens and Danitza Draskovich both lost their husbands. You said yourself that in Butte, to marry anyone is to marry death. You fear Papa dead if he comes home an hour late from his shift. Our own Uncle Vuko died in a mining accident.

"At least," she pleaded, "let me choose a man. Let me find a husband who does not work in the mines."

Papa lifted his mustache and smiled slightly, as if her words had given him some glimmer of satisfaction. "Michael Jovich isn't just a miner," he said. "He's helping us organize a reasonable union, one that protects the miners."

"That's even worse then. The Company doesn't like men who mess with their plans. Papa, please. I will put a small cot in the washroom. Baba can still have a bed here if she chooses to come. I will do chores and study and I won't bother anyone. Please don't ask this of me."

Stojan looked toward Milla.

"You raised an independent daughter, Stojan," Mama said. "One who is half boy in her ways. You took her hunting. You camped with her on the spot where your father died in battle. She knows her own desires."

Stojan pursed his lips as if he was about to speak and then stopped. He started and stopped again.

Marko, who had been quiet all this time, was the one who broke the silence. "Papa, what can it hurt to postpone the wedding so that Marika can study for a year or two?"

Papa dropped his eyes to the floor. The candles had burned out and the room had grown dark with only the dim bulb above the stove for light. He raised his head and cleared his throat. "I am your father. I have made a promise."

"It'll affect my entire life, and that of your grandchildren."

He folded his large hands around a glass of *rakija*, plum brandy, that she hadn't noticed before. The glass remained completely full. Even in the dim light she saw the decision in Papa's eyes.

"Mama?"

Milla steadied her stare on her husband. Under the table she wrapped the embroidered songbirds around her index finger. "Papa desires your happiness," she said. "And your cooperation."

Marko lit the lantern and sat in its shadow. "Mama didn't meet Papa until their wedding night," he said. "Their twentieth year will begin this fall. They're happy. You could be happy too, if you'd let yourself."

She turned on her brother. "What would you know? Of course you'll want a woman to care for your kids when you're off fighting for the causes of men buried under rock in some stupid mine so that the copper bosses can line their walls in silk. They don't care if you live or die." She slapped her hand over her mouth, catching a sob, shocked by her own cruelty.

"A single woman is not safe. You know this. You found a murdered woman last week. I couldn't protect her," Papa said. "But I can protect you. It's my responsibility and I have decided. You will attach your loyalty to Michael Jovich."

He re-lit his pipe, sucking on the mahogany stem, turning his head toward the front door as if the newcomer had just walked in and thrown his hat on the shoe bench. He blew the smoke in circles. The circles obscured his face and then disappeared into the dull light beyond the lantern.

Marika held her tongue about papa's pipe. He was dying; how he hastened the process was his own business. He had made that point clear to her again and again. She turned her gaze to Mama, whose eyes were locked on Papa. Her mother had always been locked to Papa, determined to hold onto him, ever grateful for him. Yet Mama was no one's chattel. She belonged to Papa only as much as she belonged to herself, something Marika knew but didn't understand.

She turned to look at Marko. He had carried her to the bunks in the ship's hull when she became ill from the constant motion of the sea. It was Marko who'd stopped the captain's aid when he dragged her by the arm into the rope room. Marko had said it would be good in America, where even women could make money and have a chance at something besides watching their sons and husbands go off to war to be killed. Looking at him now, with his elbows on the table, head in his hands, she wanted to apologize for what she'd said to him, tell him it was Papa she was angry with, not him. But her brother had hidden his face, a sure sign that he had closed his ears to her.

They had all closed their ears to her. Papa had made up his mind and the family had followed. Her eyes burned from the tears lurking at their edges. It wasn't proper to cry at first news of your engagement, she told herself. Engaged. The word flew around her head like bat wings in the open timbers, like the cawing ravens over a good kill. She ran her fingers through her long hair as if to shake the wings out so she could have room to think. But there was no room to think. She felt like she would burst with the fear of men confined too long in the cage.

"Papa, you don't even know this man. How old is he? What is he like? Maybe he stinks. Maybe he's gross, fat, dirty, or drinks too much *rakija*. Maybe he's mean and he will beat me and our children. How can you send me, your only daughter, off with someone you don't even know? Have you talked to him? Have you ever had him here to dinner?" She felt unreal, like she was outside of herself, watching from a distance.

Papa's eyes slit in anger, his bottom lip quivering. His pipe lay smoldering in the tin ashtray and he tightly clenched his glass of *rakija*. "Mama, you will ask your daughter to leave the room," he said.

"You're mean. This is mean. I'm a grown woman. You can't treat me this way. It's wrong. It's wrong and mean!" Marika yelled. She fled to the washroom, threw the door shut, and slammed her body against it. Let them think I'm hysterical.

She slid down the splintered wood. There was no time for dancing, no one to dance with. She was a fool to think that her father might listen to her, give her the respect he gave the men at his union meetings. She had a mind. It could think. She had a heart. It could love. But not this man they had chosen for her. She would not love Michael Jovich.

Marika pulled her knees to her chest, put her head in her hands. She thought of the game that she and Marko had played when they were kids, when their parents fought—rock, paper, scissors—the red swells rolling across their wrists. She wanted that again. She wanted someone to understand her and to share her pain. But there was no one to share her pain. This pain was hers alone.

5
WORK

Kaly watched the short man pace three steps to her cold, dark stove and three steps back to her vanity table. He did this over and over again, his face grim. Occasionally he stopped and sat on the corner chair, only to jump up and pace some more. Kaly waited on the small bed, her legs crossed under her red satin skirt.

"I couldn't breathe," the man was saying. "I was dying. I knew I was dying. All I could think about was my little girl back in Minnesota growing up without a dad. She needs her dad. But I couldn't breathe. I was dying." As he paced the floor he hummed a lullaby to himself.

Kaly wondered if it was one he sang to his little girl. "How old is your daughter?"

"All that rock on top of me, it was so heavy my chest caved in, my lungs collapsed. I saw the angels coming for me. I can still feel the dust in my lungs. I can't get it out. Do you know what it's like, Miss, to not be able to breathe, to suffocate under a ton of rock?"

Kaly did know what it was like to suffocate, not under a ton of rocks, but under a hidden past that lingered at the edge of her mind. It wasn't something she could see, or find words for, but she felt it. It kept pushing at her, trying to come through and take over. She'd push it back, but glimpses of it flashed at her in the gleam of a yellow tooth or a sinister laugh or the smell of whiskey. Her chest would collapse and she couldn't breathe, just like the little man caught under the rocks.

But she didn't say this to the man. "Are you sure it was a ton?" she asked instead. "You seem all right. They dug you out. Think of yourself as lucky."

"That's no kind of luck. You can have that luck. I'm telling you, I'm a dead man."

"You're as alive as any man I've ever known."

"No. I'm a dead man."

"Look mister, I can't know how you feel, but I've been caught in dead ends before. Once you're free, you just got to get up and walk away. That's what you got to do now. Get up and walk away. That little girl of yours still has her dad. She needs you."

"You're right. I got to walk. I'm not going back to mining. I need to find another job, if they'll take a dead man."

"You're not dead."

"Thanks, Miss." He threw two dollars on the nightstand, near the unused condom.

Kaly shrugged, waited for him to leave, tucked the money into her waistband, and walked out into the frigid air. The street was quiet and closed up. A door near the end of the Alley slammed shut. It was Pamela's crib, the syphilitic girl. She'd hidden from the deportation wagons too.

As Kaly walked uptown to the edge of Park Street, she pulled her red satin skirt around her knees, the frayed hem iced with snow. The last of a noon blizzard blew hard against her cheeks, making them sting. The city looked clean, swept white by the storm. A shadow crossed the snow in front of her. Nickel Annie pulled a sled that held a sack of coal—probably stolen—tied to the wooden slats.

One hand was tucked into her corduroy pocket, likely hiding the day's loot. Saturdays paid well on the streets. Annie would hunker down now in some hovel, until the week began anew.

Kaly felt like lost prey. She thought about the danger that had followed her since the police had taken her neighbors to some other town. The danger seemed to expand around every corner, following her down Park Street, up Montana, across Broadway, to the Silver Bow Bakery, to the Copper Tavern, past the grade school, to the brothel on Galena, and to her own tiny crib. It was in every restaurant, every bar, seeping into the streets like the gaseous air from the copper smelter.

The city offered protection too. A secret path led down the alleyways to the blacksmith from Joe's café with a door that would open at a dark hour, and gentle arms that would reach out of a white mist. Sometimes the city was like the weather, changing at a sharp corner. It would shift under fog and veil the pursued, blowing a wind so bitter it blinded the assailant. At that moment it seemed like Butte belonged to the poor and she felt the town surge through her blood. Her eyes shone like gold, and she felt at home in the dark city.

Then the moment passed. She spooked at an explosion in one of the nearby mines, swallowed hard, and touched her sore throat. Sickness swelled in her head, arrested her body, and weighted her to the boardwalk like the miner's ton of rocks. Dark clouds swallowed the last bite of blue sky. Sweat covered her forehead and she stood alone and cold, hiding in plain sight, a fugitive in her own town.

A truck full of lumber passed two horses pulling a carriage. The thin-spoke wheels of the carriage cut a narrow line in the snow. Black smoke from the truck's exhaust soiled the ice gathered on the horses' tails. Kaly saw that the city might also be hiding her own flesh-and-blood mother. The woman could be looking down on her right now, from a window on the eighth floor of the

Hirbour Building. Or maybe out from under a snow-covered awning.

Kaly sighed, her lungs aflame. She dragged her feet down the icy street to the Silver Bow Bakery. The thing to do was rest, get some tea and something real to eat, and go home with a full belly so that sleep would come easily. Make herself well. She would forget about the memory that kept trying to bully its way into her mind. She would forget about her mother.

Dan McClane was shoveling the walk in front of the bakery, the wind blowing against his knit cap. His face lit up when he saw her. As she stepped inside, the aroma of baking bread, cakes, and raised doughnuts mixed with the scent of bean soup, ham sandwiches, and grilled steak. Cigar smoke spilled out from the back room. A small, thin-boned man sat alone in a booth reading the *Daily Miner*. Kaly took a seat at the counter and coughed into a napkin.

Tara McClane wore a green, checkered apron. A green scarf captured her auburn curls and pulled her forehead back, making the pupils in her hazel eyes large and sad. The curve of her chin, the way her cheekbone looked when turned to the light, reminded her of someone, but Kaly couldn't make the connection.

"What's the soup today?" she asked.

"Split pea," Tara said, smiling a hearty, full-lipped smile that contradicted her sad eyes.

Kaly frowned.

"Colored a true Irish green," Tara said with a laugh, "or we have our everyday special of potato soup."

"How much is it?"

"In this weather, half-price, free." Tara looked earnestly at Kaly.

Her sweetness soured Kaly's desire for a decent, wholesome meal. The mixed food and smoke smells felt like an assault now, the woman's words clanging in her ears. From the back counter, two yarn dolls stared out at her. "I'm sorry," Kaly said, standing to leave. She needed less kindness. The Copper Tavern would be a better bet for anonymity.

"Miss Shane," the man in the booth said, "please don't leave yet." He had dark skin, thin sharp cheekbones, and brown eyes wide with hunger. Kaly knew him. She'd met him at the Casino during the last fight. He waved her over. "Have a seat here with me."

She slid into the booth across from him.

He pushed four quarters over to her. "Let's go together," he said, his eyes twitching everywhere, never once meeting hers. "Me and you, let's go visit."

Kaly thought about the child growing in her belly and wondered what this man's child might look like. A dark beauty, probably, with the bones of a bird.

"What's your name?" She asked.

"Frank. Frank Hoffman."

"Where you from, Mr. Hoffman?"

"Nevada. Moved up here last winter."

"You have any children?"

"No. No family yet," he said.

In a sudden protective urge, wanting him to have a real family, worried about the baby, she pushed the coins back to him. "Not today," she said.

From there, she walked up the street toward the Copper Tavern.

The wind stung her face again as she climbed. Black metal head frames on the hill blended into the dark winter day. Clouds covered the sun with a thick gray veil. Her arms ached with tightness and her fingers had gone white from the cold. Snow had settled in her brown curls and they hung frozen at her cheeks.

Inside the tavern, she shook the moisture from her wool coat, hung it on her stool and looked around for Beth, hoping she'd be here. She wiggled her freezing toes to warm them, and fought the relentless weakness that lodged in her legs and torso—a weakness that came on fast and she hadn't been able to throw off since talking with Frank Hoffman. Something in the man's eyes haunted her. He'd seemed scared and lonely, a ghost of himself.

Big Joe poured a full shot of whiskey for her. She drank it down, thankful for the heat it gave her, thinking one drink wouldn't hurt the child. Knowing she was probably wrong, but taking the drink anyway.

"You want another?" Joe loomed hesitantly above Kaly, his question booming around her. *You want a mother?*

She looked at him.

"Another?" he asked again, rubbing his black beard with one hand, the other hand holding a bottle of Old Label by the neck.

A small man at the far end of the bar, near the poker tables, yelled, "Joe, give me a shot before I get my ax out and chop this damn bar to pieces."

"Y'oughta join the army and put your hot temper to use," Big Joe said.

"Ain't nobody getting this Finn to go overseas just to kill his own brother," the little man said. "I'm gonna start a riot, and the country will think twice about what wars they join us up in. Hell, I'm gonna start a riot right now if you don't fill my glass." He got off his stool and charged toward Big Joe and Kaly. After two steps he slipped on the wood shavings lining the floor, falling face first into the sawdust. The music coming from the back room stopped just as his head hit the rough wood, adding a last loud beat to the song.

"Sure, I'll have another," Kaly finally answered.

Big Joe scratched his beard again and shook his head at the small man now covered in sawdust. He poured the shot glass to the brim and replaced the bottle on the bottom row of shelves lining the mahogany back bar. "It's on the man at the end," he said.

Down the wooden bar sat a dark-skinned man with thick black eyebrows. He was dressed in a brown suit, with a clean white shirt, and a small brimmed hat. His red tie made a sharp point where it met his vest. The man touched the brim of the hat and tipped it toward Kaly.

She gave a salute, tilted her head, and mouthed the words "thank you."

The man, Michael Jovich, stood a full six feet tall as he sauntered down the long bar and sat next to her.

Kaly caught the scents of tobacco and rose water, smells that reminded her of the summer she first left the Polly May and worked at the Goldmine Cafe. Although the work was hard, she'd made enough money to afford a small room at a lodging house on North Wyoming Street. The landlady had a policy of renting to abandoned women and children. She would put out straw mattresses for the kids, sleeping as many as five to a single room. Kaly had felt like a queen, having a room all to herself. Her room had been simple, with a small vanity in the corner, a window table and a shared bathroom. It was on the third floor and, at night, she had loved looking out on the lights scattered across the Flats.

The ladies of the line, along with rag pickers, street sweepers, and coal stealers, had come into the Goldmine Cafe for an occasional late breakfast. The ladies had red nails, dried and scaly hands, and mouths that twisted around on themselves. Beth had been among them. She was a pretty, young girl with dark hair and slim shoulders. Kaly'd felt sorry for her and befriended her. They chatted late into the night and, more than once, Kaly slipped Beth a loaf of soda bread as she left the cafe for a long morning sleep.

A year later the café owner ran into gambling trouble and laid Kaly off.

Things went quickly downhill after that. She recalled her hunger as that harsh winter had settled over the town. Kaly'd had nowhere to go and Beth took her in. The two of them lived in Beth's tiny crib, sharing a single bed. Although Beth was younger, she was the one who bought Kaly the red satin dress and taught her the rules of seduction, price, and safety—in that order. By spring, Kaly had rented the crib next door to Beth's and owned two dresses—the red satin day dress and a silk lavender gown with an ivory lace collar, for special occasions.

"Did you get where you wanted to go?" Michael asked.

"What's that?"

"I saw you walking down Montana Street last week," he said. "Hey, Big, give us a couple of those pickled eggs."

Big Joe delivered both eggs to Kaly. The white rubbery balls rolled on the napkin before her, their vinegar smell wafting up. Kaly turned her head away from them, her stomach tumbling, skin itching. She shifted on her seat.

She had worked for Michael's family the year after Anne Marie died. She wouldn't talk. Michael had tried all sorts of food to coax a word from Kaly. Here, try some lime potatoes and parsley. How about pigs in a blanket? Just say please, or yes, or hungry, he would plead. Anything. Silence isn't always golden, he'd told her. Sometimes it was just dirt-ass poor. He'd promised to feed her a hot cinnamon crisp if she said his name, or her own name.

None of it had worked. But Michael had developed the habit of supplying Kaly with food.

"You seemed to be on some secret mission," he said.

"What?"

"I saw you charging across Montana Street like a mad buffalo."

"I didn't know you were there."

"Look up when you're walking, and you'll see the whole capitalistic world around you. Where were you going?"

"Into a very bad dream," she replied vaguely. Kaly had no desire to tell him about the baby or her misplaced hopes for Miss Anderson.

"You're not gonna go quiet on me again, are you?"

"There's still nothing to say about Anne Marie's death, if that's what you mean."

"Whoa, wait a minute. I was just making simple,

friendly conversation. You know, between old friends. But you're upset tonight."

"Yeah," she said, glancing toward the door for Beth. The bitter smell of the eggs stung her nostrils and the heat started up her belly again, the invasions coming from all directions. She perched on the edge of her seat, ready to flee. She pushed both the eggs and the heat away. The little man who'd fallen was now back on his stool, brushing himself off. A full glass of water sat on the bar before him. The music started up again and a female voice sang out, course and rough.

Finally the whiskey worked its magic and she relaxed.

Michael ordered a shot for himself and another for her.

She studied the straight line of his nose and his rich brown eyes, eyes like Anne Marie's rather than the steady green of her own. She'd never noticed before how much Michael looked like Anne Marie. Adding up the years, she realized he could be their brother.

If they'd had a brother.

"I'll pass on the whiskey." She'd already had two and needed to regain her equilibrium. She knew that she shouldn't drink. She'd seen babies born to women who drank through their pregnancies. Something was always off in them. They seemed disconnected and hard to reach, sweet at times but quick to anger.

Alcohol didn't taste right to her. Half poison, half comfort. Most of the time it turned her stomach, its bitter taste shooting straight to the back of her throat.

Big Joe filled her shot glass anyway.

She shrugged and sipped at it.

"I spent the day trying to organize miners in the Orphan Girl," Michael said. "The work is dangerous and their pay is garbage. We can't get the Company to negotiate with us. The men are afraid to attend the meetings because if they get found out they lose their rustling cards. They can't feed their families if they're out of work. The IWW is talking about sending an organizer out here from Chicago. But they're too radical for Butte. All we want is a fair wage and safe working conditions."

"Safety. That's a joke. None of us are safe." Kaly palmed her aching chest, her mind filled with the empty cribs, the bruised sky. "Plus, you're mining the wrong workings, if you think the Company will pay more. They'll just shut down the mines and put everyone out of work. They strong-arm the state and everyone goes hungry."

"They can afford a decent wage," he said. "Price of copper goes up, pay is supposed to go up. But it doesn't happen. When the price of copper goes down, everyone's pay drops. Funny how that works, huh? We want ventilation, sprinkler systems, and escape routes. Escape routes save lives and they're easy to map out. There are bulkheads closing off simple escape routes. A man can get trapped in there. A reasonable union can insist on putting doors in those bulkheads so if there's an accident the men just follow the tunnels to another mine and out, to safety. It's so simple."

"Yeah, simple escape routes. What a good idea."

Michael lifted his eyebrows at her. "Butte's the largest city between Minneapolis and San Francisco. There's more than enough money coming out of these mines to help all of us. The Company exploits the poor."

"You're making my head hurt," Kaly said. "Most of the people are loyalists. They support the mines and the Company, just like they support the war."

"The war and the mines are worlds apart. It's fear, not support, that drives the miners. But no one will go hungry if we all pull together. At times like these, it's courage that moves a town forward."

"Courage." Miss Anderson's word.

"A lot of people don't support the war. In fact, there's talk of an organized protest here if America joins in and sends over forces. People say they'll be fighting their own relatives."

Kaly tilted her head, questioning him.

He nodded. "It's true. Half the town will be fighting people they ate dinner with just a year ago. I still have family in Montenegro. But we would be fighting to protect my people. The war is a complicated decision. But Butte's mining fight is clear: The Company has too much power. It's wrong."

"Can't we just talk about the weather or something?" Kaly felt sick and her lungs burned. Although the baby was too young to move, she seemed to be twisting and turning inside of her. The door opened and Tommy Monroe walked in, his dark hair covered with snow. He rubbed his red, bare hands together.

Michael acknowledged him and turned his attention back to Kaly.

Kaly relaxed at the sight of Tommy. She followed his gaze across the room to Bert Brown.

Michael pointed to a man in tattered coveralls. "It's King of the Hill, the wicked version," he said. "That man in the middle of the bar, the one with a glass eye?"

Kaly nodded. She knew the man.

"He lost his eye in a blast in the Gray Rock last year."

"The miners hurt each other," Kaly said. "They attacked the Miner's Union a few years ago, set off a bomb that killed two guys."

"That was after the Company had usurped control of the Union. Those were extreme conditions. We don't want violence. We want fairness. You're a woman, try working for a legitimate wage."

"So, go to bat for us. Five hundred women were just trotted off to who knows where and I don't see anyone doing anything about that." A strange chill swept over Kaly and she put her coat on. She didn't want this conversation. She wanted to go home, to the temporary safety of her crib. But the whiskey had pasted her to her seat.

"Remember the fire of 1895?" Michael asked.

Kaly nodded. Everyone alive then remembered the fire.

Michael dumped tobacco onto a piece of pale thin paper, caught the far end of the paper between his fingers and rolled it toward his chest. He licked the edge, twisted the ends and offered it to Kaly. When she refused, he lit it and puffed the smoke out toward the huge mirror that captured bits of their images between the liquor bottles.

Michael removed his hat and set it on the bar next to his drink. His thick black hair stood out in all directions. "I was six years old at the time," he said. "The sirens woke me."

That fire had changed Kaly's life. It erupted in a warehouse next to a hardware building that secretly stored dynamite. Miss Anderson thought it would be fun for the children to watch the fire. Hundreds of people had gathered around as the firemen tried to kill the flames. The snow had reflected the brilliant orange glow and the whole sky lit up, beautiful and eerie at the same time.

Then the fire jumped to the hardware building and a small explosion indicated dynamite. But the crowd didn't take heed. Just before the dynamite blew the buildings apart, Kaly watched Bert Brown beat a dog with a stick. She was standing next to Bert when the building exploded. Pink mucus had landed in the snow around them, and on his face. A fuming Bert wiped his face clean with his coat sleeve and walked ahead of the other children. On the way home he swung the stick like a bat.

Bert had been Miss Anderson's favorite. He was older than the others and she coddled him, especially when he was mean—which happened more often after the warehouse fire. Maybe Miss Anderson thought coddling him would calm him down. Maybe she thought she could feed the meanness out of him. Whenever Miss Anderson pulled out the Limoges China for Bert, Kaly and Anne Marie retreated to their room and jammed the door.

After the fire, Tommy moved in and Bert didn't like it. He didn't like anyone taking Miss Anderson's attention away from him. His anger got worse as time went on and the kids at the Polly May suffered escalating injuries. Five years later, the year Anne Marie died, Bert disappeared.

"No one had any idea what was stored in that building," Michael was saying. "I watched the fire from inside our house." He paused and took a long drag off his cigarette.

Kaly gulped what was left of her whiskey, this time finding comfort in the stinging sensation that surged through her mouth and down her throat, until it hit her stomach, and exploded.

Michael flipped the ash from his cigarette onto the floor. "When the dynamite blew," he said, "glass shattered all over me. I couldn't move. I just kept staring out the window at the red snow. I wanted to turn away but couldn't. There was a leg in the snow." He sucked his cigarette and stared at the back bar. "Imagine. I'm a kid and there's a leg in front of me and I don't know who it belongs to."

Kaly's hands turned to ice and trembled, like they had the night of the fire. Women's screams were like the distant whistles of trains that had jumped track and were barging through a station unhalted. Trains no one could stop. Kaly covered her ears, making the screams small and mundane, a far off hollow whine, a child's cry.

Her chills and shivering worsened, as if reliving that night was giving the fever a firm hold on her burning lungs. She shook her head, trying to shake off Michael's words.

Their real troubles, hers and Anne Marie's, had started with that fire.

"My father had gone to help fight the fire. He was blown back from the building and the explosion broke his arm. My uncles weren't so lucky. Djuro lost his sight and Uncle Luk died."

Kaly's face flushed as she thought about the tiny legs and arms developing inside of her, the leg in the snow, the red-laced arm that had shocked her sister.

Michael's cigarette rested between his fingers. "They knew it was against the law to store dynamite there. They didn't care."

Three hundred and fifty boxes of dynamite made for a mighty big explosion. All but three of the Butte firemen died. They still don't know how many bystanders died. One horse lived. A horse had been to the blackened world, withstood the blown town, lost the men he loved, and went back to haul a fire wagon to another site. Kaly held on to the horse's slim survival like prophecy. That horse had still pulled water until a couple of years ago, when he was retired and put out to pasture.

Michael put his cigarette out and downed the shot of whiskey in front of him.

The place was packed now. Kaly recognized women from the streets, women who had dodged the police wagons and deportation, women like herself and the horse—holdouts who had developed a hundred new ways to survive each year.

The music, still playing in the background, was difficult to hear through the yelling of the crowd. An old musician snored on the railing, his head tucked into his crossed arms. Beth—her friend, her safety—was nowhere to be found. Kaly caught a glimpse of Bert Brown as he walked to the front poker table, sat down with the other men, and lit a cigar.

"I'll start working with Stojan Lailich and a group of miners that meet at his house next month," Michael said.

"Marika's father?" She'd said the words aloud before she could edit them.

"You know her?"

"A little bit. She reminds me of Anne Marie. Every time I see her I feel a strange closeness to her, like a sister. But she's not my sister. She's not my family. I don't have a family." She pushed herself away from the bar, leaving the orphaned eggs to stare out at some other customer.

Michael gaped at her and said nothing.

She walked away. Let them have their families, Kaly thought. Michael had a family. Maybe one of his uncles died in the warehouse fire, but he still had another, plus his father and mother. Kaly had no one but Miss Anderson, and fat lot of good that had done her.

On her way to the door someone grabbed her arm.

She froze.

"Hey, we got a free seat. Play a game with us." Bert stared at her, spitting the words through his whiskey breath.

She looked at the poker table.

The little man who'd fallen patted the empty seat next to him.

Tommy stood in the corner watching.

She pulled her elbow from Bert's grip. "Oh, I'm lucky at poker and love," she said, folding her arms in front of her, just over Tommy's growing child. "But not tonight."

Outside the cold air stung her cheeks. Although she couldn't see them through the clouds, she knew that the Rocky Mountains were covered in snow. She imagined how they might shine under a full moon in a cloudless sky, beauty saved for another time. She started for home, breathing in the cool air. It felt good in her feverish lungs.

When she arrived home, Bert Brown stood at the doorway. He had evidently left the Copper Tavern shortly after she had and hurried down a side street to meet her.

She walked past him, saying nothing.

He captured her in his arms. "Hey."

Kaly felt an old inertia come over her. Her chest tightened as she fought the paralytic urge, pushing Bert away. He clenched her wrists in his fists and pushed her through the door.

By the time she heard the faint knock, her eye had swollen partially shut. She ignored the noise until she heard Tommy's voice on the other side.

"Kay, are you all right?"

Sheltering her throbbing eye with her palm, she opened the door. "If I'm not alright, it's a fine time for you to come checking. Go home, Tommy. There's nothing you or anyone can do for me."

Tommy narrowed his eyes. "Bert did this to you, didn't he?"

Kaly smelled the whiskey on his breath. She'd had enough for one day. She just wanted to be left alone. "Go home Tommy."

"No. You need help. You do not look good."

"What can you do? I'll heal. That's one good thing about me, I heal." Outside, a horse neighed and Kaly heard the wagon wheels rock across the snow. She gazed at the floor and back to Tommy. "Well, there might be one thing you can do for me. Your mother was a midwife before she died."

"True."

"Her friends would come to the Polly May to see you. They adored you. They must have missed your mother."

A soft flush came over Tommy's face. "They were kind. I think they felt indebted to her. They wanted to honor her memory."

"You still know some of them, don't you?"

He nodded, suspicion filling his eyes.

"You would do something for me, wouldn't you?"

"What is it?"

"Get me some tansy and arsenic. You must know someone who will supply it."

"That's dangerous stuff. What do you want with it?"

"It's not for me," she said. "It's for Pamela, the girl with syphilis."

"I don't know."

"Please, Tommy. Pamela doesn't have anyone to help her. She only had us, the crib girls. Now she doesn't even have that. She probably won't last till summer. She'll likely die of hunger or hypothermia. It's wrong. But I don't know what's right anymore. I told her that I'd help her.

She wants the comfort of knowing she can reach the end quickly if the pain of the syphilis gets to be too much."

"Why doesn't she go to the doctor?"

"Tommy, please. You know people."

"I don't know. You're sure she wants it?"

"Very badly."

"I'll see what I can do. It's not right though and I know it."

"Get a strong portion, Tommy, one with more arsenic than tansy. Get it strong enough so that, if it comes to it, she won't get caught between worlds."

She closed the door, the lie about the syphilitic girl still on her lips.

6
CROSSED PATHS

Marika walked into the small building on Broadway that housed Dr. Fletcher's office. She had pulled her hair into a tight bun at the back of her neck. She wore her brown skirt, which flowed down to the top of her boots, lightly polishing the insteps. A soft white blouse under her mother's white sweater finished the outfit, giving her a responsible look.

Although the doctor's office was clean and uncluttered, it desperately needed a paint job. Rough wooden wallboards peeked out from under a faded gray plaster coat. Exquisite furniture from the turn of the century backed up to dull gray logs. Anatomical drawings hung down the log walls. The room smelled of antiseptic and formaldehyde.

Tommy Monroe sat on a red velvet bench. She didn't know why, but seeing him quickened her heartbeat and made her forehead sweat. She hadn't wanted an audience. Let alone someone like Tommy.

Marika knew that he was one of the top contenders for the middleweight state boxing championships. He'd fought

Birddog Billy, The Red Tycoon, and Mad Madison Mike—
and beat them all.

He grinned at Marika. A long scar on his cheek turned
into a half moon. Another, thinner scar at the corner of his
left eye gave the impression of a permanent wink. His
broken nose had healed into a crooked arc.

She recognized him by matching his wounds to
Marko's stories. Her brother loved the prizefights, and
Papa allowed him to go to them. Marko would come home
late, nudge Marika awake, and signal for her to follow him
into the washroom. Behind the heavy wooden door,
Marko would give her blow-by-blow accounts of the
fights.

"Then Bailey the Bomb knocked Tommy across the
ring," Marko had said. "Then Tommy righted himself and
downed the bomber."

Her brother had never seen Tommy Monroe lose a
fight.

Marika couldn't quite believe that the man sitting
before her had never lost a fight. No one never loses. He
was probably just another blowhard who got the
community to brag on him. Barely curtailing the urge to
stare, she took a deep breath and walked past.

A booming voice from behind a large oak desk
confronted her. "Do you have an appointment?" the
receptionist asked without looking up from her scribbling.
The woman's desk barricaded her from the patients.

"I'd like to talk to the doctor about employment,"
Marika said, stepping closer, feeling queasy about asking.
Papa would be furious with her.

But he hadn't seen the men in the hospital tent in
Montenegro, their white faces, their struggles for breath,
blood flowing from gut wounds that had been torn wide
open, her own sense of helplessness. And just a while ago
there was Lacy Blue. She should have been able to save
that woman. Get her breathing again. Pump her heart.
Wave some smelling salts under her nose. Instead she ran

away like a frightened child.

She looked at the woman behind the desk. "Miss Parsons," her tag said. Miss Parsons wore short-cropped hair and circular glasses. She had dressed in a simple blue skirt with a white blouse and a blue scarf thrown over her shoulders.

Marika caught a lavender scent and spotted a row of medicine bottles that lined the shelves behind the big desk: potassium bromide to lift the spirits; belladonna to help with sleep; ergosterol for vertigo; and salicylates for aching bones. The shiny black shelves did not have a speck of dust on them.

"I'll ask again. Do you have an appointment?" Miss Parsons stared out over her glasses, which were perched halfway down her nose.

"No. I'm not sick. I'm for hire. I'm skilled at mixing medicines."

"You need to make an appointment," Miss Parsons said. "We see no one without an appointment."

"I just want to talk to Dr. Fletcher."

"I'll be happy to make an appointment for you."

"It'll only take a moment."

"Thrilled to make you an appointment." The woman's eyes narrowed into a glare.

"I'm not leaving until I talk to the doctor." Marika crossed her arms on her chest, straightening herself to her full five-feet-six-inch height, false bravado over her nerves. She hated herself for asking. Demanding.

Tommy Monroe grinned.

Marika noticed it, but ignored him.

Miss Parsons stood up and leaned over the desk, towering toward Marika. She looked appalled, her lips pursed ominously. Evidently, people usually did what she said. Shuddering, Marika understood why.

"Please, if I can just talk to the doctor," she repeated, trying a softer tone.

"You *do* need an appointment. To get your ears

cleaned. You obviously don't hear well. He can see you tomorrow at two o'clock."

"I want. To apply. For a job. That's all I want."

"Are you an overgrown child? You look about twenty, but you're throwing a two-year-old temper tantrum. Do you want the two o'clock appointment or not?"

"She can take part of my time," Tommy Monroe said.

Miss Parsons glared at him.

Marika flushed red.

"What's all the commotion?" A small bald man wearing a pair of eyeglasses identical to Miss Parsons' stepped through a door located behind the large desk. He was much smaller than Miss Parsons, but they both had round faces with red cheeks and peanut eyes behind the circular glasses. Their shoulders humped in unison. The woman's neck was longer than the man's, but they could have easily been brother and sister.

Miss Parsons glared at Marika and stepped forward, blocking the doctor from view, the blue skirt drooping around her white boots. Rumor had it that they'd been married at one time, and that she'd found him much too difficult to live with. She divorced him and, finding herself in need of an income, went to work for him instead.

Marika spoke through Miss Parsons as if she were air. "Dr. Fletcher, my grandmother trained me to care for the sick. She taught me the medicinal uses of plants and herbs. I am a willing student. I'd like to learn more. I'd like you to teach me."

The doctor instructed Miss Parsons to sit down.

Surprisingly, she did.

Dr. Fletcher walked over to Marika. "Go home," he told her, waving his arms in a jerking manner. "I have no work for a woman. Women leave jobs as soon as they find a husband and have babies. Medicine takes education and dedication. You haven't been to university, right? Not to slight your grandmother, I'm sure she's a fine woman. It's just that, well, a wives' tale is a far cry from a cure. I'm sure you understand. Now I've got work to do."

Marika wondered if he talked like this to his patients. It was as if he was speaking to a theatrical audience rather than to a real person. "I'll start anywhere—mopping floors, cleaning rooms—and I'll study at night. You'll see I have the knack."

She felt Tommy Monroe's smile and she hated herself for begging in front of him. But she was desperate to begin work before the wedding. Making her quit would be much more difficult for Mr. Jovich than denying her permission.

Permission! Marika trembled.

"Ma'am', you are making a spectacle of yourself. A 'no' is a 'no' is a 'no', when a 'yes' is not right a 'no' must suffice."

"Where a 'no' might suffice, a 'yes' would be twice as nice." She smiled. She stood up tall, twirling her brown skirt at her ankles, flipping her palms up.

The doctor smiled back, to Marika's surprise.

In the background, Miss Parsons countered all good cheer.

"Ah, yes," he said, "nevertheless, a 'no' will have to do."

The door slammed against the outside wall and they all turned toward the sound.

"Quit talking nonsense and keep your dirty hands off of me," a large woman in a red coat said to an even larger man who followed her as she tripped through the door.

Marika and Tommy exchanged glances.

"My hard-working hands, you mean," the man said, hulking over the woman. He wore bib overalls with flowers embroidered on the pockets, and huge work boots. His curly brown hair stuck out in all directions. "Besides, I haven't touched you in months. You have to tell the doctor the truth."

"Quit nagging me," the woman said, wiping her coat as if brushing him off. Her graying hair was braided loosely down her back. She swung her braid so that it flipped across the man's chest.

"See?" The man turned toward Dr. Fletcher. "See how she talks to me? She used to be sweet and kind. Now she's possessed. I don't even know my own wife."

"How long have you been married?" Dr. Fletcher asked.

Miss Parsons stood up and peered over the doctor's shoulder.

"Twenty-two years," the husband answered.

"Twenty-two years too long!" the wife bellowed into the man's face.

"Children?" Miss Parsons asked.

"They're all like him. Ungrateful, nagging know-it-alls." She stood on her toes, her face pointed at the man's chin.

"You're probably just tired," Dr. Fletcher said.

"I told you," the woman said to her husband. "I told you I was tired, that I just needed a little help around the house. But you can't listen to me. You'd rather pay good money just to hear what I've been telling you all along."

"Doc, she needs real help," the man said.

Marika felt sorry for him. He looked like he was about to cry.

"Does she have a broken bone? A bad tooth? A deep cut?" the doctor asked.

The man shook his head.

"Does she have syphilis? Pneumonia? Consumption?" The doctor waved his arms again in that jerking motion of his. "Her lungs sound good, she seems to have plenty of energy, and she's obviously strong as an ox. I think she's fine. Maybe you and your kids should just help her with chores. I can't do anything for someone who is not sick."

"Ha!" the woman said. But she looked dejected.

Marika whispered something to Miss Parsons, who grudgingly gave her a piece of paper and a pencil. Marika scribbled something and handed the paper to the woman, who squinted at it as if it hurt her eyes. Marika realized that the woman couldn't read, so she sketched simple pictures next to each of the words. A cow. The sun. A stick person walking. A bean. A field of crops.

"Eat plenty of red meat," she told the woman. "Get plenty of sunshine. Take a long walk every day. Eat vegetables and beans. Gather and eat alfalfa every day." She pushed the paper toward the woman, who stuffed it into her pocket. Marika leaned closer. "It's the change," she whispered. "All women go through it eventually, when they're done having children. It just takes your body a while to adjust."

The woman smiled, thanked Marika, and walked out the door.

Her hulk of a husband followed.

Dr. Fletcher stared at Marika, a blank look on his face, while picking up a chart and calling out Tommy Monroe's name.

Marika turned back to Miss Parsons to make another bid for employment. Through the sheer curtains of the side window she saw her father slowly approaching the doctor's office.

"Please tell Dr. Fletcher I'll be back. Please ask him to reconsider my request. And, please, please don't tell my father that I was here. Do you have a back door?"

Miss Parsons motioned to the hallway and walked in front of Marika, hiding her from view. As Marika quietly slipped into the alley, she heard Miss Parsons ask, "Do you have an appointment?"

The bruise from Bert Brown still hurt Kaly's cheek as she waited for the doctor. Doctor Fletcher would ignore the bruise and chastise her, then lecture her. Then he'd hold her hand, look at her like she mattered, and remind her that she'd been ordered to leave town—and that she'd have no support if she got caught soliciting. He'd say she had no business raising a child and that the only reasonable course of action was to give the child up for adoption. Or give the child to Miss Anderson at the Polly May. He'd remind her again that she was a whore, and babies and whores didn't mix.

She folded her hands in her lap, feeling the cotton texture of the gray skirt she'd found in an abandoned crib, something good left behind by one of the deported women. The skirt stretched at her belly and flowed over her hips. A simple cream-colored sweater, found in the same crib, gave her an acceptable, motherly appeal. The thick make-up covering her bruised eye and cheek quickly countered any civilized air she put on, Bert's brutality marking her for what she was—a street worker, a prostitute, a woman in extreme danger.

She looked out the window toward the snow-covered mountains. She couldn't help but wonder if there might be a cabin out there somewhere that she could live in and raise the child. She'd plant a garden, learn to hunt, gather water from the mountain streams—never work the streets again. The child would grow up peacefully, never having to suffer.

In her heart though, she knew the doctor's advice about giving the child away would be right. She could never raise a child. The chances were too great that she would grow up hungry, and starved for love.

Kaly also knew that if she gave her baby up, the day would come when the child would begin searching for her mother—obsessed with the curve in a stranger's chin, the arc of an eyebrow, or the shape of a nose, looking for the ones that matched her own. She would walk into the Goldmine Cafe, the Silver Bow Bakery, the Casino, the Copper Tavern as an instant member and an instant outsider, never falling off of that one edge.

Kaly would lurk in the shadows waiting for the child to learn to walk, lose her first tooth, skip by on her way to school. She'd be on the lookout for her child to excel at track or take up needlework, graduate from grade school, marry.

Worse, she'd be waiting to read the poor child's name in the paper, having met with some unfortunate end.

Could the life someone else give to her baby really be any better or worse than the life Kaly could give to her? Their mom had given them to Miss Anderson, and look at how she and Anne Marie had fared.

Last week Tommy had brought her the tansy and arsenic tincture—a potent sweet smelling potion. She'd tucked it safely away in her crib. Kaly was collecting options: here in the doctor's office, the choice was life, with the child either at her side or wrapped in another's arms; hidden in her crib was the option of death. She had to admit that it frightened her.

Whatever Dr. Fletcher said, she would make up her own mind. Nevertheless, she liked the doctor and wanted his opinion. He seemed to accept her, and to pride himself on working well for her. His profession was to tend to the sick, no matter who they were or how they conducted their lives. It was clear that he meant to live by his oath.

The man sitting across from Kaly coughed into one hand and wiped the sweat from his brow with the other. He had wide, bushy eyebrows and deep wrinkles in his forehead. His shoulders were hunched forward in a dirt-covered shirt, his skin pallid from being too long underground. He wore brown coveralls, held up by straps that bunched at the top and fell off his shoulders.

She'd watched him enter the doctor's office just ahead of her. Since they'd been there, he'd had a coughing fit about once every ten minutes. She knew that sound, the sound of dark, sick lungs. She could almost see the phantom walking next to him.

An anatomical chart of a skeleton hung on the wall a few feet away from the man. An artist's sketch of a healthy pair of lungs covered the wall on one side of the entry, and a heart decorated the other side. A picture of a man with his muscles bared to the bone dropped down the wall a few feet away. On a small table, a photo book of legs, feet, hands and arms sat neatly closed. It was strange, she thought, to cut a person into parts like that.

"Would either of you like some tea?" Miss Parsons asked.

Before either of them could answer, the door to the patient office opened. To Kaly's surprise, Tommy Monroe emerged, with the doctor following. She gazed at Tommy's dark hair, the scar across his cheek, his watery eyes.

"Come by next week," Dr. Fletcher said. "In between now and then, stay off the booze. Your body's weak. Be easy on yourself."

"I haven't touched a drop in three days," Tommy said.

"Another thing, you're in no shape to be fighting."

Tommy shook his head. "No way I'm gonna let Bert down, Doc. See ya next week."

"Well, I do not approve. I'm against the fight. Let it be known." The doctor walked over to Miss Parsons' desk and picked up a chart. "Stojan Lailich," he called out as if the waiting room was full of people. The coughing man stood up and followed Dr. Fletcher.

Tommy Monroe walked over and stood next to Kaly. A wildfire flashed in his face and disappeared, as if he'd just glimpsed a raging memory. An arm from the skeleton sketch dropped down the wall nearby. Tommy reached out and gently took her chin in his hand, tilting her bruised cheek toward him.

"You're not healing too quickly. How do you feel?" He asked.

"Bert's got a wicked punch. But like you said, I'm a fighter." She stiffened but didn't pull away. Her heart beat rapidly and her hands shook. She willed them to stop. The sound of Tommy's voice, coarse from his sickness, made that awful heat in her stomach start again. It crawled up her legs and made her skin itch. She felt unreal as he let her chin go.

Miss Parsons stood a foot away. "May I help you, Tommy?"

"Look at her face," he said.

"That's her business."

"Yes. I know." He shook his head. "I don't mean trouble, but that? That is trouble." His brown eyes darkened and his lip trembled.

For a minute she thought she saw Tommy step away from himself and toward the window, a scared boy in a snowstorm. But it was just the sun through the curtains shifting on Tommy's forehead.

"Take good care of her," he said.

He left and Kaly knew that he wouldn't be gone long. He'd be waiting just beyond some doorway, and she was glad of it. He watched out for her, even when she didn't watch out for herself. He reminded her that the past was the past, no more harmful than the shades in Miss Anderson's dormers.

It confused Kaly, the compassion she felt for Tommy. After all, she'd spent a lifetime building a bulkhead against love. Tommy was different though. She'd had a real weakness for him one night. It was stupid. She drank too much and walked under the slender light of a new moon. Within reach of the cribs, almost home, she heard someone step out from the shadows. It was Tommy. He stopped her near a storage shed and they chatted. It was a friendly conversation but her teeth chattered from the cold. He offered his coat and she took it.

"Do you ever think of me?" he asked, draping the wool coat over her shoulders. He smelled too much like whiskey and cigars to even consider his question.

"I'm tired," she said. "I'm going home." She pulled his coat tight, feeling the wine crash down on her, wanting to turn away but staying close, feeling the warmth surge through her chest and down her legs.

"Stay here with me," he said. He ran the back of his hand across her cheek, down her neck. He leaned in and kissed her ear.

She turned to leave, barely moving, but then not trying. Maybe it was the wine, or the too thin moon. Maybe it was fear or the unexpected feeling of love. Whatever it was, she softened, lifted her chin and kissed him on the mouth.

He kissed her back, holding her up, while she collapsed into him, feeling his warm body, the foreign feeling of belonging. He'd pulled her close, pressing his chest against hers, and in the dark of that winter night, she heard his heart beat.

"Baby," he whispered, like she meant something to him. And she knew it was true; she mattered. She felt his endearment, "Baby," as real as anything she'd ever known. "Come on," he'd said and they went inside. She was without protection and it was during the most fertile time of her cycle and she knew better. And his "baby" had "come on," just like that.

Now she didn't know what to do about the baby.

Miss Parsons was standing in front her when the building rumbled like a small earthquake. "A tunnel collapsing," the receptionist said. "It happens every now and then and we feel it here. The town'll fall into the mines one day, if we're not careful. Tell me now, would you like some tea?"

Kaly started to cry.

"Of course you'd like tea. Just because the sun is shining doesn't mean a woman doesn't need comfort. We'll have some chamomile." Miss Parsons disappeared through the doorway to the back room.

Kaly stepped quietly over to the big desk. Tommy's chart was on top. She opened it to the last note and saw the doctor's handwriting. *Fear and panic bouts exacerbated by alcohol use, further exacerbated by flu symptoms. Patient must stop drinking.*

"Tea coming," Miss Parsons said from the other room.

Kaly dropped the chart and stood back from the desk. The dark oak wood pulsed in her vision and the beating sound hurt her ears. She realized it was her own heart beating a terrified rhythm. She imagined that she heard another, barely discernable heartbeat, beating twice as fast as her own.

"Pacing the floor, are you," Miss Parsons remarked as she emerged from the back room. "I know what that feels like. Sometimes I can't sleep, so I go walking around the neighborhood." She set the tea tray on her desk. "But in your shape you shouldn't be pacing. You should rest."

"What shape?" Kaly asked.

"You can't hide such a thing."

"What am I hiding?"

"Come on, Kaly Shane. It was bound to happen." Miss Parsons shook her head.

"Tell me what you're talking about."

"You're pregnant."

"If I were, how would you know?"

"I've been watching pregnant women for years. The flush in your face. The way you dropped your hands to your stomach when Tommy reached toward you. You have that full sinking feeling, the sense that there is no way out."

Kaly looked down at her hands and said nothing, thinking of the man trapped in the landslide last week at the Gray Rock.

"You can't breathe," he'd said. "Your chest is caving in, all that dirt on top of you. After being buried alive, you die at the sound of each rolling pebble, each time the land shifts."

She had understood the man too well and Miss Parsons was right. On her worst days Kaly did have that sinking, no-way-out feeling. But on her best days, she was grateful that she had learned to breathe again. She wondered if this was what her own mother had felt.

"It's all right if you don't want to talk about it," Miss Parsons said.

"Do you have any adoption records for the town?" Kaly asked.

"Locked in the basement." Miss Parsons squinted her eyes.

Kaly smiled. Something misty pulled away from her,

and the air in the room settled. "What about Coral Anderson's kids, the ones never taken into families? Is there a record of them?"

"Some might be sealed off somewhere," Miss Parsons said, "but most of those kids have no paperwork."

"How about deaths?"

"Shouldn't you focus on your own life and that of your child's, rather than the mistakes made by others?"

Doctor Fletcher and Stojan Lailich came out of the back office. "Yes, yes," the doctor was saying, "come back next week and until then be easy on yourself. Rest. You're in no shape to be down in those tunnels."

"Gotta work as long as I can," Mr. Lailich said. He nodded to the women and left.

Dr. Fletcher walked over to Miss Parsons' desk, poured a cup of the barely brewed tea, and stood staring out the window as he drank it.

Kaly wondered if he was watching Stojan Lailich.

He opened the window and she heard shouting from outside.

"Down with war!"

"Kill the draft!"

"Stop the capitalists!"

She walked over to peer out. A small group of protesters was charging down Broadway. Most of them probably came from Little Finland, Centerville, or Meaderville. Men poured out of the boot shop and the billiards hall to watch the commotion, and the group picked up a few stragglers. A horse galloped toward the head frames on the hill, snow pluming up from its sharp hooves.

"The poor have rights, too," one man yelled through Dr. Fletcher's window. He shook a stick.

A cold chill swept over Kaly.

"A lot of folks are against the war," Dr. Fletcher said.

"War creates a lot of work for doctors," Miss Parsons said.

"Not good work. If they force me to stitch up soldiers, I won't like it, but I'll do it." He finished his tea, went to the big oak desk, put the cup down, and picked up a chart. "Kaly Shane," he called out into the waiting room, even though she was standing only a few feet away from him.

7
BIRTHDAY PARTY

Kaly stood across the street from Lottie Boyle's house, the visit to Dr. Fletcher still rolling through her head. The doctor had gotten very quiet when Kaly told him that she thought she was pregnant. He folded his hands, as if in prayer, then flattened them against his brown trousers. He shook his head and asked, "What were you thinking?"

With that simple question Kaly had felt shame swell in her cheeks. Her heart slammed against her ribs and tiny beads of sweat lined her neck. She had no answer for him. She wasn't thinking. She had been careless and had no excuse for it and now another child was on her way to the Copper Camp.

"Well, let's make sure," Dr. Fletcher had said. He checked her and confirmed that this summer Kaly would, indeed, give birth, sometime in August. Kaly had calculated the time. Approximately six months to find a mother for the baby.

"Can you raise this child?" He had asked, a worried look furrowing his brow. "I know you Kaly. You're a good person. You'd be good to the baby."

She shook her head. "My life is no life for a child."

"You could change your work. Do something else." The doctor's voice sounded distant, far away, like the forbidden words spoken in the dark of night. Kaly had heard the utterances a hundred times in her crib, just before the exchange of sex and money.

"I have no skills. I talked with Miss Anderson."

"And?" His eye twitched and he pressed his hand against the eyelid.

"I walked out without making a decision. She's like you. She wants me to live there, help her. Find wholesome work. But Annie died there."

"You think the baby will die with her?"

"I don't know." Kaly put her head in her hands. The shame expanded in her chest, making her feel dirty and weak. When she found the courage to look up at the doctor, she asked, "Why didn't she protect Annie?"

"Maybe she tried."

Just then Miss Parsons came in with Kaly's cup of tea. Without a word, she set it on Dr. Fletcher's desk and left. Kaly stared at the tea. Steam wafted up off of the hot liquid and ballooned into tiny swirls.

"Or maybe," she said, "she just loved someone else more than she loved Annie. And she protected him instead."

"You're blaming Tommy."

Kaly shook her head. "Not Tommy."

Dr. Fletcher sighed. Quietly he said, "Perhaps the old danger has passed. Her offer is worth considering. There's time." He motioned for her to drink the tea that Miss Parsons had delivered. "We'll figure it out."

Kaly had left his office as the sun disappeared behind the clouds and snow drifted down, landing in large flakes on her gray woolen coat. In the quiet storm she went home changed into the red satin and walked up to Lottie's brothel. As she got close to it the snow stopped and a light wind came up.

Across the street Kaly saw Beth sitting in a rocker on

the porch. A roof covered the porch and half walls offered a small protection from the weather. Beth was bundled up in a large puffy coat, her neck wrapped in red wool, her hair pulled up into a dozen loose curls. Even from a distance she was beautiful.

She wore thin white gloves as she knitted a blue scarf, a present for Lottie Boyle's sixtieth birthday. She and the other girls from the house were planning a surprise party for Miss Lottie, scheduled to start after the sun went down and the full moon came up. Of course the Madam would have been born on Valentine's Day, one more thing to make her special, to convince girls to work for her, to convince their suitors that they had, in fact, come to the right place.

Beth had certainly been captivated by Miss Lottie's allure. As she sat on the porch she studied the scarf like a foreign specimen, adding rows of yarn to it. Lost in her own world, Beth didn't seem to notice Kaly approaching. That suited Kaly just fine. She was glad for the extra time to think. She needed to make sure that she did the right thing.

Beth thought that Kaly's only safe choice was to move into Miss Lottie's house. She had insisted that Kaly come to the party, feeling that it would be the best time for a formal introduction. Watching the Butte sky change from a soft copper to a golden red, Kaly once more went over the reasons for moving into the brothel: Safety, shelter, companionship. Safety. Lottie's girls did not get run out of town. Miss Lottie had connections and her girls benefited from those connections.

Beth had called the brothel "a home for girls." "That's all it is," she had said, "a place for girls to live. Nothing illegal in that." And she looked happy enough. Embraced by the warm coat, sitting in the large wooden rocker, a roof over her head, the wind on her cheeks, she was the picture of charm.

The house was a fine two-story building with lace

curtains. A sharp roofline pointed through the soft wind and into the dark rouge clouds on the horizon. Stone steps led up the front of the building onto the large porch. Three angels carved into the dark wooden door guarded the entrance to the brothel. The walls on either side of the door had been painted a soft green.

After the Polly May, Kaly had never allowed herself to think about living in a real house. But if she had, this would be the one, strong and steady, a lovely secret where she could simply vanish at will. This house could protect her from the dangers of town, the violence, the hunger, the sheer loneliness of pushing forward day after day, trying to eek out a living. This is a home, she thought, as she let herself hope for something good.

Beyond the house, the silhouette of the Speculator mine frame sat on top of the hill like a gentleman's cap. The ruddy sky was heavy with mining vapors, the air poisoning the ground and preventing new growth. The forest around Butte had been generous at one time, but now the trees were small and deformed, diminished by the gaseous haze. Bushes and wild flowers were starved for nutrients and wilted as soon as they sprouted.

As though someone was pushing and pulling her— back and forth between hope and futility—Kaly walked toward the house one slow step at a time. Why on earth was she dragging her feet about this? She shook her head. The baby was growing. She needed a place to hold up until the baby was born. Somewhere secure. After the birth she could move to Wallace or San Francisco.

The thought of moving away set a boulder on her chest and she nearly keeled over from the weight of it. Butte was her town. She couldn't leave. Her sister was buried here. Who would bring flowers to her grave or clean her tombstone if Kaly moved?

No. She'd stay with Miss Lottie, or move back into her crib after the baby was born, or, heaven forbid, she'd move in with Miss Anderson.

Several people passed her on the street. Everyone seemed to have a few extra bucks in their pocket to spend at the dry goods store, or in the taverns. Butte's nightlife had escalated lately, spinning wildly around loose money and booze. Last month she'd seen a man get shot just a few feet from her crib. Two weeks after they closed down the line and ran most of the prostitutes out of town, an angry wife had ridden her horse through a saloon looking for her husband. She'd found him in the corner, passed out, his pockets emptied, the trouble of winter in full storm.

Kaly pulled her coat tight and stared at the brothel. She had loved Butte, especially at this time of evening, when people wrapped up the loose ends of the day and gave bad luck a second chance. Like nothing else, the city had belonged to her. But now that she was expecting a baby, she felt foreign in the town, foreign to herself. And with police and soldiers roaming the streets, even the city frightened her. She wanted out, but at the same time she wanted to belong. She hoped that Lottie Boyle's house would offer a perfect balance of being taken in, yet given little notice.

Everyone said Lottie was a straightforward woman, happy as long as others doted on her. Kaly winced at the thought of brushing the woman's hair, polishing her shoes, picking up after her. Then again, doting was a small price to pay for a home. Especially when she needed one so badly. If Lottie liked her and took her on as one of her girls, life might get a lot easier.

"Kaly!" Beth was sitting forward in the rocker, waving at her.

Kaly waved to Beth. "I'll be there in a few minutes," she said and stalled by two dark-haired girls playing jacks at the edge of the shoveled walkway. One of them caught a ball, her glove full of sharp silver stars. She smiled brilliantly at her triumph, and then at Kaly, holding them up for her admiration. A woman looked out from behind a half-closed curtain on the second floor. Kaly waved to her. The woman waved back.

"Those are some pretty stars." Kaly knelt beside the girls. "You must be two very lucky young ladies."

"They're silver like your scarf," said the girl who held the jacks. Strands of jet-black hair had escaped her knit hat and fallen in her face. Her pink snow pants were stained with dirt.

"I guess they are." Kaly touched the silk scarf she'd looped around her neck. It was a birthday present for Miss Lottie.

"And the ball is red like your dress," the girl said.

Kaly nodded. "And your red ball is the earth, in the center of the stars."

"If the jacks are the stars, and the ball is the earth, where's the moon?"

"The moon? You're the moon. Your very special world has two moons, you and your friend." She smiled at the girls. "What are your names?"

"I'm Leesy. And this is Licia," said the girl with the jacks.

"Are you sisters?"

The girls looked at each other. "We play like we are," said Leesy. "I just have brothers and Licia only has older sisters who ignore her. My real name is Jaleese and Licia's real name is Alicia, but we changed them."

"I see, so you'd be "L" sisters."

The girls giggled.

Kaly admired them and their stolen sisterhood,

"Is that your dog?" Leesy pointed behind Kaly to the wolf dog that sat about ten feet away wagging his tail and pawing the air with his large forefoot.

"No, not mine. He seems to like children." She smiled. "Come here, boy."

Leesy and Licia climbed into each other's arms. "Does he bite?" asked Licia.

"I don't think so. He seems friendly." Kaly put her

hand on his head and the dog laid down, rolled on his back, and bared his belly to her. She rubbed his stomach and he stretched his long neck toward the girls.

As if they were one, the girls edged closer. "Can we pet him?"

"You'd have to ask him," Kaly said.

"Can we?" they asked the dog in unison. The dog wagged his tail and they took it for a yes. As they rubbed his belly, the woman in the window called for Leesy to come home.

The girls went inside. The dog followed Kaly and curled up at the brothel's foundation where peeled green paint revealed a previous crimson coat. Kaly climbed the stone steps to where Beth sat in the rocker.

Even with Beth all bundled up like she was, Kaly could see that she wore the blue silk dress, its puffed skirt spilling out from under a blanket, over the rocker's edges. The dress's sharp cobalt color lit up Beth's full, blushing face and her blue eyes.

Kaly leaned over and kissed her on the cheek.

"What did the doctor say?" her friend asked. She put the knitting down and looked up at Kaly, an anxious lift of the eyebrow, lips pulled in and tight. The blue yarn ran across her lap and down the blanket, where it was attached to a ball that had rolled into a corner

"Not what I thought he'd say." Kaly waved at the air, sending the imagined conversation away in favor of the real one, not quite believing she'd been wrong about the doctors recommendations, knowing she couldn't follow his advice.

"What was your guess?"

"That people like me shouldn't have children." Kaly said. "I was wrong. He actually asked if I could raise the child."

Beth shook her head. A scowl hung on her pursed lips, her eyes twitching, making it clear that she didn't like the news. "It's for sure then? You're pregnant?"

Kaly nodded. Her cheeks felt like they were on fire, like they could burst into flames and burn down the town. She'd gotten used to the heaviness in her breasts, and the tenderness in her body. She still had the morning sickness and, at times, she felt like she'd crawl out of her skin and float off into the vapor-filled sky. But this heat in her face suffocated her. "She is due in August."

Beth's scowl turned to wide-eyed fear. "What are we going to do?"

"I don't know." Kaly felt the shame in her cheeks again.

"You can't let Lottie see that you're pregnant," Beth said. "She'll never take on the burden of a woman with child. And you've got to get in here. It's not safe for you down in the cribs by yourself."

"She'll find out eventually."

"You can't." Beth picked up the knitting and avoided looking at Kaly, tears lining her eyes. "You can't raise a child. You've seen the children raised on the line. They all end up here. Or worse."

Kaly turned and looked out at the town. A few lights had come on down in the flats. The moon peaked up over the beautiful snow-covered East Ridge. The futile dream of raising the child in a mountain cabin hit her in the gut. There was no cabin, no place in life for her and the child. She turned back to Beth and said, "I'll sort it out."

"How? August will be here in no time." Beth chewed her lower lip and shook her head. Disbelief spilled out her eyes. Beth, the one who had protected Kaly from the beginning, had nothing for this.

"You're right. Dr. Fletcher's wrong. What can I give a child?" The truth slammed Kaly in the chest so hard it hurt. She leaned into the sidewall of the porch drawing in a deep slow breath, dropped her face into her hands and started to cry. "Miss Anderson will take the child. She has to!"

Beth leaned forward in the rocker, the legs creaking against the wooden porch boards. "She's not safe there.

You told me."

"Safe. Where in the world will she be safe?"

Beth stood up and wrapped the blanket around Kaly's shoulders, hugging her. Her soft dark curls fell against Kaly's face. When Kaly finally stopped crying, she pushed away from Beth and stared out at the flushed horizon. She ran her fingers down the silver scarf that she'd brought for Miss Lottie.

A light came on inside the brothel and she turned toward it. Through the large window she could see the girls gathering there, filling the dining table with food and drink, adjusting pillows on the sofas, sweeping little bits of dirt from the carpet, getting ready for the grand party.

"I don't know what I'll do," she murmured.

"We have to think of something," Beth said again. "Otherwise, you'll end up begging in the streets. Miss Lottie will say no to the baby."

"Of all the people in this town, she should understand," Kaly murmured. "Maybe if I explain it to her, she'll let me stay on as the maid or something, until the child is born." Kaly's shoulders tensed. Her heart pounded in her chest. She looked down, counting the rotting floorboards in the porch.

When she looked up, Beth shook her head. "It won't work."

Kaly felt her body go quiet. She thought about the tansy hidden in her crib.

"It's no good," Beth was saying, pacing, the dress dragging on the floor behind her. "You'll be in the streets. Alone. And how, pray tell, will you pay a birthing fee?"

"I don't know."

"And who will watch the child while you work?"

"I don't know."

"And what do you think will happen to her while you're out working?"

"Bethy. Please. Let's not talk about it anymore. Let's just enjoy the evening. I'll talk to Miss Lottie. If she doesn't understand, I'll figure it out from there." The hair rose on her arms and a sour taste stung her throat. She felt trapped and began to cry again.

Beth brushed Kaly's brown curls aside. She patted her shoulder through the gray wool blanket. "You gotta stop crying."

"I know. It's just that at times like this I wish I had something."

"A family?"

"A mother. To hold me and tell me everything will be fine. That I'll be fine, the baby will be fine, and we'll figure it out together." Her tongue felt large in her mouth and she resolved again to work hard at the brothel, to mind the rules, to be an asset. "Lottie will see that I'm worth it, if she just gives me a chance."

"Come here." Beth took her by the hand and led her to the rocker. She gestured for Kaly to sit down and when she did, Beth put the blanket over her lap.

"You need to finish your scarf," Kaly said, trying to smile.

Beth knelt down by Kaly. "I'm almost done. It'll wait."

Beth leaned in close. "It's gonna be just fine," she whispered. "We'll figure it out. We'll be each other's mother. When the baby is born you can send the poor thing off to live with Miss Anderson, if you think it's right. She won't say no."

Kaly swayed in the rocker with Beth at her side. Chatter, laughter, clanging dishes, and light footsteps drifted out to them from inside. Through the window Kaly saw that the big room was decorated in reds and yellows for the party.

"Now there's a fine sight." The voice came from the porch steps, where Dan McClane stood in the half-dark evening. He held his work clothes and hardhat under his arm in a bundle. His hazel eyes sparkled. "Two grown women holding each other and crying. You girls didn't lose at poker again last night, did you?"

"Hey, Danny." Kaly tilted her head back. "Looks like you're off to work."

"On my way to the Orphan Girl. Just thought I'd pop in and say hello."

Kaly heaved herself out of the rocking chair, feeling large and awkward. She wondered if Dan knew she was pregnant. But that was silly. Other than the red dress getting snug, she hadn't begun to show yet. She'd like to tell him. She had known Dan for years and she trusted him. Instead she teased him, a safer strategy.

""I saw you dancing with that girl. At the Silver Bow Bakery. You know, the Slav? She laughed so hard, tears ran down her face and she looked like she carried the light of angels. Marika Lailich, that's her name. The girl with the soft, easy smile. She your girl now?"

"She looked like she needed cheering up." Dan said. He took his cap off and ran a hand through his light brown hair. "That's all."

"Nothing wrong with that girl, except that she's too innocent for you. You gotta be nice to her. She has a special place in my heart."

Dan tilted his head in a question.

"She looks like my sister. Every time I see her I feel a sense of family. Like maybe somehow I can stop Annie from dying and keep her close."

Dan's eyes softened. "I'm sorry about Anne Marie. That would be so difficult to lose a sister like that."

Kaly shrugged. "It's hard. Just be kind to her. She seems like a nice kid."

"I'm pretty sure she can take care of herself."

"She fell in love with you before the first dance steps."

"Oh no. You're dreaming, Kaly. I'm grateful for the compliment, but no woman has ever fallen in love with me that quickly." Dan held his cap to his chest. Where the hat had pressed against his forehead, his hair stuck to his skin. A few strands stood straight up.

"You underestimate yourself, Danny Dear," Beth said.

She stepped forward, pulling her coat tight against the wind. "Girls fall for you all the time."

Kaly nodded. "You'll break her heart in a second, just like it's nothing. Then you'll act like nothing happened, all pleased with yourself."

"I barely even know her."

"You swing a woman in your arms like that, and she'll fall for you every time." Beth looked at Kaly and they nodded to each other.

"I see. It's some women's secret," Dan said.

Beth smiled sweetly and nodded.

He looked back and forth between them, as if urging the secret from the duo. When neither of them revealed anything he said, "Well, for all the world to know: that was simply dancing. No more. No less."

"The dance of love." Kaly drew "love" into two syllables, her voice lilting.

"If that was all it took." His voice dropped a notch and he looked down at his boots. "Love would pour out of the bakery instead cigar smoke. The whole town would be in love. Even the mining bosses. But those bosses got a mean streak. They love nothing."

"Yeah, especially late miners," Kaly said, feeling guilty for keeping him. "You better go before you miss your shift."

Everyone in Butte knew the foremen were sticklers about time. They lowered the cage five minutes after the whistle, and anyone who missed the cage dropped a day of work, sometimes got fired. A man could always rustle a new job the next day and sometimes even get back on at the same mine, but eventually word got around. Then a man might spend days—weeks even—in the rustling line before working again.

Kaly touched her stomach. She felt the tiniest bulge under her wool coat. Suddenly she had a crazy desire to let him into her intimate life. He could be a sort of uncle for her unborn child. She wanted to confide in him as if he were her brother, feel his air of protection. Kaly reached out her hand to him.

As if reading Kaly's mind, Beth shook her head "no," a primitive urge to protect her, Kaly thought. It worked. Kaly stopped, looked down the hill toward the flats. Lights had come on all across the town, stretching like fingers to the East Ridge, where the crimson moon appeared, full and beautiful now, high above the mountains.

Dan stepped toward her and took her hand. Nearly six feet tall, he looked down, meeting her eyes. He held back slightly, as though putting a protective distance between them, and held her carefully. She knew he should leave immediately. But Kaly threw her head back like a schoolgirl and laughed a sweet laugh.

Dan McClane swung her in his arms and danced her across the wooden porch.

"Two not-so-complete strangers dancing on my front porch." Lottie Boyle bellowed as she climbed the stone steps. A line of men—including Bert Brown—followed her. "That's a fine spectacle." Her course voice boomed in Kaly's ears, jarring the night.

Dan gently let go of her and walked toward the stairs. "I'm sorry, Ma'am. I was just leaving. I'm on my way to work."

"No. Stay. We're having a birthday party for some decrepit old maid. It's a surprise." She laughed, walked over to Kaly, and pulled the silver scarf off her neck. "Thank you. You're welcome to stay for the party but you're much too old to be one of my girls."

"How did you know we wanted to ask you that?" Kaly slipped her eyes from Lottie to Bert, who just shrugged, and then to Beth, who hid her face. Kaly's heart thudded in her chest. Heat rushed to her cheeks again, capturing the shame, humiliating her, and reminding her that she was alone. Unbelievably alone. The knowledge stunned her, and she could barely stand.

"Deary, I haven't come to be in charge of the finest

home in town by keeping my nose in silt. I have a few secrets up my own puffed skirts." She looked Kaly up and down as if she'd just examined a bad cow and was ready to move on to a better slaughterhouse. "As far as that bastard child of yours goes, don't even give it a second thought. I'm less interested in that kid than the dirt on the mister's work boots there." She wrapped the silver scarf around her neck, walked over to the rocking chair and picked up Beth's scarf too, the blue yarn unraveling as she sauntered into the house.

Kaly froze. The heat hit her stomach hard and her breasts drooped heavily, her breath catching like the red ball in her throat. The world went fuzzy. She hadn't had a chance and she hadn't even known it. The mine whistle blew for the late shift, and the wolf dog howled. Kaly looked at Beth as if she could make it right.

Her friend winced and shrugged, tears spilling down her cheeks.

At the bottom of the stairs, Dan held up his hand, offering Kaly a graceful out.

Lottie stepped back out onto the porch, took Beth by the arm and pulled her into the house, the two scarves trailing behind them like flags. "Let's cut the cake!" the woman hollered, and the girls cheered.

Dan would miss the cage and likely get canned.

But there was nothing for it.

She stumbled down the stairs and took his hand. With Dan and the dog, under the pregnant red moon, Kaly fled into the street.

8
A DOCTOR'S WORK

Marika placed the essentials in her bag: tape, Mercurochrome, smelling salts, scissors, a needle, and thread. She went to the back door and listened to her parents stacking wood. They were trying to get the chore done before it rained. Marika slipped on her father's canvas coat and snuck out the front door. She hated herself for slinking away like this, keeping her ears wide open, hoping to be long up Montana Street by the time her parents walked inside.

Her self-loathing grew with each step she took away from Papa's imagined gaze, the one that would demand she stay home, marry Michael, carry out a woman's tradition. She chastised herself for stealing dreams instead of honoring family loyalty. There was no honor in deceit. In spite of her good heart, she'd turned into a liar. Another thing she hated.

The wind blew in gusts and rattles, shutters swinging on their hinges, stray papers soaring down the street, telling her to go home where she belonged. She bit her lip and threw a shoulder into the wind, bracing herself against it. She thought about this match between Tommy Monroe and Bert Brown and how badly she wanted to prove that she was worthy of a job with Dr. Fletcher.

The sun dropped over the edge of the western valley as the rain sped in. It beat at her with tiny hands. Her skin pimpled up and she shivered. The cold rain quickly turned to sleet that whipped against Marika's face. She'd tied her hair in a bun at the back of her neck, exposing her cheeks to the wild weather. They were bound to be as red as the cotton skirt she wore.

As she approached the Casino, she glanced around, looking for Papa's friends. If any of them saw her there, they would race off to tell him. Eyes intent and focused. Taking care of his little girl. With a kind smile Papa would thank them. Then he would come to get her, drag her home, and ruin her chances with the doctor.

Just walk, she told herself. Shut up your mind and walk.

From across the street she watched the Casino doors open and close as people flooded into the tavern. Laughter rolled out the doors, toward her, inviting her in. You too. Walk into the magical world beyond the gateway. The dazzling, reckless, outrageous Casino where you can watch men beat each other to a pulp. And here she was trying to do something good about it.

The doors swung out and a man stumbled past her. She took a deep breath and marched into the smoky lights, stood on her tiptoes, and gazed across the crowd. The bartender caught her eye. Not wanting to be noticed, she slipped down out of his sight, the throng hiding her as she pressed herself against the wall.

Heads turned. Lips moved. Faces nodded. Arms waved. But no one seemed real. It all seemed like slow motion, everyone talking at once, words blurred together, the buzz palpable. A man slammed a glass onto a table and startled her. The bartender dropped a bottle of whiskey, and Marika jumped. The noises struck her ears like gunshots, reminding her of Montenegro. She found a secure place to stand and looked out through the moving bodies. On one side of the bar, a wiry man was roping off a boxing arena. People were jamming into the rows of chairs surrounding the ring, chattering over their drinks.

Marika turned sideways to make her way through the mob. She looked at the floor where the men would compete. It was dirty and bloodstained. She cringed, imagining a boxer with an open wound landing in the dirt there, infection an eager badger. She imagined other wounds too. A cheek cut open from sharp knuckles to the face, a concussion from hitting the floor too hard, a broken hand from slamming into a rigid body. She was hoping she could make it through the night without losing her nerve. Just slide in, like a true medic, and take care of the injuries. It wasn't so much to ask.

"Hey, Blossom," said the wiry man, stepping out of the ring lights and into the shadows. He had a narrow face with a sharp chin, and clear blue eyes. "You here for the fights?"

Her heart raced as she bit her lip, clutched her bag, and nodded. "Dr. Fletcher sent me." The lie slipped out of her mouth so easily. She was willing to bet it wouldn't be the only lie told tonight.

The man laughed. "That's a big, fat waste of time. The only way these guys'll allow doctoring is if they're out cold."

"Dr. Fletcher has faith in me and so should you," she countered. She looked around. "Where's the doctor's station?"

"Well, Doc Blossom, wherever you're standing, I reckon, is the doctor's station." He turned and pulled a chair from a stack in the corner for her, and set it behind a chair occupied by a tall, wide man. The wiry man flashed her several smiles as he set up the remaining chairs and benches. Smiling back at him Marika waited until he wasn't looking, and then moved the chair to a place with a better view.

Her eyes watered from the thick smoke in the room.

She kept glancing over at the doors, dreading the moment the doctor walked in. She'd rehearsed a speech to convince him to hire her, but her mind went blank when she tried to remember it. She would have to be like the fighters and think on her feet. She would have to trust fate, punch from the gut, and speak from a clear mind. Although, with the crowd, the smoke and the lies, nothing in this room was clear.

"Can these guys actually see to fight?" she asked the wiry man when he passed by. She waved a hand through the bulky gray haze blanketing the room.

"Sure, they're used to it," he replied, motioning for her to follow him. "Here's a chair closer to the ring, and I've cleared a space. A bucket of water and an extra towel for you are here. There are two more in each corner. If you need something, ask me and I'll get it."

"Thank you. What's your name?"

"Ted Framer. I'm a miner, at the Speculator."

She nodded, felt her chest go rigid. Her breath caught in her throat. If Ted worked at the Speculator he probably knew Papa. "But you work here."

"Sadly, refereeing don't pay the bills. I gotta put food on the table."

Baba used to say a man has to put food on the table. She felt her grandmother's ethereal hand reach across the ocean, reminding her of her purpose, imbuing her with the soft glow of courage. "I'm Marika. What time does Dr. Fletcher usually show up?"

"What?" Ted lifted a questioning eyebrow.

"Dr. Fletcher. He'll be here soon, won't he?"

"He don't come to these things. Ain't that why he sent you?"

Marika slipped off her father's coat, sat in the lonely chair, and felt her cheeks flush, feeling every bit the imposter that she was. Three men near the door roughhoused with each other. A girl who couldn't be older than fourteen stood by and watched. Kaly Shane sat at the bar, the red satin dress hugging her back. She tilted her amber cheekbones defiantly toward the blunted light.

From this far away Marika couldn't see her eyes, but she knew that they were the color of the sea, large and changing, full of mystery. Perhaps she should pity the woman. Mama and the priest would both encourage sympathy. More than feeling sorry for her, Marika wondered what possessed the woman to so boldly command attention. She wanted to go talk to her, but decided against it, staying put and waiting for the match to start.

"Why do men fight?" Marika had asked Baba one day during the Balkan Wars. They'd been on their way to the medical tents to take care of the wounded soldiers.

"Words are empty without the actions to back them up," Baba had said. Her brow had furrowed under her black and gray hair. She'd cut it short to keep it out of the way. She had worn a long dark skirt and a dark top, a uniform designed to hide dirt and blood. "Good men stand by their words," her grandmother had told her.

Marika had given Dr. Fletcher her words and now she would act. If all went well, she would convince him that the boxers should have a regular doctor attend the fights, and that she should be that doctor. Never mind that she wasn't a doctor. It would be good for business though. It would be good money, and an essential service to the town. The Doc would see for himself that she had a talent for it. That she could learn. Then he would finally take her on as an apprentice. It was the one thing she wanted more than anything else: to study medicine.

"I don't get it," Ted Framer was saying, shaking his head. "The doc's never sent anyone over here before. He's never even attended a fight before. And why didn't he just do it himself, if he was going to be here?"

"You said he doesn't come to these things."

"Guess I was wrong. He's at the bar next to Michael Jovich."

Marika snapped her head toward the bar. There was Dr. Fletcher, next to a tall, dark-haired man, Michael Jovich, her fiancé.

Of all her heart's luck.

"Mr. Framer, can you keep a secret?"

Ted sealed his lips.

"My grandmother taught me about healing and I want to learn more. Last week I tried to get Dr. Fletcher to hire me, and he said 'no.' I thought he'd be here, and if he needed help I could show him that I'd be of use."

"Whooh Boy, you called that one good. He's here alright."

"Well then you said he doesn't come to fights, so I thought I'd just impose myself as the doctor." She was talking fast, so that Ted would not rat her out. "He won't like it that I lied to you. But I didn't know what else to do. Did he see me?"

"Like I'd know." Ted's voice had grown cool. He frowned as he looked at the special seat he's put out for her, evidently deciding against retrieving it. "Let's hope you know what you're doing."

Marika shook her head. She felt light and airy, ready to float away into the Rocky Mountains and settle, like an owl, on a dark branch. Just then there was a commotion at the bar. Some man had Kaly Shane pinned to the counter. She was slapping and pushing at him as if he was a pesky fly.

Dr. Fletcher stepped in, flapping his arms and saying something. The man let go of Kaly and dove for Dr. Fletcher, who quickly stepped aside. The man fell on his face. Several men at the bar laughed. Kaly froze for a brief moment, then, fists clenched, eyes wide-open and bruised looking, her face tight as a bolt, she disappeared into the smoky haze.

Marika watched her red satin dress fold into the crowd. We're alike, she thought, looking down at her own red cotton skirt. We are two sides of the same woman. Marika was strong, independent, bull-headed and trying to prove herself in a man's world. Kaly was vibrant, independent, stubborn, caught in a dangerous job of catering to men.

"Why does she put up with it?" She mumbled through clenched teeth. She told herself that she ought to leave too, before Dr. Fletcher spotted her. Before Michael spotted her and, heaven forbid, introduced himself. She located the back door. She would use it, if need be.

Ted shrugged, head tilted, a baffled look on his face.

"Do you know her?" Marika focused on the spot where Kaly had just disappeared, and, as if by some magic trick, she'd reappear with a rabbit in hand.

"Who doesn't?" Ted asked. He pushed his toes against the floor, drawing invisible, hesitant lines on the wood, ones he might not cross over. "Nice kid. Got herself into a load of trouble early on. She'd better be careful, though. A whore over on Idaho, Lacy Blue, got herself killed last month."

Marika suddenly felt weightless, helpless, the soft spirit of the dead woman whispering in her ear, telling her to protect Kaly.

"Maybe she could do something else," she said.

"You might save your breath on that. Her life's hard. She didn't have much of a chance from the start."

"What do you mean?"

"She had nothing to stand on from the get go. Some girls and boys with no one to raise them, they don't make it. Children that have at least one parent can go to the Paul Clark Home, giving them a better chance at life."

"One parent or no parents, what's the difference? They still don't get to live with their families." Marika had a family, she reminded herself, a simple fact that would never change. No matter what she thought of Mama and Papa's rules and traditions, she had spent her whole life with them. Something no one could take away from her.

"At the home, there's a hired staff round-the-clock. So the kids always have someone to go to."

"How many kids live there?"

"Twenty to twenty-five. Kaly, she has no home to go to." Ted rubbed his chin hard with his forearm, drew in a breath of the thick air and looked over to the spot where Kaly had disappeared.

"You seem to know a lot about it," Marika said.

"I lived at the Paul Clark Home for a while. My pa died when me and my brother were young. My ma struggled. A widow only gets five bucks a month per kid from the county. I don't know about you girls, but boys can put away a lot of food. And if the boys work, the county takes that money away from the widow. I don't know what Silver Bow County expects."

Marika thought about that, thought about Papa's black lungs. "Which do you think is more dangerous, mining or prostitution?"

"Ain't no neither nor, Doc. The two go hand in hand."

Suddenly the doors slammed against the inside wall as a tall husky man strutted in. He looked mean and mad-dog scary, dark eyes staring out under tense eyebrows, shoulders pushing through the swarm. He raised his clenched fist in the air and punched at an invisible foe. The crowd yelled. He took off his shirt revealing a solid mass of muscles rolling across his chest. He slid the shirt across the shiny wooden bar to the bartender, who gave him a pair of boxing gloves and a shot glass full of whiskey.

"Bert Brown," Ted said.

"He looks familiar." A sick feeling crawled across Marika's chest, Lacey Blue coming like the wind, whispering in her ear again, holding out a vaporous hand.

Bert drank the shot and pointed to a brown bottle on the back shelf.

The bartender filled the glass a second time.

Bert slugged the booze down and caved his mouth into a circle. His massive chest trembled as he growled out a loud, horrible sound. Marika had heard sounds like his in the hospital tent, when the recovered men readied themselves for battle. His fans surrounded him blurring Marika's vision and she was glad of it. The man eked a kind of cruelty that slapped a hand over Marika's mouth, shutting her up. Closing down her breath.

Breathe, she told herself.

And breathe she did, sitting herself down in her doctor's seat.

But she didn't stay there, standing quickly when the door opened again. This time Tommy Monroe entered. His shoulders slumped and his head drooped. He shuffled his feet toward the bar, waiting feebly for others to move aside, the exact opposite of Bert. Looking like he did, it was hard to believe that Tommy had never lost a fight. He didn't look like he could win, didn't even look like the same man she'd seen at the doctor's office last week. His skin drooped on his face, pale and oxygen poor, as if he'd been weak and in bed for days.

Marika knew the outcome here. Tommy was already beaten.

The two men climbed into the ring with Ted Framer, and took their corners.

The crowd cheered. Tommy. Tommy. Bert. Bert. Bert.

Tommy looked toward the bar.

Bert jerked his head in that direction.

Kaly Shane had reappeared and stood at the bar, calm and composed. She had pinned her hair up into perfect curls, full of shine, shimmering with their own little lives. She squished herself in between two men, one of them Dan McClane. His tall straight back, his light brown hair, his green laughing eyes. Marika's heart missed a beat.

Of course he'd be here. He looked so comfortable beside Kaly, like best friends, nothing else in it, she thought. She hoped. She closed her eyes as a wild, dizzying wave swept over her. For a sad second she wanted to feel his hand on her waist again. Forget it. He's gone. She'd never get a relationship with him past Papa.

Kaly stood next to Dan with relaxed, happy shoulders.

She held up a hand, fingers formed in a soft inviting curl, as if asking the stars to attend. Her lips glowed with an easy smile as she gazed toward the men in the ring. The strength of the woman's rebound was so complete that it dazzled Marika. What kind of courage, or desperation, pushed a woman to transform like that, and in so little time?

Bert bowed toward Kaly, bounced around, and punched the air. His red hair flopped against his ears, partially covering a mass of freckles there. His cold blue eyes looked menacing. Marika would not want to be on the other side of them.

Tommy sat on his stool, shaking.

"Ted," she said, loud enough to be heard over the crowd. When Ted looked at her, she shook her head, warning him off of the fight. She glanced over at Dr. Fletcher. He didn't seem to notice her. More importantly, he didn't seem to notice Tommy's sickness. He should have. The doctor had just seen him, likely told him not to fight in the first place. And here Tommy was, proving the doctor right. Indignation beat at Marika's chest.

Ted glanced at her and called the two fighters to the center. Tommy peeled himself off of the stool, his face all red blotches and white spots, and shuffled toward the referee. He stood there panting, sweat beading on his forehead, his dull brown eyes watery and rimmed with red, his gloved fists hanging loosely at his sides. He'll go down quickly and not come up, Marika thought, as though thinking it would make it happen.

Guilt toppled the indignation and its acid taste hit her throat.

She should have minded Papa. Here, where she could only see devastation, she couldn't do anything to stop it. But then, when men died in the hospital tent in Montenegro, she hadn't even tried.

Marika stood and shook her head again.

Ted checked the fighters' gloves.

"Wait," she said.

A hundred eyes turned to her, including Dr. Fletcher's and Michael Jovich's. And Dan McClane's. She felt the burn of his eyes, like all the others. The most cursed, wicked fire, though, came from Bert and Tommy. She didn't care. Tommy was really ill. He was in no shape to fight.

"He can't fight," she told Ted.

"Sit down, Doc," he said.

"He's ill. There's no fairness in that."

Framer looked at the two men. "Ready?"

They both nodded.

The bell rang and Bert lunged toward Tommy. He threw his first punch at Tommy's face and missed. The fist flew through thin air.

Tommy's knees had already buckled, and he crumpled to the floor.

Marika jumped into the ring. She felt Tommy's forehead. He had a fever.

"Listen, Blossom, you're about to get kicked out of here," Ted said, smiling at the crowd, whispering sideways through his teeth. "Doc Fetcher doesn't look too happy. Not to mention all the others who want to see this. You're breaking regulations. I'll thank you to take your seat."

Marika didn't like it, but she sat down.

Ted started the fight again.

Tommy stood and butted his fists together. His brown eyes wavered as he bounced heavily in place.

Bert wasted no time. He grinned sharply and caught Tommy in the stomach with an upper cut, then slammed a fist into his jaw, not once or twice, but three rapid hits, winding Tommy's neck into a ghostly arc.

He went down again.

Framer counted to six before Tommy got to his knees and pushed himself up onto his quivering legs. He blew his breath out heavily, and Marika saw the large thick exhales that brought him here, risking his life for fame, or revenge.

She didn't know which. She only knew that it was wrong.

The bell rang and Tommy took a seat in the corner. Someone toweled off his face and gave him water.

Marika imagined what the coach was telling Tommy. Step sideways, let Bert's weight carry him off balance, then come in with an uppercut to the chin. A move that he was bound to execute too slowly. She held her breath, waiting helplessly for his demise.

The bell rang and the fight resumed, Tommy weaving into the middle of the ring. Bert smirking.

Bert faked a punch.

Tommy flinched.

Bert faked another, and laughed, looking around at the crowd, pulling their amusement into it, a melody of sick joy. He faked one more punch, but this time he followed with a right upper cut to Tommy's chin.

Tommy went down and didn't get up.

At the end of the count, Ted raised Bert's hand.

As the audience cheered and booed, a man approached the ring and whispered something to Ted.

Ted nodded and raised his hand to silence the crowd. The two fighters would have a rematch in two weeks, he said, looking to Bert for agreement.

"Yessiree!" Bert yelled, bouncing around and punching the air.

Ted climbed out of the ring. Marika rose to talk to him. He pushed his palm toward her, shaking his head. Shoving his way through the crowd, the referee disappeared to the back of the Casino.

At the edge of the ring, Tommy sat staring vacantly in her direction.

When Marika stood to go to him, he growled.

She sat back down.

Bert headed straight for Kaly Shane. When he reached her, he passed his gloves to the bartender, retrieving his shirt in return. Kaly started to move away from Bert but he flipped the shirt over her head, capturing her at the waist and pulling her toward him.

She pushed him away.

It looked like an innocent game of tug-of-war, but Marika saw the fear on Kaly's face. Bystanders were caught up in their own conversations. Dan had already left and, in a tavern full of people, Kaly seemed to be on her own.

Tommy looked like he saw it too. His legs trembled as he stood, like they'd collapse under him. Still, he lumbered toward Kaly and Bert. When he got to the bar he threw a slow-moving fist at Bert.

Bert easily blocked him, and hit Tommy hard in the face.

Tommy fell backwards.

Bert snickered, his scowl twisted into something inhuman, and picked up a whiskey bottle. He held it menacingly above Tommy's head. "Stop now," he snarled loudly. Marika moved closer to hear better.

Michael Jovich stepped between the two men and stopped the potential violence, grabbing hold of the bottle. "Not this way fellas," Michael said.

Bert stared at him and finally let go. Michael passed the whisky bottle over to the bartender.

Marika was glad that Michael stopped this fight. Something she hadn't been able to do with the one in the ring.

"You wanna fight outside the ring," Bert drawled, stretching his head around Michael to glare at Tommy. "The rules change."

Tommy took a seat at the bar. "Gimme a whiskey," he said.

"The doctor told you to lay off the stuff," the bartender said as he poured a shot.

"Ya, ya. I know. It's medicinal. And it's my business."

Kaly freed herself from Bert and bolted to the far end of the bar.

The two fighters ignored each other.

Michael ignored them both.

Marika walked over and stood by Kaly. "Are you ok?" She asked.

"Yeah. Fine." Kaly stared at the back bar. A glass of water had appeared in front of her.

"Bert's a mean man. What's wrong with him?"

"He's been terrorizing me and Tommy since we were kids," Kaly said. "You don't want to get mixed up in this."

"Where is your friend, the other woman who is usually with you?"

"Beth? I don't know. She's off on her own somewhere. Or she might be home in bed. She wasn't feeling so good today." Kaly frowned, the grimace setting low in her jaw. She took a sip of water as if sealing her lips, confusing Marika. Marika wasn't out for blood or money. She was just trying to understand. And be friendly.

When Kaly spoke again it was with a deep whisper that rattled Marika. "You don't want in any of this," she said. "Go home. This is no life for you."

The words cut like a knife, slicing at her desire to be a fight doctor. As though weighted to the saloon floor she shuffled back to where Ted cleaned the ring. This was a world Marika didn't understand. The smoke hurt her eyes, and she rubbed them. Kaly's words stuck in her chest and made her arms feel weak.

She'd been completely useless here. She'd destroyed Papa's trust in her, and for what? To stand hopelessly aside and watch a sick man get hammered? She was pathetic.

Kaly was right. She should go. There was nothing she could do here. She pulled Papa's coat off of the chair and put it on.

"The best man doesn't always win," Ted said.

"You think I made a fool of myself," she said. "But I think you should've stopped the fight."

"You already pissed off enough people. You think I should piss off the rest of them?" Ted had already restacked most of the chairs. He pushed a broom across the floor, gathering up small mounds of sawdust and leaving them to be picked up later. The half-finished job irritated Marika. But it wasn't her business. Why should she care?

Having been dismissed at every turn, she wiped her hands on her skirt, wiping away the bitter failure of the night. But the rejections clung to her. "Bert could've killed Tommy tonight," she told Ted. "At least I spoke up."

"Dr. Fletcher didn't seem to mind the fight. He was sitting right there."

"He wasn't close enough to see how sick Tommy was. I was, and so were you. There was nothing fair about that fight. It was like letting a full grown man beat an invalid."

"Better not let Tommy hear you say that. Besides, he'll have another chance."

"Yeah. Some chance."

"I'll walk you home," Ted said.

"No," she said, avoiding his eyes. She also avoided looking at the bar, where Michael Jovich and Dr. Fletcher sat. "I'm fine."

Her hair and every stitch of clothing she wore reeked of smoke. Maybe the smell of Papa's pipe would disguise the Casino smell. Outside the sleet was coming down hard. Hazy amber light from the streetlamp cast angled shadows through the moisture. Marika pulled the coat up over her head.

"Miss Lailich."

She turned. Dr. Fletcher stood in the doorway of the Casino.

"Are you thinking of opening your own practice? Hanging out a shingle? Wooing patients with witchcraft and wives tales? There are laws and morals, and I'd suggest you pay attention to them if you want to serve people well."

"I'm sorry." Marika nearly swallowed the words. "I thought I could show you that I'd be of use. I was hoping to prove myself to you."

"Rethink your strategy. Stay away from the fights. You're likely to get yourself in trouble, or killed." Dr. Fletcher turned with a flip of his arm and the Casino absorbed him back into its dark haze. "Oh, and Miss Lailich," he added, popping his head back out the door, "you don't stop a fight in the ring. It's not your place. Wiser men than you have stepped aside when two good fighters step in."

"I'll remember that," she said, wondering what on earth she would tell Papa when she got home.

9
BOXING MATCH

$\mathcal{S}$weaty and breathless, Kaly was stuck in the nightmare. The blue scar moved toward her, making her hurt all over. The boot, the pale face, the smell of whiskey. They all followed that horrible scar.

When the dream vanished, the dread hung on like fever. Kaly woke up in a quiet despair, her heart racing, a chilly pressure filling her chest. Her head was dull and thick, as if full of water. She rubbed her eyes and shivered, to shake off the feverish feeling. Pouring rain had ensued during the two weeks since Tommy and Bert's fight and should have taken the bad dreams away. Instead the rain had stolen the snow and, at night when the temperature dropped below freezing, the rain spread glassy ice across the city, leaving Kaly alone with the nightmares that began when her sister died.

The smoldering fire warmed the room. Outside, the relentless rain had turned to slush and then to snow falling softly from the fickle sky. The dream and the snow reminded her of Anne Marie. "Winter," her sister used to say, making the word sparkle with enthusiasm. Anne Marie had created a wonder of delight as the twins stepped off together into that glittering, darling world—with only Kaly to return, separate and singular, alone.

Winter. When they were young, the word from Anne Marie's lips had warded off the bad feelings and taken away all things dark and dirty. Her sister's word had turned their lives as brilliant as the sun. Radiant and clean. Winter. Yet, Kaly could not reconcile her twin's notion of such magic with that one dark thief of a winter that took her sister into its murky oblivion where she vanished forever.

Kaly'd had the nightmare many times, and now the images sharpened. The old, scruffy boot with missing laces kicked the snow just below the pallid face. It was a pallid, smirking face with yellow teeth that were pushed forward and to one side, as if a shovel had banged into them. The blue scar stretched across someone's collarbone, glaring at her with a terrible, grinning life of its own. When she tried really hard, she could almost see the face above the blue scar. The boots, the awful teeth, and the scar held some secret key to Kaly's past—a past she wanted to leave buried.

She shuffled to the small vanity table against the crib wall. A kerosene lantern hung from the ceiling. The eight-by-eight room held all of her belongings: a photograph of Annie, two dresses, the wool coat, a red sweater, a shawl, a pot for water, the snow lily plant, a tin of condoms, and a simple painting of white roses.

Kaly pulled the red dress over her slip. She buttoned the front of it and fluffed its wide skirt. Pulling it underneath her as she sat on the low stool, she pressed her palm flat against the mirror. Her reflection was pale and sickly. Her brown tangled hair was flattened to the side of her head. Her sharp cheekbones cast dark shadows down her face. Blue half-circles cupped her dull green eyes, and she wiped the sleep from them.

The red dress fit tightly around the waist now. She'd be in real trouble if she grew out of it. A new dress was hard to come by, and expensive. With the pregnancy, her cleavage had burst to life in a new way, delightful and heavy, invitingly charming. Kaly smiled at that. Evidently, she hadn't completely given up the idea of love, even if her breasts did serve another purpose.

Before she'd ever acquired the red satin, someone had painstakingly sewn tiny cloth buttons up the front of the dress. She admired them now, the ease with which they afforded her to dress and undress, such a delicate device for such a brutish job. The dressmaker had sewn a beautiful cream lace along the collar, giving it a modern elegant look.

And here she was looking old and tattered, her face wrinkled and used up, her belly swelling toward that one final moment. Miss Lottie was right. Kaly was far too weathered for such a lovely dress, far too wrong to raise a child, far too old for this horrible trade. It should have already killed her.

The dream. It kept crashing in at her. She tried to shake the bad feelings off. "A dream is just a dream," she reminded herself, words she'd used to comfort her sister when she'd wake up screaming. "It's OK, Kaly's here," she'd told Anne Marie. "No one will hurt you. You're safe. I'll keep you safe."

But she hadn't kept her twin safe. Bad things had happened, really bad things, and Kaly hadn't protected her. Each time the nightmare groped Kaly, she woke up thinking about Anne Marie and the storm that killed her. Thinking about Tommy leaning over Anne Marie like a viper. Thinking about the blue scar. Thinking about her own terrible mistakes. If she'd kept a tighter rein on things, her sister would still be alive. If she'd paid attention, kept her sister close, asked for help, Anne Marie might still be here at her side, not here in the crib, but both of them living in a home, managing a store or doing housekeeping somewhere.

Clean work. Proud work.

The thought took her breath away. She leaned in

toward the mirror. Pain whipped across her shoulders, tightening them into a solid pulsing muscle. The pain grew until she thought she'd pass out, wanting only to go back to bed and find a dreamless sleep. But that wasn't possible. She needed the night. Needed to go out. Needed to work.

"You're a trapped and dirty mess," Kaly told the mirror. She poured water into a metal washbasin, set it on the small stove and tried to ignore her lurking thoughts. A dream was not just a dream. It was information. That winter day when Tommy had leaned over her beautiful, silent Anne Marie, the snow had captured a second set of footprints—footprints much larger than Tommy's. The footprints of someone else who'd been there that day. The large prints pulsed through Kaly's bad dream like a child playing catch-me-if-you-can.

Kaly could catch him. But she didn't want to. She just wanted him gone.

"Hey doll, you about ready?" Beth stood in the doorway in the same blue silk dress she'd worn for Lottie Boyle's birthday party. Her steely blue eyes shifted dreamily as she glanced back at the girls from the brothel. Three of them stood waiting for her, all of them with that same dreamy look, all of them in glorious new gowns.

Kaly knew that Beth and the others had been to the opium dens. She wished they hadn't, and she wished she didn't know. But then, how could she complain, she had the tansy potion set aside, in case she simply couldn't bear this life any longer. She'd been trying, but she'd never had an easy go of it. Perhaps she should try the temporary relief that the opium offered. Probably better than that final portion of tansy and arsenic she had tucked away. She hugged her arms tightly and motioned for Beth to come in and close the door.

In a dark, sleepy voice Beth told the other girls to go on without her. She sat on Kaly's bed and looked into the mirror, while Kaly struggled with her tangled hair, attempting to muscle it into shape. Feeling hopeless, Kaly finally gave up on trying to style her unruly mane and marveled at Beth.

Beth had pinned her own dark locks up onto her head, allowing long tresses to cascade down to her smooth neck. She had dark blue, mysterious eyes, soft, full lips and cheekbones sharp, high and lovely. She moved with the agile body of a dancer, full of story and grace. Even the air around Beth seemed rich and full of meaning.

Beth's strong muscles in her arms and legs, the strength of her good heart and determination, made the blue dress lovely. On anyone else it might have looked fragile and bird-like. But on Beth it was beautiful. Still, Kaly couldn't help but wonder, how long it would be—if she kept with the opium—before her heart turned, and her body weakened, turning her sick and wretched.

"We can watch Tommy get creamed tonight," Beth said with a smile, her salty, slow voice dancing around the small room. She loped her eyes at Kaly. "After that last pathetic fight, the crowd will be hungry for blood. You know how men are after a good match, they just want to keep fighting." Beth took a playful swing at Kaly's arm and missed.

Kaly started to cry. Tears dropped onto the red dress, leaving dark, blood like splotches that would later dry, and disguise her pain as beauty. She leaned forward on the vanity, letting her tears fall onto the poorly painted table. Someone, a previous tenant maybe, had smeared a white coat across it, leaving tiny snow-like ridges in the wood.

"Hey Kay Kay, I didn't mean it to hurt you. Here, try some of this." She pulled an opium pipe out of her pocket and pushed it toward Kaly. The skin on her hand was dry and flaking, bright red from the cold. It looked like the skin on Kaly's face, undernourished, poorly cared for, pushed to some invisible limit.

Kaly shifted her thin shoulders and shook her head. "The baby."

"Just a little won't hurt, it'll help with the night." Beth's dark ringlets bounced lightly on her shoulders, working with the opium to make her look soft and fairylike, someone who could wave a magic wand and disappear all bad things.

Kaly wanted that, wanted the dread to go away. She wanted to feel free and easy again. But she hadn't felt that since Annie died, and, as far as she knew, there was no remedy for death.

"No," she said. "I better not. Just help me with my hair."

"Yes, you are a wee bit of a wild wreck." Beth slowly untangled Kaly's brown hair, twisted it into a French roll, and secured it with black hairpins. Pulling a lock of bangs out, she draped it across Kaly's forehead. "There you go, transformed into a real beauty. Now let's get out of here."

Outside of the Casino, Beth rushed ahead to see the fighters, leaving Kaly to lumber behind. A group of teenage boys converged on her. She recognized one of them from the fights last Fourth of July. He was a slim muscled boy with a broad forehead, a square jaw line and skin blotched with pimples. After those fights, he'd tried to parade his own independence with her. When she rejected him, he came at her in a vicious rage. "Whore!" he had yelled at her then.

"Whore!" he yelled at her now.

"Slut!" one of his friends yelled.

"Crawl back under the boardwalk, where you belong," another jeered.

Kaly pulled her wrap tightly and turned away.

The Fourth of July boy grabbed her, smudging the red satin with dirt, hurting her arm. She slapped at him with her free hand. When his grip tightened she pulled her skirt out of the way and kicked him hard with her heeled boot. This only enraged him further and she felt like a rag doll in his clutch.

As the other boys closed in, Beth showed up out of

nowhere, without a care in the world, as strong as a fallen angel. She walked into the center of the attackers and calmly lifted the boy's fingers off of Kaly. "Get lost," she snarled.

They scattered.

Beth wrapped an arm around Kaly and walked her into the Casino. It was a kind gesture, but Kaly felt no safer than she had when she first woke up from the nightmare. The dread clung to her like mining dust. She had a bad feeling about the night.

The bouncer motioned Kaly and Beth through the door, into a cloud of smoke. The place was jammed with people. A few played at the billiards table. Others played a sullen-faced poker. Bare bulbs hung from the ceiling throwing off a mild light. At the center of the room, two teenage boys prepared to box, testing their amateur skills and warming the crowd for Tommy and Bert.

Kaly was surprised to see that the Fourth of July boy had made it so quickly into the Casino and was one of the first fighters up. He wore loose shorts and no shirt. Bruises rippled down his ribs. A red rash covered his left shoulder. He didn't look like he'd put up much fuss. The other boy didn't look much better. He was tall and lanky, skin barely hanging on his bones. Sparse stubble grew on his chin. A dull sheen crossed his eyes, his lips thin and fragile, giving an empty vacuous look to his face.

She watched the two boys with pity and curiosity, wondering why two such unfortunate souls would get in the ring together. The bell rang and they shuffled across the fight floor. The Fourth of July Boy threw a slow, almost absent-minded, uppercut toward the other fighter. The tall boy danced around the ring, dodging the punch and answering it with a left jab to the head, knocking the Fourth of July Boy to his knees. She saw then that the red rash also covered his back, as if he'd already been in a fight and lost. Kaly almost felt sorry for him.

He stood up, looking brave, and moved toward the tall

boy. But he was heavy footed, still in a stupor, and the daze fastened him to the floor. The tall boy rapidly spun his fists. The Fourth of July boy took a solid hook to the face, his face going blank and far away. After a flurry of punches from the tall, lanky boy, he crumpled to the floor.

"Get up." Kaly threw the thought at him as hard as she could, as if her mind could overtake his inertia. She didn't know why she cared. He didn't get up. It was a knock out.

The crowd cheered.

Ted, the referee, counted to ten and declared the tall boy the winner.

"There's some good old fashioned justice for you," Beth said, with an edge in her voice, shifting her eyes back and forth, the opium wearing thin. "What goes around comes around. I've never seen a bully yet who didn't get what he had coming to him." But Kaly wasn't so sure anymore. The kid looked like he had big troubles of his own, that rash, those bruised ribs. Someone had already lathered him in anger.

Beth winked at a man across the ring. He blushed and turned his head. "Your loss," she shrugged, turning her attention to those at the bar.

During the brief intermission, spectators lit up cigars and pipes.

The thick smoke choked and nauseated Kaly. She ordered a soda to calm her stomach. When the crowd cheered again, she looked up to see Tommy Monroe saunter into the ring. He wore red shorts and a white towel draped over his shoulders.

Unlike the fight two weeks ago, Tommy's brown eyes were rich and fresh, attentive to each small movement. The scar on his cheek smiled at the crowd. He stood tall, with strong shoulders and a straight back, his stance solid. He pushed his brown hair away from his broad forehead, set his jaw and bounced around his corner punching at the air, clearly recovered from his sickness, ready to fight.

In that dark bar with the dirty floors, Kaly surprised

herself by thinking about the future. She hoped the baby would look like him with dark brown hair, deep brown eyes and an agile, narrow back, with strong muscles and long legs. But more than that, she hoped the baby would have her father's attitude. He didn't give up. And he took care of others. The child would need both strength and compassion to survive the rough haul of growing up in a mining town.

Bert Brown stepped up to his corner stool, his red hair hanging down past his chin. His watery blue eyes full of vile made her shudder. He wore black shorts and a white T-shirt.

The crowd's cheers thundered across the tense, excited room.

Beth joined the shouting and waved her arms.

Even with the last fight's mishap, Tommy was still favored to win. Most of the crowd considered Bert a madman looking to get hurt. As far as Kaly could tell, they cheered for the possibility of his pain. It was a cheer she'd join later.

"I'm a fan of the underdog," Beth said.

"Bert scares me." His face struck a bad chord in Kaly, making her want to slink away and hide. He stared at her and that sense of being hunted prey pulsed through her legs, making them heavy, as if she were running through deep snow.

Beth watched him, then squinted at Kaly, something akin to jealousy shining in her eyes. "Bert scares you more than that big Monroe?"

Kaly fanned away the cigar smoke that had drifted over from another table. "Tommy's a friend. He confuses me, but I trust him."

"You OK?" Beth asked. "You look pale."

Kaly pressed a protective hand against her stomach. The mistakes in her life swirled around like the fallout from an ice storm, loneliness crashing down on her, the changes solid and bound to last. "The pregnancy is making me sick."

"At least it's temporary," Beth said flippantly, countering Kaly's sense of pending doom. The dark-haired beauty looked over at Bert, obviously having other priorities.

Ted Framer called the fighters into the ring, held up his index finger, and yelled, "Round one!" The bell sounded, the crowd went wild and Framer took a step back.

Tommy wasted no time. He dove at Bert, throwing a right hook that caught him square and hard in the chin.

Bert's head bounced back like a shortly tethered ball. He recovered quickly and ducked out of Tommy's next punch.

Tommy followed with a left jab that glanced off Bert's shoulder, and a right upper cut to Bert's ribs.

Bert dropped to his knees and took the count nearly to its end before he stood again.

Kaly leaned forward and back, her legs twitching under the red satin with each hit, acting as Tommy's trivial second. It was clear: Tommy had not only recovered from his illness, but also strengthened his resolve. He jabbed, and Bert took the jab square in the face.

Kaly cringed as Bert's head jerked back.

He stumbled and recovered. Fury gathered like a dark cloud around him, blurring his red hair and blue eyes into a gray ash. He lunged toward Tommy, throwing a right roundhouse that caught Tommy square on the cheek, breaking it open into a bloody mess. Bert connected with a left punch, turning Tommy's other cheek for him, backing Tommy off. Then Bert slid in with an uppercut, which Tommy managed to block. Bert threw another right roundhouse, pounding Tommy's wounded cheek. Bert slammed him with a left punch and an uppercut to the stomach.

Tommy stumbled, and Bert nailed him in the ribs.

Leaning in close, Bert whispered something in Tommy's ear.

Tommy exploded with fury, coming out of his stupor. He raged through Bert like a wind-whipped grass fire.

Bert tried to block the punches, but wasn't fast enough.

Tommy's uppercut slammed into Bert's chin, jerking his head back. Something cracked. Bert went down like a felled tree and never got up.

The crowd roared.

The referee raised Tommy's hand.

Tommy ran his eyes across the crowd and stopped them on Kaly. She knew those eyes. The kindness in them frightened her. She looked away.

Twenty minutes later Tommy stood in front of her, dressed in tan trousers, a red plaid shirt and black boots, his wet brown hair slicked straight back, his cheek swollen. His dark eyes twitched under his broad forehead, shining in the light. He smelled like whiskey. Kaly had long ago grown tired of the smell of heavy drinkers, and with the pregnancy, her revulsion nearly turned her heels to run.

"Glad you're here," he said.

"You fought well."

"Can I buy you a drink?" With a half-closed fist, he caressed his own forearm. His hair fell forward and he smiled at her, his eyes pressing her to agree.

She felt her heart go still. A sharp pain shot through her like broken glass. She didn't want to love Tommy. She didn't want to love anyone. Love hurt. People died. And she was left alone.

"I don't know," she said and looked away.

"Stay and dance with me, at least. It's a celebration."

"A celebration of battles. How long will you two carry on your childhood wars?" She had watched them vying for power, fists to the face, bloody knuckles brought to Miss Anderson, always blaming each other like they had no control over their swinging limbs. When they were young, it had been scary, but always with the matron's end in sight. Now, nothing stopped them from killing each other if they wanted to take it that far.

"As long as it takes," Tommy said. He reached out and pulled her close. The fight ring was now a dance floor and he twirled her to the band's music.

Heat spiraled up her belly. She wanted nothing to do with him, and everything to do with him. His salty rough smell dizzied her will in a way that would lead to a pile of crumpled clothes by the bedside if she didn't stop it now. She didn't understand herself, but she did understand the smell of whiskey. The smells on Tommy—of the fight and his drink—pulled her too near to the dream and the blue scar. Dread barged in, stomping the floor, slamming doors, taking over all sensibilities, stealing love right out from under her fingertips. She had to get out of there. She spotted Beth across the room, laughing with Bert and his fans. Beth held an ice pack to Bert's jaw.

An old man walked past. "Good fight, fella." The man winked at Kaly. "Keep him happy, doll."

"Or," Tommy said, as if reading her mind, "me and you, we could get out of here together."

Once again, she yearned to tell him about the baby, ask him for help, but the paralyzing inertia covered her, wrapping her vocal chords in a dark gauze. "I'm not well," she said, hating the coldness in her own voice but helpless to do anything about it. "I'm going home."

"Want me to come with you?"

His whiskey breath permeated the air. His body reeked of sweat.

He held her arm too tightly and it hurt.

Anger rose up in her and she yanked herself free of his grip. "I need to go find Beth." Kaly walked away from him. The smoky air surrounded her, floating like hazy shadows that tracked her every wrong move.

But Beth didn't want to leave. "Now, during the best part?" She winked and curled her arm around Bert Brown's waist. "Not a chance."

Kaly did her best not to glare at Bert. She wanted to

bust her knuckles across his cheek, the one that Tommy had just broken open. But she knew it would get her nowhere. She pulled her sweater around her shoulders and said, "I'm leaving by myself then."

Beth pointed across the room. "Your friend is sitting at the bar. I bet you two had some fun the other night." She sounded like her mouth was full of sweet corn, and her eyes were half shut.

Kaly wanted to slap her out of the opium and into the reality of the night. Instead, she followed the line of her pointing finger.

Dan McClane stood at the bar talking to a short, bald man in a leather shirt and leather pants, a wood worker who ran a shop on East Galena. When times were slow the man worked at the Speculator.

"Dan took me for tea at the Goldmine after Lottie's so-called party, and then walked me home. That's all." Which was more than you did, Kaly wanted to say. But didn't. She left Beth hanging on Bert, and walked toward Dan.

Tommy intercepted her and gently took her arm. "Hey Kay, I thought that we were all made up."

"Let me go, Tommy. I'm no good for you."

"Let me decide that."

Her aching lungs had weakened her and she felt the fever spread across her face. But still she resisted the urge to relax into him.

"Hey, the lady doesn't want to go with you." Bert now stood on Kaly's other side. He grabbed her free arm.

Tommy tightened his grip and pulled her toward him.

With her arms stretched between the two men, Kaly's head spun. Something cold as the dark lake in the Highlands froze in her veins. She tried to pull her arms in, yanking them both toward her chest. The two men blended into one horrible monster.

"Let go of me," she yelled. Disinhabited faces with deaf ears floated in front of her like specters. She swung her elbows back and up, struggling with a fierce heart. Like a wild animal she would chew off her hands to escape their grip. She twisted her neck and reached for Bert's rugged flesh, biting down hard. A pain hit her head, flashing a brilliant white light filled with doubtful angels.

The night caved in on her. She struggled for air. The pallid face and the grinning blue scar swirled around the room. The nightmare face smelled of whiskey and lunged at her. Not now, not here! Kaly struggled to push the demon nightmare away and stay alert to the air of the Casino and Tommy Monroe and Bert Brown's fingers pinching her bicep. She finally freed one arm from Tommy, and slammed her fist into Bert's broken cheek.

Bert grabbed her hard and shook her.

He seemed unreal, far away, laughing. With a last surge of strength Kaly dug her nails into Bert's wrist and slammed her head into his bruised chest. She twisted her neck and bit him again.

"You bitch!" He snarled, loosening his grip on her. His eyes narrowed to twitching slits. He doubled a fist and swung hard, hitting her square in the face. He swung again and slammed her nose. Her head flew back and forth like a banked billiards ball. White fire raged up her spine to her brain and she dropped like a rock to the sawdust floor.

Kaly didn't feel Bert kick her stomach, didn't see Tommy lunge for Bert's throat and bring him to the floor beside her. She didn't see Tommy's fist crash into Bert's wounded face, or Bert smash Tommy's head against the floor.

Kaly floated far from the crowded Casino into the dream, the white dog at her side, the icy air filling her lungs, the odor of whiskey, sweet and pungent. The black boots stood at her feet. The blue scar coiled and grinned down someone's collarbone. A white ashy face laughed and leered and rough hands pressed into her. The face hovered over her in anger and descended on her, pinning her arms to the pure white ground, where they stayed frozen under the silver, silken snow.

Wake Up Jim, Mountain Con, Orphan Girl, Neversweat. Never ever sweat now, be sweet now, Wake Up Jim, she says, wake up Jimmy. It's time to get up and go home.

Kaly floated from the bad dream of the leering face and the scar into another dream, a lovely, fresh dream where the winter sun shone brightly and Anne Marie lived, and the blended conversations from the festive night murmured into cold silence.

1895
THE WHITE DOG WATCHES

*W*hen the old-time miner finally leaves his body and soars into sky, the air in his lungs is clean and fresh. His legs are strong again and, if he wants, he can run to the top of the East Ridge and back without a single gasp. He might've known he'd die in an explosion, but he never thought, in all of his wild, vapor-infested dreams, that he'd explode as a spectator in the streets of his own town where a warehouse caught fire.

If he could cross back over and talk to the living, he'd tell them that he's free and it's a great day to be free. He'd say that going suddenly has its advantages. There is no enduring pain, no years of suffering, and no longing for the future. He can hang around the earth for three days, or until the burial, whichever comes last, and watch. During that time he slides comfortably between two worlds—one filled with wonder and awe, the other laced with sobbing and loss.

On this night the ghostly white dog makes his way through the splintered wood in the smoke-black snow. Medical wagons carry people away from the fire. A man digs a hole in a pile of ashes. Another splashes water on the pile and the hot spot bubbles and hisses like a snake pit. Steam rises into the smoldering night like cloudy ghouls. Two women place a charred body in a horse-drawn wagon. The blackened arm from another body hangs loosely over the front wheel. All night long voices flare. Among the dead, people find the living. As morning approaches, the shrieks and commands fade away. In a cold silence, everyone works together.

The milky sun reveals blood-soaked snow covered with soot. The white dog steps around the bodies and the shattered bricks that cover several blocks. He avoids the broken glass and the scattered workers trying to clean the streets. They toss debris into a separate wagon, careful not to throw debris into the wagons that hold legs, arms, torsos, feet, and bodies.

The men and women of the cleanup crew came to watch the fire department extinguish another flame. But this time the firemen couldn't put out the flame. This time the wind had blown the blaze to a hardware building where dynamite hid, waiting. The firemen had no chance of surviving the explosion, and they didn't even know it, leaving the cleanup to the town's people.

Somewhere nearby, a young woman pulls a boy of about ten from a burned body. "Shhhh. It's ok. We'll take care of her," she says.

The boy yells and lurches from the woman, grabbing the singed body by the shoulders. Pieces of burnt flesh rise and glide on the north wind. He hugs the melted face to his chest, rocks the body back and forth, rocks her like she might have rocked him when he was a baby.

The woman wraps her arms around both the boy and the corpse. "What's your name?" she asks, her voice gentle.

"Tommy."

"It's OK, Tommy," she tells him. "Come with me. They'll take her to a place where she can be cared for and she won't hurt anymore." The woman whispers the words as if casting a spell.

The boy softens in her arms. He slowly loosens his grip on the corpse, and two men in soot-covered overalls pick it up and place it in the dead wagon. When the horses pull the wagon away, the boy tries to sprint after it.

The woman tightens her hold on him, cooing that he'll be safe, that his mother is gone, that the town will take care of him now.

The next day, the white dog visits the Polly May and the boy from the fire sits at the kitchen table between the look-alike girls, across the table from the tall, copper-haired boy. The boy from the fire stares at something on the far wall and the dark haired girl stares with him. It's as if they're mesmerized by something magical, something only the two of them can see.

The white dog, a simple spirit of himself, walks over to the girl and puts his head under her hand, as if asking her to pet him. But she doesn't pet him. She takes her hand from his head and places it in her lap, as if shaking off an unseasonable fly, as if he isn't even there. The white dog goes to the boy from the fire and puts his head in the boy's lap. When the boy doesn't respond, the dog nudges his leg with his nose. When the boy still doesn't even look at him, the dog follows the woman who fed him two days before. He trots behind her to the back of the Polly May where there's a long room filled with books and a bitter, wild smell.

The room is so full of frightened children.

One little girl cries and clutches her blanket to her chin. Another squishes her eyes shut and refuses to open them. A small boy watches with glazed eyes from a dusty corner. The woman passes out muffins to each child. She stops to pat a young boy's head. She pulls a tear-soaked girl close, wipes the hair out of the girl's face, and hums a lullaby.

The white dog and the woman return to the kitchen. The dog whines, his whine floating off into the smoky air, unheard by any. He slinks over to his empty food dish, and lies down. The children at the table eat quietly. After breakfast no one comes over to scratch the dog's ears, or rough up his fur, or roll their heads across his belly. Even the woman is oblivious to his presence. She doesn't fix any food for him and his water dish remains ash-dry.

The streets are as quiet as fallen snow, as thick as a paralyzed dream. The dog drags himself through the drifts. No one reaches out a mittened hand to pat his head.

Something is wrong.

Their strides are heavy, their faces pale below hair frozen stiff by the wind. One man tethers a solitary horse to the rail edging the icy boardwalk in front of the blacksmith's shop. Another gathers the last body parts from the neighborhood surrounding the warehouse. Homes and hotels are now hospitals and people comb through temporary morgues.

Wherever the white dog goes, the people ignore him. It's as if he has disintegrated into dust and no longer exists. He pulls at their hands and whines at their sides. He sleeps just beyond their doorways. When they still don't see him or hear him, the fur on his back stands straight up and he bares his teeth to the crowd. His eyes flash. He howls like a wild wolf enraged and digs through the snow to the rock hard dirt. Still no one notices. The change in the blackened city has already spread like smoke and plumed, downy and light, into the frigid sky.

SPRING 1917
10
THE BLUE SCAR

Two days after Bert's vicious attack, Kaly was still unconscious, unaware of the material world. In another world somewhere, her vision blurred. There was Anne Marie, who didn't speak but rather, put one quiet finger to her lips. Her hand glided through a golden light, stretching gracefully through an azure mist and washing Kaly's face with a warm, sweet cloth. The bright sun floated in through the crib's window like a smile. The electric blue room was brand new, transcendent and heavenly. Her make-up shone on the vanity table. The red satin hung on the wall like a sunset. The tiny door next to her bed radiated a shimmering clean yellow. Even the polished floor glowed with the life that had once pulsed through its maple roots.

Anne Marie's face brightened, then faded. Kaly could not hold onto the image of her sister, or hear her precious laugh. A high wind picked up outside and rushed under the door like the tiny hands that kept swooping in to cover Kaly's eyes. She swooned under the pressure of those hands, hands that now turned the damp air dark and cold. A fierce ash spun around her face. The room filled with the voices of little children crying, laughing, and begging for attention. They were the ones who came to live at the Polly May after the warehouse fire took their parents. The children had been cut wide-open and sewn back together again. One boy lost his vision, another his ability to make coherent words. Miss Anderson took in the flood of children, and food was scarcer than ever. The faces and tiny bodies wiggled around Kaly, bumping her, causing tiny prickles to race down her spine.

When the ghostly children left, Kaly felt Anne Marie's hands and the tepid washcloth on her face. She slid her elbow under her like a crutch, but it collapsed. The soft bed feathers swallowed her up and she couldn't breathe. Anne Marie lay next to her now, silent and cold as a winter log. Kaly turned on her side and, with a leaden arm, dragged the snow-white blanket up over her sister's chest to warm her.

A vaporous hand reached out from under the covers and capped her mouth shut. The disembodied hand dragged Kaly through the feather bed and back into a dark memory, back to the hard, cold ground outside the Polly May where she'd found her sister frozen.

Kaly and Anne Marie were ten. The back door of the Victorian house opened into a jungle of trees painted white with freshly fallen snow. A storm had ravaged the pines and they built a fort with the fallen branches.

"Take only the branches that are already broken, and be careful," Kaly told Annie.

"Why can't I break the limbs off? The trees don't care."

"They do care. The fallen branches are ready to be used. The other ones haven't given us permission to use them."

"Trees can't talk," Anne Marie said, pointing to the

back door where Bert Brown stood swinging a stick. His red hair straggled down past his cheeks. A sneer hung on his lips. He was a tall, heavy boy by then, old enough to leave the Polly May and live on his own. He'd been standing in that doorframe for a while. Icicles had already begun to freeze in his hair.

"Ignore him," Kaly said, turning back to her sister, the hair on her neck standing up. Wind circled through the tops of the trees and howled down toward them. She braced herself against it, holding strong, staying with the game. "If the branches haven't fallen, they're not ready to be a fort." She explained it to Annie with the voice of a wiser, older sibling, even though they were the same age.

"You mean they still want to be a tree?" Annie kept her eyes on Bert.

"Yes."

Anne Marie frowned as she finally looked back at their fort. Kaly let go the breath she'd been holding. Together they gathered the nearby branches and searched the far borders of the white forest for more limbs.

"Let's make a home that's just ours, and maybe Tommy's," Annie said. "But no one else's."

"Not Tommy," Kaly said. With Tommy there, Anne Marie would ignore her and Kaly would feel alone. When Anne Marie went off on her own, looking for more broken branches, the snow blew hard against Kaly's frozen cheeks and she collapsed the fort. The branches fell into a disorganized pile. She felt happy about ruining the fort and forbidding Tommy's entry. Plus, she knew that Anne Marie would forgive her.

A sudden cold scream shook her silly. It was long and low, as if from a wild animal. The sheet-white day enveloped her as she ran to find her sister. She heard a sound scrape across the snow. "Annie?" she whispered. "Is that you?"

Silence. Just silent snow and wind filling the sky.

Something moved, fast as the wind and growing like a

hailstorm. The branches rustled and snapped as big feet crashed through them. Kaly picked up a branch, clenched it tightly. "Go away!" she hollered. "Leave us alone!" That was when the world went black, and then, not too long after, a sharp pain jabbed the base of her neck and her back slammed against the ground.

Kaly tried to get up. The pain jumped from her neck to her head. She couldn't move. Lying there on the forest floor, she saw work boots with mud and snow caked on them. The laces were missing. She wondered where the missing laces had gone and why the feet inside those boots hadn't frozen from the snow that was packed around the ankles. A large hand dropped out of the white snow, the long fingers gripping the broken stick, the smell of whiskey in the air. Kaly's heart beat in her head. She felt her pulse inching around her face.

She tried again to get up, but her arms jerked out from under her. Someone pulled them over her head and flattened them against the ground. Laughter broke out. Eerie, deep laughter. Mean laughter. Above her, a head loomed, disconnected and foggy and grinning. A stocking hat was pulled down over his forehead, nearly closing his eyes. The man, the boy, the boy-man, was a misguided hunter. He must've mistaken her for a wild fawn or a downed eagle, spreading its broken wings across the drift.

He growled something, a blue scar snaking down his collarbone. Terrified and furious, she kicked at the scar with her small pointed boots. The head disappeared and then her legs were spread, grabbing the ground like her arms. The floating grin descended on her. The weight of a thousand mountains crushed down on Kaly's chest. The pain in her head shot through her neck and arms. Sharp pain sizzled down her torso, to her pelvis and legs.

Wake up Jim, Wake up Jim, Kaly Jim. Orphan Girl.
Wake up, Kaly.
Wake up.

Finally the numbness came. The pain in her pelvis was

the last to go. She curled up inside herself, a tiny fetal ball hiding inside her own belly. She floated above herself, above the man's matted hair sticking out from under the stocking cap. Kaly flew in the golden clouds for moments—or hours—waiting for him to be done with her. Waiting for her body to be her own again. The white dog—the dog from the fire—sat in the clouds beside her. Together they watched the hunter as he poached his prey.

When she came to, Kaly wandered through the storm trying to find the Polly May. Or a street, or anything familiar. She wanted her sister or Miss Anderson. The pure white blinded her in every direction. She walked into a tree. She ran into a fence. She fell in the snow, where it dropped into a deep ditch. She was trapped and she panicked. "Help!" she called, the word muffled by the snow and frozen in mid-air.

When she finally found Anne Marie, Tommy was leaning over her. Kaly could not awaken her sister. She shook Anne Marie, but her sister was in a deep sleep. She turned on Tommy and he ran for Miss Anderson. Whatever Tommy had done to Anne Marie must have made her very tired. Kaly would take care of it; she would simply take Annie home and put her to bed. She would miss dinner, sure, but old Miss Anderson probably wouldn't feed them, anyway. She never fed them when they came in late.

Kaly pulled Annie across the ground and stumbled, aching from the forest snow. Anne Marie slipped out of her grip and fell limply, all shoulders and legs, on top of her. She stood up and dragged her sister, the heaviest thing she had ever moved, to the smashed fort and tried to crawl inside of the crumpled pile, tugging the branches over them and sat there until Tommy returned.

"You have to come inside," Tommy said. Miss Anderson's head peered over the top of his.

"Go get the police," Miss Anderson told him.

The police came with the ambulance and took Anne

Marie away.

Tommy pulled Kaly from the ambulance and held her tight. "It's OK," he kept saying. "They'll take her to a place where she won't hurt anymore."

He helped Kaly back to the Polly May. As they entered the back door, a policeman came in behind them. He grabbed Tommy's shoulders and pried his hands off Kaly, leaving long bruises on her arms where Tommy had tried to hold fast.

Kaly climbed the stairs to the second floor. She walked down the hallway past pictures of the fine men and women who donated money every year to help Miss Anderson keep the Polly May open. The children thanked God for them each night at dinner. From her bedroom window she watched the policeman pack Tommy into the back of the Model T and drive away. When the sun disappeared, Kaly crawled into bed and covered herself with the warmest quilt, the one she and Anne Marie usually fought over.

Anne Marie never came home from the hospital. Kaly wrestled that night and woke up sick, pushing away the remembered screams, the fetal position, the staring after something dark. By the time Kaly walked downstairs for breakfast, she didn't understand why she'd been sent to bed without dinner, why her little belly was cramped in its emptiness. She didn't understand where her sister was.

So many polite and kind people came to Annie's funeral. Kaly thought she might drown in a landslide of black sweetness. After the burial, she looked for Tommy. His were the one pair of hands that might dig her out from under the rubble of her shattered life. When she couldn't find him, she knew that her worst fears had come true. He had disappeared with her sister.

A woman dressed in a downy gray suit stood apart from the crowd. She touched Kaly's head as she passed. Kaly thought the woman might take her. Then she'd disappear like her sister and Tommy. But the woman didn't take her. She simply touched Kaly's head and vanished.

Bert Brown glared at her from the edge of the cemetery. A cold wind sped up her spine, circled her neck and held her breathless. Her chest hurt. At first, she glared back at him, never having told anyone that he'd been there the day that Annie died, knowing that Miss Anderson wouldn't believe her. He held his glare, never even flinching, cutting her courage with that look, until she turned away. By the time she looked back, he too was gone.

Kaly tried hard to wake up from that deep and dreadful sleep, to make her way back to her simple crib. She could feel herself emerging, just behind her eyes, knowing it would only take a little more effort and she could come out of this stupor, sit on the edge of her bed and throw cold water on her face. She knew the blue scar. She didn't want to know it and had tried to push it away, letting the past die, letting sleeping dogs lie, as Miss Anderson had said. But she knew.

She also knew why she'd never told anyone. She'd been paralyzed with fear after he raped her. And then her sister died and the world became surreal, untouchable, someone else's horrible dream. She couldn't reconcile the rape with Annie's death. Grief swelled so large inside of her that it allowed no room for memory or pain. The numbness of that day had followed her like an old dog.

When the police took Tommy away and blamed him for Annie's death, Kaly knew right away that something was wrong. But she had no proof of anything. It wasn't Tommy, and she had a good idea of who it had been. But she hadn't even pointed a finger in that direction.

Under her closed eyes her mind twitched and circled, reaching for breath, coming back to this dark fog, not awake but not quite asleep. She heard sounds outside of the crib, the rain patting against the roof, horse hooves clopping down the street, the sirens of a shift change. The smells of sulfur, exhaust, and horse dung wafted in through the window. The bed suffocated her and she wanted out of it, but she couldn't move. Her arms were too heavy, her head fused to the pillow, her eyelids fastened shut. She wanted to call out to someone for help, but she couldn't move her lips to speak.

The light beyond her eyes rippled like metal bars of the jail that she was stuck in, and somewhere among the layers: Tommy and the baby. But only one person kept banging against the bars. She knew it as if Anne Marie, light as the mountain air, sat on the bed next to her, swinging her legs, counting to a hundred, effortlessly flipping the jail key from one hand to the other.

Bert Brown.

He banged against those bars, loud and terrible, demanding her silence, demanding her oblivion. He'd been the one person never accounted for at the time that her sister died. Had he gotten to Annie before he pinned Kaly's back to the ground and sat on her like a horrible monster, the worst of thieves? No. Not the worst. Someone had stolen Anne Marie's life. Someone had reached into that tenth year of her youth and snatched away Annie's future like it was a bright orange ball.

When Kaly finally opened her eyes and looked at the ceiling of her crib she hurt all over. The wind whispered under a crack in the door. A fire had been built and stoked to keep the room warm. The golden sun glimmered through her window, weightless and gentle, causing the room to glow like a mystical supper. She turned toward the chair at her bedside, and then toward the vanity table. No one was there.

She could feel the remnants of the past landing on her like dark confetti, too light to break the skin, but nevertheless hurting every small bit of her body. The thief that had taken Anne Marie's life had left an invisible scar, just over a pain so deep it shot down to the center of the earth. Just under the surface of the stories told, just under Kaly's frozen façade, the blue scar across Bert's collarbone haunted her.

11
FAITH AND MEDICINE

*T*he sun inched above the East Ridge into a foggy blue sky. A soft morning wind blew a flurry of dried weeds past Marika as she left the house to check on Kaly. The woman had been punched hard and Marika had come out of the shadows to help her. Papa had been fuming mad when she got home so late the night of Bert and Tommy's rematch, but she'd assured her father that she was through with disobeying him. From now on, she'd promised, she would behave like a good daughter.

At the time she'd meant it.

Marika entered the alley behind Mercury Street, trying to put Papa out of her mind. He wasn't that easy to forget, though. His commanding voice roared in her head as she hurried to Kaly's crib.

She simply could not obey his rules, not with Kaly needing her so badly. Papa would do exactly as she was doing. He would step in and offer vital help to any person who needed it. He would never leave a person in danger to fend for herself. After all, he had brought ice and food to Tara McClane for over a year. He risked fighting with Mama for the secret alliance with Dan's family, an alliance that still mystified her. And that's what she'd tell him if he asked.

She pressed her palms together and felt her heart beating fast in her chest. The wind came on stronger now, and slapped a warning against her face. She ignored it, pushed into it even, and forged past the brick buildings and down through the narrow passageway to Kaly's crib.

The alley was strange and unnaturally quiet. The tiny rooms of the empty cribs huddled next to each other like cold, lost soldiers. Leftover paper flowers and old scarves decorated the doors. Torn curtains and lengths of rope tied the doors shut. Broken bits of glass littered the entryway to Kaly's crib, halting Marika's heart, worry blazing down the alley like wildfire. Had Bert gotten back to Kaly and finished what he'd started?

Marika knocked lightly on her door, pushed against the thin wood, and peeked into the room. A bruised face poked out from under a white quilt. A white stone cross, attached to a leather strip, lay at Kaly's neck. Her brown hair fanned out across the pillow, making her look like she'd already crossed over and was waiting for a proper burial. In a painting above the bed, three white roses bloomed. The ceiling lamp flickered, giving off a soft amber light. The scent of lavender, sweet and fragrant, hit Marika's nose.

"Well come in or don't. But either way, close the door." Dr. Fletcher sat in a chair to the side of Kaly's bed. He wore a white shirt and brown trousers, his shoes polished and shining. Light poured in from the window and across the large chair that nearly swallowed him, making him look slight and fragile. But his intent gaze at Marika dismissed any semblance of weakness. "You keep barging in on a professional practice. Or are you good friends with the sick girl? What are you doing here? And what is that in your hand? Let me guess. You thought the girl might benefit from magical herbs and chants."

His words assaulted Marika and she stopped abruptly in the doorway. "I thought maybe I could help. There are no laws against friendships, are there?"

"But that's a medicine bag in your hand." His voice was deadly calm as he stared at her. A bead of sweat had formed on his baldhead, most likely from the warm, still air in the room. He wiped it away, picked up a pencil and jotted something on a pad in his lap.

"It is," Marika said, the cat with the canary in her mouth.

"So you have just decided to take up practicing medicine in town whether or not you know what you're doing. Don't you see the dangers you put others in? They believe you. Belief won't cure an infection or deliver a baby..."

"She's pregnant?"

"Never mind!"

"If you'd believe in me, I could be of use. I welcome your guidance, but you're stingy with your knowledge. Why won't you just help me?" She stepped in and shut the door behind her.

"For one, you're a liar. You told Ted Framer that I sent you to be the fight doctor. For two, you're presumptuous. You presume to have knowledge it's taken me years to gain. And three, you're stubborn and impatient. You don't listen. You're like a child who keeps grabbing for what she wants and needs her hand slapped."

Marika put up her arm to stop the flurry of insults. She felt her face go hot. "I will learn doctoring one way or another. I'm not giving up. If you won't teach me, I'll find someone who will."

"Like, for instance, medical school? You'll end up in big trouble if you keep misrepresenting yourself." He shook his head. "Because I feel an irrational need to take care of the wayward young, I've decided to try to keep you out of trouble, to keep you from causing harm to those you take it upon yourself to heal. But, understand, to be a proper doctor, if that's what you want, you must get yourself into a medical school."

She stared at him.

"Have a seat." He motioned to a spot on the bed next to Kaly.

Marika hesitated. She didn't trust his sudden change of heart.

"She won't bite."

She sat. The bed had a soft, uneasy feeling to it.

"She continues to go in and out of sleep. I believe she's got an infection in her lungs, bronchitis, most likely," Dr. Fletcher said, cleaning his spectacles with a handkerchief. "When she wakes up, get her some clean water and food."

"Of course," Marika said, calming herself, too innocent to reign in her enthusiasm, her suspicions scattering like dust. "I can try smelling salts to wake her. I can bathe her in eucalyptus and make ginger tea."

The doctor took a deep breath.

She watched his Adam's apple rise and fall as he swallowed.

"Tell her stories if you want," he finally said. "Ask questions. Get her to respond. But please keep your wives' tales and herbs in your bag. We do not wave a magic wand to cure a patient. I'll be back tomorrow morning."

Tomorrow morning. Papa wouldn't like it if she stayed the night. Her parents would worry. Even at her worst, she knew she couldn't stay the night. But Kaly needed her. The doctor needed her.

Dr. Fletcher got up and went to the door. "Keep in mind, Miss Lailich, that a doctor's work is confidential. No one's business is no one's business."

Kaly did not look good. Her swollen lip had seven stitches. A purple mound left only a narrow slit for her eye. The cut on her forehead already bulged with infection.

Under the quilt her whole body seemed bloated and it looked wrong. Marika studied the blue veins in her uninjured eyelid. It was smooth and young, a sad match to its mangled twin. Just looking at it hurt.

In the corner, a red satin dress hung on the wall. Behind it was a lavender colored dress, more stylish and proper, like Mama's. Marika took the red satin and held it to her, admiring it in the vanity mirror. She imagined herself in the ballroom at the Columbia Gardens, where Dan twirled her across the floor. What would it be like to dance in puffed petticoats and a stiff corset? Marika had never owned such a dress. She looked down at her own gray skirt. It was a plain, practical skirt, hanging in simple cotton folds to her ankles. She put the red dress back.

Wringing the water from a warm washcloth, she touched the wet rag to Kaly's cheek. The woman flinched and Marika smiled. She'd wake up soon. As a girl, Marika had watched Baba lead injured soldiers out of a worse kind of battered sleep. One man had slept through several sunsets. Baba had tended to him and prayed over him. His comrades outside the hospital tent had been singing "Battle of the Blackbirds."

"Long ago, far away on a field like any other, Heaven above, heaven below, bird hearts called each brother. Blackbirds fly, blackbirds sing, for their ruby homeland, sky shines through, earth bells ring, warriors take their stand."

Ten years old at the time, and not her first visit to the hospital tent, she'd listened to the singing and later, to the cold air hissing through the birch branches. Squirrels ran for cover as the tent's canvas billowed in the wind. The sound of distant gunshots made her queasy and the smell of burned flesh made her want to flee.

Instead, she sat near the entrance and watched Baba move from one injured man to the next, disinfecting wounds and stitching cuts. She had seen her grandmother cauterize the stump of a patient's missing thumb. The soldier had turned his head away, his face squeezed tight.

Marika finally calmed her nerves and, when Baba asked, she brought the cloth to her grandmother, stood at her side and held the scissors. The man passed out before Baba finished dressing the wound. At dusk the soldier still slept. He'd stayed asleep for three days.

Papa had argued with Baba. "Marika is too young," he said. "A child has no place on the battlefield." He'd ruled the hospital tent off limits for his daughter.

A few days after Papa said she couldn't help Baba, Marika snuck out of the house, slid under the canvas, and watched from a corner. When Baba stopped at the sleeping man's bed, Marika crept to her side. The man woke up screaming, his face covered in sweat as he tore at the missing thumb.

Baba sent Marika home. From that day on, Baba agreed with Papa: Marika was too young. "You must wait," Baba had said.

Now Dr. Fletcher was giving her a chance. She didn't have to wait any longer.

Alone with Kaly, in an official capacity, Marika was suddenly afraid. Anything could happen. Kaly might stop breathing. Her heart might convulse and squeeze shut. Marika wouldn't know what to do. She'd have no way to contact the doctor and Kaly could die.

She pulled the woman's hands from under the covers and washed her long, elegant fingers. The nails had been cut and cleaned. Her arm was lax, thin, and pale white. Water from the rag dripped down her arm and Marika caught it by wrapping her palm around her bicep.

A knock sounded and the door opened. Dan McClane's mother stood there, wearing a long skirt and a brown knit shawl. She smelled like freshly baked bread. Her hazel eyes scanned the room as if snagging images on a hook, but stopped and narrowed when she saw Kaly's bruised face.

"Come in," Marika said.

"I have some turkey soup." She handed a large jar to Marika.

"That's very kind. Thank you." She paused politely and watched the woman. Dan's mother here—visiting Kaly, bringing soup—sent a small, troubling quiver through her.

Mrs. McClane stepped closer. "How is she?"

"She's fine. She needs rest. Her wounds will heal." She set the soup on the nightstand. Again, she left a pause for Tara McClane to speak, to give a reason for taking the time to check on Kaly, for bringing food, for such a show of affection to the woman.

Tara nodded. "She's been through so much. And the baby?"

Marika said nothing.

"She looks peaceful," Mrs. McClane said, turning to go.

"Wait," Marika said, grasping for an explanation. "Can I...do you want me to tell her something?"

"No, dear, nothing to tell. Enjoy the soup. There's enough for both of you." Tara McClane ducked out of the crib, closing the door behind her.

Marika put the soup on the vanity table and noticed the string of pale pink beads wrapped around the lid. A worn silver cross hung from the beads. Marika lifted the rosary and hooked it over the bedpost. It was a good omen.

"This town's a mystery," Marika said to Kaly. "Dan's mother brings you soup with no explanation. The doctor leaves me with minimal instructions, when he could have told me more."

Marika opened the door and looked outside. Fog filtered the sun, giving it a vaporous look. Snow capped mountain peaks stood above the mist. Somewhere, far in the distance, she heard the faint call of an owl. The cool air felt good. A light breeze cleared the room, granting Marika hope for Kaly.

She closed the door and opened the window. The flowered curtains billowed forward. The white roses in the picture above the bed glowed like dawn, her favorite part of the day. Marika loved that solitary moment when the dark night gave way to a fresh new beginning, when everything was possible. It was God's moment. But usually, it disappeared as quickly as it arrived.

"Pssst." The sound came through the window.

She stood on her tiptoes and peeked outside.

Marko fiddled with his hat, shifting from one foot to the other. "Let me in," he said.

"You could just knock like other people."

"I don't want Papa knowing that I'm here." He kept shifting from one foot to the other and shoved his hands into his pockets.

Marika shrugged and opened the door for him.

He gazed anxiously at Kaly and slipped inside.

"Where are your dark clothes and stocking cap," Marika asked, "so you can blend in like a common burglar? I've never seen you so sly. It's not your nature."

"How is she?"

"Not great. She'll need some time to recover. Why are you here?"

"Papa's been ranting and raving all morning," Marko whispered. "He wants you to quit this foolishness. There are arrangements to be made for the wedding and he wants you home helping Mama. He's coughing up a storm and sounds terrible. You gotta come home!"

Marika thought hard and fast about how to ward off that grim trip back to the house. Even Marko—even Papa—could see that she couldn't leave Kaly alone in her current state.

"I can't," she said. "Look at her. I'd never forgive myself if she died while I was gone." As soon as she said it she knew it was true. Kaly's life was at stake. She'd already watched men die in Montenegro. She'd been right there and still hadn't been able to stop Lacy Blue's murder. She wasn't going to leave Kaly and risk letting her die too.

Marko shook his head. "I'll go get Dr. Fletcher. He should be here anyway." He was pleading. Having their father's fierce pride, it was something he didn't do easily.

"I finally got him to agree to teach me. If I walk out

now, I'll wreck it. Go home and calm Papa. Get him to rest. Ask about Uncle Vuko. He loves to talk about his brother."

"I tried that."

"And?"

"He called you an impudent child."

"What did you say?"

"If the shoe fits..."

Marika raised her eyebrows and twisted her lips.

Marko shrugged. "No, really. I tried. He won't be soothed."

"Take him to church."

"Doesn't want to enter with such grief in his heart."

"That's what church if for! Those are his words?"

"Mama's. Please just come home. You're making it hard on all of us and it's not fair. You're trying to become something and me and Mama are just trying to keep Dumitor from falling on us."

"Marko, you have to help me." She looked at the white roses. Their tiny spirits lifted off of the painting with the breeze and sailed small bits of courage to her heart. "Remember the story Papa tells about what a great painter his brother was? Go to the hardware store and buy some paints and canvas. Ask Papa to show you some of Uncle Vuko's painting techniques. He'll do it. He loves to talk, and teaching will give him something to think about besides me. Plus, you might like it."

"Buy? With what, my good looks?"

"You could charge it to Papa's account."

"I don't know." He put his hat on.

"Go. It'll make Papa happy. I need more time. I might make it home for dinner. You can show me your painting then."

"I'll be at work. I'm on the late shift."

"Then I'll admire it in your absence. Papa will forget all about me and my insolence. On second thought, you better tell Papa that I might not be home until morning."

Marko gasped. "He'll be furious. He'll come get you himself!"

Marika shook her head, thinking about Tara McClane. "Papa understands helping the unfortunate. You can see for yourself what terrible shape Kaly is in. She can't be left alone. Even if he won't admit it, Papa knows why I'm here."

Marko left and Marika heated tea water on the small coal stove, trying to think of stories to tell Kaly. Nothing seemed bearable. How could Marika's simple struggles seem worth anything when Kaly had nearly been killed? Marika had to stop complaining. Papa was easy compared to Bert Brown.

The woman suddenly opened her good eye and looked at Marika, who jumped, feeling like an intruder, a fake and caught in the sham.

She hadn't expected her to wake up yet. She took in a breath and leaned forward. She was here now; she might as well be useful.

"How do you feel?" Marika asked.

"Like I've been in a barroom ball—brawl. What you doing here?" She pulled her elbows under her and struggled to sit up. When Marika tried to help her Kaly gave her a one-eyed glare.

Marika backed off. "Dr. Fletcher asked me to look after you," she said.

Kaly shook her head and winced.

"Hurt?"

"All over."

"Imagine yourself strong." Baba had told her that the mind is powerful, what you can see, what you love, loves you and will come into being, and she wanted to portray that to Kaly now. "Imagine yourself dancing in the lavender gown, swaying across the ballroom at the Columbia Gardens."

"With whom shall I dance?" Kaly's voice was weak. She closed her good eye.

"You have someone who is in love with you. We all do. The moment you see him, you'll recognize him."

"Of course," Kaly laughed and grimaced. "Are you boiling water? I'd love a cup of warm broth."

Marika handed her a cup of tea. "My grandmother would say that you probably felt the spirit of someone with you at times. Following you around, saying, hey, it's me. I'm here. Look now, I'm right in front of you."

"Just my luck. My true love's a ghost." Kaly took a sip and put the tea aside, a shadow crossing her face and swelling. "Tommy," she said. Her voice sounded far away and of another world.

"Tommy Monroe, the fighter?"

Kaly nodded. "We grew up together. He has a bad habit of watching out for me." Her eyes twitched like she'd just witnessed something terrible. Trembling, she folded herself back into the covers, her head heavy on the pillow, and closed her eyes.

Marika waited, but Kaly said nothing more. Finally, she asked, "Is he the baby's father?"

Kaly looked at Marika. Even in her injured state Marika could see the woman sizing her up. It was unfair of Marika to take advantage of Kaly, when she wasn't quite herself and too sleepy to guard her words. But Marika's intentions were good. She just wanted to help.

"How do you know about the baby?" Kaly asked.

"Dr. Fletcher told me when he left me here to care for you."

Kaly looked aside, toward the crib window. "I'd rather not say who the child's father is. Life is too unpredictable, as witnessed by recent events. There is not much chance for either one of us."

Marika shook her head. "It's not true. We can help. People care about you. The doctor was here. I'm here. Tara McClane was here. She brought soup."

"Dan's mother?" Her mouth twisted in bewilderment.

"Yes, she brought the rosary beads too. I thought you'd

know why she came by."

As if a shade rose up and crossed the room, Kaly went perfectly still. She burrowed even deeper under the covers, covering her neck and chin, leaving only her bruised face visible, leaving Marika to feel that she'd said something terribly wrong. Before she could respond to correct it, Kaly was fast asleep again.

Marika's spine shivered. The light had shifted. Outside the fog sang a dark song. When she opened the door, it rushed into the room like a clandestine lover.

Marika left Kaly that evening and closed the door softly behind her. The woman had awakened, but now she slept soundly. She wouldn't miss her for the half hour she'd be gone. A golden lantern threw hazy shadows across the deserted street. Night hadn't begun in earnest and she could still see the tops of the Highland Mountains where snow absorbed the last beams from the setting sun and cast off a crimson glow. The eastern sky rippled with pinks and reds.

Marika found Dan on his way home from his shift at the Speculator, covered in dirt with a bundle of clothes under his arm. He crossed the street toward her. "Aren't you out late for a young woman?" he asked.

A strong wind kicked leaves off the street as she fell in stride beside him. Her dark hair spun in her face and she locked it behind her ears, turning her face away from the squall. "I heard that you got let go from the Orphan Girl," she said when the gusty weather let up. "And started at the Speculator. How do you like it?"

"It's OK. It's underground and it's dirty. One mine's as good as the next. They're all suffocating, dark and dangerous." He sounded tired. And she wanted to take that from him. But she couldn't. His weariness was his own to deal with. Those were the rules Baba had said.

"I thought they were making safety improvements at the Speculator, that you preferred the Speculator," she said, walking fast to keep up with him.

"Nevertheless."

"And Michael Jovich, does he work with you?"

Dan narrowed his eyes at her. "Yes."

"I mean, did he show you around, talk to you?"

"About what?"

"Things. Your plans." She was revealing a hand she had wanted to keep hidden.

"He talked to me about mining."

"But you and Michael. Are you friends?" Marika didn't like the idea of them being friends, but she had to know if Michael talked about her.

Dan nodded. "He helped me get on at the Speculator. Come on, I'll walk you home."

"I'm going back to Kaly's crib. I'll be spending the night there." Her throat closed a little, stifling a panic, wondering how Papa had accepted the news. He'd be mad. But he should be proud of her. But he wouldn't be. He wouldn't listen to her. There was one way in the family. His way.

"Then I'll walk you back to the cribs. How is she?" Dan asked.

"She's been thrashing about. Her dreams are filled with demons."

"Does she have an infection?"

"In the lungs. Grief."

"What?"

"My grandmother says that the body carries grief in the lungs. Anger in the liver. Secrets in the small intestine. My grandmother reads the body like Dr. Fletcher reads his medical journals. Kaly's lungs are filled with infection. That's grief."

"She's had plenty of it."

They opened the door to Kaly's crib. She still slept. Her legs had fallen out from under the covers and Marika tucked them back in.

"According to my grandmother, if you can resolve the

grief, you resolve the disease. Dr. Fletcher thinks it's all voodoo magic. But it's not. He thinks she's suffering from bronchitis."

Dan nodded. "Grief."

"Look at this nasty cut on her forehead," she continued. "It's infected, too. I've got some Mercurochrome. Dr. Fletcher said he'll send over something stronger. She's going to have a nasty scar."

"What does your grandmother say about scars?" Dan asked.

"Our lives are written in our wounds."

"Poetic. What wounds do you have?" His voice softened.

"If I have scars, they are well-hidden. Baba says that at my age, most bruises are mild and will heal quickly. She says I have the blood of a warrior and it takes more than a sharp blade to create a wound that'll last."

"A warrior who heals. Not many wars would go far if all the fighters were doctors." Dan reached out, touched Marika's chin, and turned her face toward him. "You really miss your grandmother, don't you?"

"I do."

His hand was warm and strong. Her spine shivered like a thousand flowers opening to the sun. She pulled away. "What else did you and Michael talk about?"

Dan backed up, shrugged and moved close again. "He's got influence with the bosses." He took her hand and pulled her into his arms, kissing her on the mouth.

Marika liked how his lips felt on hers, sure and strong. She kissed him back.

He tightened his grip on her hand and pulled her closer yet. He kissed her neck, brushing his lips up to her ear and over her eyes. He nuzzled his face into her cheek. A swift, beautiful warmth flowed through her, and she wanted to remember this night forever. She leaned into his solid chest, loose and unthinking, breathing in the smell of rich earth and salt. The room swooned gold and silver around her.

Over his shoulder she saw Kaly sleeping peacefully in her bed. Somehow, Marika's life had intertwined with Kaly's. It had taken one of those unreal turns and here—in this moment—she relished the turn. She relished Dan's strong shoulders, his arm around her waist, his hand tenderly tracing the line of her jaw.

The shiver sizzled through her torso. She backed up and looked at him. The lamp illuminated one side of his handsome, angular face while casting the other in shadow.

"You just can't decide who you want to kiss, can you?" A large woman in a gray satin dress and blue knit scarf stood in the doorway. She clicked her heels against the wooden floor like a gavel.

"Excuse me," Marika said, blocking Kaly from the woman's view, a futile attempt to protect her privacy. "Who are you?"

"Aren't you pretty? Well, the man's got taste, anyway. Fickle, though. Very fickle. A girl like you shouldn't be working out of a place like this. You come with me and you won't have to worry about anything again." The woman cooed, then coughed and cleared her throat. Her sickness sounded like Papa's.

"Who are you?" Marika asked again, holding Dan's hand.

"Lottie Boyle, proprietor. I own these cribs. Bought 'em last week. Only one person is supposed to be living here. But for now, I won't tell the police you girls are still working out of here. I'll have to charge you double though. Rent is due today. As I understand it, the rent on this crib is already weeks late. Pay up or move out," she said, and lassoed the air with her scarf. "You," she added, pointing to Marika, "can always move into my sweet home for girls. But decide fast. Youth don't last forever."

Marika stared at the woman, horrified by her rapid-fire accusations.

"Suit yourself. I'll give you two weeks on the rent. No

more. After that, I call the law. I'll tell 'em Miss Kaly Shane still entertains men in the Alley. Or maybe I'll have my bouncers dump her in the street. It won't be pretty. But then street whores are used to being dumped. It's their lot in life." Lottie turned, flipped the scarf over her shoulder, tipped her skirt in the air like a rabbit tail, and heel-clicked her way out the door. A mean pine smell trailed after her.

"You really get around, don't you?" Marika said, turning on Dan.

"What are you talking about?"

"'You just don't know who you want to kiss, do you?'" She mimicked the woman.

"She's a bitter old witch. She wants to poison you against me."

Marika stood to go. She was itchy and restless. Suddenly she just wanted to go home to Mama and Papa. Where she belonged, where, beyond anything else, she was loved. Let Dan keep watch over Kaly. This was his town, after all.

"Lottie Boyle will hurt whoever she can," Dan said. "She takes pleasure in other people's pain. Don't let her turn you against yourself."

"I'm tired. I'm leaving." She grabbed her sweater and stepped outside, slamming the door behind her. The air smelled bitter and heavy, the wind thick with the smell of arsenic.

Lottie Boyle leaned against the building across the street and smoked a cigar, a smile on her lips.

Marika leaned against the wall of the crib. She heard muffled voices through the door of another crib. The sounds of a fight came from a nearby alley. Down the street a tavern light blinked out. Smoke from Lottie's cigar swirled in circles and glowed under the street lamp. The woman coughed into her scarf and again she sounded like Papa. When she stopped coughing, Lottie's eyes seared into Marika.

Marika waved her off and opened the door to Kaly's

crib. Leaving the door open, she went back in. Dan was wiping Kaly's forehead with the washrag.

"You're back."

"I recover quickly," Marika said.

"Her fever seems bad." He put the rag in the washbasin and stood to leave.

"Wait," she said, suddenly fearful. "Are we still meeting at the Columbia Gardens opening weekend?" She hated herself for asking. Telling another lie, she added, "Because Dr. Fletcher asked me if I'd go up there and set up a medical station."

In the alley, a group of soldiers clopped by on horses. A bottle crashed and shattered, sending the scent of whiskey wafting in through the doorway.

"We're officially at war," Dan said.

"We don't have to be. I'm sorry about that little fit. Let's not fight."

"Not us. The country. The town will soon be short on men." He smiled. "You should be nice to us while we're still here."

"There are plenty of people in town who are not happy about the war. Are you joining the military?"

"A conversation for another time. I've got to go now."

"Me and you then, at the Gardens?"

"Yes. I'll be here at least through opening weekend."

"You'll meet me to catch the trolley car?"

He nodded. "On the corner of Park and Main."

Marika stood in the doorway and watched him disappear into the night. Lottie Boyle flipped her cigar onto the ground and slipped into the shadows.

12
SMOKY DREAMS

*I*t was a full two weeks before Kaly was able to walk out of her crib alone, with no one watching. She'd had a rough time. All week she'd been dreaming about the day her sister died, about the day she'd been raped. She'd never told anyone about the rape. With her sister's death, there was no room in her young mind to think about Bert and his cruelty. It was incomprehensible. What child could understand a world so brutal? Kaly had buried the memory away in the dark coal bin of her past, never to be thought of again.

Until last week's dream. Anne Marie whispering in her ear.

Now the nightmare images kept flopping in front of her like poker cards: the blue scar, the boot, the looming grin. Bert Brown. His weight crushing her. And where had he been, what had he done before she felt the massive boulder of him pinning her to the earth?

She remembered the man caught in the landslide. What was it he'd said? Even though you walk out, you never breathe again; you die every time the land shifts. No wonder she'd understood him so well. That horrible weight had collapsed her chest and lungs and crumpled her heart, her arms and legs slammed against the hard white ground. And at the end of it all, when she'd finally been able to stand again: Anne Marie dead.

Beth would help her. Although nothing could bring Annie back, Beth's good nature and kind words would put the rape back in the coal bin. Then Kaly could toss it into the fire, never to be seen or felt again. Beth would take her hand and save her from the horrible dreams. She needed Beth and she knew where to find her: underground in the opium dens.

The afternoon sun made the snow on the East Ridge glow like shining angels looking out over the valley, protecting the town. The peaks were solid and steady, one enduring symbol of strength in Kaly's life. She turned her back on the beautiful mountains and walked down the dark alley, to a dingy, shot up door where Nickel Annie stood shaking her head. Her blue wrinkled eyes wobbled with the motion. Her dirty hair hugged one cheek. Hair on the other side had been pulled back and fastened with bobby pins. She wore a threadbare wool coat over a tattered skirt.

"No," the woman said, holding out her hand to be paid for the simple prophecy.

Kaly placed a coin in her hand where her fingers poked through her gloves.

"No, don't go," Nickel Annie said.

Kaly shrugged and opened the door. A smoky film greeted her. She waited for her eyes to stop watering and adjust to the dimness. A wooden stairway led down to the basement. A weak light from a bare bulb revealed two tunnels that stretched like arms in different directions. Kaly chose the one with the most laughter wafting out. She passed curtained rooms where couples lounged on beds and moaned softly, the opium pipes set momentarily aside.

"Hey, Sugar, what brings you into the den of long, beautiful nights?" Beth lifted herself up from a bed and leaned on one elbow. Her half-open eyes motioned for Kaly to join her. Her dark hair hung in messy curls past her shoulders. She wore the blue dress, now wrinkled and smeared with grime. Miss Lottie would not be happy.

Bert Brown slept soundly on the other side of Beth, his eyes closed, looking almost innocent, not looking at all like the liar and rapist that he was.

Bad idea. Coming here was a bad idea.

Kaly clenched her fists and turned to leave.

"Don't worry about him," Beth said. "He's out cold."

"Whose friend are you? He nearly killed me that night!" Not to mention when she was a kid. And who knows what harm he'd done to Anne Marie. But Kaly didn't say that. A bitter, sharp taste shot up her throat and she planted her feet to steady herself.

"Come on, Kay," Beth said. "We've both been through worse. I can't know all the sordid details of your history with him. And I don't want to know. But me, I gotta love someone. He's not all bad. Stick around, you'll see."

"Who's not all bad?" Bert sat up and rubbed his eyes. His hair hung in ratted tangles past his ears. He wore brown trousers that had been torn and stained and a flannel shirt, unbuttoned at the top. That terrible blue scar crossed his collarbone and sent a jagged fear through Kaly.

"I guess he's not out cold," Beth said, roughing up his red hair.

"Look who's here," Bert said. With heavy eyelids and a slow turn of the head he reached behind the mattress and pulled out an envelope. A brown paste stained the broken seal.

"One smoke and the night will be all fine," Beth said. She patted the bed next to her. "Sit down. Join us in the den of gold."

"I need some peace. I hurt and I have bad memories. It's too much. I keep seeing my sister in that snowstorm. I can see every detail except for who killed her." Kaly glared at Bert. "I need to calm my mind. But I don't know about opium, you know." Kaly patted her stomach.

"Don't worry so much. It'll be fine," Beth said.

Kaly shook her head, no conviction in it. It would not be fine.

Bert opened the envelope. A storm raged in his face. "Wait a minute. This is empty. You smoked the last of it? Without telling me?"

Kaly felt her eyes go wild with fear. She felt the land shift and the crushing weight on her again, but it passed when Beth ignored Bert.

He settled back on the bed, fading into the smoky air.

"He's having a rough night," Beth said. "He got canned from the Orphan Girl."

"There's plenty of work. He'll get hired again."

"Yeah, he already got on at the Speculator. Starts tomorrow. Look, I'll get you some smoke. Do you have any money?"

Kaly pulled several coins out of the waistband of the red dress.

Footsteps came up beside her. "No," Nickel Annie said.

"An angel in disguise," Beth said. "Annie, be a dear. Find Pauley and buy some good smoke for us. That way I don't have to leave my friend here alone with my beau. It's her first time, and, well, you know these tunnels aren't always sweet."

Nickel Annie floated her hand through the blue smoke. The timbers in the wall behind her loomed like watchful guards. Someone had splashed a coat of paint on them, but the rough wood still showed through.

Beth gave her the coins and sat back down. She spread her skirt across the bed, smoothed the wrinkles from it and lounged next to Bert.

He moaned and turned aside.

"I didn't expect to see you down here," Beth said to

Kaly, her voice soft and pliable. "But I'm glad you're here."

Kaly sat next to her. "Remember how I told you I spent a year not talking? I long for that quiet again. The worst noise is in my own head. I want to know who killed my sister. Our parents should never have left us there without protection. A part of me wants revenge. Another part says never mind, it's no use, forget it. I'm fighting myself." There was no way to tell Beth about the rape, not with Bert lying next to her.

"Tonight, you call a truce."

"This is no life for us Beth. Think about Lacy Blue. Someone killed her."

"You can't let it get to you. If you do, you'll end up in a dark hole. You have to look forward, do your work, and survive." Beth slurred the last words, her eyes closing. A gentle wheezing came through her lips. Within moments, she was sound asleep.

Kaly looked at the low ceiling of the tiny half room. Silky smoke floated up to the chipped paint. Nickel Annie appeared out of the smoke like an apparition, her ragged skirt sweeping against her worn boots, her empty hand held out again.

Kaly fished around in the pocket of her waistband for more coins and dropped them into the gloved palm.

Annie put the coins in her pocket and floated her hand out again.

"I guess I'll go," Kaly mumbled, following the sweet floral scent through the tunnels. She tried to note markers so she could find her way back to Beth: a burned out light bulb, a wooden beam leaning against the wall, a mattress on the floor with a crumpled blanket and two men sleeping on top of it. The deeper she went into the tunnel, the thicker and more intoxicating the smells became. Everyone she met was calm and welcoming, their limbs melting into the darkness.

One man looked up through milky eyes and stared at her. It was a kind stare and he patted the bed beside him.

Two women near the wall lay wrapped in each other's arms.

Kaly sat down.

"We've been waiting for you to join us. You in your beautiful red. Sit. We'll share." The man's words seemed to float from his mouth and ride easily on some underground wind. He handed Kaly a pipe and held a long match to the black tar inside of it.

Blue smoke wafted up in front of her face. She touched the stone cross at her neck, leaned close, and drew on the pipe. Her throat hurt as she took in the opium. She waited while the man inhaled his own deep peace. The pipe drifted back to her and this time she pulled the smoke in softly, her throat a gentle pathway to a new world.

The opium took a little time to affect her. Slowly it entered her senses, dulling the tension in her arms, covering her vision, softening her hearing. She was light and beautiful and in control. Here in the womb of the earth, life protected her as tenderly as any mother might. She felt reckless and tipsy and so, so young, the child of a beautiful woman. Pure. Precious. Lovely. The dear city above held her at its true center. At some point, she stood to leave. Her legs wobbled and she gently sat down again.

The man with the pipe had set it aside and stretched out next to the others, his feet dangling off the end of the bed.

Kaly didn't want to sleep. She wanted to be wonderfully awake. Even her stomach felt odd and disjointed, not quite her own. Well, it isn't your own, said her blue cloud of thoughts. This stomach belongs to the baby. The baby.

Dread and regret now hung in the blue smoke, clouding her vision and pushing against her heart. She had just hurt the child and she hadn't even been born yet.

"I have to go," she said to the man on the bed. He turned aside and moaned.

Drifting through the tunnels, the dread evaporated as

she followed a path through the smoke, a natural path someone had created just for her, to guide her. It was the path of her life. If she kept her eye on the smoke she would always know where she was going. Look around any corner and she would see the future. It was so simple. How had she missed it all these years?

"Welcome back," Beth said. Sweat poured from her forehead. "Look, I can't leave Bert alone. Keep him safe for me, will you? Don't let the watchers in the corner get at him. You got to keep him safe."

Kaly looked up and down the tunnel and saw no watchers anywhere.

"Over there. Look. You can't miss their leering red pupils. They stalk us. They want to snatch our happiness away."

Kaly squinted. She saw nothing but beautiful, glorious dirt.

"I got to go find some more smoke. I'm cramping up and sweating. My heart's beating about a thousand times a minute. Wait here. I'll be back with more sweet stuff."

Kaly waited a long time. On the other side of the bed, next to where Bert slept, and tucked between the wall and the mattress, glittering blue beads poked out and winked at her. She reached across Bert, ran her hand across the tiny pieces of smooth glass, lifted the thing, and settled it on her stomach. It was a very pretty, mostly blue, beaded purse. It reminded her of something, but just then she couldn't remember what. Something Beth had said. She absently tucked the beads into her waistband. Soon the blue beads were a shining boat taking her across gently rocking waves into a silver sleep full of wonder.

But the nap turned into rocky dreams. She was in charge of a child. She forgot about the child. By the time she remembered, the child was dead. Kaly bolted awake, her heart racing. Her head hurt and her insides felt as if they would splatter across the floor. Sweat smattered her forehead. She prayed that she hadn't harmed the baby. She looked frantically around.

A syringe and a strip of cloth lay on the tiny table just inside the cubby, the likely cause of Bert's long sleep. His face looked young again.

Kaly remembered him at the warehouse fire. He had grabbed her arm and yanked her down the street toward the Polly May.

"Stop it!" She'd yelled. "You're hurting me!"

"Am I?" He'd ripped her arm harder, pulling her off the ground. "Does that hurt too?"

The next day, when Tommy showed up, he'd stared wide-eyed at Bert.

Bert's face had puffed up like a balloon and he stomped his work boots around Tommy. "What you looking at?" he'd jeered. "Think you see something funny. Damn baby." Bert towered over Tommy and squeezed his shoulders.

Kaly watched Bert's hands shake from the effort.

Tommy just kept staring.

The next morning Kaly saw Tommy leave the bathroom, shirtless. Nasty bruises covered his shoulders like football pads.

Her throbbing head brought her back to the cubby, the gloom of the tunnel walls descending on her. Memory was no good. She'd been foolish to come here. She had to get back above ground.

"Smoke this, then we'll wake him," Beth said, emerging from the darkness.

Kaly felt a hand on her shoulder.

She turned to see Tommy.

He wore brown coveralls and carried his work bundle under his arm. His narrow nose and sharp features looked out of place in the dim light of the tunnel. He stared at her, his sloped brown eyes incredulous. In an instant they narrowed with determination.

"She's coming with me," he said.

Beth shrugged and smiled. "Her choice."

Tommy gripped Kaly's wrist and tugged her through the tunnel.

"I can walk by myself," Kaly said, yanking her arm free. The beaded purse from her waistband fell to the ground. "I better take this back to Beth."

"Leave it. She won't need it tonight. You can tell her where to find it tomorrow."

"No. I'm taking Beth her purse."

"You're not going back in there. Leave the purse here or take it with you."

Kaly glared at Tommy and spun on her heels.

Tommy grabbed her wrist again and pulled her toward daylight. "There's no good end to this. You're getting out of here right now, and I'm taking you. If you hate me, you hate me."

Suddenly she didn't feel well. Beth seemed far away. Kaly found an empty cubby and stuck the purse behind the mattress. She looked around and noticed a chipped light fixture. Tomorrow she'd tell her friend exactly where she'd hid the purse.

Tommy was quiet as he led her out.

Back on the street, Kaly was surprised at the daylight. The beautiful snow-covered mountains glowed with a trace of pink. She smelled the sulfur in the air and anger flared in her nostrils. It flushed through her body. "Who do you think you are, interfering in my life?"

Instead of answering, Tommy quickened his speed.

She had to run to keep up. "Don't you think it's time you stopped playing big brother and let me live my own life? You're like Miss Anderson, always picking at what's wrong with me, thinking you can save me. If I could be saved don't you think I'd have done it myself by now?" She stopped in the middle of the boardwalk and started to cry.

Tommy looked at her.

She wiped at the tears and glared at him. "Go save yourself. You're so keen on being a white knight. I'm a lost cause. I'll only hurt you."

Tommy bit his lip and spoke through his teeth. "You go into the dens and that's the end of your life, good or bad. Those people down there will own you. You won't care. You'll be begging them to own you, just so you can get another smoke. The tunnels will steal your soul, Kaly. Your soul's one thing you haven't given up on yet. Plus, you have more to think of than yourself."

"What?" Kaly palmed her stomach.

"I wouldn't want a friend anywhere near what goes on down there. Every breath of that smoke you take goes right to your death. You want to ruin your life, and I don't like it. If you want me to stop rescuing you, stop putting yourself in danger. You and the baby."

Kaly stared at him. "You know?"

"Oh, it's really difficult to notice. The bulge at your stomach, your barrage of tears, the flush in your cheeks and your sudden preoccupation with something. You're acting just like my mom did when she was pregnant."

"You saw your mom pregnant?"

Tommy nodded.

"Your mother had another child?"

"The baby was never born."

"She miscarried?"

Tommy shook his head. "The warehouse fire took the baby along with my parents."

Kaly's lungs hurt. "I'm sorry."

He looked away.

"I was thinking about the warehouse fire today," she said. "When you came to live at the Polly May, Bert left bruises on you and you just stood there and took it."

"I thought my mother would come and get me. I thought she was at the hospital having the baby. Later I pretended that Anne Marie was my little sister, that my mother was at the grocery store or the pub. It was crazy. But youth is crazy. You're not young anymore, Kaly. And you're not alone."

Kaly struggled through the blue opium fog. She wanted to tell him that he wasn't alone either, that the child was his. She yearned to tell him. But again the words stuck in her throat, hurting her. The old grief clamped her mouth shut.

The moment passed.

Kaly crossed her arms and looked up at the rose tinted sky.

"You can't stay in your crib," Tommy said. "It's too dangerous. With the other girls gone, you have no protection."

"There's Pamela."

"I saw her earlier. She looks done for." Tommy looked away again. "You have to stay at the Polly May. Miss Anderson will give you a room. It'll keep you off the streets until the baby is born."

"Tell me why you care."

"It's a good question, isn't it?"

"You must know something about my sister's death. You went to corrections, but you didn't kill her. Something frightened you and that's why you wouldn't tell what you knew." They stood at the door of her crib and Kaly held the knob ready to push it open. "What scared you?"

A loud commotion prevented him from answering. A scream came from the direction of Pamela's crib.

Tommy motioned for her to stay back while he went to help Pamela. After a few minutes he returned to Kaly. "She's alone. It's the disease. She's swatting at things that aren't there."

"We can't leave her here like this."

"She won't listen. Tomorrow we'll talk to Dr. Fletcher. See if he can't get her some help, maybe put her in the hospital for a while, keep her safe."

"Safe?" None of them were safe.

"Yeah. She must have decided not to use the tansy tincture that I gave you for her. I'm glad of it. I've felt terrible about that. I keep waiting for her to turn up dead, knowing it'd be my fault. I should have gotten it back from you. Did you give it to her?"

Kaly rubbed her eyes with the palm of her hand. The problem with lying was forgetting a lie that she'd told and then almost revealing the truth. She flattened her fingers against her stone cross where it hung from her neck, pressing it into her chest.

"I threw it away," she said, lying again.

Tommy nodded. A look of relief crossed his face. "Come on," he said. "Let's get you to Miss Anderson's. There's nothing we can do for Pamela right now."

"There've been looters. They'll take everything I have in my crib if I leave."

"There is no looter. It's just Pamela."

"But they'll come if there's no one to stop them."

"Thieves are crazy in this town. They'll shoot you on the spot just to take that cross off your neck. No. We're going to the Polly May. You'll be safe there."

Safe. That word again.

She moved toward Pamela's room.

"Where are you going?" he whispered.

"I can't just leave her."

She opened the door to Pamela's crib. The room was in shambles. The vanity table had been tipped and the drawers spilled. Make-up sprawled across the wooden floor. A blanket lay crumpled next to a winter coat. An opened book had fallen near the stove. Pamela wore a dirty slip with a man's shirt over the top. Her yellow dress had been thrown in the corner and lay abandoned like a stray dog, hungry and alone, verging on mean.

"You're coming to Miss Anderson's house with us," Kaly said. When the girl didn't respond, Kaly stepped closer. "Pammy, come on. We'll help you."

The girl crossed her arms on her belly and moaned. She sounded like a sad hound.

Kaly waved her arms in front of Pamela.

The girl still didn't seem to know she was there. As a

last resort, Kaly grabbed the dress and reached for Pamela's elbow to guide her out of the crib.

Pamela pulled away and cringed in the corner.

Kaly looked at Tommy, wild-eyed and helpless.

"She'll fight me all the way," he said. "The police will be on us and we'll all go to jail."

"She might be safer there."

"We'll go to the doctor in the morning. Till then we can have people check on her. We can't do much right now."

"I can stay with her." A shoe flew past Kaly's head. A cup hit the door.

The girl was quickly crouched back in the corner.

Kaly shrugged, folded the dress and put it on a chair. She looked at her one last time and went to her own crib. The string of pale pink rosary beads hung on her bedpost. She lifted them up and dropped them into her palm as a loud crash came from yet another crib. Was that a looter going through the abandoned rooms?

"You're going to get us killed," Tommy said.

"Whoever that is, he won't go where people are." Kaly left Tommy standing guard as she slipped back into Pamela's crib and hung the rosary beads on the girl's bedpost.

At least it was something.

At that point, though, Kaly doubted that it was enough.

Miss Anderson opened the door. "Ah, the prodigal girl. I figured you'd be back. Have you told him yet?" She tipped her chin toward Tommy.

"Told me what?" he asked.

"So, you haven't told the young man he'll soon be a father."

Tommy's stunned face reminded Kaly of the strange zombie stare he'd had when he first arrived at the Polly May all those years ago. Turning away from him in panic, she stepped across the threshold with Miss Anderson, and shut the door on Tommy. She sank onto the wrought iron bench, and cried.

"Rudeness has never been allowed in my house," Miss Anderson said. "You open the door right now and invite Tommy in for tea. It's time you two talked. Go on. Open the door and apologize."

Kaly's mouth twitched as if she was six years old and in trouble again. She did as she was told. She opened the door. The last of the melting snow on the ground in front of the Polly May shone pink under the setting sun. An owl hooted from somewhere nearby. Nickel Annie dragged her feet toward the flats.

Tommy was gone.

13
ASSIGNMENT

Marika picked up a file from Miss Parsons' desk and arranged the notes in it. The storm had blown the sulfur out of the town, leaving the day sweet and fresh like the fields surrounding her home in Montenegro. It wasn't just the freshness of the day that reminded her of her beloved *Crna Gora*. Periodic explosions on the hill reminded her of the wars in her homeland. But in Butte, the only ongoing battles were with landslides, fires in the shafts, poisonous gases—things that could instantly kill a man. Those and the battle in her own home between her and Papa.

Miss Parson's leaned over a clothing catalogue, sighing and turning pages. Her short hair framed her round glasses, rosy red cheeks and small face. She was a single woman in a dangerous town. She had a job and a life of her own. Somewhere along the way she'd seen fit to divorce the doctor and forge her own living, albeit with the doctor, but still! If she could do it, so could Marika. And Papa would just have to live with it.

As she waited for Dr. Fletcher to finish with a patient,

Marika dusted the bottles on the shelves. Then she dusted the pictures on the walls. She straightened the chairs in the waiting room. Gliding with easy quick movements, she nearly floated across the room, her simple cotton skirt flowing around her ankles. She'd tucked her ivory colored blouse into her waistband and it puffed out in a balloon like fashion, slimming her waist in a way that made her look lean but not skinny. She needed her heft, needed to present as strong enough to lift any patient that required support, strong enough to impress Dr. Fletcher.

She was hoping for an assignment from the doctor, hoping that he'd put another patient under her care. The door creaked open and, to her surprise, Papa slouched out of the doctor's back office. His soupy eyes and messed up hair made him look ragged and worse for wear. At first he didn't seem to see her, but when his dark brown eyes finally lit on her, he did a double take.

The stare went right to her heart. At home she'd found ways to defy Papa—little things that drove him to drink too much *rakija*, like forgetting to bring in firewood, serving cold, bland dinners, leaving washed clothes in dirty water, or coming home late. She'd act like she didn't hear him, or she'd ask him to retell his stories, pretending not to understand, just so he'd have to struggle with new ways of saying the exact same thing. It was mean, but so was not listening to her.

"Mama," he would say, "behave your daughter."

Finally, last night, after a long coughing fit that ended with him on the floor unable to breathe, she stopped. As she helped Mama get Papa up onto the bed, her mother glared at her and told her to quit her foolishness. "I will, Mama," she said.

But Papa shook his head. Through raspy breaths he gave her permission. He had conceded that if she wanted to study medicine it was her choice. However, medicine would not interfere with the marriage plans. And she must stay away from that Dan McClane.

Marika had agreed.

The victory had been all hers. But now it didn't seem so sweet.

"I didn't know you had a doctor's appointment today," she said. "You had a rough night last night, didn't you?"

He combed his moustache with his fingers, and pushed his thick black hair off of his forehead. Beads of sweat gathered in the creases there and he wiped them away. "In more ways than one." He smiled a tired smile at her.

"I'm sorry we fought," Marika said. And she was. She had just wanted him to see things her way so that she could get on with her studies, and so that they could get on with being a happy family. But Papa was stubborn. And so was she.

"You're growing up, making your own decisions. I'm sure more than one war has been started on the edge of adulthood."

"Here's your medicine." Dr. Fletcher emerged from the back room. He looked tiny in his white coat, which had been made for a much larger man. The shoulder seams crossed his biceps. The arms belled out wide and needed to be rolled up. But none of that seemed to bother the doctor. He looked over the top of his glasses at the bottle. "It should help. Rest. The key factor is rest, sir."

Miss Parsons lay a palm over the open magazine and sighed. Papa put the bottle in his pocket. "Thank you Doctor," he said. And to Marika, "How is Kaly?"

"Fine," Marika replied. "Much better. Good enough to be on her own. I need a new patient." She looked at Dr. Fletcher who ignored her and busied himself with looking over Miss Parson's shoulder at the catalogue.

Papa collapsed into a coughing fit. His chest and legs shook and he put his hands on his brown trousers to steady himself as he caught his breath. Waving at the air in front of him as if he could ward off the consumption with a flip of the wrist, he sat down. But the miner's con was easily as stubborn as Papa and the spasms continued.

Marika got him a glass of water and waited for the coughing to stop, feeling pleased that Papa had asked about Kaly. Was it possible that Papa did feel proud of her for helping Kaly? The thought was like soothing water on a parched lilac bush, making her smile. She let it grow inside of her. But it quickly withered when Papa pushed against the bench and pulled down a breath, his face turning red with the effort. When he recovered, she noticed that something was missing in him. His fight had diminished. He looked beaten, resigned. She felt a cool, brief wind on her cheek, something clammy and not of their world. Her heart broke like Mama's beads from the old country.

"Mama's preparing a nice dinner," he said when he could breathe. Although his voice was raspy and rough, it sounded gentle and full of kindness. "Be on time."

"I will, Papa. I won't disappoint you again."

"You have a question, I presume," Dr. Fletcher said as Papa left the building. "But your father's business is your father's business. He'll tell you all he wants you to know."

"I'm not wondering about my papa," she lied. "His sickness is obvious." Of course she was wondering about Papa. He seemed to be sliding rapidly down a steep hill, further from health every day. But Marika shifted the doctor's attention to another patient. She pushed her hair behind her ears, a reflexive twitch to hide her discomfort. She tugged at the blousy chiffon sleeves, pulling the elbows tight. "It's Kaly Shane I have questions about."

"Yes, Miss Shane. What can I tell you about the dear girl?" He held a chart and a pencil. He scribbled something with a flourish before he looked up at her.

"She seems lost, out of sorts. She talks like she doesn't have much hope. Like her life is already over. A danger to herself."

"Have you always acted so perfectly yourself?" Dr. Fletcher asked, holding the chart at his chest and crossing his arms over it, looking hard at her. Underneath his glasses his eyes were blue and clear.

At first the question seemed mundane and then stopped her cold. She drew in a short breath. "My father talked to you about me?"

"You must assess yourself first, Miss Lailich, and then assess your patient."

Marika blinked. Her lip twitched. No, Papa wouldn't tell family business. "Did he complain about me? You agreed to let me to take care of Kaly."

"Yes. To get you out of my hair. The best way to solve a problem is to give that problem a job." He nodded his head and smiled thinly, as if congratulating himself on choosing such a reasonable solution.

Behind him Miss Parsons laughed quietly.

"But no. You father did not talk about you. I suspect that he would have been in here dragging you out, if he hadn't consented to you being here. But back to Kaly Shane. By knowing your own heart, you will be able to take proper care of Miss Shane's heart."

"It's not her heart I'm worried about, it's her mind."

Dr. Fletcher put the chart on Miss Parson's desk, pulled off his glasses and cleaned them on his lab coat. After a very long pause, he looked up at Marika. "You'd be lost, too," he said, "if you'd lived her life."

"She's scaring me."

"She took a serious blow to the head and that takes time to heal. Desperation, confusion, and a slow wit are all possible side effects of such an injury. Or it could be preoccupation with the pregnancy."

"Is she acting like herself?" Marika blew out a frustrated breath. Why couldn't he just answer her?

"Supremely."

Supremely, she mimicked to herself. "So this is normal?" she asked, pulling teeth. She should have gone into dentistry.

"As normal as anything is," Dr. Fletcher said.

"Anything else?"

"Maybe she's scared that Bert will come after her again. Or maybe it's like battle fatigue. She's worn out and startled from the slightest sound. We could give her Chamomile. It's good for relaxation. Or Frankincense for her spirits."

"Wives' tales, my dear." He picked up the chart and scribbled something more inside of it, folded it shut, and handed it to her. "Please file this."

Marika huffed a breath. This doctor! Nothing was turning out the way she'd hoped. As she took the chart to the back room to file it, she noticed Papa's name on it. His face had turned so red today. What would cause that? She stood in front of the file bin and sighed, her fingers itching to open the chart. No, I must not look, Marika told herself sternly. I mustn't invade Papa's privacy. "Respect," she said aloud, dropping the file into its bin like a piece of hot coal. *No one's business is no one's business.*

She heard the outside door slam open and shut. She bolted out of the file room to see Bert Brown charge through the door to the doctor's private office. Miss Parsons turned an incredulous look at her.

"What was that?" Marika asked.

"Seems the man is not too happy."

"Or in desperate need of a doctor. Demanding brute, isn't he?"

Miss Parsons nodded, openly agreeing with her.

After a while both the doctor and a wild-eyed Bert emerged from the back office. Bert's knuckles had been banged up and he held his hands gingerly at his sides. Looking at his torn plaid shirt and the scrapes on his face, Marika wondered if he'd just come from a street fight.

Dr. Fletcher pulled a bottle of medicine from the shelf and handed it to Bert.

"Take this three times a day, without fail," he said. He leaned in close to Bert and whispered just loud enough that Marika heard, "for the sake of others, no nighttime or other activities with women."

Bert snatched the bottle out of the doctor's hand and left with a swing and a slam of the door, exiting in much the same way he'd arrived. Dr. Fletcher wrote something in his chart and handed it to Marika. "File this please," he said with out much flourish. He poured himself a cup of tea and returned to his office.

Marika retreated to the back room, which smelled dusty and damp. The air caught in her throat. She opened Bert's chart. *Syphilis.* A dark shadow lifted off of the file and hung in the dank air. One low-watt bulb dangled from the ceiling, shedding its stingy light on the secrets stored there.

She was tired of secrets. What could it hurt? Opening the middle drawer of the cabinet, she filed Bert's chart and flipped to the "L's." Marika pulled Papa's chart out and opened it. Dr. Fletcher's writing slid wildly across the top page in large, loopy letters. She heard the front door open and shut. She stood motionless and listened. Only silence. Miss Parsons was going to get the mail. Exhaling with relief, Marika read the last entry Dr. Fletcher had written.

"Lungs holding up well under the circumstances. Trend is downward yet subject stubborn toward illness. Might have another good year in him. Advise: Rest. Quit smoking. Regular treatments."

Marika smiled. Papa's red-faced effort at breathing hadn't been the worst. Papa was ill, but he was strong in his illness. He'd probably live longer than any of them expected. What a relief, to let go of the idea that Papa might die any day. A lot could happen in a year. New treatments could be found, new medicines discovered, a cure developed. She closed the chart and filed it carefully. She'd get some Myrtle oil for him. It was good for the lungs.

Miss Parsons returned with an armful of catalogues and plopped down with them. Marika smiled meekly at her. She had made herself comfortable, sitting at the end of the big desk, reading about consumption.

"Miss Lailich," Dr. Fletcher said from the doorway. "Go down to the Alley and check on a girl named Pamela. She's at the end of the cribs and will most likely be the only one left living there. She missed her appointment earlier, probably thought I'd get free to go to her. But I can't get free today. Although, you two seem to have gotten free." He stared at the catalogues and the medical journal.

"Should I take anything with me?" Marika asked.

Dr. Fletcher sighed. "How about some good sense?"

Marika turned on her heels and stomped out the door. Why was everyone so mean? What happened to common courtesy? Maybe it was the fumes day after day, making people on edge. She heard a blast come from the mines.

Or maybe it was fear.

She walked down the row of cribs. Windows were broken and doors left ajar. She peeked inside one. It was stripped bare except for a few dishes and a make-up tin. Blood smeared the walls. The next one was the same, empty and ghostly. Even Kaly's crib had been abandoned.

She came to one with the door flung wide open. A heavy-set woman with disheveled hair sat on a cot, a floral scarf tied loosely around her arm above the elbow and an empty syringe on the blanket next to her. She looked up through matted hair, her eyes half-closed. "Are you an angel?" she crooned.

"Are you Pamela?"

The woman shook her head. "She's at the end of the row. Poor thing."

"No offense, but you don't look that great yourself. I'm from the doctor's office. Do you need help?"

The woman shook her head again and lay down on the cot, waving Marika away. "Pamela needs you. She's the one who needs an angel, I've already got my angel right here," she said cupping a hand over the marks on her arm.

Marika stood in the doorway for a moment and watched the woman drift off to sleep. She wanted to bring her to Dr. Fletcher. He knew how to help people with this sickness. She closed the door and she left.

The final door in the row of cribs was shut.

Marika knocked.

No one answered.

She knocked again, harder this time. "Pamela? Dr. Fletcher sent me to check on you. I'm Marika Lailich. Please open the door." She shifted from foot to foot. The sun felt surprisingly warm and nice on her shoulders. Spring was finally here. "Pamela," she called again.

Again she was met with silence. Maybe the girl was out running errands. Not wanting to intrude into the woman's room, she sat on the boardwalk, leaned against the warm wall, and closed her eyes to the sun.

"Funny place to find you." A rich voice materialized from somewhere. Marika looked up, squinted her eyes into the sun, and nodded. Her heart leapt, beating too fast. She jumped up and brushed her skirt down. There stood Michael Jovich, his work clothes bundled under one arm, dirt smeared across his face, outlining his dark eyes. His dark hair and thick mustache looked a lot like Papa's. He was much taller than Papa, and his nose narrower. Other than that, he could have been Papa's son. Clearly *Crnagoski*. A man right out of her homeland.

"I'm here by doctor's orders," she said, standing tall.

"Really? This is a funny place for the doctor to send a young woman for a cure. What is your ailment?" His smile challenged her for a real answer.

Well, she had one. She was here on official business. Pushing her hair behind her ear, she straightened her back. "Not me. I'm here to check on a patient. I work for Dr. Fletcher." She lifted her chin a little. "He trusts me, says he couldn't have asked for a better student." She folded her arms across her chest and smiled. That would let him know exactly where she stood. It was a kindness to let him

Milana Marsenich

"A patient," he said, looking at the wall. "A boardwalk ghost? Forgive me, but you don't look like you're tending to anyone. In fact, I could have sworn you were taking a nap in the sun. By the way, I'm Michael Jovich."

"I know who you are. Think what you want, Mr. Jovich. My patient is not home. I thought I'd wait for her, but now I see that I'll have to come back later."

He lifted his eyebrows and narrowed them, a look of concern crossing his face. "Pamela?"

"I can't reveal a patient's name to you."

"Pamela hasn't been out of her crib for two days. People have been bringing food and checking on her. Last I heard she was in no shape to go anywhere. You sure she's not here?"

"I knocked and knocked."

Michael reached for the doorknob.

"Wait," Marika said, stepping in front of him, so close that her skirt brushed against his trousers. "She has a right to privacy. If she's not answering, there must be a reason."

Michael looked at her, a question in his dark eyes, shook his head and pushed the door open. She stood aside, exasperated, uncertain why she'd let him pass. She peeked into the room. A girl lay sprawled on the floor, her bluish skin dark in the gloom. She couldn't have been more than fifteen!

Marika rushed in and knelt beside her. She put her fingers on her neck, checking for a pulse. Nothing. She listened for breath, watching for the rise and fall of her chest. Nothing. She pinched the skin on the girl's arm and watched for a reaction. Nothing.

Michael closed his eyes and opened them. "Pamela," he said softly.

"Oh no," Marika said. She pulled in a breath, opened Pamela's mouth and pushed the oxygen into it, watching again for the rise and fall of her lungs. When the breath didn't take she pumped the girl's chest. Nothing changed.

192

Panicked, she did it all again. Dazed, she checked again for a pulse. Still nothing. Signs of breath? Nothing. The girl lay as silent as last winter's fallen snow, here and gone. "Please. Go get the doctor."

"It's too late," Michael said, his voice gentle, kind. It was the voice of a person who'd known hardship and heartbreak. She'd heard it in Papa when he talked of Uncle Vuko's death. She'd heard it in Mama when they left Baba for the new world. He put a hand on Marika's shoulder.

She lifted it off, her eyes darting around the room. Chaos littered the crib. Someone had tossed it thoroughly, either in anger or looking for something. "No," she said. "We've got to do something. I should've just opened the door and come in. I should've checked on her right away. I thought I'd be intruding. I should've walked right in. We've got to do something." Marika wobbled back and forth on her knees, her face damp.

"I'll get Dr. Fletcher. We'll find someone to stay here and you come with me." He stood so tall, close to six feet, so confident, but she could not leave the girl, not like this.

She shook her head. "I'll stay here."

He shrugged and left her to the strange solitude of Pamela's crib. The girl was gone, but all earthly signs of her life remained, including her ravaged body. Bruises marked her face. Her hands were scraped up with dried blood on them. Blood had smeared on the yellow dress she wore. She'd been beaten before she died, and the beating might have killed her.

While waiting, Marika sat on the floor next to her. She wanted to clean her, straighten her legs, pull her dress smooth, push her hair out of her face. She wanted to pick her up and rock her like her mother might have done. But, with the taste of the girl's death on her lips, she did none of these things.

In Montenegro, her grandmother had always been with Marika when death struck. That was war. You expected people to die during war. But here in America, you expected good things. Here in America, there was no reason for a girl to die so young.

It seemed like Michael had just left when he returned with the doctor. Dr. Fletcher had changed out of his lab coat and wore a brown suit. His stethoscope dangled from his neck and he carried a medical bag.

"I see," said Dr. Fletcher. "The girl didn't have a chance. The sickness ate away at her. But look at those bruises. I'm not sure it was the sickness that killed her."

Marika looked around the room again. A lamp lay broken on the floor. The water basin was turned upside down near the dumped vanity table. Pamela might have struggled to get help, but most certainly, she had struggled with some intruder.

"Michael, help me get her into the wagon. We'll take her down to the undertaker. He'll rule on her death. Miss Lailich, you return to the office and do what you can there. Our work is with the living."

Marika looked at Michael. "*Hvala*," she said. Thank you.

He cocked his head, that question in his eyes again. "The doctor gives you the tough assignments," he said. "I see that he does have faith in you."

Marika nodded, glad that Michael knew about her work. As she made her way back to the office, the weather turned bad, the town sick with the drizzly, gray rain, which matched the sick feeling in her heart. At Park Street two automobiles passed a horse and buggy. The horse tossed his mane against the halter. The wind had stopped and the smog poured back in, mixing with the rain. Her stomach twisted up on itself. Her legs trembled. If she'd just walked in, Pamela might still be alive. Instead, Marika had stood there telling Michael what a great doctor she'd be someday. Marika should have just opened the door to Pamela's crib and walked in. She should've saved the girl.

14
VISITORS

Kaly woke up to sirens wailing up the hill. Now what? She dropped her hand over the side of her old bed at the Polly May, shaking it as if to shake off the terrible dream—the terrible blue scar. Why had she smoked that opium? How foolish. Two days later and she still felt dread. She hadn't been thinking right. She'd been angry and careless, wanting to blind herself to everything, not thinking of the baby.

The sirens signaled another accident. She sat up on the bed, removed her gown, and pulled on the ashen cotton dress she'd borrowed from Miss Anderson. She fastened her brown hair at her neck in a low ponytail as she walked over to the fire escape. Through the window she saw the problem. On the hill, a thin line of smoke snaked up into the sky from one of the mines. It looked calm, almost innocent, not at all like the true danger that even a small fire in a mine could cause.

A while later, she heard a door slam shut. Kaly spotted Bert Brown storming away from the house and up the sidewalk. She hugged herself and shivered. A chill swept over her and deepened, settling into her spine. Shifting her weight, she rubbed her round belly. "Hey, little monkey," she said, wondering again if the baby could be safe at the Polly May. Something in the hallway moved.

"Who's there?" she asked.

No one answered.

A sound came through the door and she turned quickly.

No one was there.

"What a silly scaredy-cat I am, afraid of my own shadow," she said out loud.

Someone knocked on the door, and she jumped.

"Here's your breakfast." It was George, the boy she'd held in her arms last winter, balancing a tray of juice, scrambled eggs, and toast. His dark hair fell into his large brown eyes. He wore a red plaid shirt that hung low on his thin shoulders. His torn trousers folded onto his bare feet, too long for him.

"Shouldn't you be at school?" she asked.

"They sent me home."

"What did Miss Anderson say about that?" She glanced out the window and noticed other children playing in the yard. "Were you all bad?"

"They sent our class home. There was an accident in one of the mines. Teacher's husband was up there. Miss Anderson told me to bring you breakfast." He lifted the tray.

"Place it on the dresser," she said. Miss Anderson making her breakfast? There had to be a catch to it. Or had she changed?

He put the plate down, pushed the hair out of his eyes and sat on the floor. When he pulled up his pant leg, she saw a scar that ran along the smooth curve of his foot.

"You can sit in a chair. You don't have to sit on the floor like an animal."

"I'm not supposed to bother you. Miss Anderson said."

"Well, then, you better mind her." Kaly could hear a

196

door downstairs open and close. Miss Anderson welcomed someone in a bright high-pitched tone.

Moments later Marika walked in hugging a bag of groceries. She wore a simple gray skirt with a blue cotton top under a white sweater. Her hair had been pinned up into a bun and several stands of hair had fallen out, framing her face, outlining her high cheekbones. A small girl followed her. Julian and two older girls stood in the hallway and peered through the door.

"Shoo," Kaly told them.

All but George scattered.

"Oh, good. You're awake," Marika said. She put the groceries on the vanity table.

"You don't need to bring me food." Kaly tilted her head toward the tray. "Miss Anderson made breakfast this morning."

"How are you doing? Are you worried about the baby?" Marika asked. "Your hand's resting on your stomach."

"I am. Whenever there is an accident it worries me. Have you heard anything about it? If anyone died up there today?"

"I don't know much yet. It was at the Orphan Girl and the fire wasn't as bad as it could have been. It happened during a shift change so not many men were down in the tunnels. My father is up there. I'm sure he'll know more when he gets home."

"Your father was working?" A cold chill went through Kaly.

Marika shook her head. "He had some union business to tend to. Thank God he and Marko, my brother, work at the Speculator. That mine is safe."

"I hope anyone down there got out ok."

"Me too. We'll know soon enough."

Worry rose up in Kaly and she tried to push it down. "Do you know if Tommy or Dan were on shift?"

Marika seemed startled at the question. "I don't think

so. They wouldn't be over there. They both work at the Speculator now. Dan just left the Orphan Girl while you were recovering from your injuries." She pushed a loose strand of hair behind her ear. "How do you know Dan?"

"He's a little younger than me, but I grew up with him."

"You grew up with both him and Tommy?"

"The town wasn't always so big. Most people, other than the newcomers, know each other."

Marika flinched at that and looked away. She was uncomfortable, but there was nothing Kaly could do about it. The girl had come over from Montenegro, a recent transplant. It felt funny to be the one who suddenly belonged. Kaly didn't know if she'd ever had that feeling before. Still, she didn't mean to be unkind, so she changed the subject.

"Doctor Fletcher was by yesterday and said the baby is just fine." She flipped her arms like the doctor, and deepened her voice. "'That's a baby with an unbeatable will, a baby that begs to be born.'" She pulled a shawl over her shoulders. "Tommy told me you're engaged to Michael Jovich."

"Don't remind me. He could be the King of England and I wouldn't want to marry him. I want to be independent, earn my own living."

"I'd marry a king," George said from the floor.

"But to have a man love you, care for you? To rest in the arms of your loved one and know you're safe, to know that if you're ill, someone will be there? I'd give anything to have that."

"What about the child's father? He could be there for you."

Kaly shook her head. She hesitated to tell Marika, or anyone, her thoughts. Then the girl smiled at her, a smile that she'd seen a hundred times before, on her sister. Her heart softened and a seed of trust took hold. "It's just so hard for me to ask for help," she said. How could she explain this to Marika? She looked so much like Anne

Marie. She even moved like Annie, pushing the hair out of her face, standing with a hand on her hip, that bright and beautiful smile on her lips, ready to jump in and take care of things. "Tommy and I used to fight over my sister. I spent years not liking him for that reason. I blamed him for taking my sister away from me."

"What does your sister say about it?"

"Nothing. She's passed on."

Marika went quiet. Finally, she said, "I'm sorry. How old was she?"

"Ten years old. You look like her—like she would have looked if she'd lived to be your age."

"What was her name?"

"Anne Marie. We were twins, but she looked more like you than me."

A small smile graced Marika's face, like she liked the idea of being Annie's other look alike. "Tommy is the baby's father?"

Kaly nodded.

"You two must have made up since childhood." Marika tilted her head in a question.

Kaly laughed. She felt her shoulders soften and relax. "Oh, we did. Still, I'm used to handling things myself. I like it that way. I don't like counting on others. Plus, he might not want to help me."

"If he doesn't want to help you, maybe you could marry the king, Miss Shane," George said.

"It'd take courage to ask him to help," Marika said. She looked down at her sweater sleeve and rolled it up over her slim wrist. "He could only say 'no'." She lifted her head and looked at Kaly with her dark brown eyes, eyes so much like Annie's that Kaly felt the spirit of her sister move across the room. "You've survived worse things. Go to him. Ask. He could also say 'yes'. Then you wouldn't be so alone."

"As parents, neither of us would be any good."

"Mama told me that children change people," Marika

said. "They find love and strength they never knew they had."

"Isn't that a lot to ask of a child? Here kid, fix Mom and Dad. Help them grow up. I'm so stupid! How did I get myself into this mess? When we were young Tommy got blamed for something he didn't do."

"What was it?" Marika asked.

"Killing my sister. I didn't know what to think when the police arrested him. When he never came home, I thought he'd just disappeared too, along with my sister. I blamed him for taking her away, but not for killing her."

"Do you know who did it?"

Kaly shook her head. "But Tommy is the one who paid for it. Four years in the state reform school. I'm sure he must have hated me for that."

"That doesn't look like hatred to me," Marika said with a lopsided smile, pointing at Kaly's belly.

"Things have always been complicated between us." Kaly needed someone safe, someone with resources and kindness, to raise her child. "Maybe you and Michael could adopt the baby. You two could raise the child properly."

George popped up from the floor. "Miss Shane," he said, pulling on her sleeve, "I'll raise the baby."

"I've seen you in action," she said, remembering how he'd slung the knife into Julian's shoulder, instantly hating herself for talking to the boy like that. What on earth was wrong with her these days? "Go get your coat and we'll go for a walk in a minute."

George slumped out of the room.

Marika shook her head. "I don't know the first thing about children. Plus, I'm trying to delay the marriage as long as I can—if I can get around Papa. I'll marry the man I choose. In about ten years."

"You're good at caring for others. You took good care of me. You'd make a great mother. And marrying Michael isn't such a bad idea. He's a good man. He'd make a good father. Imagine the horror of a life the child would have in my care."

"You're wrong, Kaly. You're not bad. Give yourself a chance. Give the baby a chance to know her mother. Even the darkest dream has an angel inside it."

Kaly shook her head. She had the back up plan of the tansy and arsenic. She just didn't know if she could use it. "Some angel," she said. "Maybe that's what we should do, join the angels. If neither of us are here the baby won't ever have to live a life like mine." It should have been that simple. But the words made her whole body hurt.

"Death?" Marika's eyes widened. She slowly closed her fists.

Kaly folded her arms across her chest. She shouldn't have said anything. She'd made no decisions. She'd only been collecting options and there was no need to trouble anyone else with those options. But then, to use Miss Anderson's words, when hadn't she been trouble?

"Death is no joke. It's final," Marika said, her voice soft and steady. "Your sister died and it broke your heart. Pamela is dead. Michael and I found her. I kept thinking she would move, but she was gone. Forever gone."

Kaly's breath caught in her throat. "Pamela's dead? How did she die?" The girl had been ill but very much alive when Kaly'd last seen her. How long had it been? Too long.

"I should've saved her," Marika was saying. "Dr. Fletcher sent me to her."

Kaly stared out the window at the smoke on the hill spreading across the sky and disappearing, like nothing had ever happened up there. "I'm right, then," she murmured absently, more to herself than to Marika. "With me, my daughter will have a fate no better than Pamela's."

Marika went to the window, stood in front of Kaly, and held her by her shoulders as if she were a small child. "Look at me." She waited until Kaly looked at her. "You almost died after Bert beat you. What good is surviving if you take your own life, and the baby's? Prostitution is dangerous. Give it up. Raise your child."

Kaly shook her head. "I'm no good."

"You're wrong."

"No." Kaly thought of Marika's father, Stojan, the time she'd seen him at Dr. Fletcher's office. His pale face. His coughing. She imagined him standing protectively over Marika, like Marika stood by her now. At one time Kaly had liked that feeling of protection. But since Bert's beating she'd wanted all hovering, all protection, to stop. The only thing she wanted now was to throw herself into the black void of her life and come out somewhere else. The air around Kaly darkened. She swooned, and held onto the bedpost. "There is no good life I can give this child."

Both women turned at a gasp from the doorway.

George stood there wide-eyed, his coat hanging loosely on his shoulders.

The small bit of her that still felt human wanted to protect the boy. But something else, something bitter and vile, wanted to get rid of him. To get rid of all of them. "Go back to your room," Kaly told the boy. "Go," she said, turning back to Marika. "Leave me alone."

"Give yourself and the child a chance," Marika said, looking like she might burst into tears. "Promise me."

"I'm in no position to promise anyone anything." Kaly looked out again at the smoke from the mining accident. It was almost gone now. Just a vague haze hung in the air. She turned toward the hallway.

George pulled a cigarette from his pocket.

Kaly walked over and grabbed the cigarette. She crushed it on the floor. "That's bad for you, and against Miss Anderson's rules. How old are you? Ten?"

"You haven't given up on him," Marika said, nodding at the boy.

"Yeah, foolish of me. Someone better stick around to take care of him." She took a breath to calm her racing heart and gave Marika a weak smile. It wasn't a promise, but it was the best she could do. "Bert Brown was here today. When I saw him I felt scared."

"He nearly killed you that night at the Casino."

"It was more than that. I wonder where he was when my sister died."

"You think Bert killed your sister?"

"I don't know."

"Pamela had bruises on her," Marika said.

"She probably gave them to herself. She was crazy when I saw her."

George coughed from the doorway.

"Come on, we'll walk you home," Kaly said, grabbing a sweater.

That night it poured rain. Kaly could hear the rattle of the storm on the roof, feel its chill in her chest. A sad, hopeless feeling swelled in her heart and she tried to push it back. She sat on the bed, wondering what she would do about the baby, about herself. A knock on her window interrupted her thoughts, punctuating the steady strum of rain. Kaly turned toward the sound.

There was Tommy, outside, standing on the fire escape. His shirt was wet, his dark hair pasted to his forehead.

"You're not allowed in here," she said, opening the window.

He ignored her comment and climbed through the opening. "The old place hasn't changed much, has it?"

"What do you want?"

"I felt bad about running away that day. I wanted to see that you're OK."

"There's a door downstairs."

"A door you can shut in my face. Plus, I don't want to explain to Miss Anderson the reasons I'm here." He wiped a drizzle of water off his forehead. "Did you hear about Pamela? They found her dead in her crib."

"I heard. Stojan Lailich's daughter told me. I feel bad

about Pamela. There was nothing for it, though. She was so sick."

"Something's haunting me."

"Welcome to the land of ghosts."

"Did the Lailich girl say how Pamela died?"

"Seems clear enough. The syphilis ate away at her brain."

"It was a natural death then?"

"Why? What's wrong?"

"Remember when she was fighting some sort of demon that day after we left the opium dens? I asked you if you'd given her that tansy and arsenic mixture? You said you hadn't and I was glad of it. But you were really quiet after you said that, like you knew something more." He ran a hand through his wet hair, wiped the moisture off on his brown trousers. "Are you sure you didn't give it to her? I'm worried you did and didn't want to tell me. I'm worried she used it to kill herself."

"No, I didn't give it to her." Kaly told him the truth. But in her next breath she found herself lying again. "I dumped it, tossed the bottle in the garbage. Pamela died of the disease, not her own hand." She said nothing about the bruises Marika had mentioned earlier.

"Oh, I'm glad." His face softened and he looked relieved.

Kaly shrugged. "Look, Tommy, you can't just show up here uninvited. Come back in the morning. Miss Anderson will pitch a fit if she finds you here like this. I promise we'll talk tomorrow."

"Bert's up at the Tavern ranting about someone stealing something from him. He's going on about dirty whores can't be trusted. Be careful, Kaly. He seems to have a grudge out for you. That night he hurt you in the Casino, I meant to keep you safe. That's all I ever wanted. It's been my biggest failure."

"Thank you. I know you've watched out for me. But if you want to keep me safe you should go now. If I get kicked out of here you'll worry about me again. Now that I'm here, I realize I'm running out of places to go."

"I'll take care of you," Tommy said. "You're the closest thing to family I've got."

Family. There it was again. The word sat on Kaly's chest and hurt. A chill despair reached in and dislodged any good feeling the word might have to it. "I have no family," she said. "Without Anne Marie my life is nothing." It was true. Her life had amounted to a simple nothing.

Tommy bit his lip and looked at the floor. "I loved Annie too."

"You just happened to be there when I found her dead. Imagine what it was like for me to find you two together, and Anne Marie without a breath left in her."

"We've been over this, Kaly. I would do anything to change it. Annie's been dead for nearly twenty years and we're still playing tug-of-war with her ghost. Can't we just talk about it like adults? We can help each other."

The muscles in Kaly's arms tightened, the icy cold spreading through her torso, down her pelvis, and into her legs and feet, that winter day swelling up around her and disappearing.

"Someone else was there that day," Tommy was saying.

Kaly nodded and hugged herself. The years were unraveling. She wanted to wrap them back up and put them away like an old ball of yarn.

Tommy stood near her as if she was ten years old again.

Outside, the silence hummed. The rain stood in reprieve. Kaly's stomach cramped and she doubled over the baby in pain. The image of Bert at the Polly May doorway the day her sister died rose and fell in her mind.

"Before I found her that day in the snow storm someone else had been there with Annie," Tommy said a second time. He wiped his brow with his wet sleeve and sat on the bed. "Whoever he was, he ran into the bushes when I showed up. When I found her, her coat was torn off and she looked so cold. I managed to get it back on her before you found us."

The air went out of Kaly. Her face was burning up. "Did you tell the police that?"

"I did. But they didn't believe me." He moved closer to her. "I was the person there when you found us. I was the one to go and get Miss Anderson. There was no one else to implicate. They must have figured it for a simple open and shut case. But I didn't kill her. I never would have hurt Annie."

"I know that." And she did. "But who ran away? And who killed her?"

"I wish I knew." Tommy took Kaly's hand in his.

She froze, the old inertness sitting down on her like an unwanted friend.

"I thought I could make up for her death by watching out for you. I thought that someday, with time, things would get better between us," Tommy said. "It broke my heart to lose Annie, but we still have each other."

His words swirled around her and she felt herself drowning in hope, self-pity, and bitterness—the emotions mixed inside of her like bad electricity. She heard Marika's words from earlier. *Give yourself and the baby a chance.*

"There is another reason I'm here tonight," he said and took her in his arms.

She let him. His warm body felt good to her. He ran his hand down her neck, past her pregnant breasts, and over the hard mound of her belly. "Is it true? Am I the child's father?"

Kaly imagined his hand floating through her skin and touching his child's head. She swooned, not sure if it was desire or despair she felt.

A knock on the door startled her and shook her to reality. She pushed Tommy away, without an answer.

"Miss Shane, you have a visitor," George said through the door.

He should have been sleeping. Where was Miss

Anderson and why was the boy escorting visitors at this time of night? Something to do with her good friend the gin bottle, no doubt.

"Who is it?" Kaly asked.

"That woman who always comes here," he said.

Marika must have forgotten something. But the last thing Kaly wanted was more talk about how she should raise her own child. "Tell her to be like the gold and vanish. She can come back tomorrow. And you. Go back to bed."

"She says she really needs to talk to you."

"You have to go," Kaly whispered to Tommy.

"But is it true?"

Kaly went numb, words that she should have had the courage to speak halted in her throat and refused to budge. Why couldn't she just tell him the truth and ask for his help? Finally, with a baffled look on his face, he crawled through the window back to the fire escape, back out into the night.

Kaly ran to the sill. "Wait!"

He turned back to her.

"It's true. The child is yours."

His eyes widened. He nodded, his bright, open smile crossing the sky. "You and me, we're family," he said. "We'll raise the child together."

Kaly shook her head and watched him climb down the narrow wooden stairs of the fire escape. His spirit lingered for a moment. Then the air in the room went still and empty, as if Tommy had never been there.

"Miss Shane, can I let her in?" George sounded sleepy and afraid.

What the hell. "Sure. Come on in." Everybody, come on in, she thought. It's a regular circus in here. She lay on her bed, staring at the ceiling and preparing for whatever news the girl might hurl at her next. Shivering, she pulled a brown afghan over her feet.

The door opened and Mrs. McClane walked in. She wore a shiny scarf over her curled brown hair.

George slid down the doorframe and sat on the floor.

Kaly sat up. "Hello. Bad weather for a stroll," she said. Why on earth was Dan's mother here?

"I'm here to ask you for a favor," Mrs. McClane said.

"Well, don't beat around the bush. Get right to the point."

"Dan just told me he's going to join the army."

"And?" Kaly couldn't have been more baffled. It was unlike the woman to ever address her without pleasantries. In fact, Kaly was pretty sure that pleasantries were all that they had ever exchanged.

"They'll send him overseas."

"That's where the war is."

"He could die."

"Why are you telling me? And why the urgency in this storm?"

"I want you to talk him out of it."

"Like he'd listen to me," Kaly said, shaking her head, wondering, perplexed.

"He respects your opinion."

"Respect! A word I don't hear often. Dan's adult enough to make up his own mind." Kaly looked toward the fire escape. For this, she sent Tommy away?

"Please, talk to him. Ask him not to go."

"No offense, ma'am, but why should I? Why me? Obviously, I can barely manage my own life." Kaly cupped her stomach. Tears edged her eyes. That hopeless feeling swelled in her chest. In spite of it all, curiosity swirled in her brain. What was this woman up to?

"He'll listen to you. He's...your family."

"Excuse me?"

"He's your family."

"I have no family," Kaly said.

"Your brother," Mrs. McClane said.

Kaly stared at her.

"Your half-brother. He had a different father than you."

"No, I have no family," Kaly said again. *You and me, we're family*, Tommy had said just moments before.

"You have a brother." Mrs. McClane took off her scarf and folded it into a square. She sat down on the wooden chair near the dresser, looked toward the door where George's legs sprawled across the opening. "And a mother."

Kaly jerked her eyes away from the woman, then back where she was looking at Kaly and talking. She watched Mrs. McClane's mouth move in slow motion as marbled words spewed forth. They bounced off each other and rolled in all directions.

"What are you saying?" Kaly asked.

"You have a brother, Dan, and a mother. Me."

Kaly blinked twice, wide-eyed, and threw her hands at the woman as if to push her back into the wall and out of the room. The vat of stored bitterness inside Kaly spilled over. "Get out," she said, her voice trembling and her throat tightening as if around barbed wire. "Now."

Mrs. McClane didn't move. "I watched you at Anne Marie's funeral."

A black hole opened and Kaly fell into it. The rain began again, the sound of it drumming in her ears. She tried to breathe and her chest seized up. She remembered the woman in gray at Anne Marie's funeral. Kaly had stood beside the sooty snow that was piled up by Annie's grave, alone, bone-frozen, lost.

Under the dull clouds the woman in gray touched Kaly's head and the wind turned on the woman's fingers. A splinter broke away from Kaly's frozen heart where icicles had formed, and she'd watched the woman walk through the cemetery gate back into the underworld of momentary people.

"The one thing I felt good about was that you girls were in a safe home. I was shocked to hear about Annie.

My heart broke, seeing you there that day."

"Don't call her Annie. You don't know the first thing about my sister."

"I've made mistakes. Big ones. I can only hope that the mistakes I made were smaller than the ones I would've made."

Smoke from the kitchen stove wafted up the stairs and the smell of burning wood filled the air. Thunder boomed outside. When Kaly finally heard her own voice in the rain, it was through a night anchored in grief. "Is that what you call an apology?"

Mrs. McClane shook her head. "The girl who left you with Miss Anderson is gone. She died the day she walked away from you and Annie. She froze up to keep from feeling the pain. She died from her sorrow."

"How poetic."

"Will you talk to him?"

"You talk to him."

"He won't hear it from me."

"Let him decide. Dan is a man, completely capable of running his own life." Kaly looked out through half closed eyes. She pulled the afghan up to her chin. "Please. Do one thing for me."

"Yes?"

"Go away. That's all I want from you. Just go away." She turned her face into her pillow and stayed there, away from the deranged night.

Tara McClane moved in her chair and the legs creaked. "That day of Annie's funeral. I wanted to hold you, tell you that it would be alright, take you away. But I had Danny by then and I hadn't told his father about you and Anne Marie. I was afraid he'd leave me and I'd be left with another child I couldn't feed. I was afraid I'd lose Danny, too. That's when I started the bakery and made a plan: As soon as it was successful and I could support you, I'd come and get you. Then Danny's father died, and the bakery barely supported us. Before I knew it, you had grown up."

Kaly said nothing. She breathed into her pillow. It was like pulling the last air from the rocks of a landslide.

"I'm sorry for the way things have turned out. I wanted to keep you safe. I wanted what was best for you."

Muffled sounds throbbed through the room—the rain, the woman's breath, Kaly's heartbeat.

After a long while she heard Mrs. McClane shake out her scarf and walk toward the door. "I guess that's a 'no.' I'm still glad I came here tonight. I put off telling you the truth for far too long. I rehearsed it a thousand ways. None of them included a request for help."

Kaly lay so still she thought she'd halt the rain. She heard footsteps go down the stairs. Then tiny, light footsteps stopped at her bed. The quilt crawled up over her shoulders. She opened her eyes and saw George. "Thought I told you to go back to bed," she said.

"I couldn't sleep," he said. "I had a bad dream."

Kaly pulled the cover back and moved over. "You want to sleep in here?"

He nodded, climbed into bed, and cuddled up with his back to her belly.

"Miss Shane," he said, his voice softened by the covers. "If your mommy makes you cry, I'll take care of you."

Kaly wiped away the tears she hadn't even known were there. "That'd really be something, Georgie, wouldn't it," she said. "A little boy like you taking care of a full grown woman like me. That'd be a real backwards something." She pulled him in close, right next to the baby, and held them both tight.

15
A GUEST COMES TO DINNER

Marika cut up carrots and potatoes for the Lenten stew. Earlier that day she had attended Pamela's funeral, along with Kaly, Michael, and the minister. It was a shiny, bright day perfumed by fresh rain. Surprisingly, the minister's words had comforted her. Marika hadn't expected that. She was convinced that she could've helped the girl, but didn't. What was it the minister had said? That Pamela would now go home, to the arms of her Father. No longer hurt or judged, sick or neglected; she would be held in love—pure, simple love.

Marika quickly quartered the potatoes, watching them weep milky tears. She could still see Pamela that day when she found her. She was lying on the floor, her face blue, her yellow dress wrapped around her knees. She tried to shake the image from her head. Think about something else, she told herself. Think of Papa's latest tale of the homeland. Or her brother's stories about the fights. But her mind immediately went back to Pamela's eyes. Had the girl been terrified during her last moments? Or was Marika remembering her own terror when she found her?

"You finally saw fit to come home," Papa said as he walked through the door. Marko trailed behind him. Before either of them could dump their work bundles, Papa pitched into a coughing fit. He wheezed and struggled for breath, holding the doorjamb to balance himself.

"Sit," he said when he recovered.

Marika looked at Mama.

"Go ahead," Mama said. "You can help me later."

She sat down. It was not good news, if Papa wanted her at the kitchen table with him.

"I spoke with Milosav Jovich today. We set a date for the wedding. All things permitting, it'll be August 8. I still need to talk with the priest to see if he's available that day. If he is, we will announce your engagement next Sunday."

Marika was glad she hadn't been alone when she found Pamela, and grateful that Michael had gone for the doctor. Nevertheless, she didn't want to marry him. She knew she must be careful about what she said to Papa. She didn't want to send him into another coughing fit. One of these times, his lungs would simply explode from the pressure, and that would be it. He'd be gone forever.

Her stomach clenched and her heart dropped at the thought of losing Papa. She felt hot and sudden droplets of sweat dotted her forehead. Guilt lodged in her throat and blocked her breath. The idea of going against his will, when he was dying, terrified her and she hated herself for her next words.

"There are things you don't know about Michael," she said.

Papa nodded. "I know enough to be happy that he'll take you. Be happy, my girl. You'll see that this is a good thing. If not today, tomorrow. Or next year. Be happy."

"I don't want to spend my life wishing it was something else."

"Don't, then," Papa said. "Accept your Papa's decision. It's a good match."

"It's a cliff and you push me off." Marika wrung her hands in her lap. "Why?"

"You're young. You can't be expected to know more than you know. I see the world from having lived. Saying you don't want to marry is like saying you don't want to eat. You'll get used to marriage. It'll be like the precious air someday, a thing you cannot live without."

"I can live without marriage."

Papa held a handkerchief to his mouth and coughed again, backing his chair away from the table and leaning over his knees. His face turned scarlet. His arms shook. His legs trembled.

She should stop her foolishness. Just give Papa this. She loves him. Why can't she just do as he says, like a good daughter. Her chest filled with helplessness. Couldn't she control just one thing? Make Papa happy. She could give him that. But by throwing her dreams away? No. It wasn't possible.

Marika's lips quivered as she tried to stop the chatter in her head. She turned away and got a glass of water for him. "Here, Papa. Drink this."

He stood and wobbled to the washroom, ignoring the water.

Marika moved to help him, but he threw her a fierce warning glance. She turned and helped Mama instead.

Marko slid into the chair Papa had just vacated. He propped his knee against the table and leaned back on two legs of the chair, balancing in a precarious position. "You can't fight him," he said. "You should just give up."

"You wouldn't. You'd find a way around him."

"I don't fight him."

"You go around him all the time."

"Yes, I'm a genius about getting my way, but I don't push my luck." He locked his hands behind his head, leaning back further, making the chair topple. Her brother tumbled to the floor, bringing a smile to Marika's face.

"Smarty pants," she said, stifling a giggle. "Now you might learn how to sit in a chair. It's very complicated. But you're a genius. You'll come up with a brilliant system."

"Ha. Ha. Very funny." He stood up and righted the chair. "I'm going to bring in some wood."

Behind the washroom door, Papa let loose another string of coughs.

Marika covered the table with a white crocheted tablecloth. Already the stew and corn bread smelled wonderful. The warmth from the fire covered Marika's bones like a thick blanket. Mama set her gold-trimmed china out for five people.

"Five plates?" Marika asked.

"Yes. Five." Mama took the lid off of the pot and steam curled up to the ceiling. She stirred the stew with a long wooden spoon.

"Who's coming for dinner?"

"Your fiancé. I thought Papa told you."

"Michael?"

"What better day than today? He's already shown you kindness. That makes me happy."

"I met him in the Alley, outside of a prostitute's crib. He was at her funeral today." She decided not to mention that she'd seen him at the Casino the night Bert Brown had ruthlessly beaten Tommy Monroe.

"He was at Pamela's funeral showing his respect. Very kind of him. Not unlike yourself. The sooner you get to know him, the sooner you can get over your fear that he's a horrible person. You never know, you might actually like him." Mama took the corn bread from the oven, set it on top of the stove, and wiped her hands on her apron. "Go clean up. Be a good daughter. He'll be here any minute."

"Is the whole world against me? Because he was kind, does that mean I have to marry him? It's my life. My life!" The words sounded meaningless and hollow and she knew Papa would take them that way. Something inside of her had hoped Mama would take her seriously.

Mama just shook her head. "Count your blessings. Papa wants the best for you, for your life to be good. Be happy, my girl. Make Papa proud."

Marika threw her arms up, sighing. All right, she'd behave. For one night.

In the sleeping room she pulled a purple dress out of the trunk and put it on. She yanked the brush through her hair several times, tipping her head to one side and then the other. Maybe they were right. Maybe this was the best way. Maybe she should let tradition dictate her life.

Mama came in, pulled off her dirty apron, and her brown skirt. She changed into the lavender dress and put on a clean apron. She patted the bun at the back of her head and caught the loose strands of hair with bobby pins. Glancing at Marika and back to the mirror, she hummed a simple tune. An icon of the Holy Mother sat on the vanity table near the mirror. When she finished fixing her hair, she crossed herself and kissed the icon.

"Are you ready?" She asked.

Marika shook her head. "I wonder if Pamela believed in God," she said, pointing to the icon. "What do you think will happen to her?"

"Not much more can happen to her now." Mama looked concerned. She pulled her skirt under her legs and sat down on the bed, motioning for Marika to join her. Marika sat down next to her.

"But will she go to heaven? The minister at her funeral said that she would, but what would our priest say? She worked out of the cribs. I can't stop thinking about how helpless and weak she looked when we found her. They say prostitution is the devil's work, but will God take her age into account and make an exception for one so young?"

Mama took her hand and held it in her lap. Marika felt safe and secure next to her mother on the bed. "Honey, that's between God and Pamela. I believe God knows our hearts. If we didn't make mistakes, we wouldn't be human. A child like Pamela was likely still suffering from the mistakes of her parents, or the mistakes of a town. We do our best, that's all."

"You think she did her best?"

Mama put her arm around Marika and pulled her into a hug. Her warm body felt good to Marika and she let herself settle into the comfort of it. Tears had welled up in her eyes and they now spilled onto Mama's clean apron. Finally, Mama spoke. "Yes," she said. "Yes, I do. I'm sure that Pamela did her best."

Marika lifted her head off of Mama's shoulder. She looked at the icon and said, "I really hope God sees it that way."

By the time Michael arrived, Marika was looking her best. The white lace collar on the purple dress set off the olive tones in her skin, and her dark hair was loosely fastened at the nape of her neck. A few tiny curls spiraled down, resting on her shoulders. Promising to behave, she had composed herself, her back straight and graceful, her hand stretched out in greeting.

However, when Michael kissed her on both cheeks in the traditional greeting, implying an intimacy she didn't feel, she stiffened and jerked away. Instantly flustered, she felt her face heat up. He was too handsome. No doubt a lady's man. His words were as smooth as velvet. She couldn't trust him. She couldn't trust her family either, the way they had disregarded her, and evaporated her opinion from the purpose of her life. Marika dropped her composure and began the evening seething inside.

Mama's lavender dress twirled as she moved around the table to serve the rich vegetable stew, giving Michael the healthiest portion.

He attempted to pass it over to Papa and then, when Papa refused, he tried to pass it to, of all people, Marika!

"Thank you but no," she said, trying to sound calm.

"You eat it."

"It smells wonderful. Thank you for having me over." He placed his napkin in his lap, folded his hands, and waited.

"Lord, thank you for this good food," Papa said when all the plates were filled, "for the love of our families, and for bringing Michael here tonight as our dinner guest. Please watch over us and guide us tonight and always. Amen."

Michael unfolded his hands and began to eat.

"Remember when the Moulton Dam blew up?" Papa asked.

Michael nodded. His eyes went dark and serious. "That accident is really disturbing. They don't even know what caused the explosion. They're still investigating it, but all this time has passed and it's still a mystery."

"That was a real shame," Mama said. "People lost their homes. The mine owners promised to make good on the damage done, but how do you ever replace personal items?"

"Books, letters, clothing," Michael agreed. "Sleep. A sense of security. Lots of things money can't replace. These accidents keep knocking the feet out from under the town, but somehow people find the strength to carry on. Still, so many men die, it's amazing there's anyone left to work."

"A good reason for women to have their own livelihoods, don't you think?" Marika said, glancing sideways at Papa.

"You'll never have a shortage of workers," Papa said to Michael. "You've got a constant flow of men to the area. That's one reason we're having trouble with the union. Miners are afraid to stand for their rights, afraid they'll be black-listed and denied a rustling card. Somebody owns this town, and it's not the people."

"It's not just men who die," Mama said. "It's mothers too. They die from diseases, poverty and broken hearts.

Children are left alone."

"It's true Papa," Marika said. "So many women are left on their own with children. Women need education and training to have good work."

Mama cut a potato with her spoon and Marika thought she could see the edge of smile in her lips.

"When the Moulton tailings from the dam hit?" Marko said, nodding. "One mother told the paper that the tailings knocked her house right off its foundation. A pile of mud slid through the window. She climbed on top of the roof in the middle of the night, holding her baby."

"That's strong love, the love of a mother for her child," Mama said.

"The strength of a woman," Marika said.

"Mining accidents are like the weather, and you can't control the weather," Marko said. The others nodded to him, *responded to him*.

Marika felt her own words like whispers that vanished in a strong wind. Sitting there at the dinner table, she was nothing. Well, not exactly nothing. More like a poisonous vapor that evaporates unnoticed, but waits in the clouds.

"The thing is that we can limit the number of accidents that happen on the hill," Michael was saying. "We can make the mines as safe as possible. Safe work is every person's right. That's why I have so much respect for the safety precautions they're putting in up there at the North Butte Mine Workings, at the Speculator and Granite Mountain mines right now. Good lighting. Electricity. Everything helps." He dipped a piece of cornbread into his stew.

Marika watched the hair on his long fingers as he put the cornbread in his mouth. His hands seemed strong, certain, too certain and confident.

"They've improved the ventilation system in both mines," Papa said. "Fresh air reduces the risk of poisoning. They're scheduled to put a new sprinkling system in soon. The way that the Speculator hooks into the Granite

Mountain it'll make for better working conditions in both shafts."

"This year has been pretty quiet so far," Mama said. "Knock on wood." She reached out and knocked her knuckles against the table.

"Amen," Papa said. "Let's hope it stays that way."

"Would you like more?" Mama asked, gesturing to Marko. He had already eaten most of his meal. Only the carrots, which he hated, were left orphaned on his plate.

"No thank you," he said.

Marika didn't know how he could eat so fast. She forced down a bite of turnip and broke her cornbread into small pieces. She'd eat. If they acted like she wasn't there, she would act like she wasn't there. She would act like nothing was happening. Because nothing was happening. Nothing but this stupid, boring dinner conversation. She had to be there, but she didn't have to like being there.

"Not to belabor the point, but I just want to mention the fire in the Pennsylvania Mine," Papa said. "Twenty-one men died in that fire, bless their souls."

"Do you think that's why they raised the pay to $4.75 a shift, the dangers involved in mining?" Mama asked. She brushed crumbs off of her skirt.

"No," Michael replied. "It has to do with the war. Copper is worth a pretty penny, now that they're using it for bullets. A sure sell. The more copper they can put out, the more money they can make. It's worth it to them to pay a pittance more to have the product. They're making a killing, pun aside."

"Killing is not a joke, Mr. Jovich." Marika picked up her plate and stood. She gathered the empty plates and carried them all to the washroom. She had to get away from the table and this dinner talk, trapped, right there in her own home. She needed a moment to think, to gather her wits. *To behave.* Yes, for Mama and Papa, she would behave. After all they'd done for her, she could at least be polite.

After dinner, Michael and Papa sat at the table while Papa smoked a cigar. The fumes nauseated her and expanded her hopelessness. She helped Mama put the food away and cut *povetica* for dessert.

By the time Papa broke out the after-dinner *rakija* Marika had said very little. She had definitely not said anything kind or welcoming. Not that anyone seemed to notice. Or care.

Papa filled five glasses. Apparently on this grand occasion, even she and Marko were people. They, too, were welcome to the celebratory plum brandy.

She wasted no time drinking it. When she finished the *rakija*, she pushed her glass toward Papa.

Much to her surprise, Papa re-filled it.

The brandy's effect was magical. Marika found her voice. "Mr. Jovich, as you know, I've been taking care of Miss Kaly Shane," she said. "As you saw today at Pamela's funeral, she's doing well. She speaks highly of you." Marika smiled, a smile that greatly broadened when she saw the shocked look on Papa's face. Now Papa would know what kind of man he had promised his only daughter.

"She's a friend of mine," Michael said. "She's been through a lot. I'm glad the doctor engaged you to care for her."

"Funny choice of words," Marika said.

"She needs help," Michael said. "I'm grateful that she is in good hands." He looked directly at her. His eyebrows were thick and bushy, like Papa's, his nose narrow at the bridge like Marko's. Michael was clean-shaven and his dark hair had been recently trimmed. All remnants of the dirty mine work had been washed away. He seemed like a different person from the rugged man who'd walked into Pamela's crib with her.

Marika took another sip of her brandy. "Let me get this straight: You're glad your fiancée is caring for a woman of ill-repute."

"Sweetheart," Mama said, "he is happy for her. Let's

leave it at that."

"A working girl, a prostitute," Marika said, "whom you claim as a friend."

"Marika! Mind your manners," Mama said. She scooted her chair back an inch.

"A claim you make at the dinner table of your future in-laws? Please. Won't that tarnish your reputation?"

"That's enough." Mama grabbed Marika's elbow. But she let it go right away, as if burned by a hot coal. "Mr. Jovich is a guest in our home."

"It's fine," Michael said. "I have nothing to hide. She is right to question my motives with other women if we're to be married."

Finally! He said it! He named the reason he sat at their table. If she hadn't been so adverse to the idea of him, she'd have admired him for speaking directly. She caught Papa's slight nod out of the corner of her eye.

"Go on," Marika said.

"I've known Kaly since she was a young girl. She cleaned my parents' house after her sister died. After losing her sister, she went mute. She didn't say a word to anyone for a very long time. Seemed like forever. Miss Anderson thought the work would do her good."

"Did it?"

"I think so. Eventually, she talked with us, and even began to laugh again. I thought of her like a sister."

"How noble," Marika said.

"I wouldn't call it that. She'd been through a lot. I felt sorry for her."

"You still feel sorry for her?"

"I feel sorry for her past. She makes her own decisions now."

"Working for the unions. Cheering the underdog. Tell me, now that we've joined the war, will you enlist in the military, too?"

"I know that a lot of people are against the war. Most of them having just come over from Europe. They say that they'll be killing their own people over there. War can be a terrible oppression of the poor. Yet, if we don't fight for good, who will?"

"But are you enlisting?" Marika understood many people were against the war, and she understood why, but she didn't want a philosophical discussion. She just wanted a simple answer from Michael. It could help her make her case to Papa.

"I've been down there. They won't take me with my poor vision. I'm waiting for eye glasses." His expression softened.

For a moment, Marika felt foolish. She was behaving badly. She wondered how bad his eyes could be. What emotion had Baba said the eyes held? She would say that he was hiding from something, or that he couldn't see beyond the end of his own nose. Or would Baba have said that the eyes signify fear of struggle, fear of being humiliated? Marika couldn't recall. Perhaps more *rakija* would help. Draining the last of her brandy, she pushed her glass again toward Papa, motioning for him to refill it another time.

Papa's fist tightened around the slim neck of the bottle, his eyes as wide as owl eyes in a pitch-black night. But he did not lift the bottle from the table.

In the street an automobile backfired and Marika jumped.

Marko smiled. "Papa, they're just talking. He said he doesn't mind."

Marika made a face for Marko's benefit—and to test Michael's vision. Michael didn't react at all but Marko's smile widened.

She pushed her glass closer to the bottle. "May I have another please?" She really wanted some more plum brandy. She hadn't known she was so brilliant.

"Me, too, please?" Marko asked.

"Yes, let's all have another and then we'll have dessert and coffee," Mama said.

Marko made the same face his sister had made earlier. They had triumphed. Papa filled their glasses.

"You and your brother really look alike," Michael said. "Especially when you squish up your noses like that."

The two of them went red.

"We always do that," Marko said.

"We just never grew out of it." Marika giggled and covered her mouth with her hand. "How can you think of going to fight?" she asked. "Like you said earlier, our relatives *are* dying over there. And so are yours."

"A Slav started the war," Michael said. "We have an obligation."

"To keep the war going?" She palmed her glass and watched the rich purple liquid swirl.

"To bring peace to the continent."

"To build the market for copper bullets," she said.

"Time for dessert!" Mama brought out the plate of *povetica* and placed it on the table.

Marika laid a large piece on a small plate. The dark circles of filling snaked though the thin bread. She slid the light pastry into her mouth and the buttery, rich honey and walnuts soothed her tongue. The taste stole her attention and she reveled in it.

"Mr. Jovich, please forgive me," Papa said. "I've made a mistake. I may have saddled you with a terrible imposition by agreeing to your father's request that I allow you to marry my Marika. I'm afraid my daughter is not mature enough to marry. She is old enough so that she won't be a child bride, but evidently she is not old enough to stop acting like a child."

Marika swallowed the *povetica*, hiccupped, and nodded.

16
GHOSTS IN THE BASEMENT

Kaly knew what her sister would've done. Anne Marie, who never even uttered the word mother, had always been better at loving easily and freely. She would have sat up on the bed and called for tea for the woman. Annie would have welcomed Tara McClane to tell her stories, and then she would have told her own stories too. Annie wouldn't have to forgive Tara McClane. She never thought anyone needed forgiveness. She would have simply loved their mother, because this was an opportunity for love.

But then again, Annie had never found her sister dead in a snow bank.

Kaly didn't like it but she had to admit that she was a slave to the past. Plus, she needed to be certain that Tara McClane really was their mother. She remembered what Miss Parsons had said about the files on the Polly May kids. *Locked up tight in some basement somewhere.*

So when Miss Anderson went through the forbidden door to the Polly May basement, carrying an armload of papers, Kaly catalogued the information and waited. She poured herself a cup of coffee and a flutter skimmed across her stomach. The coffee disgusted her. It clearly disagreed with the baby, forcing Kaly to dump it down the sink and put on tea water.

The warm stove scented the room with fir and cedar, conjuring up old memories. The memories blended into the morning light and spit off sparks, like the warm fire. For the moment, remembering felt good. Annie, Tommy, Bert. The youth they all shared: ribbons tied in bows on the Christmas trees; Annie splashing dishwater on Kaly while cleaning up after dinner; stitching yarn dolls together late at night in their room; sculpting snow angels.

"I am your angel, and you are mine," Annie had said. Later that day they made a wonderful winter arch for the angels to fly through. That spring they planted iris bulbs for Miss Anderson along the southern fence. The irises never bloomed. They simply rotted in the ground.

Today the basement door loomed, mysterious, loud. She and Anne Marie had never gone near that door. The dark monster lived behind it. When they heard voices or sounds come from it they ran and hid under their quilt. In their own bed together, they were strong. They were at home and warm. Nothing could hurt them. The cradle of their small room held them safe. That tiny world was all they had needed.

The teapot whistled as Miss Anderson rose from the basement, arms empty. Kaly poured a cup of coffee for her and put it on the kitchen table. She poured hot water into a rose colored teapot for herself. "Remember when I came to you this winter, asking you to take the baby?" Kaly asked. "The day George stabbed Julian?"

"Yes, I remember." Miss Anderson sat and spooned sugar into her coffee.

"You said I sent one of your best boys to the state reform school."

"You did."

"You said to ask Tommy about what happened the day

that Anne Marie died."

"You have quite a memory. What is it you're after?" Miss Anderson poured cream into her coffee and stirred it slowly.

"You knew Tommy didn't kill Anne Marie."

Something like fear flickered across the matron's face but vanished immediately, leaving her reserved again. "I'd always known he was wrongly accused," she said. "A mother knows her children."

"You're not his mother. But never mind. Here's what I don't understand. You blamed me for saying Tommy killed Annie. I was just a kid and so was Tommy. Why didn't you look out for us? Why didn't you tell the court that Tommy didn't do it?" Kaly couldn't believe she was asking Miss Anderson this question. She'd spent a lifetime too scared to ask the matron about that time.

"They would've thought I was being overly protective. Reform school isn't so bad. A boy gets fed; he stays out of trouble."

"You believed he was innocent and you let him go to corrections anyway? How could paying for a crime he didn't commit help him?"

"Nothing I could have told the court would have changed their minds about him."

Kaly took a breath deep into her lungs and let it go. Words lodged in her throat, stuck there. She poured her tea and looked out at the stunted lilac bushes. When she looked back, Miss Anderson was reading the morning paper. Finally Kaly asked, "Do you know who killed Annie?"

"If anyone knew who killed her, Tommy wouldn't have spent time in corrections. True justice is a ghost of some future time. It's not something that flourishes in a mining town." Miss Anderson dumped her coffee in the sink. "I've got chores to do. You need to fix up your room for the baby."

"What was Bert doing here?" Kaly asked.

"What?"

"Bert Brown. I saw him leave. He looked mad. Does he still come to you to bail him out of his mess of a life?"

Miss Anderson raised her eyebrows. "Ask him yourself."

"I had a visitor the other day. George brought her to my room. You, I suppose, were downstairs sleeping with a bottle of gin."

"You'll speak respectfully in my house or not at all."

"My mother, supposedly. Tara McClane. You knew all along. She lived right down the road."

"Tara was here?" Miss Anderson looked out the window as if she could see the shades of the irises there. "That's good. No more secrets. I'm tired of other people's secrets."

"Why didn't you tell us?"

"You know how it is. Someone comes to you with trouble, you don't want their troubles, but you reach out your arms anyway. They tell you to guard their secrets and you do. Not because you want to take care of them, but because it's what you do. Your mother did her best. I just figured it was her job to tell you, not mine."

"I'm looking for a small room to rent," Kaly said. "If you won't keep the baby, I'll find someone else to adopt her."

"Another secret, another mistake. You never could appreciate what you had. You have an opportunity here. You don't have to keep walking the line. A whore's life is a short life. You've already run out your luck. Stay here and raise your child. It just takes a little courage."

"Maybe you're right," Kaly said, thinking of the golden cross on Anne Marie's picture, the white twin cross around her sister's neck in the picture, "but I doubt it."

Later on, when Miss Anderson went uptown for groceries, Kaly walked to the wrought iron bench in the entryway. The children's pictures gazed toward the front door, stuck in the past, longing to burst out of the Polly May and live in the free, sooty air of the mining town. She scrutinized the pictures of Tommy, Bert, and Anne Marie. There was a picture of Miss Anderson holding Bert when he was about five years old. Miss Anderson was not smiling. She looked stern, as if ready to battle some unknown force.

Near the wall of pictures, the forbidden door to the basement beckoned.

It wouldn't open when Kaly turned the knob. It was locked. She felt the old rumbling in her chest, the same feeling she'd always had when she and Annie had hidden under the quilt from the monster. Suddenly her sister was there, sharing her fear. Kaly held Anne Marie's tiny hand, soft, smooth and ghostly. A lilting whisper blew across her face. The smell of coffee wafted out from the kitchen. The baby fluttered in her belly, bringing her back to the present and she was alone again, Anne Marie gone.

Going against her better judgment, Kaly searched for the key, but she found nothing, not even dust, under the dancing doll lamp, above the door, or under the Oriental rug.

She poured herself another cup of tea. Chores always helped her think. She did the dishes, and cleaned coffee grounds and toast crumbs off the counter. Then she felt tired. In the calico light of the morning kitchen, she concluded that it was fear—the fear of searching alone for the truth—that was wearing her out. Sitting down to rest, she picked up a spoon and clinked it against the sugar jar.

That simple rhythm made her think up a host of new places to search. Of course Miss Anderson would have hidden the key in the kitchen, her domain. Kaly looked under the dishes in the cupboard, and in the drawers. Finally she found a cup full of keys in the third drawer down. One by one she inserted them into the keyhole.

The door swung open.

She felt around in the damp, dusty dark for the light

string, found it and pulled, spilling light down the dirty staircase. Spider webs cluttered the edges of the stairwell. The stairs were steep, leading to a dirt room piled with boxes. Yarn dolls peeked out from one open-slat box. Winter clothes and tiny mittens reached up from another.

Kaly found a box filled with papers. On top, Tommy's papers from the Montana State Reform School seemed to stare her down. Feeling like a common burglar she read the papers. Four years for unruly behavior, they said. But there was nothing about Tommy going to the reform school for having killed Anne Marie. *A woman knows her children.* Miss Anderson had lied. She'd said that he'd gone to corrections for killing Annie. But why did she lie?

Kaly found the documents granting Miss Anderson care of Tommy, signed by his uncle in Ohio. The uncle had signed temporary custody over to Miss Anderson early in 1895. Taped to the back was an obituary dated November of that same year. Tommy's uncle had died before he could retrieve his orphaned nephew. Poor Tommy. He'd almost had a home.

Kaly dug deeper into the box. Under the documents about Tommy were her and Annie Marie's birth certificates. Twins, they said, mother Tara Marie O'Leary, father unclaimed. Kaly stared at the papers, her mouth going dry. The yellowed certificates had small tears along their edges. They looked old, and Kaly wondered if they'd been down here behind the cursed, forbidden door all along. Proof that Tara McClane really was their mother. Kaly sank onto a dusty bench and held back her tears. She wouldn't cry over an absent mother, a lost sister, or even a real, live brother working on the hill. Fate had had its way with her. What did she have to offer Tara or Danny McClane now? Kaly was certainly no one's angel, much less anyone's savior. And she didn't expect anyone to save her.

She took a deep breath and closed the box. She would leave the ghosts to themselves. As she started up the stairs, she heard the wind whipping the lilac leaves outside. Near the top of the stairs, she reached for the light string but then stopped herself and turned back down into the dirty cellar. On the box she could see her fingerprints in the dust. She opened it again and dug deeper. At the very bottom she found what she was looking for: Bert Brown's birth certificate. Born 1883. He was seven years older than Kaly. Only one parent was named—Coral Anderson. Father unknown.

Kaly dropped the tansy and arsenic potion into her coat pocket and walked uptown. The baby felt heavy as she climbed the steep streets of Butte. She was winded and her thigh muscles burned. What was it Miss Anderson had said? *Another secret, another mistake.* She tried to get the words out of her head, but then the image of Bert Brown's birth certificate popped into her mind. A merry-go-round of unwanted words and images tortured her as she made her way down Mercury Street. She felt the ghosts chattering in her brain.

In the Alley, a woman poked her head out from a crib and told her there'd been a raid last night. Girls who'd come back and had been hiding in the cribs were now in jail. The woman repeated old news: Pamela had killed herself last week. Kaly held her tongue about her suspicions that the girl had been murdered. Further down the row Beth sat on a bench in front of Kaly's old crib, her cheek swollen and deep purple.

"What happened?"

"Bert hit me," Beth said, "because I'd asked about Lacy Blue."

Kaly looked away, trying to conceal her fury. The wind blew litter down the alley. Beyond the city smog the beautiful Highlands reached toward the blue sky. Somewhere up there the Emerald Lake glowed brilliantly next to the red mountain rocks. Up there, the larkspur and pink monkey flower lay just under the spring snow, ready to grow and bloom, to reach toward the sun.

"I shoulda just let it be," Beth was saying.

"Sounds like you're blaming yourself."

"He's had a tough life."

"He put me out of commission for weeks. Look at you. He might have killed Lacy for all we know, and that's why he got so mad when you asked about her. You're making excuses for him. The more excuses you make, the more likely you'll be next." Kaly didn't mention her suspicions about Pamela, that someone had killed her too. She also didn't mention that Miss Anderson was Bert's mother. And again, she let the rape be.

"You don't know him like I do. He's got a kind heart. Sure, he gets mean some, but really he's just a scared little boy." Beth looked up at the sound of an automobile approaching. "I gotta go."

Lottie Boyle sat in the back seat of the auto, staring over at them.

The Casino was empty except for Ted Framer. It smelled of last night's whiskey. The smell twisted her stomach. "Hold on little one," she whispered to the baby. Ted wore stained trousers rolled up past his ankles and ran a swamping broom across the room. Piles of dirt and wasted cigar butts dotted the floor. He looked up as she approached him.

"Hi, Teddy. Is Bert around?" Kaly twisted the tansy and arsenic vial in her pocket.

"At the gym, training for his next fight. His mean streak is growing." Teddy smiled. "You okay?"

"Think he'll mind if I look in on him?"

Ted shook his head. "Don't know why you'd want to. The man's mean but he's not crazy. He'd never turn away a beautiful woman. But be careful. He's a bitter man."

"Thanks," she said. A few doors down the dank, cold alley she opened the gym door. The stale smell of old sweat hit her hard and her hand went to her stomach. She could hear the popping sound of taped hands hitting a heavy bag. A pile of jump ropes lay on the floor like curled snakes.

Bert wore a red thermal shirt and old trousers cut off at the knees. He pivoted right and threw a left jab followed by a right punch, double hitting the bag at the center. Then he pivoted left and threw a right jab followed by a left punch. He was sweating and breathing hard.

"Hope your next fight's in the ring with a real fighter," she said. "Instead of with a street girl. You touch Beth again and I'll make sure you pay for it."

He paused and went back to hitting the bag. He stopped and turned to her. "You're mighty brave to be here alone, without Tommy. Course, you always were a gutsy little loner. Something Tommy never could figure out."

"Not always. I had a sister once. I'm telling you, leave Beth alone."

"Girl's got her own mind. She knows what she likes."

"She doesn't like a man hitting her."

"Isn't this precious? One common whore defending another. You, Beth, and the Blue girl, all have a lot in common. That grand sense of nothingness. Even when the police kick the whole mob of nothingness out of town, you stay. Why don't you report me? I'll let the authorities know that you were down there whoring in your crib after the notice went up for 'all women of ill repute' to leave town."

"You've been warned. Keep your fists away from Beth." Kaly tightened her fingers around the tansy and arsenic. A few drops in his drink and Bert would be on the floor clutching his stomach. "You were at the Polly May last week."

"No crime there." Bert hit the bag with a double punch and stopped. He turned back and looked at her. "What do you want?"

"Peace of mind. None of us had it that good. We all

had troubles and losses. My sister died a violent death. I have questions."

"That crime is history, paid for by your dear friend, Tommy Two Shoes himself."

"Actually, he went to the reform school for reckless behavior. Today I saw your birth certificate in the basement. Miss Anderson is your mother. That's why you came back, isn't it? To collect an inheritance?"

"I work at the Speculator. I make my own way."

"I bet that just rubs you raw, those kids down at the Polly May getting what's rightfully yours. You had the run of the place until Tommy's parents died and Miss Anderson took him in. Even then he was your only real competition. Did she like him better than you, was that the problem?"

Bert glared at her, his fists tight at his sides. "I told her she shouldn't let you stay there again. I knew you'd be trouble. Some people just don't know when to let the past alone."

Kaly ran her thumb across the lid of the tansy vial. It was better than courage. "She sent you away after Annie died. She sent you somewhere far away and safe."

"I go where I want, when I want."

"You were there that day. She didn't want you telling what you saw."

"You know, Little Miss, it's dangerous to dig up old graves. You should leave the past where it belongs. That's where you'll find your peace, for yourself and that bastard child you're carrying. I've got a fight to prepare for." He went back to punching the heavy bag.

Kaly watched him dance around the bag, looking for a clue, searching for something about her sister's murder. That something kept gnawing at her but she couldn't see it. Finally, she gave up, silently slipped into the alley, and walked back into the Casino. It was useless. She was useless. She'd forget everything. Drink herself silly.

But when a tiny flutter skimmed across her stomach

and lit just below her heart she left the Casino and went back to the Polly May. A light wind blew her skirt against her legs. White, fluffy clouds rested near the top of the Highlands where the Red Mountain looked down on her. She dreamed of climbing to the Emerald Lake and sitting on its shore in the sun, somewhere far away from here, somewhere that the harsh and beautiful town couldn't touch her.

At the Polly May she cooked noodles for dinner, steam rising like smoke in the opium dens. The steam reminded her of the purse she'd found in the den, the one she'd hidden in another den, the blue and silver beaded purse. Now she remembered what Beth had said. Lacy Blue had a purse like that. She wondered if it was still there, or if Beth had found and retrieved it.

17
LOVE AND DEFIANCE
AT THE COLUMBIA GARDENS

May hadn't quite said good-bye when the sun arrived. Birds chirped in the bushes and the crisp morning air stung Marika's cheeks. Wearing a simple cotton skirt that swirled around her legs in the wind, she hugged her medicine bag. Dan waited at the trolley car, dressed in work pants and a brown jacket. He reached out a hand to her and smiled as she took it. The ride up the hill wound through fields thick with sage and wild lupine. Marika looked back at the Copper Camp, littered with black metal head frames and tiny houses stacked up next to each other. Houses where good, honest people lived, people who told the truth and didn't lie.

"I'll only lie a little bit," she said, as the city grew distant. "I'll tell Papa that I spent the day alone at the gardens doctoring skinned knees, black eyes, and hurt feelings."

"Why not just tell him you went with me?" Dan asked.

"I will tend to injured children. That part is absolutely true."

"Partial truth is like partial war. People still get hurt."

"See, I'm learning new things, being exposed to people who challenge my opinion. Not that Papa doesn't."

"Why do you have to lie to him anyway? Tell him we're friends."

Marika shook her head. "He's way too stubborn for that."

When the trolley car pulled into the Columbia Gardens they stepped out onto the boardwalk in front of the white dance pavilion. Strolling to the midway, Marika inhaled the sweet, fresh breeze from Elk Park. The snow had melted off the lower East Ridge, leaving only the mountaintops white. Below them, a smog lake held Butte under its gray cloud. As soon as the wind turned and roared out of the north, the smog would pour into the Gardens, covering the slides and cowboy swings.

With the town's lack of vegetation and the air fouled by the smelter smoke, the Gardens, with its lovely pansies and grassy knolls, seemed like a wonderland. The copper baron, William Clark, had bought 21 acres of land east of Butte for the Columbia Gardens in 1899 and built this incredible amusement park. Most likely a political move, the people exclaimed, but they didn't care. The gardens had won a soft spot in their hearts, with its roller coaster, merry-go-round, electric airplanes and Ferris wheel. There were carefree streams and trumpeter swans swimming across the ponds, children laughing at their own antics.

The place was magnificent. Above the Gardens the snow-capped mountains assured that the streams would run full and hard throughout June. The Columbia Gardens contrasted so sharply with the smog-filled town that Marika felt like she'd stepped into a fairyland. It was magical.

Folks with cabin fever had burst free from their winter shelters. They packed the fairway and crowded the boardwalk. They played games, won prizes, and bragged about their luck. The Columbia Gardens was a bright spot on the hill, a momentary vacation from the dark, sooty mines. Marika breathed it all in, a deep sigh of relief, the new air spinning in her lungs like gold.

"Three balls, three hits, and you win a stuffed animal for the little lady," a brightly dressed man said. He stood behind a counter, in front of a pillar of empty milk cans. He pointed his red face and brown beard at Marika and Dan, pinching a cigar between his fingers. He twirled a softball on his index finger. "A prize she'll never forget. One she'll cherish her whole sweet life."

Dan put a coin on the counter and took a ball in hand. He missed the cans completely with the first three throws.

"Come on, let's go," Marika said.

"Not yet. I'm warmed up now." He smiled, his green eyes sparkling, put more money down and threw three more balls, missing with each one. His face turned red as he bought a third set. This time he hit the cans with the first ball, tumbling them to the wooden floor.

"Not bad for a beginner," the man said, handing over a stuffed flop-eared rabbit. "One more time, just for beggar's luck."

Dan shook his head. "That's good enough."

He gave the rabbit to Marika and took her hand. She clasped the rabbit and the medical bag in her other hand. Dan pulled her past the soda fountain, cotton candy machines, and popcorn, toward the roller coaster. She could hear kids screaming. Slow tracks pulled the yellow cars full of people to the top and dropped them toward the ground like dumped ore, only to rescue them at the last minute.

"The pride and joy of the Columbia Gardens," Dan said.

"I can't go on that thing," she said and pulled her hand out of Dan's, clasping the flop-eared rabbit to her chest.

He took her elbow. "You can."

"No."

"You're just afraid because it unfamiliar."

"I'm scared of heights. It's three tiers high." She yanked her elbow free and made for the ice cream parlor, where she sat on a green stool.

Dan followed.

"I'll watch," she said.

"I promise you'll be safe. I'll be with you."

"No."

"Come on then, let's walk." He took her hand again.

Dangling the rabbit and unused medical bag in her other hand, she followed Dan. They walked in the sun. Pansy butterflies spread their wings. The flowers had recently been transplanted from large hot houses where they had been cultivated and grown. In the open air, their velvet petals floated toward the sky.

"I repeat my question," Dan said.

He sounded serious. Although she didn't know which question he was repeating, Marika felt panic rise in her throat.

"Why not tell your father that we're here together? I work with him. He's always been good to my mother and me. He seems like a reasonable man."

"To you. Not to his daughter."

"Suppose he would mind. You plan a secret meeting and bring your medical bag along like a protective friend. It doesn't seem right. He'll learn the truth eventually. Plus, Dr. Fletcher won't mind if you take a day off."

"Dr. Fletcher won't mind if I go away altogether. Even at my best, I disappoint him."

"Your father will find out. You'll disappoint him, too."

"See that Balsam Root? The Indians roast and grind the seeds into a flour. They mix the seeds with grease and form little balls. That yellow flower is food for them. See that Arnica? It's used to raise the body temperature, dissolve a bruise, and temper muscle aches. There is so much to learn, to know. I want to study medicine, to be a doctor."

Dan shook his head and pointed to a spiky purple

flower. "How about this one?"

"Milk Thistle. Good for the liver." She felt good about knowing these things. She wanted him to think of her as her own woman. A woman he might love. That was crazy though, when others dictated her life. She couldn't return his love.

She walked over to the boardwalk and sat on a bench. A softball crashed into three stuffed polar bears. Someone with a good aim. She looked over and saw Bert Brown. An unpleasant shiver hit her spine. She turned back to Dan and the safety of his company. "What's your real question?" she asked him. "The one you have hiding behind the others. A wise friend told me that it's better to tell the truth."

Dan looked out on the town and back to her. "Are you engaged to Michael Jovich? If you are I shouldn't be here with you. He's a good man. He works hard, plus he's done a lot for the miners."

"You should've asked me that before we boarded the trolley."

"Are you?"

"I'm too young to marry. Papa knows this."

"I thought you would've told me," Dan said, looking pensive. Finally he sat down next to her.

"Papa has the idea of it. I've said 'no.' I think Papa is considering my opinion." Considering it and disregarding it, she added silently to herself.

"Look," Dan said. "You should know; I've joined the army."

Marika stared at him. "You'll die over there." She'd never see him again, she thought, her heart sinking in her chest like a chunk of lead pipe.

"I'm just as likely to die in a mining accident. I'll be back, Marika."

The way he said her name sent a shiver up her spine. She couldn't speak. What if she never heard him say her name again? He couldn't go to war. Her mind went blank and she felt her face break into a cold sweat. She had to say something to stop him.

"You can't." I love you, she wanted to say, but she didn't know if it was true or just dramatics. Out of the corner of her eye she noticed the Ferris wheel start to spin. "Joining the army, it's a mistake," she said.

"When I come back, I might have a chance at something other than mining." He was looking at her, something in his eyes pleading for her to understand.

She shook her head, her voice rising. "People are restless and angry about registering for the selective service. They say they'll be killing their own cousins."

"A man can't be loyal in two places, he has to choose," Dan said.

Marika tied the rabbit's long ears under its chin. "When do you go?"

"The end of June."

Marika clamped her mouth shut and squinted to hold back her tears. A month. A month that would fly by like it never happened. And he'd be gone, maybe gone forever. Her heart slammed against her ribs. It was hard to breathe. She knew too much about war.

Staring down at her hands in her lap, she remembered the boys she knew who'd died in the Balkan wars. Marika had witnessed death in the hospital tent. A soldier at war had little chance. His life depended on where the bullets flew.

Even if Dan managed to survive and come back to Butte, she'd probably be married by then.

And he'd be changed.

Dan stood and walked away from her, through a friendly sea of hats, to the roller coaster. She watched him board a yellow car with two young children in it. The tracks carried the car up to the third tier, the high point, where it curved slowly around the first loop and dropped like a hard rock. Her breath caught in her throat and tears blurred her vision. The metal teeth screeched as they dragged the car to the top of the second tier for another round. The tracks hissed, singing a morbid, taunting song.

Dan had joined the army.

She took a deep, ragged breath, trying to let his news sink in. Crows cawed overhead, which Marika took as a bad omen. Her head pounded. She inhaled deeply again, struggling to calm down. She turned her face into the hot sun and took more deep breaths, the heat warming her skin.

Baba hadn't responded to Papa's letter about the wedding. Maybe that was Baba's way of suggesting that Marika decide for herself whether or not to marry Michael. Had Mama decided for herself and actually chosen Papa? Was that what made her so happy with him?

Finished with his ride, Dan rushed to her, his soft jacket flying in the wind. His hair blew out in all directions, looking feral and free. His hazel eyes glistened in the sun. They were bright and full of wonder. His strong body seemed light, ethereal, as though he had just been transported from another world. How could he be so happy when he was going to war?

The flush in his face brightened as he pulled her to her feet, caught her in his arms, and spun her around. "See?" he said. "Nothing to it. I'll hold you and when you're ready, I'll let go."

Let go.

If she let him go, she would lose him. She felt as if her heart was sealing itself off and opening at the same time, spinning out in erratic directions. Knowing he'd joined the army, Marika wanted to go wild. She wanted to be close to Dan, to feel him close. She wanted him. Forever. Suddenly she had an urge to climb into the yellow car with him, ride the roller coaster in his arms, and stay suspended up there with him, high in the thin mountain air.

"You won't let loose until I say?" She smiled into his oval shaped eyes, eyes that now seemed to transport her to another world. His smooth, clear skin, his soft eyebrows, his full lips all called to her, insisting that she join him.

"On your word," he said.

As they walked to the ride, he locked his arm around her waist, pulling her close to him. She felt the heat and pure comfort of his body, felt the muscles under his shirt. The wind blew softly against them as though they were one. Popcorn and cotton candy smells drifted down the midway. The Ferris wheel creaked as it climbed and threw off a slight smell of grease.

Two laughing kids ran past them. The girl wore a red dress with matching red ribbons in her hair. The boy reminded her of Marko before they'd left their beloved Montenegro. He was thin and dark, his face painted with dirt. For a vivid instant she could smell the earth of a yard garden with children running around. She could smell the morning coffee that she'd make for Dan in their simple home. For the first time she wondered if she'd completely missed what was happening between them.

When they reached the roller coaster Marika and Dan stood under the archway and looked up as a yellow car zipped past, nearly vertical. For a second, she lost her courage. But she forced herself to stay.

She would face this fear, leaving them all behind— Mama, Papa, Marko, Baba, Michael. Baba couldn't decide for her, and neither could any of the others. Only with Marika's permission could they dictate her life.

In an instant she knew what she had to do. It happened that quickly in her mind—as swift as wind lifting the pansy butterfly wings.

She would give Dan a reason to return from the war.

She would make her own decision.

She would tell Papa "no."

Stepping into the yellow car on the sunlit day, Marika chose her own path. She sat on the black leather seat next to Dan. The metal teeth caught the car underneath, jerking it and lugging it up the tracks.

Dan put his arm around her shoulder.

She leaned into him, gripping the bar that held them in.

Slowly they rounded a corner and picked up speed. They dropped like a boulder off the edge of the earth. Marika gasped, her heart racing. It was as if she'd left her stomach behind, in mid-air. As other riders screamed, she held her breath and swallowed hard. Her hair flew straight out behind her as she leaned into Dan's warmth. His arm tightened around her as they hit the bottom of the tier and made their way back up the tracks on the other side.

This time Marika looked around from the top of the crest, smiling into Dan's handsome face and resting her head against his muscular shoulder. From up here the midway danced in colorful, swirling scarves, men's caps, and ballooned dresses. Arms waved like insect wings. The sound of softballs crashing into metal cans rose to greet them. The car dropped into another exhilarating dip. She held her breath again but in a split second it was over and they were going up to the next crest. They raced around the tracks—crawling up and crashing down—until the metal teeth pulled them home.

Dan didn't drop his arm from her shoulder until they stepped out of the car onto the wooden platform. She felt dizzy but happy. The whole time they'd zipped around the roller coaster, he'd never once let go of her. She hadn't given him the word and he'd kept his promise.

"Next," he was saying as he pulled her down the stairs, "the Ferris wheel!"

Marika stared at the wooden seat rocking at the top of the large wheel. The wheel creaked and began a slow circle. The bucket seats fell forward and back. A young boy laughed. The wheel picked up speed and a woman screamed. Marika didn't know if she could get on the Ferris wheel. For a girl afraid of heights, that was high.

"One hurdle down, one to go," Dan said in her ear.

A girl rode a blue carousel pony on the merry-go-round beside them. The ceramic horse had a long pink mane and a yellow saddle. The girl smiled at Marika on her way around. The painted horses looked much more inviting to Marika than the Ferris wheel. "I will, but first let's go on the horses," she said. A happy breeze brushed her cheeks. The afternoon air smelled like fresh pine. "I'm a wild pony, let loose from my corral. I'm ready to ride across the sky!" She flung her arms out, spinning.

Dan laughed, caught her in his arms. As he let go, Marika spotted her brother standing next to the gate of the electric airplanes. Marko's hair was messed up, his eyes red. "What's he doing here?" she murmured, walking toward him.

"Come home," Marko said, his face deadly serious.

"I'm not going home until I'm ready." A quick-burning fuse lit up in her head. This was too much.

"Marika. Please." Marko looked rough, like Papa did after a bad night of coughing.

"Tell Papa you couldn't find me," she said, taking Dan's hand. "I'll be home in time for dinner." This was her afternoon. Hers. The one, single, solitary afternoon that was all hers.

Marko stood quietly, looking toward the East Ridge. "I can't tell Papa," he finally said, so softly she could barely hear him.

"Of course you can't tell Papa. No one can tell Papa anything."

"Something's happened. It's his lungs."

Her anger flashed to worry and back again. If Papa was sick she'd be there soon enough. He could wait a couple of hours.

"It was an accident at the Leonard. Papa went to help. Mama said that he'd never forgiven himself for getting off of the cage just before it fell, that first year we were here. As if it was his fault that those men died."

Marika looked at Dan. Dan's father had died in that accident. "Marko, spill it out. What happened?"

"They fixed the cage at the Leonard, but on the way out of the grounds Papa's lungs collapsed. They rushed him to the hospital. The doctors could do nothing for him. He's at the house now."

So duty actually did call. She had to leave this beautiful day. "I've got some Anise. It'll help clear his lungs." She started toward the trolley car, then stopped and turned to Dan. "I've got to go, I'm so sorry."

"Me too," he said. "I'll take you home."

"It's no use," Marko called, running after them.

"Papa's alright," she said.

"At first we thought he'd be OK."

"What are you saying?" She stopped again, staring at her brother.

"Mama doesn't think he'll last."

"No," she said, her chest tight. "He'll last. I can help him, brother." The air thickened like smoke around her. She couldn't breathe. Her skin burned and a bullet of pain shot through her head.

"Mama's waiting for you."

Marko's words rolled about in her ears, crashing into each other. Moisture left the air. The spring mud dried into solid earth, cracking. Surely all of this was a mistake. She had stumbled into something crazy, like a haunted house. When she walked out the other side, the sun would be shining and the bad news would dissipate.

Yet, the sky was still blue. The electric airplane ride buzzed. Children ran and laughed. Roller coaster cars crawled up the tracks. The Ferris wheel turned. The carousel horses galloped toward home over and over again.

Nothing had changed.

"Marko. Mama's right to worry. It's natural."

Marko shook his head.

Something throbbed inside her. She saw the pansy gardens, the velvet petals falling. The earth turned off kilter. Marika rushed along the boardwalk toward the dark lake of the town, to the trolley car, Marko and Dan beside her. Numb-lipped, she perched on the seat between them and gripped her medicine bag with her elbows, twisting the rabbit's ears tight as a spring. She wound them up, first one direction and then the other, the unraveling popping in her head again and again.

18
THE GOLDMINE CAFE

*T*he air was balmy as Kaly made her way through the sunny, springtime crowd toward the opium dens. She would just go down there long enough to retrieve the blue beaded purse. Right away she'd get back up here where the streets where alive with activity. A street vendor was selling tulips, daffodils, silk scarves, and handkerchiefs. Another sold children's candy and baked bread. Yet another had beer and tobacco for sale. The smells wafted out, enchanting and rich.

She spotted Dan crossing the street toward home, his work bundle tucked under his elbow. His hazel eyes shone in the sun. His hair was light brown, his skin lightly colored, like Kaly's. His face creased into a wide smile as she ran up to him.

"Your mother paid me a visit the other night," Kaly said.

Dan laughed. "Don't tell me. She wanted you to talk me out of joining the army."

"At least she cares about what happens to you." Kaly dropped her head and looked up at him through half-closed eyes. "She told me she's my mother. That makes

248

you my brother."

Dan bit his lip and nodded.

"You knew all along, didn't you?"

He nodded again.

"Why didn't you tell me? I don't understand either of you."

"I wanted to, but she said it would hurt you."

Kaly narrowed her eyes. "How kind. Knowing you have family didn't hurt you, or her. You two had each other. I have an old quilt, some yarn dolls, and memories—not all pleasant."

"I'm glad she finally told you," Dan said. "I don't blame you for being angry. I would be too. I'm glad I can finally, openly, be your brother."

Now. A lifetime later. How convenient. Kaly looked away. She saw Coral Anderson walking toward the opium tunnels. "My old matron," she mumbled. "Wonder what she wants underground."

"She was always kind to me," Dan said.

"Yeah, but she's a mean drunk." Kaly tucked a curl behind her ear, fidgeting to hide her anger. She looked at the curve of Dan's jaw, his eyebrows, his smooth forehead, his clear, hazel eyes. Like hers. "It hurts a lot to lose a sister."

"I know."

"No, you don't."

"I know it was wrong. I've known since I was eight years old that it was wrong. But I'm a man now. And I want to help."

"Such a sweet sentiment. You're joining the army. So, how many more days do you plan to be around? Twelve? Fourteen? No offense, Dan, but that doesn't add up to much help."

"It's something. And I'll be back."

"No. You'll get yourself killed. That's what happens to my siblings. Better that you stay the half stranger you've always been."

"Anne Marie was a tragedy. It doesn't mean I'll meet the same fate."

"I'll manage. Nothing has changed. I'm better off taking my chances in the streets than depending on sporadic truth tellers." Or liars.

"Maybe you'll think about it."

"Sure. I'll think about it as long as the two of you thought about it. How long was that? Twenty-seven years?"

Now she had two reasons to go underground: to find the blue purse and to see what on earth Coral Anderson was doing in the dens. Kaly left the soft daylight behind as she descended into the dank air. The gas light above her flickered and went out as the door shut behind her. The clammy air was stifling. A little way into the tunnel something fell and she whipped around toward the sound.

Nothing was there.

Kaly's heart raced. Her palms felt clammy and cold. The place was dangerous but she kept going, looking for the broken lamp near the cubby where she'd hidden the purse. She spotted a broken light, but there were no beds in the area. Up ahead were two more broken lamps. She couldn't remember anything else that might mark the right den. Whiskey bottles lay on the floor, a bunched-up blanket next to them. She heard the sound behind her again, and jumped.

This time it spoke.

"Everyone has the same interest today. But you won't find what you're looking for." It was Miss Anderson. "Bert already found it. He created quite a ruckus until he did. Said a very important girl gave that purse to him." The woman pulled the blue beaded purse out of her big bag. "He gave it to me for safekeeping."

Kaly shrugged her shoulders. "What are you doing down here?"

"A better question is, what are you doing down here?" Miss Anderson put the purse back, pulled a pin from her hair, and repositioned it. "Never mind. I'll buy you a soda at the Goldmine Café."

Kaly was happy to get back above ground. The Goldmine Café had long been a safe place for her. She and Beth had started their friendship there. Beth had helped Kaly leave her lonely, troubled life behind. Other troubles had begun, but those of her youth had ended.

You live in a haunted town, you live a haunted life, Beth had said. You choose a path, you walk down it and never look back. Kaly wondered if she'd ever had a choice of paths. Or had all the paths out of the Polly May led to right here.

They sat down in a booth at the café. She leaned across the table. "I know that Bert is your son."

Miss Anderson raised her eyebrows, shrugging. "Doesn't take a genius. Bert says you're stirring up old trouble. Says he told you to let it be. I already told you that the only person who might elaborate on what happened the day of Annie's death is Tommy."

"I think Bert knows more than he's saying."

Miss Anderson folded her hands in a spot of sunlight on the wooden table.

"Protecting a false accusation is wrong," Kaly went on. "Evidently the police and I were the only ones fooled. Now I think with a woman's mind, not a child's."

Miss Anderson raised her eyebrows again. "Then you'll do the work of a woman. Put the past behind you, tend to the child who will build a future. She can't live in what's gone by, and neither can you."

Kaly shook her head. "Actually, the police weren't even fooled by the story that Tommy killed Anne Marie. I read Tommy's papers from the Montana State Reform School. He went to corrections for unruly behavior. On that charge they may as well lock up the whole town and throw away the key."

"You've been in my basement."

The sweet smell of spring wafted in and mixed with the

gin on Miss Anderson's breath. Kaly sunk lower into the booth. "This child will not experience my sister's death," she said. "She won't have my life. I want a safe home for her. I just can't tell if she'll be safe at the Polly May, even if I am there. Anne Marie wasn't."

Miss Anderson folded a napkin into a tiny triangle, and flipped over the points turning it into a doll-sized diaper. "I do my best to give the children in my care the strength to carry the burden of their lives. I gave up trying to save them a long time ago."

"Did you really try to protect us? Or did you only protect your son?"

Miss Anderson slid the tiny diaper across the table to Kaly. When she spoke, her voice had a silver sad sound to it. "Bert thinks it's better if you don't stay at the Polly May anymore. I think he's wrong. I'm concerned for you and your child. No good comes to a child who falls into the world with no arms to catch it." She lifted her silken eyes to Kaly's. "For what you know, the child could be anybody's, even Bert's. She could be my grandchild. If she is, she'll be safe."

"She's not your grandchild. Tell me the truth about my sister."

"Some people would rather have a home than the truth," Miss Anderson said.

"My choice."

"You're mining a tunnel rich in fool's gold."

"I'll decide what it's worth."

"It looks to me like you girls are running out of decisions to make, what with the law closing you down. Word is they're closing the brothels next. Some girls got out. They married. Your child needs a family. Let her have the family you refused."

Something vile rose up in Kaly. How dare Coral Anderson blame her for not having a family? "I lost something at the Polly May, something more precious than all the copper in that hillside. I think Bert took it. If that's true, this child I'm carrying will never be part of your life."

"Kaly, you need a way out. I'm offering you one. I'll even raise the baby if it comes to that."

Kaly bit her lip. "Tell me what you know about Anne Marie's death and then we can both make good decisions."

The silence was heavy. "Maybe you shouldn't throw your chances to the wind," Miss Anderson finally said. "Some girls on the line don't end up so good. "

"Are you threatening me?"

"It's a dangerous town, that's all."

"The truth won't stay hidden forever. Someone knows what happened to Anne Marie, and someday I'll know too. Girls end up in a bad way, true. Men get hurt all the time. Stepping outside the law is easy for someone with nothing to lose. Someone like me."

Miss Anderson twisted the silver bracelet at her wrist. A bead of sweat rolled down her neck, washing a clear line through her make-up. The skin showing through was mottled and gray.

"Sorry it took so long to get to you," a thin waitress said. She looked like she was about fifteen. Her smoky gray eyes seemed like eyes that would follow a man like Bert into the opium tunnels. "Would you like something to eat?"

"Tea," Kaly said. "Black tea."

"I'll have soup. Get her a grilled cheese, pickles on the side," Miss Anderson said. "We need some sustenance. We'll be here for a while."

Kaly had been waiting for so long to talk about what had happened to her sister that she hadn't realized how hard and fast the story would hit her. Miss Anderson didn't wait for the food to arrive before she started.

"Tommy had an alibi for the day that Annie died. He'd been with me in the parlor," she said. "He never really liked how close you and Anne Marie were and felt that it was unfair that you got to spend so much time with her.

He complained that he had no one to play with."

"She was my sister!"

"Nevertheless, he said that you were hogging her attention. I told him to buck up or find another friend. He stayed nearby until dinner was ready. That's when I told him to call you girls in to eat."

Kaly traced the lines of the wooden tabletop as she listened, her heart strumming wildly in her chest. She could still hear his voice all these years later.

"That's when he found Annie."

Kaly looked up to see Miss Anderson staring at her. She froze, clamping one hand over the other, the image of her beautiful sister standing right in front of her, next to Miss Anderson, arriving just in time to hear the story. She let out the breath she'd been holding, nodded for the woman to continue.

"Oh, I knew all along that Tommy was innocent," the matron said. "When the police came, Tommy, fierce as smelter fire, kept yelling some unintelligible thing: 'He did it! He did it!' But he gave no name. When the police tried to quiet him he struck an officer. A bad move in Butte. The officer cuffed him and took him to jail."

"You could've gotten him out, told them the truth." Kaly felt her breath short in her chest, heard her voice rise.

Miss Anderson shook her head. "No. Things had gotten out of hand. I didn't know what he saw, if he was in danger."

"Him! What about me? I was out there with the killer." A horrible thought hit Kaly right in the gut. "You thought I did it!"

Miss Anderson shook her head again. Her gray eyes looked sad, resigned. "I knew it wasn't you. But if they came after you, I couldn't save you. You were only ten years old at the time and you had nowhere else to go. I was your safest place. I knew that you would have ended up on the street."

"Like I didn't."

"With a few more years behind you. But, yes, it is regrettable." The waitress delivered the food. Miss Anderson took a bite of her soup, chicken noodle, and motioned for Kaly to eat her sandwich.

Kaly flipped the sandwich over on her plate and left it there.

"You need to eat."

"I know. Go on."

"I refused to take Tommy back into the Polly May and they sent him to the state reform school. Word spread that Tommy was there for murder. I let the gossip build its own head of steam. If I'd said anything, everyone would have thought I was protecting my children. Which in a way, I was. I let the best possible outcome take its course."

"And Bert? Where was he?" Kaly knew the answer to this question, but wanted to hear what the woman would say.

"Bert had been at the neighborhood grocer at the time. I, of course, feared that they'd turn to him next, if they saw Tommy as innocent."

"The real reason you let Tommy go."

"Not the only reason. But yes. I was afraid of losing Bert and I kept my mouth shut. You don't know what it is to have a child, when a child was all you ever wanted," Miss Anderson told Kaly. "See, my parents contracted typhoid fever when they were on the way west with me. They both died. My Aunt Polly took me in."

"The Polly May is named for her."

"She named it." Miss Anderson paused, presumably to let the implication sink in.

Kaly understood. The Polly May. Her aunt's strongest love was herself. A tinge of pity started in Kaly's heart but it quickly dissipated when Annie's ghost sat down next to her.

"I was no angel, a wild girl at the time," Miss Anderson blushed and looked down. "I got pregnant at fifteen. I thought I loved the boy, but he left me alone with my shame, ran off to the California gold rush with his father. Aunt Polly took Bert away from me, and raised the boy for her own. I had to watch from the sidelines as she disciplined Bert, locking him alone in his room, sometimes for days. Polly would slide a slim bowl of cold cereal to him. She also locked him in his room when she didn't want to be bothered. I begged Aunt Polly to let me play with him, to let me take care of him. No, Aunt Polly said, I had to learn that bringing a child into this world was not without consequences, for all involved." Water rimmed her gray eyes, sadness spilling down her cheeks.

Kaly held her breath to keep from crying, but the tears welled up anyway. Against her own desires, she felt the woman's heart break.

"At night, I snuck muffins and bacon to Bert," she continued. "He would snatch them from my hands and crawl back to his corner. Aunt Polly found out about the food one day and put a lock on Bert's door. After that I sat by the door and sang lullabies. It was all I could do. When Aunt Polly unlocked his door he came out of there fighting mean. I tried to console him, but to no avail. I didn't hold my own son's heart. I didn't even hold him in my own arms until he was five years old. That was when Aunt Polly died.

"But in those five years, a lot of damage had been done. He drew pictures of men and women hanging from trees. He stole bread and hid it in his room. He set fire to the sofa one night, and the fire department had to be called. One time Bert tried to drown my cat. I rescued the feline and, figuring he just needed to be socialized, I started taking in orphaned children. I would help the children, and the children would help my son. But Bert didn't like sharing with the others. He figured out how to use them to meet his own needs. He became secretive, lying and covering up his misbehaviors."

Kaly didn't know what to say. "I'm sorry. It was hard."

"I tried. I discussed child rearing with neighbors. Spare

the rod, spoil the child, they said. A child needs good work, they told me. Don't pamper him. I applied their advice to all the children in my care—all, that is, except for Bert. Trying to make up for his wretched past, I rarely punished him. I tried to talk sense to him, and I smothered him with love and kindness. But he grew up and left home with no good handle on his anger."

"Angry enough to kill my sister?" Kaly asked.

"Anger doesn't make a person a criminal," Miss Anderson said. "I know him. He wouldn't go that far. Anne Marie's killer probably didn't mean to leave her dead. That person probably slipped out of town, never realizing what he'd done, never to be heard from again. It was a bad thing, but it's over. Let it stay over."

At that, Miss Anderson dismissed the topic. "I've answered your questions in the best way that I can. Now, I hope you can let the past be so we can all live in peace." She finished her soup in silence.

Kaly stared at the cold sandwich on the plate in front of her. How on earth could Kaly live in peace? Miss Anderson's answer was that Butte was a mining town. The very thing that supported a mining town toppled it. Good luck and hard luck were irretrievably intertwined. There was nothing personal in it. Nothing a person could do about it.

What kind of answer was that?

She still didn't know who killed her sister.

Miss Anderson paid the bill and stood to leave. She stopped at the end of the table with a look that cut at Kaly's heart. "If you won't stay at the Polly May and raise that baby," Miss Anderson said, "I would be glad to take on the job. If you argue about it, I'll go to the authorities, who will want the child in proper care."

Kaly looked her straight in the eye. "Now you are threatening me."

"Just letting you know where I stand. Choose wisely." She walked away without waiting for an answer from Kaly.

The ghost of her sister stood in the woman's place, the threat drowning any pity or relief that Kaly might have felt at hearing Miss Anderson's story. Now she felt only dread. She thought of the blue scar. She was sure of one thing: Miss Anderson had lied about Bert going to the store the day that Anne Marie died.

A woman who refuses to face the truth about her family throws fuel on the flame. Kaly didn't care what Miss Anderson's authorities said. Now she knew: No child was safe at the Polly May.

19
SOMETHING LOST

*I*n the evening, a thin ray of light beamed through the high, narrow window and landed on Papa's pale face. Marika could not get his fever down. She slumped back in the chair next to his bed, exhausted and helpless. No matter what they did, Papa grew weaker by the moment. A cup of peppermint tea sat cold on the nightstand. A bowl of yarrow lay abandoned next to the tea. In between sat Papa's pipe. Between the pipe and the mines, her father's poor lungs never had a chance.

Marika rubbed the back of her neck and looked around the room, dazed from crying. The late evening light reminded her of a long ago time in Montenegro, sitting up with Papa as they camped on a hillside where a battle had taken place. She was a girl of five that evening. Papa had wanted her to know what her ancestors had endured to keep their land. They'd fought hard so that Marika and Marko might have a good life. They fought so that the children wouldn't have to fight.

"Fighting, it's a terrible waste," Papa had said. "We spray the beautiful land with the brave blood of the young. I don't like fighting, but, like the ancestors, I will always stand for what is right."

"Is Ancestor a friend or an enemy?" Marika had asked.

Papa had smiled down at her. "Some would say both. They would say our pride is our enemy, our courage is our friend."

Marika didn't understand, but sat quietly that evening and watched the sky turn red and then dark gray with clouds. It didn't rain until the next day and she and Papa barely made it home before the storm. The following year, Papa took Marko to camp near the battle of their ancestors while Marika stayed home to help Mama.

Now the fight in Papa was weak. She choked back tears as he coughed up blood. Again. When he finished coughing, she wiped the sweat off his forehead and chin.

Marko sat in a chair on the other side of Papa's bed and poured him a salted brandy. The brandy had been a comfort, but did no trick to cure the consumption.

"It's so nice to see Vuko again," Papa whispered. "My brother says it's time to cross the sea and go home." He paused. When he continued his voice was so low and raspy that Marika had to struggle to hear his words. "The mines are clean where he lives. Men heal while they work, and there are no accidents." Her father lifted his chin, turned to her and then Marko. "Vuko looks bright and young. I didn't think I'd ever see him again. He's so proud of you two."

She looked at Marko, but he wouldn't look at her. "You and Mama raised good kids," she said. "You were everything a father could be."

"He wants me to talk to the Father. I don't know what I'll say." Papa closed his eyes and slept. A while later he woke up, his eyes wide, motioning to Marko.

Marika wiped his forehead with a cloth and he brushed her away. "He wants something," she said.

"What is it, Papa?" Marko asked.

But Papa's voice was gone. He tried to rise on his elbows and it made his arms shake. His head dropped forward. With a sudden surge of strength, Papa lifted his head and thrust his feet out from under the covers and over the side of the bed. He wobbled there a moment and planted his feet on the floor.

Marko helped him. "I think he has to go to the bathroom," he said.

Marika went to the washroom for a pan, gave it to Marko, and pulled the sleeping curtain closed behind her. She heard Papa moan as he stood. His feet shuffled a little way across the floor.

Mama stood at the stove making soup. "Are you OK?"

Marika nodded. "He's just so frail. Papa's always been so strong. I didn't know he was in such bad shape. I should've seen it. But I didn't." When she heard him slide back under the covers, she pulled the curtain back and returned to his side.

Marko's face was the color of ashes. "The pan's beside his bed," he said.

Marika took and emptied it. When she returned to the room Marko still didn't turn his head toward her. She wondered why. Suddenly life was so hard. The world had turned upside down. In a day she'd watched her father become a child. A strange mix of gratitude and grief exploded inside her. Again she fought to keep back the tears.

Mama brought hot coffee for Marko and Marika, and took the pipe out of the room like an unfinished meal.

The sleeping room was sweltering hot, the sour smell of Papa's sickness permeating Marika's clothes. Even with her knowledge and her work with Dr. Fletcher, she couldn't help Papa. How could she have so much desire, be so determined, and yet still be so ineffective? Dr. Fletcher had told her there was only one way out for Papa now. In the morning he'd send over some paregoric to keep Papa comfortable.

When Papa first told her that she was engaged to Michael, his lungs had been strong. "You are my daughter," he'd said. "I do what's best for you." But she wouldn't listen. She was definitely his daughter, she thought, letting out a little laugh at the thought.

Marko glared at her across Papa's bed.

She sent him an apologetic look. If only she could take back the last few months, just start over. Marika wanted to tell Papa how sorry she was. But it wouldn't help. Talk was cheap when he could barely answer.

He winced in pain and started coughing, choking on his own phlegm.

She used a handheld suction pump to get it out of his throat and mouth. If only the doctor would send the paregoric right away!

Marko pulled the quilt up to Papa's chin.

Marika stared at the quilt with dull, tired eyes. It looked like it was draped over a child. That's how thin their father had become.

Papa opened his eyes and almost looked at them.

He was seeing something they didn't, she thought. Marika picked up the cup of cold tea and lifted Papa's head so he could drink. The tea spilled out the sides of his mouth and dripped down his shirt. She wiped it off of his chin and neck. The peppermint was no match for the consumption that clouded his lungs. She set his head gently down. His eyes had a gray sheen to them as he turned toward her. He wanted to tell her something, but she had to guess what it was. "Are you scared, Papa?" she asked.

"He's not scared," Marko said. "He's done his last confession. He knows Father will bury him and help him cross over to the other side. He's an honest man. He's worked hard. He has nothing to be scared of."

Regret stabbed at Marika more sharply. Her younger brother knew more than she did about Papa. He'd been there to listen. He'd been there while Marika was sneaking around behind Papa's back. She should've been home. She was the one who wanted to be a doctor. She should have helped her father first. Instead of fighting him, she should've told him how much she loved him, how she admired him for his strong faith. She should have told him how she appreciated his hard work to fill their bellies, to build their homes, even to find her a proper husband. Because it was work.

Marika slumped back in her chair again, holding her head in her hands. She was getting a bad headache that made her temples throb. It was true. Papa had worked hard to find her a proper husband. Even though plenty of men lined the streets of Butte, finding a suitable match to someone like Marika had been no easy task. Papa had cared enough to try. He'd had her best interests at heart. And she'd all but spat on his ideals. Her face was hot with the shame of it. She yearned to tell him all of this, but the words stuck in her throat.

It was too late.

Papa had pushed his life as far he could. Soon his spirit would fly out the door of this world. Marika knew it. They all knew it. It was easy to see that the color had gone out of Papa's face. A blue tinge had crawled up his arms from his hands. As he struggled for breath, his lungs barely moved to let the air in.

Mama joined them by Papa's bed.

"How long will he last, Mama?" Marika asked.

"Could be a night, could be a month. There's no way to know for sure. I wish that Dr. Fletcher would bring the paregoric tonight. He deserves whatever comfort we can give to him."

"Mama, I'm sorry I wasn't here when you brought him home from the hospital," Marika said.

"You two may have your differences, but your father loves you. He loves both of you more than you can imagine. You're a good daughter. You've got nothing to be sorry about. It's the love you shared that's important. Remember that."

Marko obviously felt very differently. Something dark

and angry lay in his eyes.

Mama got up and went back into the kitchen.

Marika tried to catch her brother's attention, but he still wouldn't look at her. She waved her hands over Papa. Marko ignored her. Finally she gave him the squished-up face she'd given him the night Michael had come to dinner.

"Do you think Papa can hear us?" Marko asked.

"I'm pretty sure he can hear us wherever we are. Papa has the ears of an elephant." Then she said something she only half believed, but hoped was true. "I'm pretty sure Papa will always hear us."

"Nevertheless, lets step outside for a minute."

Outside in the cool night Marika asked, "What is it?"

"Mama may forgive you, but I don't." He was shaking. "His last days were plagued with his misery over your behavior. That shouldn't have happened. I wish that you could've thought of him just one time."

Tears smeared down Marika's face, anger heating her cheeks. But why should she be mad at Marko for saying the very thing that was in her own heart? It was the truth. Her actions the last few months were unforgivable. Mama was too kind, Marko too honest, and Marika too selfish. "Marko, I did think of him," she said. "All the time."

"It wasn't fair to him. That's all."

"You think I don't know that now? I'm so sorry. To him. To you. To Mama. I'd give anything to change it." Grief twisted her stomach. She had to make him understand. She couldn't lose Papa and Marko.

Just then a shooting star flew across the sky. They both caught their breath at what seemed like the same time and looked at each other.

"Papa doesn't like us fighting," Marko said.

Marika shook her head and smiled. "Will you please forgive me? We are going to need each other."

Marko dropped his head, looked at the cracked sidewalk, looked back up at the sky. "Ok sister. This time.

Because Papa wants it." He took her hand and held it.

Back inside they sat in silence. Papa slept and woke up and then slept again. In the early morning Papa gurgled. A rattling sound came from his throat. A smile slipped across his pale, thin face. Then the smile went lax. Then his breathing stopped. Dusty light filled the room and surrounded him.

Marko's eyes widened at Marika. "Is it over?"

"I think so," Marika said. "He's not breathing. But there's a slight movement in his skin. Someone better go get the doctor. Do you want to stay with him? I'll go. Or do you want me to stay and you go?"

"I'll go. In a few minutes."

"I'll get Mama."

A knock came at the door.

Marika hesitated. When she opened the door, the smell of arsenic wafted in. A mine whistle blew.

Michael Jovich stood there with a bottle of paregoric. "Doctor sent me with this," he said. "How is he doing?"

"I think he's gone," Marika said, her voice strangled and numb. "But I don't know for sure. We need the doctor."

"What do you mean gone?"

"I think he's passed over."

"I'm sorry. I'll go get Dr. Fletcher."

Thank you, Marika meant to tell him. But he was out the door before she could get the words up and out of her chest.

When Michael returned with the doctor, he stood back, away from the family.

Dr. Fletcher nodded his head and closed Papa's eyes.

"That slight movement that you see is simply the body letting go of residual air," he said. "Some people say that it takes a while for the spirit to gather its essence and completely leave the body. However, modern science has determined that it's the simple closing down of the

265

biological process. I'm sorry."

"Good thing you didn't decide to be a priest," Marika said.

The doctor smiled a sad smile. "I'll bring the death certificate by later. I will stop in and let the priest know. In the mean time, you and your mother will prepare your father's body for the wake?"

Mama nodded. "Thank you, Doctor."

Marko had tightened his grip on Papa's hand, as if he could will him to stay.

Marika sat back down in her chair. She felt absent, as if in a dream. As if she were someone else entirely. She sat there watching Marko and Papa until the light flickered and dimmed.

Mama came in and laid out clean clothes. Then she brought in a pan of warm water.

Michael entered and put his large hand on Marko's shoulder.

Marika stared at Michael's long fingers. They went in and out of focus.

"Come on," Michael was saying to her brother. "Your mother needs wood. I'll help you cut it."

Marika and Mama pulled the covers down to wash Papa's body.

Tears filled some remote part of her. Was that what she'd seen Papa release? His uncried tears? Maybe he was releasing his unlaughed laughter. How about his unfought fights? And everything he'd held inside all his life. Now it all gently floated into the air and drifted up, up and into the mountains.

They'd send word to Baba. When things settled down, after they'd buried Papa, she would ask Baba about these slight movements of his. They haunted Marika. Maybe Papa wasn't really gone. Shouldn't they be doing something more for him?

Mama looked over at her. "I see it too, honey. In our country they call it finishing up. The soul gathers itself to cross over to the other side. This usually takes about three days. In the beginning, the soul just stands in awe of the beauty between this world and the other. The light is so wondrous that a spirit can hardly keep from passing through right away. But they cannot leave even the slightest part of themselves behind. They feel a certain sadness, leaving their families. It lasts only a moment though, because they know that in no time their loved ones will join them. And it really is no time to a soul on the other side, because there is no such thing as time on the other side."

Marika stared at her mother. "Baba told you this?"

"The elders kept no secrets in our country. We grieve. It's a human thing to grieve. There is no shame in crying for your loss. But remember: Papa's not suffering any longer. He's happy."

"You're not sad, Mama?"

"I'm sad. But your father and I knew this was coming. We talked a lot about it. The priest talked to us about it. It helps."

"Did he talk to Marko too?"

Mama nodded.

"Where was I?"

"Working with Dr. Fletcher. Papa tried to tell you the priest was coming over. I'm sorry he didn't get the message through to you. Whatever you think, this was not your fault. It was the natural course of your father's life. He lived a good man, and he died a good man."

She knew where she'd been when they talked about Papa's pending death. Begging Dr. Fletcher for his approval. Trying to prove Papa wrong. Planning how she would escape marriage to Michael. Pursuing Dan. All things of insignificance. She set the water and rags on a table in the sleeping room.

Mama took a rag and lifted Papa's arm. She gently slid the cloth across his shoulder. "He walked a proud path, and you're walking your own path. Given time, you and

Papa would've respected each other's walk in life. You mustn't blame yourself. His death belongs only to him. He'd spite the person who tried to take it from him."

Marika laughed at this. Mama was right. Papa surely would fight to keep what was his, all the way to the end. The sound of an ax splitting wood reached her ears. Marika had already forgotten that Michael was helping Marko cut wood. They'd need the wood. There would be a lot of company. A lot of cooking.

"He blames me." Marika nodded her head toward the back door.

"Your brother is scared. He also feels bad that you weren't here to talk to Papa when the priest was here. He thinks Papa missed something by your being gone. Marko will get over it. He's finding his way too."

A reverent silence cocooned the room. They moved Papa to Marika's bed. He was surprisingly light. Marika saw now what she had missed. Her father had been wasting away. Before her eyes his stature had been diminishing daily. But somehow she had not seen it. Where, oh where, had she been looking?

They dressed Papa in a clean suit. It felt wrong and awkward to Marika to have power over her father. She lifted his leg. He let her. She turned him sideways. He didn't object. When they finished cleaning and dressing him, Papa looked handsome. He was a man with class and style, despite his life as a miner. They made up his bed with clean blankets and laid him on top of it.

Mama touched his cheek and then Marika's elbow. "Come, we must cook. People will be arriving soon."

Marika nodded. She held her father's hand and said a quiet prayer. It was not a prayer for the dead, or a prayer that she had memorized. It was one that she made up, a prayer of promise that poured from her like tears. When she was finished, she laid Papa's arms across his chest in the shape of a slanted cross. He had everything to be proud of. Everything, that is, except his daughter.

20
A WALK IN THE CITY

Kaly watched George drawing in the hallway. He colored a picture of a house with a bright sun in the corner. The house had red and black lines scribbled over the top of neatly drawn walls and windows. Smoke raged out of the chimney. Kaly reached down and took the picture from him.

He looked up at her. "Are dreams real?" he asked.

"Get your coat," she said. "You can come with me."

"Where are we going?"

"A few places. None of them are going to be much fun. But it'll be better than sitting here scribbling over the top of great art all day." She wanted to show him something good. Today, though, was not the day for good things. "Go now, get your coat."

"I don't need a coat. It's not cold out."

"A proper coat, not one of those ragged things you and Julian play in." She stopped by the kitchen, where Miss Anderson sat drinking tea and reading the newspaper. "I'm going to Stojan Lailich's funeral, and George is going with me," Kaly told her.

"He hasn't done his chores yet." Miss Anderson looked up from her paper and glanced around the room.

Following the woman's eyes, Kaly took in the piled breakfast dishes and overflowing garbage. She spotted the blue beaded purse behind the flour canister.

"Since you moved in," Miss Anderson said, "no one does what they're told anymore."

"I'll help George with his chores when we get back."

"After the chores are done he can go. Not before." Miss Anderson rubbed her pale hand across her forehead. "The funeral isn't until this afternoon, so you have plenty of time."

"I'll help him now." Kaly put her purse down in front of the blue purse. "You're right. Things have gotten out of hand."

"He can do them himself."

"It'll only take a minute."

"My horoscope today says that all signs point to a terrible underground explosion," Miss Anderson said. "They could be talking about the way this house looks."

"It doesn't take the stars to predict an explosion in a mining town."

"George managed his chores by himself before you moved in; he can manage them now. Have some faith in him. That's what he needs. Not your coddling." She closed the paper and stared out the back window.

"You mean like you coddled Bert?"

"What?"

"By your own admission you protected Bert, coddled him. That's what he was doing here the other day, coming home to claim his inheritance."

"A pittance that is."

"When we were young, you should've told us he was your son. You shouldn't have kept that secret. He would've been important in his own right, just by having a mother. You should've told us."

"Should've done this, should've done that. No one can

change the past. You're better off just facing reality."

"Like you?" Kaly pointed to an empty gin bottle.

Miss Anderson shrugged. "Bert had a propensity for trouble. He was nearly eighteen, and I knew he'd be better off getting out of here. Butte had nothing to hold him. I was afraid they'd try to peg Annie's death on him. I was worried about him, as I am worried about you right now."

George walked in.

"I'll wait outside for you," Kaly told him.

"Can we talk about my dream then?" George asked.

"Yeah, sure." Kaly picked up the blue beaded purse along with her own, but she didn't grip it tightly enough. The purse slipped through her fingers to the floor. The pink rosary beads she'd placed on Pamela's bedpost and a white cross slid out. Her knees went weak and she felt her sister's breath ripple across her face like an errant wind. "That's Annie's cross," she said.

Miss Anderson shrugged, looking at the purse. "I'm telling you again," she said, "let things be."

Outside, the balmy spring day dropped a gauzy shroud over Kaly, smothering her. She could barely breathe. Annie's memory spun through the trees like the golden sun. Fear sharp as ice crystals lodged in her throat. Why was Annie's cross in the blue purse?

The wolf dog, who evidently lived there now, wagged across the yard to see her.

"Hey, boy," she said, ruffling the dog's thick fur. George came out with a rope, which he looped around the dog's neck.

"He'll follow you without that," Kaly said. "He won't like being tied."

"But I don't want him to leave me." The dog twisted his head around and grabbed the rope in his mouth so that he was leading the boy.

"I thought you were afraid of him."

"That was before he put his head in my lap. He was

really nice then."

"He hates that rope."

"No, he doesn't."

The dog loped ahead, dancing and playing with the rope, twisting it around himself, making her laugh. The day smelled like sulfur. The town blazed out before them, stretching up Montana Street toward the head frames on the hill.

"I had a bad dream last night," George said. "A man chased me into a black room. Everyone was crying, except the ones sleeping on the ground. There were a lot of people sleeping on the ground. They were all really quiet. I couldn't find you."

"Dreams can't hurt you. Just tell the scary thing to go away and leave you alone. When I was a kid I saw a bad fire. I'd dream about that fire and wake up scared silly. Then one night I said to myself, 'I'm dreaming of something nice tonight.'"

"Did you?"

"Yes. I dreamed of a beautiful white horse. He ran through a field of long grass and his mane flew in the wind. When he stopped to eat, his tail hung softly. Sometimes in the dream I would pet his side. He'd just stand there quietly and let me."

"That's a nice dream."

"Yeah. There was a real horse that lived through that fire. It's still alive, pastured down on the flats somewhere. One day we'll go see him."

"Can my dog come with us when we go?"

"Your dog. Sure, he can come. So, you just tell those bad dreams to leave you alone. Tell them you've got to dream about taking your dog to visit a white horse."

"I dream of bad guys, too."

"If someone is mean to you in a dream, tell them to stop. Tell them 'No!' in a loud voice, that you aren't going to let them hurt you."

"Do you think a dream will listen to me?"

"Sure I do," she said.

When they reached Lottie Boyle's brothel, Beth waved to her from a perch on the porch steps. She wore a pink cotton dress with embroidered roses. The bruise on her cheek was barely yellow now and fading fast. "I didn't think you'd ever visit me here again," she said. "How are you feeling?"

"Other than losing my home, my livelihood, and my best friend, and being on our way to a funeral, not too bad," Kaly replied.

"Stojan Lailich. I heard. Too bad."

"Yeah, and the Polly May might soon be off limits."

"Miss Anderson put you out?"

"She threatened me." She didn't mention the blue purse. Or Bert Brown.

Beth looked back over her shoulder toward the brothel. "I can't bring you in here. I would if I could. The hospitality's not mine to offer. Not sure how long I'll last. Cause trouble and I get canned."

"George, honey, will you take the dog around back and play with him? I need to talk to Beth. I'll come and get you in a few minutes." She watched George round the corner. "Canned from a whorehouse. There's a first time for everything."

Beth laughed and her face softened. "This was not on your way to the funeral."

"No. Mr. Lailich's daughter took care of me when I was laid up. I feel bad for her. The least I can do is show my respect."

"Mr. Lailich was a good man. It's been a tough month for all of us." Beth patted the step next to her.

Kaly accepted the invitation and sat down. "It wasn't all loss, Beth."

"What do you mean?"

"I'm not sure where to begin. I wanted to talk to you about it the other day, in the Alley, but you left."

"Miss Lottie called."

"When I woke up from the beating, Mr. Lailich's daughter was watching over me. She looked so much like Anne Marie, I thought I had died and my sister had come for me. Then I realized I was at home, in my crib. I felt horrible, like I'd dragged myself out from under a landslide."

"You didn't look that great, either."

"Then the cribs got more dangerous, the law watching 'em, the looters robbing 'em, and Pamela dying. In the mix, I ended up back at the Polly May. Tommy snuck into my room one night. It was like the old days, me and him figuring where we stand with each other."

"Was it about the baby?"

"Yes. But that wasn't all. He said he was sorry about everything, especially about Anne Marie. He went to jail for unruly behavior, not murder. I found papers that verifiy that."

Beth crossed her arms over her chest. "So he tells the truth."

"I dreamt about a man—an older boy really, nearly a man, a very mean man. I'd always had a certain dark knowing, like being caught in the dead air of an end tunnel." Kaly paused, trying to decide how much she wanted to tell Beth, listening for George. She heard nothing.

"Go on," Beth said.

"On the day my sister was killed, I was raped."

Beth pulled her dress sleeve down over her wrist. "Weren't we all?"

"Losing my sister was enough tragedy for my young mind. I couldn't face the rape, too. The man in the dream is the worst kind of vulture, vicious, and absolutely vile." Kaly played with the hem of her skirt, curling it to her knee and back toward her foot. The vein over her anklebone shone blue under the white skin. "I think the man who raped me is the same one who killed my sister."

"You are really, really messing with fire, Kaly! If you

think your life hasn't fallen apart enough, just set flame to this. Let the past be. Some things should not be dragged into the daylight." Beth pointed to the brothel. "Every woman in there knows that."

Kaly nodded. "It's so wrong though. We all keep our mouths shut and rape and murder goes on." She paused and started again. "That's not all. When Tommy was in my room, Mrs. McClane showed up."

"Mrs. McClane? Suddenly you're more popular than the queen."

"It gets better. Or worse. She said she's my mother."

"What?" Beth's mouth was hanging open, her eyes wide.

Kaly nodded again. "Says she wants me to talk Dan out of joining the army."

"What did you tell her?"

"I told her to leave." Kaly stood and brushed her skirt down. She paced from one edge of the building to the other.

Beth stood and followed her. "Dan is your brother? Does he know?"

Kaly shrugged. "Yeah."

Beth sat back down on the stairs and put her face in her hands.

"How many times have you imagined what it might be like if your mother finally showed up and claimed you?" Kaly asked. "To finally belong, to have a family, a home." She poked her head around the corner, listening for George, hearing nothing. "But it wasn't like that. It was like a stranger had walked into my life, asking for directions, only worse. I hated her. She was poison to me."

Beth peeked out from under one hand and patted the step next to her again.

Kaly waited until she heard the dog bark, running feet, and George's laughter before she sat back down beside her friend. "She didn't come to claim me. I can forgive her for leaving me, but I can't forgive her for not claiming me. I mean, I've been living in the same town as her all of my life. She came to my sister's funeral."

"Her daughter's funeral," Beth said.

Kaly shook her head. "No. She was never a mother to us."

"Why did she leave you with Coral Anderson?"

She shook her head again. "She said she couldn't take care of us. But, Beth, she didn't have a life on the street! She had a bakery. A bakery! Now the questions keep gnawing at me. Someone has the answers. That's why I'm here. After the funeral, I want to go to the bakery to ask her. I'd like you to come with me. I'm not sure I can find the courage alone."

The brothel door opened. Lottie Boyle hovered in the doorframe. "Time for you to come inside, Beth," she said.

The woman seemed massive to Kaly.

"Ask her if I can go with you," Beth said in a quiet voice.

"You can't decide for yourself?"

"Not without a lot of trouble. Just ask her. I'm sure it'll be alright."

Kaly shook her head. She had promised herself never to speak another word to Lottie Boyle, never to give her the satisfaction of having any power over her. As she stood to go, she heard George laugh again. And, as if his laughter was a salve that healed the wound, Kaly turned, faced the madam, and stepped up onto the porch.

"May Beth meet me at the bakery this afternoon?" Kaly asked, looking at the green floorboards.

"Is someone speaking?" Lottie said. "If so, to whom are they speaking?"

A low rumbling started in Kaly's chest and rolled down her arms into her hands. She tightened her fingers into fists, and then felt her hands relax as the anger flowed out of them. You don't own our friendship, you mean woman, she thought. She raised her eyes to meet Lottie's. "Miss Boyle," she said, "I'd like Beth to meet me later. Will that be alright with you?"

"Oh, it's the poor little pregnant girl," the woman growled. "You want me to let my little girl go with you and your bad influence. No. She may not go out and play with you. Come on, Bethy. Inside."

After a frozen minute, Beth shrugged and stood.

Kaly stepped aside and waited for Beth to pass by the woman, back into their sanctuary. Once their skirts twirled out of sight, she looked for George. Her mind was racing. How dare that woman treat her friend like that! The Beth she knew had been so strong, so independent and defiant. But now she'd said nothing to Lottie on her own behalf. In that moment of Beth's silence, Kaly knew the difference between wanting respect and requiring it. She may have lost her friend to that woman's madness, but Kaly had won a small victory of self-respect by facing Lottie Boyle. She couldn't think about it much right then, though, because she couldn't find George and the dog. Did Lottie have him locked inside her petticoats, too?

"Miss Shane."

Kaly whipped around toward George's voice.

His head was peeking out from a thicket of bushes. "We're stuck," he said. "Will you help us?"

"You and I are good at getting into messes," she told him. She loosened the bushes around him, untangled the dog's rope, got them free, and brushed the dirt off George's coat. Then she ran her fingers through the dog's fur, loosening twigs.

Beth poked her head out the back door. "You're not taking the boy to the funeral, are you?" she whispered.

"He doesn't need coddling," Kaly said, wondering why on earth she was quoting Miss Anderson, of all people.

"Leave the boy with me."

"Not a chance. Look, Beth, I need your friendship, not your judgment." Without waiting for a response, Kaly took off down the hill like a steam engine, George and the dog chugging behind her.

Twenty minutes later they tied the dog to an iron fence near a wailing woman in a dark veil. Kaly and George made their way through the crowd into the Holy Trinity Serbian Orthodox Church. She purchased two candles and gave one to George. Together they followed the marble floor to the side and lit the candles.

Kaly bowed her head, folded her hands, and closed her eyes.

George nudged her. "What should I do?" he whispered.

"Say a prayer."

"What prayer?"

"You decide.

"Like talking to a dream?"

"Yes. Only you're talking to God."

The choir sang as they made their way to the back of the church. Stojan Lailich's gray coffin rested in front of the steps to the inner sanctum. Marika stood on the left side of the church between a woman who might be her mother and Tara McClane. Dan and Michael stood with another man, maybe Marika's brother, on the right side of the church.

"Are those angels?" George asked about the choir.

"Not angels, just messengers."

The priest came through the doors of the inner sanctum and blessed Stojan's body with smoke from the incense. He then turned toward the congregation and, walking down the aisle lightly swinging the censer, he said a prayer to bless them too.

George was quiet.

The priest began chanting. The song was beautiful and filled her heart with a sad warmth that spread through her chest to her arms and legs. Tears filled her eyes and she thought she felt Anne Marie slip in beside her, fold her hands and bow her head in reverence.

"Will that man wake up?" George asked.

Kaly nodded. "Not here. When he wakes up, he'll be

278

far away, in a place more beautiful than anyone can imagine."

"Will his mother be there?"

"I don't know," Kaly said, a wave of grief washing over her. That was something she would love to know. She'd imagined it a hundred times, what it would be like when she died. Would Anne Marie be waiting for her? When she was younger, she'd held onto the hope of seeing Annie in heaven, the thought a security blanket to Kaly. But as she'd aged, cynicism had poked and torn at the blanket's frayed edges.

"How will he get there?" George asked.

"Where?"

"To that place more beautiful than anyone can imagine?"

"The angels will take him."

"I want to go there."

"No, you don't. Not yet."

An older gentleman from the right side of the church motioned for George to join the men on that side.

George looked at Kaly.

She nodded.

He let go of her hand and crossed the aisle.

The priest looked out over the many people there. "Stojan Lailich follows his brother, Vuko, into God's hands. His brother will be waiting for him, to help him pass peacefully into the brilliant light of God's heavenly kingdom. Let us remember Stojan for his kindness, his strength, and his devout heart. Lord have mercy on his soul. May his memory be eternal."

When the service was over, Kaly and George walked outside and joined everyone in telling the family how sorry they were for their loss. Marika greeted Kaly and George with a weak smile. She was pale and her eyes were red. She leaned into Michael like she could barely stand.

Kaly dodged the McClanes. Her questions could wait until later.

George untied the dog from the iron fence and they started their long walk back uptown. The dog had gotten used to the rope leash, and pranced along as if he'd always been right there next to the boy.

"We sure are getting our exercise today, huh?" Kaly said. Climbing the Butte streets always made her thighs burn. She'd never gotten used to it. But now, carrying the extra weight of the baby, her muscles were on fire.

At the bakery, George didn't want to leave the dog to go inside.

Kaly helped him find a quiet spot in the alley near the back door of the bakery and left him there, gripping the dog's rope so tightly his knuckles were white. She shoved her way through the crowd to the front door of the bakery. The smell of fresh bread was conspicuously absent. She tried the door. It was locked. On the door a sign said, "Gone to a funeral." Kaly looked up and down the street. Other businesses were closed too, but the town was still brimming with people.

She made her way back to the alley.

George was happily rubbing the dog's belly.

"Let's go to the Copper Tavern. They never close." She led George and the dog around the corner and found a safe place for them to wait.

"Kaly?"

"Yes?"

"What's the moon doing?" George asked and pointed to the sky.

Kaly looked out at the East Ridge. "Coming up over the mountains."

"But it's still daytime."

"I guess it's a moon with a mind of its own."

"A wild moon."

"Wild and precious. Like you."

She walked through the door of the Copper Tavern as a group of men at the end of the bar were singing "My

Country 'Tis of Thee." Another group near the poker tables popped up at the end of the song and yelled, "Damn with war." Through the smoke she spotted Beth walking toward her.

"When the bakery was closed, I figured I'd see you here," Beth said. "Things are a real mess out there. Everything is closed and the town is still packed. You get through alright?"

Kaly nodded. "How'd you escape?"

"I am an artist," her friend said, wiggling her fingers in the air.

Kaly ordered a sandwich for George and asked Big Joe if he had any scraps for the dog. He recovered a steak bone from a miner's plate. She thanked him and took the food out to the boy. "You okay?" she asked him.

He nodded.

"Don't go anywhere. I'll be right back."

The noise of the tavern hurt her ears. But she didn't leave. She was there for a reason.

Mrs. McClane walked in by herself and slid into a booth. How perfect, Kaly thought. And Beth was there. The two of them joined Tara McClane. Big Joe set three beers on the table.

"You were right," Mrs. McClane said. Her eyes were red and sad, the skin under them drooping. "It's Danny's choice, whether or not to join the army. A mother needs to know when to let go."

"Or when to hold on," Kaly said.

"You think I gave you two up carelessly." The woman pulled her beer close. "I didn't. I was young and scared. Having no means to care for you, I didn't think I had a choice."

"You must have thought about keeping us."

"I did."

"What happened? Why didn't you protect Annie? Me? You were here all along." Kaly kicked at the sawdust under the table, her blood singed with the soot of old rage. She would never understand.

Mrs. McClane said nothing. She wiped the moisture from the sides of her beer and sipped it.

"You owe me that much," Kaly said.

"I heard your father's name today," Mrs. McClane said.

Kaly's hands shook. She clamped her teeth together to keep them from chattering. Her father's name. "Do you want me to guess? Do you want me to feel sorry for you?" She stood to go. What had she expected? Open arms? A soft bed? Motherly advice? The truth?

"Your father was Orthodox. I was Catholic. My father never would have permitted us to marry. We ran away to Helena and got married by a Lutheran pastor."

Kaly sat back down next to Beth, fixing her pale eyes on Mrs. McClane's.

"I stayed with friends of the pastor in Helena while your father came back to Butte. He had to work. Once we had enough money for our own house, we would tell my parents. But there was an accident. Your father was killed in the Little Minah the first day he returned to Butte. We didn't even have a chance to tell anyone that we'd gotten married before he was gone. In a fluke accident, my parents shortly followed. I was already pregnant. I had no one. I had no money. I was scared you'd starve." She paused, looked out across the crowd. "And later I was terrified to tell Danny's father about you. I thought you were safe. I was so wrong."

Kaly shook her head. "What was his name?"

"Your father?"

She nodded.

"Vuko. Lailich. Stojan's brother."

The wind went out of Kaly. She slumped in the booth. Stojan Lailich had been her uncle.

Under the table Beth took her hand.

Beth's hand was moist and soft, like it felt when Beth had first taken her into her small crib and shared her bed with Kaly. Her friend had been a small refuge in a lifetime of storms.

"Every day I've thought of you," the woman was saying. "For that first year after Annie died, I sat at her grave most nights until the sun rose. I'd go home just before Danny's father would rise for work."

"The grave next to Anne Marie's?"

"Vuko's."

"My father."

"Dan knows?" Beth asked.

Tara McClane nodded.

"How long?" Beth asked.

"I told him when he was eight. That was wrong of me too...to ask him to keep that secret."

"The food you brought to the Polly May," Kaly said.

"It was all I could do. It was nothing."

"We buried my uncle today." And she didn't even go out to the cemetery for the interment. "Did he know?"

"He knew. He tried to help me."

Kaly felt a hand on her shoulder. George stood there, his eyes watery and wide. Next to him the wolf dog sat as still as a fallen bird. "Maybe you can talk to them in your dreams, Miss Shane," the boy whispered to her.

She wiped his eyes with her handkerchief.

"I hope I can talk to my daddy in my dreams." He slid into the booth next to her. The dog nuzzled in under the table.

She put her arm around George and kissed the top of his head, remembering the first time she'd held him in her lap. It was after he'd stabbed Julian. A feral rage had leaked out of him. That day she'd wondered if she would ever find her mother, her family. She sat here now, with the boy and Beth beside her, the wolf dog at their feet, with Tara McClane across the table, and a wild, precious moon outside. Like it or not, she had found them.

1895
WAKES AND FUNERALS

The old-time miner knows how it works: Give a man a week in Butte, and the Copper Camp will either capture his heart or send him running forever. The miner knows he doesn't have much time now. Some day soon they'll thaw the ground for his body. He finds the white dog, a sweet spirit, under a dark table where the woman prepares the bodies for burial.

Children from the dusty room lock their eyes on the woman.

A man helps her, a child clinging to his leg.

The look-alike girls bring buckets of warm water and wring the water from the rags. In the days after the warehouse fire people of the town flood the big house. They stumble in from the winter storm, glad for shelter from the freezing cold. They come to view the bodies of the men, women and children killed in the explosion. Sometimes all they can view are closed caskets. Occasionally someone knocks at the door and claims a living child. The dark-haired girl retrieves the child's coat, and the child leaves the house.

The other children float like ghosts between the rooms

that the woman has arranged for the bodies, and the separate rooms that she has arranged for the men and the women to sit, to mourn. The white dog wanders through the rooms with the children, though none of them call to him. In the parlor, men speak well of the dead and laugh at death. It's as if laughter can keep the specter out of their building, or mineshaft, or store.

In the kitchen the women consider funeral and burial arrangements. They wonder about living in a town like Butte, a town now thick with smoke.

Early one cold morning, wagons come to get the bodies.

Later that morning, the white dog sits on the corner of Wyoming and Broadway as the men load caskets one by one into black wagons and funeral carts. The men hitch the horses to the carts and wagons, climb up onto their crackling seats, and drive down Montana Street to the cemeteries.

The dog runs, camouflaged in the snow-white day, behind the parade of black to where the flats stretch an open hand toward the Highlands, the beautiful snow-covered peaks that glow red in the muted sun. He reaches the first black iron fence surrounding the gray stones. The yard is already filled with people.

Women cry.

Men look solemn. Snow blows in their hair and on their shoulders.

The women pull on scarves and brush at the flakes. Several are on crutches or in splints. All are bruised in some way.

The children from the big house stand near the woman who is now their matron. They stare into the snow. The merciless wind blows hard off the Rocky Mountains and slants their eyes back.

The white dog walks behind the children. He sees the light-haired girl turn in his direction and crawls under her shivering, mittened hand.

A few shallow holes have been partially dug in the frozen ground and abandoned. The caskets will be stored in a temporary shelter until a fire can thaw the ground.

Men in black robes say words over the wooden boxes.

The men in black suits climb back onto the wagons and proceed to the second cemetery. The white dog follows, running to keep up with the horses. More men and women people the yard. The relentless, sharp wind freezes tiny teardrops like ice shards to the women's cheeks. The children and the woman from the big house descend from their wagon again. The look-alike girls stand between two tall boys and watch as the boxes slide into the men's arms. Turning their heads away from the blowing snow, the men lower the caskets from the wagons.

At the third cemetery, one of the tall boys stares at two wooden boxes. He runs to the one nearest him and throws himself onto it. The woman from the big house puts her arms around the boy. Time passes. Dark clouds and blowing snow block the sun, and the woman stays with the boy.

"Come on, Tommy," she says. "We'll go home soon."

The boy's frozen hands let go of the wooden lid and slide into a pocket of the woman's coat. The other children lean into each other like friendly timbers and the white dog nuzzles between them, welcoming their warmth. The children don't seem to notice his fur touching their thighs, or feel his breath on their tiny hands. He seems no more a presence than the wild snow on the wind.

The men in black robes pray for the souls of the dead. In the storm, their robes turn white. The woman carries the sad, tall boy, his face tucked into her shoulder, his legs dangling like ropes at her sides. The men and women head home, the final graves to be dug after the ground fires loosen the earth.

The white dog runs after the children's wagon as the horses pull it up the hill. When they reach the big house, the children disappear inside. They close the door, leaving the dog behind. The white dog tries to howl, but only a whimper rises from his throat. He lies near the porch, where snow is piled in a mound like dirt from an uncovered grave. He pulls his large tail in close to his body and tucks his head between his legs. And here, he rests.

SUMMER 1917
21
EMBRACED BY STRANGERS

Marika tugged the sleeve of her mother's wedding gown down past her wrist bone and turned sideways to view herself in the mirror. Baba had crocheted the dress with fine sheep's wool, and lined it with silk. It was a simple, straight pattern. The years had worn and softened it. She lifted one of her wrists to her nose. It smelled damp and dusty, like Montenegro. She looked beautiful in it, and unreal, like no one she'd ever known, like the imposter that had stepped into her life and taken over.

Mama turned her around and nodded approval. "You are stunning."

Marika smiled weakly, thankful for her mother's help. After Papa died she hadn't been able to think. But one thing had been clear, and now with Mama at her side, she knew exactly what she'd do. She'd marry Michael.

The ceiling light in the sleeping room cast slight shadows on the walls below it. A square of daylight shone through the small window. All but one of the beds had been neatly made. The mattress closest to Marika had been stripped, the bedding rolled and packed into a large trunk that also held her medicine bag, clothes, and books. The trunk sat at the foot of the bed, ready to go. They had left Papa's bed alone.

Papa. Her heart sank.

They had buried him a week ago. Then, with her permission, Michael's parents and Mama had rushed the wedding forward. Michael would take care of them now. Marika would grant Papa his last request. It was the least she could do. Regret punched her in the throat as she remembered how she'd behaved during her last months with her father. She would do anything to turn back time.

But time, she was learning, was the one thing no one could turn around.

Plus, with Papa gone she needed to be practical. Marko didn't make enough money as a nipper to support the family. If her brother had to get more work, it would pull him out of school. She, herself, made next to nothing at Dr. Fletcher's. And Mama had never worked for money.

"Papa would be proud. You'll be happy. Just give yourself a chance."

"I will, Mama."

"Before they come to get you I want to tell you something. I don't know when I'll have the chance to talk privately with you once you're married."

"What is it Mama?"

"Your father shared some secrets with me before he died, things he wanted you and Marko to know."

Marika nodded.

"Papa really was proud of you for taking care of Kaly Shane. Not only proud of you, he was grateful." Mama hesitated, looked away, took in a breath and turned back to her. "You see. She is Vuko's daughter. Your cousin."

"What?"

"She is our family."

"What? How? Did he just learn this?"

"Remember, Papa and I fought when we first came to

America. He brought food to Tara McClane. She is Kaly's mother. In secret, she and Vuko had married. Before they could tell anyone, Vuko died in an accident. She made sure he had a proper burial. But she had already gotten pregnant and had no way to support the girls."

"Girls?" Then Marika remembered Kaly had a sister.

"Yes. She gave birth to twins. She had no way to feed them. They went to live with Coral Anderson at the Polly May. But Tara had never told Kaly, so Papa couldn't tell you. It's true that Papa wanted you to marry, but he did not want you to give up your medical dreams, especially after he saw how happy they made you. He just didn't know how you could both marry and attend a medical school. Nevertheless, he was grateful that you took care of his brother's daughter. He just couldn't tell you."

Loud clapping and singing came from outside.

Marko rushed in. "They're here."

She put one last pin in her hair. Kaly was her cousin. What?

Mama took her hands and rubbed lavender oil on her wrists. She held them up and kissed them.

Mama's kiss and the sweet scent calmed her. But her words rumbled around in Marika's head. Kaly. Anne Marie. No wonder Kaly kept looking at her like she knew her. They were related!

"We're here for the bride," a voice boomed as the door flung open. There stood Michael's oldest brother, Tomo, tall and strong like Michael. He had thick, bushy eyebrows and dark eyes. He was dressed in a black suit and his beard had been freshly trimmed. "May I take your daughter away with us, to marry her groom?"

He sounded so formal.

Mama stepped out to greet him. She nodded and unfolded two shawls, wrapping one around Marika's shoulders and the other around her own.

Marko slipped his arms into the same gray suit coat he'd worn to Papa's funeral. It was too big for his shoulders, making him look like the boy he was, not yet grown into his manhood.

A second Jovich brother, Stephan, came up behind Tomo. Smaller and younger, this one had soft blue eyes and blond hair. His cheeks and lips, however, were the same as Michael's—determined, richly colored, and full. "May we escort you, Mrs. Lailich, to the house?" Stephan asked.

"Of course," Mama said.

He took Mama's arm and helped her up the steps of the wagon, where she sat on the bench beside the driver.

Marko followed.

The horse swiped the ground with his foot, as if counting passengers.

Tomo picked Marika up and carried her like a precious swan egg to the back of the wagon. There he nestled her into an overstuffed chair, then sat like a knightly guard on a wooden box beside her. She held her breath, feeling ridiculous, giving the imposter full control. She'd never liked being the center of attention and she could feel her cheeks grow hot.

They dropped Mama off at Michael's house, where the women were preparing the wedding feast. The day after the wedding, Marika would cook a traditional "stranger's" dinner for her husband. She ran a hand across her heated forehead as the horses clopped in unison toward South Idaho Street. Toward the church. Toward her fiancé. Kids in the street waved at her and she waved back, the unlikely queen of the parade.

Only a week ago these same horses had pulled Papa's coffin to the flats. Now, after all of her resistance, she would marry Michael Jovich.

Men in suits smoked pipes in front of the church. They huddled together, talking in loud voices and gesturing with their hands. Another large group of men shadowed the church steps as if it was some uptown tavern.

The bright sun turned Marika's dress hot and itchy. A

fly buzzed around her neck. Get away, she thought, swatting at it.

Suddenly her calm evaporated. She must get away too!

But there was nowhere to go.

She pushed the urge down. She tried to think reasonable thoughts. Michael was kind. He'd been kind when Marika found Pamela. He was kind at Papa's funeral. She was grateful for his kindness.

Now she knew that people could suddenly die, just vanish from your life forever. They wouldn't always be around for one more chance to make up after a bad quarrel. People were here one minute and gone the next. Losing Papa wasn't like watching the soldiers die in Montenegro. She'd barely known them. This was Papa. Her Papa. Gone. She'd been mad at him and hadn't even told him how much she loved him, hadn't thanked Papa for teaching her, for arguing with her. She hadn't told him he was a good father and that, no matter how she fought with him, she admired him more than anyone. She hadn't said these things while he was here to listen, and now she regretted her silence.

As the wagon rolled along, Marika's mind raced. What about Dan? What would she do about him? Nothing, she guessed. Their time had come and gone, like a roller coaster ride that was forever finished as The Gardens closed at sunset. For a moment she disregarded the grief weighing on her chest, and smiled at her own melodrama.

A large man on the steps smiled with her. He had red, curly hair and looked familiar. Then she remembered: He was the man in bib overalls who'd accompanied his wife to Dr. Fletcher's office last winter. His wife had sought help for her late-life mood swings. The woman's gray braid had flipped against her husband's chest like a horsetail when she moved. That moment, Marika was sure, was the one that had won her Miss Parsons' respect. The large man, now wearing a suit, was applauding Marika. Then he bowed to her. Well, she thought, her advice that day must have helped settle things at home. He must be a miner, a friend of Michael's, a friend of Papa's too.

The wagon stopped in front of the church.

Tomo lifted Marika from her throne. "This way." He grabbed her hand and pulled her toward the church steps. "He is waiting for you inside." She stopped, paralyzed with fear, her legs suddenly too heavy. But Tomo didn't notice and pulled her forward.

As they climbed the stairs, the men quieted and split apart, creating an aisle into the church. They bowed to her respectfully. Marika hadn't expected respect. She spotted Dan, tucked behind two other men. He tipped his hat to her. He had taught her to face her fears. And here she was, facing them. She wished she'd had time to talk to him, to explain. But then what would she say? Nothing. Nothing could change the future she entered. Her chest felt tight and her arms tingled. Her world had twisted itself out of her control.

Tomo swept her into the church, the heavy doors closing behind her.

She lifted her face to the large chandelier that hung from the ceiling. The scent of incense hit her nose, and the images from Papa's funeral swung into her mind like a sledgehammer. She could still see his body in the casket, in the place where the marital altar now stood. She smelled his pipe and turned toward the smell, confused. Portraits of Jesus, Mary and the saints lined the iconostas. Mary held Baby Jesus on her lap, His head tucked under her chin, looking both sweet and sad.

Tomo stood by Marika's side, smiling as if it was his wedding. Her lungs filled and her face flushed hot. She let out a heavy breath, unable to think.

Michael, stood near the icon table. His hair was freshly trimmed. New eyeglasses perched neatly on his nose. He wore a black suit with a white shirt, and a beautiful, wide smile. Smiles were everywhere in the church. Michael's was the biggest and brightest. It lit up his face. Marika wished she felt more for him, looking at her groom. She was certain he was a good man. And, in his suit, he was so handsome. Papa had told her that marriage was not in the intercourse, but in the consent. Papa had insisted on this. In the end, she had consented.

The choir sang in Church Slavonic as the priest entered in his long white and gold robe, the air thick with incense. He invited Michael and Marika to the back of the church, where he blessed the rings and the bridal pair. They exchanged the simple rings, and the priest prayed over them. "Lord, establish in them the holy union which is in Thee."

Marika felt dizzy. And hot. Too hot. So much had happened in the last week. Too much. The colors from the stained glass swooned around her as the crowd behind them settled into a solemn silence. Preceded by the priest, Marika and Michael moved in procession to the front of the church to the marital alter for the crowning service.

"Do you, Michael Jovich, have a good, free and unconstrained will and a firm intention to take as your wife this woman, Marika Lailich, whom you see here before you?"

"I have, Father." Michael looked at Marika. For the first time, she realized that the arrangement has been made on his side too. His father had requested his compliance. Michael had also consented.

"Have you promised yourself to any other bride?"

"I have not promised myself to any other."

The priest turned to her. "Do you, Marika Lailich, have a good, free and unconstrained will and firm intention to take as your husband this man, Michael Jovich, whom you see here before you?"

"I have, Father."

"Have you promised yourself to any other man?"

"I have not promised myself to any other." She hadn't had a chance to promise herself to Dan. She'd never had a chance with him. She saw that now.

The priest prayed over them again.

The choir sang.

Marika wiped a hand across her cheek, in the exact spot where tears had streamed during Papa's funeral. New tears welled in her eyes.

The priest placed the crowns on their heads to show that they were queen and king of their world, equal partners and partners with God. The deacon brought the Common Cup and the priest blessed it. He gave it to Michael, and Michael drank from it. He gave it to Marika and she also drank from the Cup.

She looked up to steal a glance at Michael. A soft wind crossed her cheek and she felt the bones of the dead settle somewhere far away. The priest led them three times around the icon table to seal their union. Dizziness came on fast and she grabbed Michael's arm to steady herself. He looked at her, his eyes kind and full of love. How could that be? He didn't even know her.

Afterwards, the men spilled out of the church and made their way the few blocks to Michael's house. There, everyone feasted on a delicious, spectacular banquet of lamb, beef, turkey, roasted potatoes, early greens from someone's garden, *povetica*, and rich cakes. Guests drank *Rakija*, plum brandy, or *Kruska*, pear brandy, maybe even brought over from the old country.

Accepting congratulations one after the other, Marika hardly saw Michael throughout the meal. She looked for Dan. She wanted to explain. But he hadn't come to the house. Marko grabbed Marika and the two of them danced the *kolos* of home. He danced with her like Papa would have done. That made her cry and then it made her smile. They danced like they had danced when they were kids in Montenegro, wild and free, the smoke from the campfires lilting toward the sky.

Mama was the star of the feast. She wore the lavender dress and piled her dark curls on top of her head. Her face was bright and full of laughter as she bounced from one guest to the next. Her long skirt flowed and twirled as she danced and served food and danced again.

Even Papa, wherever he was now, must have been satisfied.

That night, after Michael went to bed, Marika stood at the window in her nightgown, a blanket wrapped around her shoulders. She couldn't stop shivering. Already she missed Mama and Marko. As the lights went out across the city she thought about Papa. She wanted so badly to talk to him. If only he could have been at the wedding. It should have been his day too. Finally, she slept on a bed in the living room of a tiny apartment attached to Michael's family home. Feeling small and frightened, she could not yet bring herself to the marriage bed.

On the second night, fog rose up like a shroud outside her window. Marika thought of going to Michael. She knew she should go, make things right. But she was scared and it wasn't right.

Her life would never be right again.

She imagined Papa in his grave, silent and still, the wind blowing over the freshly laid dirt. Was he at peace? Now that his murky lungs no longer gurgled and spun dark mucus up his throat, now that his lungs no longer collapsed on themselves, was he resting in peace? Please let Papa rest in peace, Marika prayed, curling up on her side on the bed. Here she was, left in this world without her Papa. Could anyone have changed the course of his life, of their lives? She knew only this: she was here now with Michael, and she should go to him.

Custom demanded this of her. She had, after all, stepped into Custom's swirling tirade. Papa's traditions were hers now. She could hold onto Papa as she carried out his will. She would hold onto him, take over where he'd left off, slap her knee when she drank *rakija*, help Michael with the unions. Papa would want her to behave as Custom demanded.

Her shoulders tightened, nausea swirling around her chest. No. She wouldn't let her life fall down around her like loose boulders. She was caught in an end tunnel, gasping for dead air. She couldn't get out. There was nowhere to go. She lay there and covered her face with her hands, longing for comfort. Not just any comfort. The comfort of her father's arms, his smile, his voice telling her that everything would be fine.

She uncovered her face and opened her eyes. Gazing at the window, she watched the fog spin and swirl out there. A red tinge colored the mist on the hill. She curled up tighter, pulling the covers up to her chin. She closed her eyes again. When she opened them, Michael stood at the end to her bed. Moonlight edged through the fog and curtains and threw a strange, beautiful light across his eyes.

"May I?" he asked, his voice gentle.

She nodded, not knowing what he asked. She was already the odd person out in the marriage. She no longer knew herself. Her old life had let loose of her, but this new life had not yet stitched her in its hem.

Michael sat in a rocker at the foot of her bed, the flop-eared rabbit Dan had won for her slumped over his leg. Outside the summer wind picked up. She smelled smoke high on its ashy wing. She was surprised to find herself glad to see her new husband. She had married Michael for Papa, and for the family. Or so she'd thought. Now she was not so sure that her motives were all that generous. Papa's death broke open her heart, leaving the door wide open for Michael to walk in.

"I couldn't sleep," he said. "Maybe we could talk or go for a stroll."

A walk sounded good. If the wind blew the smoky air out toward the flats and the fog lifted, the stars would shine on them. Papa would see his good daughter. She nodded to Michael and motioned for him to turn away while she dressed. But before she pulled back the covers, yelling broke out in the street.

Michael rose to attend to it.

For the first time, she smiled at him. "Let it go," she whispered. "It's probably pranksters. It doesn't sound serious." Her heart turned on itself, desiring his company. She wanted to feel the cold air on her face, to walk with Michael in the foggy night as the city lights blinked out around them. She didn't know what the night held. For the briefest moment she wanted to protect their simple beginning.

The quick, high trill of a mine whistle sounded over the yelling. Then the shrieks of several mine whistles clouded the air.

Marika covered her ears and flew to the window. The red tinged fog on the hill! The smoky air! A column of flames leaped up from one of the mines. Thick orange fingers lashed the sky. Smoke blackened the moon.

Someone knocked.

Marika grabbed her clothes and rushed to the washroom. An accident!

The knock came again, harder this time.

"There's a fire!" The wooden door muffled a woman's voice.

Michael went outside.

As the door opened and shut, Marika heard the many voices. The wailing mine whistles exploded and popped, twisting and lapping over each other, cutting at her ears. She couldn't make out the words being said by those in the street, but she heard the urgency in them, mixed with the desperate sound from the hill. It must be bad. Really bad.

Michael poked his head back through the door. "Miss Parsons and Dr. Fletcher are here for you," he said.

She threw on a simple brown shift and wrapped a shawl around her shoulders. Before leaving the house, she grabbed her medicine bag.

Outside Michael, Stephan and Tomo talked with a group of men.

Miss Parsons waited nearby. "It's at the Speculator,"

she said. "Doctor needs your help."

"What happened?" Marika asked. The chill night sloped toward her.

"A fire in the shaft. They've called all medical units out."

"I'm coming with you," Michael said, climbing into Dr. Fletcher's automobile behind her. "Tomo says an electrical cable must have caught fire in the mineshaft. Workers got it stuck earlier today. Some late shift fellows were checking it out, trying to loosen it and drop it down. One must have gotten too close with his carbide light, touching it to exposed insulation. The whole thing likely went up in flames immediately. There's twelve hundred feet of cable down there." Michael turned his head toward the open window, where fog lined the streets. He wiped his face with his hand and shifted back toward Marika. "The electrical cable was for the new sprinkling system. It was to protect the mine from fires."

Marika felt the crushing pressure in her throat as Doctor Fletcher turned the automobile toward the mine. Her heart raced. She wiped the sweat from her cheeks. The night was so hot!

They drove past large groups of people rushing up the hill, toward the fire. Eventually the doctor pulled the big car up next to the fence surrounding the North Butte Mine Workings, where the Speculator's Granite Mountain mineshaft blazed a hole in the sky.

"What's happening to the miners?" Marika shouted as they ran to the yard. Her legs burned and her lungs already hurt.

"Some will have escaped through adjoining tunnels." Michael's eyes reflected the firelight.

"Papa's work toward safety?"

"Not enough. In fact, at this point, the ventilation system is most likely spreading the fire. A lot of men are down there still. Nearly five hundred men were on shift."

Marika chilled to a stop, the full awareness hitting her.

"Was Marko working?"

Michael shook his head. "He's not scheduled to start swing shift until next week. He should be fine. I'm sure he'll be up here to help."

She looked across the housetops to the East Ridge where the sky had briefly cleared. The snow had mostly melted out of the mountains. The beautiful jagged peaks seemed to reach for the moon. She didn't want to ask Michael, but there was no one else. "Was Dan McClane working?"

He nodded. "I'm sorry."

Her mind turned cloudy, like a dark, smoky lung. All luminescence dried out of it. She struggled for air, pumping it into her body. It felt as unnatural as the mine's ventilation system. "Has he come out?"

Michael shook his head. His shoulders lifted slowly and feathered down, stretching time. "We'll know more soon."

A black plume rose and billowed toward the sky, filling the June air with sour smoke. Sirens swarmed in the night as people everywhere rushed toward the head frames, looking for their loved ones.

My son?

Missing.

Have you seen my father?

Missing.

My husband, he was supposed to be off at midnight. Is he here?

Missing.

My baby brother?

Missing.

My uncle. My neighbor. My friend.

Missing. Missing. Missing.

Dan was nowhere.

In the midst of the clanging night, Marika heard her name and turned toward the sound.

Kaly and Beth clipped past an ambulance and caught

up with them.

Sirens wailed from all sides. A dead wagon pulled through the gates and parked next to the southern storage shed. Fire plumed up the Speculator's Granite Mountain shaft, turning the blackened yard an eerie orange. Copper smoke spilled into the sky and dipped down to greet them. The hill looked like the war field where Marika had helped Baba wrap the wounded Montenegrin soldiers. The scene pushed her back in time. She smelled the flesh burning.

"What happened?" Kaly was asking.

"A cable caught fire and lots of men are trapped. Or worse." Marika's lips were thick with other people's blood. Their images swirled around her. And now this: Kaly was Uncle Vuko's daughter. Did she know? Should she tell her? No. She should do nothing but try to get her bearings.

"They couldn't stop it?" Kaly asked.

"I think that the shaft sucked the fire up the cable," Michael told her, "setting fire to the entire thing instantly. The ventilation system is probably spreading the fire and gas. We have to reach survivors quickly or they'll perish."

"A snap of the fingers and everything as you know it disappears," Beth said. "How many men are down there?"

"Five different mines connect to the Speculator and Granite Mountain shafts. If you add the possibilities, hundreds, maybe as many as a thousand." Michael's voice funneled through the rushing sounds of the crowd. "Some will have made their way to the Badger. Even if they escape the flames, they still have to contend with the smoke and poisonous gases. And the heat." Michael rubbed his elbow, his eye twitching.

"What are the chances of survival?" Kaly asked.

"It's a matter of timing. Doctor says that a few have been treated for gas exposure and released. But as time goes on, the odds get worse. The men at the scene of the initial fire probably died instantly."

In the dim firelight, rescuers scurried with their helmets and oxygen masks like moles across the dirt.

Marika heard them yelling to each other, but couldn't make out the words.

A batch of workers disappeared into the dark.

"Dan was down there," Marika said.

Kaly arched her back, her round, pregnant belly pushing through her too-thin frame. A blue cotton dress gathered below her breasts and above her ankles. She wore a black sweater over the dress. She folded her arms across her chest, at the top of her stomach, just above the baby's tiny heart, and tucked her hands like hidden mice into the opposite sleeves.

Kaly Shane had not faired well. Bad news had piled itself upon the woman. Marika felt sorry for her and grabbed the sympathy like a lifeline. She cared for her. She would always care for her. They were cousins.

"Tommy?" Kaly asked.

"We don't know," Marika said.

Kaly shook, and tightened her arms, hugging herself.

Michael reached out and held her steady for a moment, until Kaly unwrapped herself and linked arms with Marika and Beth.

They followed Michael to the head frame, where Dr. Fletcher waited.

Helmet men, the men brave enough to go into the mine tunnels to look for survivors, were already bringing out bodies. Their helmets protected them. The oxygen connected to the helmet masks kept them from succumbing to the deadly gases.

"In my car you'll find a tarp for supplies," Dr. Fletcher said. "The ambulance will have whatever I don't have. Let others focus on the dead while we focus on the living." Dr. Fletcher was calm and steady, unlike his usual fidgety self. Perhaps he was conserving energy. He must have known, like Marika knew, that the night before them would last forever.

Emergency workers pulled cots from ambulances. They spread canvas across the ground and set up workstations with medical supplies and resuscitators.

Marika and Kaly dragged the tarp from Dr. Fletcher's automobile to an open spot on the hill.

Two men carried a limp man in a blanket. They placed him on the canvas. His eyelids fluttered. His tongue pushed out his mouth, his lips and skin bright red. He let off a slow whine like an old siren.

Marika wanted to hold him and comfort him, to rock him like the child he'd become. But she didn't. She couldn't. The noxious air had poisoned him. He needed the hospital immediately. There was nothing Marika could do. She stood there, frozen by his huge, urgent need.

"I'll get an ambulance," Kaly said.

A helmet worker brought over another man. "He just stopped breathing."

Marika snapped to, putting the respirator on him and pumping hard. Pressing the mask's levers and letting them go, she held her own breath. She stopped and felt his pulse. He had a heartbeat, but the resuscitation wasn't taking.

She thought about her grandmother's quiet way with soldiers, calmed herself and prayed. The breath came back into her body and she stood firmly in the night, useful again. She prayed for the man's spirit to live there, in his body, to make him whole again. She tried pumping the oxygen again.

The man drew a breath and then two. Soon his breathing was regular and automatic, a simple match to his heartbeat.

She helped transfer him to an ambulance, and moved on to the next man. In the rush to leave the tunnels he'd fallen and twisted his arm backward nearly severing it at his elbow.

The next man had had a burning timber fall on him. His face popped out yellow like a bulldog.

Another man had fallen and broken his arm.

Marika splinted it for him, something she could do.

"Are you OK?" Michael asked.

"I'm fine," she said. "Will you help me?"

He nodded. Michael spent the next hour triaging and walking or carrying the bandaged men to ambulances.

She followed his back as he faced into the dark. He moved carefully, quickly, his spine flexible, his shoulders strong.

Kaly and Beth disappeared into the crowd about the same time Mama and Marko showed up.

When the call came for more helmet men, Michael and Marko volunteered.

"No!" Marika blurted. But she quickly added, "Be careful." Speaking the obvious. "It's dangerous in there." Her heart flipped around in her chest. She couldn't lose anyone else, but she couldn't stop them from trying to save someone else's loved ones.

They nodded in unison and put on their helmets. The oxygen hoses rattled and they were gone.

Fire poured out of the shaft, burning the fog from the night air. She watched the greedy flames lash toward the stars. She knew that innocent men in the tunnels beneath the flames had signaled for a cage to be sent down to them. They had signaled for some way to be raised up out of the mine.

Marika froze for a moment, clutched in the horrible knowledge that the miners would signal again and again with no possible response.

Until finally the signal bells would go quiet.

Dread seized her. It was like an icy claw gripping her heart.

The helpless townspeople stood around her.

All of them were struck dumb by the tragic horror they were witnessing.

Tommy Monroe walked up to her station in a rescue helmet carrying an agitated man.

Tommy! Kaly would be glad Tommy was here.

Marika focused on the raving man in his arms. He was

delirious from the poisonous gases, unable to state his name. Tommy, who was wet and covered in mud, gently placed the man on a cot.

The man twisted toward Marika. "Listen!" He seemed to be hearing something she couldn't hear. "Help them! They're calling me. I have to go to them!" He threw himself off the cot, stumbling back toward the mineshaft.

Tommy caught him, led him back to Marika.

"It's OK," she said, knowing that nothing was OK. Nothing would ever be OK again. "We have men in there to help them. You rest. We'll take care of it now."

Tommy backed away, a stricken look on his face, and vanished into the engulfing night.

"There's gas, though," the man on the cot told her, wheezing. "And it's so hot! They're melting! I ran. I tried to carry him. His arm. I held his arm. I have to go to him! He's there alone. In the dark. It's so dark in there! Do you know how dark it is, Miss?" He held his hand up as if he held the melting man's arm.

Marika realized that he meant it. He thought that he'd held the man's arm and, in the intense heat, that it had detached from his friend's body, an orphaned hand waving to the night. She shook her head. "We'll take care of you now."

She gave the man air. He sucked it in and calmed down. Or perhaps he was going deeper into shock. Marika couldn't tell which. Within moments he recovered enough to walk away toward his wife and child. It struck Marika as a miracle, as some sort of odd luck in the middle of this ghastly night.

Dr. Fletcher summoned her over to the cage shaft. Two men had insisted on being lowered into the tunnels to warn the men and bring out as many as they could. One of the men who had gone down there was the foreman whose carbide light had caught flame to the cable. Feeling responsible for all of this, he'd been hell-bent on getting as many men out as possible.

It had already been forty-five minutes since they'd gone down.

The rope man waited and waited for their signal to raise the cage. Now he said he'd waited long enough. Now he would bring them back up.

Dr. Fletcher wanted Marika there to help, in the event that the two men were still alive.

The cage rose to the top of the shaft, molten hot and glowing in the morbid night.

The fire crew sprayed water on the cage to cool it. The water hissed and bubbled and sizzled, creating a cloud of smoky steam.

No one could live through that.

A fireman opened the cage.

Two charred bodies lay crumpled inside. One man's leg had burned off and dropped to the second deck of the cage.

Marika clenched her jaw, steeled herself, and went back to her work station.

She spotted Mama resting on a bench near the storage shed. She wanted to tell her to go home. Mama was frail. She had just lost Papa. She'd just married off her daughter. She shouldn't be there in the midst of this deadly horror. She wanted to tell Mama to let the young take their turn reining in tragedy. But it would be useless to tell Mama to go home. It would be a waste of Marika's energy. Her mother would stay and work with the rest of the town until all of the work was done.

Soldiers arrived. They threw a cordon around the mine, permitting only physicians, rescue squads, and undertakers to pass through, forcing family members to watch the horrific scene through slats in the tall wooden fence.

In a pale morning light, corpses were lined up like fallen trees after a windstorm.

As far as Marika could tell, none of them were Dan's.

Michael, Marko and Tommy had worked hard, pulling

bodies from the mine. Several of them were bloated and twisted, beyond recognition, poisoned by the fatal gases. The more time that went by, the more difficult it would be to identify the recovered bodies.

Dan could be any one of them. Or he could still be down there. He could be alive, although Marika doubted it. There were fewer and fewer survivors as time went on.

Tommy placed a thin, small man on the cot and lifted his oxygen hose to speak. "He's still breathing. I hope you can work your magic on him." He dropped the hose back in place and headed straight back to the shafts.

Marika wanted to thank Tommy, and tell him what good work he was doing. She yearned to ask him what it was like down there, and how he was holding up, if he'd seen Dan. But he was instantly gone, as quickly as a flame flickers, an angel of mercy in the midst of this gruesome morning.

Marika looked at the man before her. Before she could do anything for him, he hissed a rattled breath and let go, his spirit soaring away on the smoky wind. All Marika could do was wipe the dirt from his face.

It was Ted Framer, the referee from the Casino. He smiled a silky, soft smile at her. "Out," she said, and held her hand gently above him. She closed his eyes and asked a helper to take him to the temporary morgue.

The work didn't stop. Doctors. Rescue squads. Helmet men. Ambulance drivers. Undertakers. Priests in black robes. Women cooking. People praying. They all worked on. Food was brought in, but much of it went untouched as crews plowed on toward the evening.

The black smoke still plumed. Marika wondered how. The fire fighters were dousing the flames with five hundred gallons of water per minute. That much water should have counted for something, drenched flames, extra lives saved, the end of tragedy, something more than the dozens of dead bodies pulled from the earth.

Long past midnight of the second day, Marika took her first break. She sat on a log at the edge of camp, breathed deeply, and brushed a damp strand of hair off her forehead. Her fingers were stained with gray soot.

"You've done enough for now." It was Dr. Fletcher's voice. He stood like a phantom in the smoke. "They haven't brought out a live man for hours. Go home, get some sleep, come back refreshed. You'll be more useful then."

Michael stood nearby, his helmet in his hand. He, Marko, and Tommy were being sent home to rest. Some of the helmet men had become reckless from lack of sleep, and had nearly met their own demise in the gassy tunnels. Now the rescue workers were only allowed to stay on shift a limited number of hours without a break.

The undertakers were already busy enough.

She hesitated.

"Marika?" Dr. Fletcher said her name as if it was a fragile bird. The sound of it made her feel afraid.

"Yes?"

"Thank you," he said.

She only nodded.

The wind blew smoke across the dark sky as she and Michael left Marko with Mama. Michael took her hand in his, and she was glad of it. She wanted to forget the disaster for one minute, for an hour even. She would hold onto this moment, right here, right now, with the moon, the brisk wind, the lights of the flats, the gravel under her feet, the smell of horses, and Michael's warm hand. Tomorrow would be a new day, with more bad news and she'd need to prepare herself.

Her legs hurt. Her back stung. The image of the molten cage beat at her eyes.

When they got home she washed her face in cold water. The water felt good on her skin. She scrubbed at her eyes where the scarred faces had burned into her eyelids.

Dan was gone.

She wanted comfort, needed comfort. Who was she, though, to think of her own comfort when the whole town had lost its life? Smoke had replaced the fog and the summer stars were lost behind ashes. Only the moon stole through the curtains, spreading light like embers across the room.

She washed up and put on her blue nightgown.

"You okay?" Michael asked.

"I'm fine," she said numbly.

Michael retired to the bedroom.

Marika rocked in the living room chair, rubbing the flop-eared rabbit's belly. Poor things. You and me. Dan won us together and now look at us. We've gone from desire to disaster in a moment's time. The chair creaked to a stop and she climbed into bed, still tightly clutching the rabbit.

She heard Michael's breathing from the other room. It was the unnatural breath of a survivor. It was thick with dreams she couldn't enter. It was the breath of a man who loved safety and justice, whose love of the union had forced him to carve one small hole in the steel ball of oppression.

Marika had loathed the idea of marrying Michael. She hadn't wanted him, but here they were, married, the wedding feast behind them, king and queen of their world, strangers united. The marriage was done and there was nothing for it.

In the last forty-eight hours, Marika had faced tragedy the likes of which she'd never known existed. She had smelled its acrid stench, felt its disintegrating touch, heard the range of its high and low voices. She had seen tragedy and Michael was not it.

No. He was her gift. From Papa. From God. Yet, she had chosen Michael, to please Mama, to take care of Marko, to make it up to Papa. To one day look at Papa's grave and say, "Look, I'm your good daughter, I've kept your word." For whatever reasons, with Papa gone, she, herself, had chosen to uphold her father's promise. Michael was her family and here, in the deathly night of forever, she wanted to be close to him.

She got out of bed, propped the rabbit up on the pillow, and pulled the covers over him. The flat wooden floor against her feet cooled her toes, sending little shivers up her legs. She stood in the doorway to Michael's room. The still outline of his body rested under a thick, rose-colored quilt that lifted and fell with his breath. The wind blew the curtains in circles.

He was awake when she slid into bed next to him. He turned toward her. "Are you sure you want to be here?" he asked.

She nodded.

He folded her in his arms like a sad pony, and pulled her close.

Lying there with him slowed down time. His heart crooned a soft harmony underneath his skin. Marika didn't cry. She listened to his heart song, each precious note winging her soul upward. Toward a golden forgiveness.

After a long while, Michael passed his hand across her cheek. He kissed her eyes, one and then the other, his lips blessing the thin skin on her lids, brushing across her eyelashes. He pressed her toward him and kissed her on the mouth.

Marika tasted his sure, earthy courage, and twisted into him.

With the wind blowing through the curtains, Michael rose up on his elbows and looked at her, his eyes strong, safe beacons. His face answered a million questions as he pulled her nightgown off her shoulders and laid his bare skin against hers. He dropped his hand down her thigh where she waited, silky and pure.

She pushed herself up against his hand. It was strange and succulent, pushing up into him. It was somehow delicious, reaching out for him. Reaching out for her husband, her friend. Reaching for release from her shattered heart.

In the smoky night, under the light of an outlaw moon, Michael took her past the pain of the first moments.

Marika no longer knew her own body. On this desperately sad night she twirled with Michael under the windy curtains, until the night disappeared. Until heat quivered through her limbs. Until silver threads spun all around her. Beyond the fallen bodies, far away from the fire, she opened to Michael and felt the utter goodness of him.

When she was ready, he pressed into her so that Marika's spine shivered and curved. Like wild flowers, like fresh water, like grace, she sweetened wildly under the weight of her husband's solidly beating heart. She folded into him. Marika was light and free, and she was dancing.

22
RESCUED LIVES

Kaly searched for Miss Anderson at the Speculator fire. She spotted her in the massive crowd gathered behind the fence where people waited to get word of their relatives and friends. Kaly wanted to offer a truce to the matron, or at least some kind words. But before she could go talk to her, John Hurt, the undertaker, poked his head around the fence. He pointed to Kaly and motioned for her to come into the mine yard.

On the other side of the fence, the mine looked unreal in the soft pink light of a partially hidden sun. Even the sun seemed afraid of what it might see. A slight wind blew, carrying the rank scent of decomposed bodies, warning of the task ahead.

They passed the medical station where Marika was helping a man to the ambulance.

"Tommy's safe!" Marika told her. "He's helping with the rescue. I'm sure you'll see him soon."

"Thank you!" Relief filled her heart. Tommy was alive! In all the chaos she hadn't known for sure. A thousand possibilities had gone through her mind, none of them good. Now she just felt gratitude.

Tommy was alive.

John Hurt led Kaly into a newly framed building.

She gazed at the peaked ceiling above them. Stark pine boards walled a vacuous space. Benches lined the temporary floor inside. On each bench lay a body. The corpses were still and light as ashes, like they might float away at any moment. The putrid smell attacked her, making her stomach lurch. She pulled her scarf up over her nose for little protection against the assault.

"Can you tell us who any of these men are?" John Hurt asked, pointing to the row of benches on the west side of the building. "No one seems to know them."

She took a deep breath through her scarf. She must calm down and concentrate. Kaly looked at the men. They all lunged at her at once.

"In time," she said, speaking to their spirits.

The undertaker nodded.

There was one she recognized immediately. He had told her his name was Frank Hoffman, although Kaly doubted that he'd told her his real name. He had a sharp angular face with a V-shaped chin, a thin body, and beautiful dark skin. Now that skin was bloated and bright red. A dark mole sat just under his collarbone. Kaly had thought about running her finger across that mole several months ago. He'd moved to Butte from Nevada, he'd said. He had no family yet. He'd been a kind, unassuming man and, in moment of self-protection and concern for the child she carried, she had told him no.

Next to him was a man from the east. He'd come west to work on the railroad in Taft. The job had proven too tough for him, and after witnessing his third murder in a month, he'd moved to Butte to work in the mines. He'd visited her several times, but had never told her his name. He did tell her a lot of other things, though—that he was in love with a girl back home who he hadn't seen in years. But as soon as he made enough money he'd send for her and they'd marry. Kaly wondered if his true love had ever made it out west to be with him or not.

Looking down the row, she knew them all. Possum James, from the south, married and divorced with grown children. Alby Voich, who'd traveled by sea from Montenegro. Micky Shea from Ireland. Shelby Jones, a short timer. The Fourth of July Boy. The boy who limped. The man with the arm that cracked. He had done magic tricks for her.

Kaly gave the undertaker as much information as she knew about each man. She helped him wrap the deceased in canvas, tag him, and pack him into the dead wagon. As they emptied the benches, the helmet men brought in more bodies to fill the spaces. She recognized two men from a war protest, and several from the Copper Tavern. One had scurried out of the red light district one morning last fall. Another she'd bumped into at the fights. So many dead men. And there were bound to be more. It was unlikely that any had survived the gases and flames beyond the first day or two. She looked around again.

Tommy was alive, but Dan was nowhere.

Kaly worked all day with John Hurt. Her mind shut down. Her overwhelmed heart rolled into a dark hole, hiding from all of this.

One of the helmet men stopped to talk to her. "Thanks for your help," he said.

She looked up to see two accordion hoses that dropped down from the mask covering his face. Dark hair swooped over his eyes. Tommy! She reached toward his face. The helmet felt cool and hard.

"You're here. It's really true. You're alive." In a burst of joy she threw herself into his arms and hugged him. She struggled to keep back the tears. This was no time for tears. "I was so scared I'd never see you again."

"It's OK," Tommy said, pulling his mask off.

She backed up and looked at him. "Marika told me you were safe. I didn't know."

"I'm sorry about Dan. He's still missing. I know that he

was your friend."

Kaly didn't want to hear about Dan in the past tense. But she knew Tommy was right. In the space of a few weeks she'd gained and lost a brother. Pain seized her heart. She'd forgotten how much having family could hurt. "Any signs of life down there?"

"Wish I could say yes. It's a cloud of poisonous smoke. Broken through nearly every bulkhead."

"That smell, what is it?"

They turned. Two men were carrying in a heavy lump of what seemed to be burnt hair. They hunched protectively over the thing, their knees bent. They staggered under its weight. The odor was putrid.

Kaly had to step outside to get a breath, so she wouldn't get sick.

Tommy followed her.

Pulling the scarf off her nose, she doubled it, and tied it back across her nostrils and mouth. "You look like you could use a rest," she told him, wanting to say more. She wanted to say something reassuring, something grateful or kind. She cursed herself for freezing up like this, even now, in the middle of horrific loss and death. As relieved as she was that Tommy was alive, that he was standing here next to her, she couldn't tell him how much he meant to her.

He sat on the ground near a shed to rest a moment, and she went back into the temporary morgue. She heard John identify the lump. It was the severed end of a workhorse. She looked at the undertaker.

"Four of them so far. They had to cut them apart so they'd fit in the cage to lift them out."

It was too much. She wondered if the baby knew where they were and what was going on here. Could the little one sense the disembodied spirits rising through the smoky air? Could the baby sense her father just outside of the morgue? Could she be hurt by actions taken before she was born? Kaly waved the thoughts away as if they were an even worse stench. "Will we bury them?" she asked.

"Probably at the edge of the cemetery."

She cut a large piece of canvas.

"They started the burials today," John said absently. "The paper said twenty-three unidentified men were laid quietly away. It won't be the last of the unidentified. We can't wait for family members to claim them now. The bodies are decomposing too quickly. The danger of disease is too strong."

A rescue squad brought each of the found horses up in five separate pieces. She helped wrap each part carefully, smoothing what was left of the mane or tail, trying to find anything to give dignity to the huge animals. Workers helped pack the horse remains into the dead wagon.

Kaly walked back over to the shed where Tommy sat and slid her back against the wall, sinking down next to him.

A helmet man came to the surface gasping for air. He stumbled and landed right in front of them. His eyes were red, wide, and turned up. The veins of his arms bulged out in rolling blue hills.

"That's the gases," Tommy said, "seeping into the blood through the skin." He jumped up, leaving his jacket on the ground beside her, caught the man, and walked him to the medical station.

When he didn't come back, Kaly returned to the morgue.

"How many mines are closed?" she asked John.

"Most of them, I believe. Once we clean up the accident, operations will start up again. Look at this one." He pointed to the man's throat, where severe gouges laced across each other. "He was gasping for breath. His fingers are stained with blood too."

"Poor man." Kaly knew him. He'd spent an afternoon with her when he did nothing but talk. He'd been caught in a landslide at the Gray Rock and barely made it out alive. He'd said he didn't think he'd go back to mining after that. Now this. She felt bad for him, his luck collapsing two times in a year.

"He was probably trying to move solid rock," John said. "I'd go crazy, trapped like that."

"Me too," she whispered.

The bodies were coming in bloated and disfigured. Even close family members had a difficult time identifying them. They'd run out of caskets. More had been ordered from Spokane. The gates had been opened the previous night for several hours and a long line of people had trailed through the temporary morgue looking for loved ones. Looking for the sad blessing of at least a body to bury. Of knowing with certainty what had happened to their man.

Only one man was identified. John Aeson. Son. Husband. Fine father of two boys. Boys who would probably grow up to be miners.

Kaly was so tired. She wanted to just lie down somewhere safe, to protect her child from the only life she could see spread out before her. Her. She'd always thought of the baby as a girl, and now she fervently hoped the baby was a girl. A girl wouldn't end up dead in the mines. But then again, plenty of things happened to girls, too. She knew plenty of girls and women who'd died under the same conditions Kaly had survived.

Here, now, in this nightmare lodge of the dead, she saw it. With this baby, she had a chance. She didn't know yet what that chance was, but somehow this tiny being had sought refuge in the mess of Kaly's life. Suddenly she didn't want to let either of them down.

"Miners are fatalists by nature," John was saying. "I read that in the paper today too. I think it's true."

"How about undertakers?"

"Naturally, yes, of course."

Michael Jovich and Marko Lailich brought in another man, a large fellow in bib overalls with curly red hair. She looked at his bibs. They had flowers embroidered on the pockets. Most likely a recent transplant from a mine in the east. Poor guy. He was probably teased relentlessly about those overalls, since no Butte miner would dare decorate his bibs.

Moments later they opened the gates to the public. Kaly stood aside and watched while a large woman in a red coat with a long gray braid wailed over the man in the flowered bibs. Finally, the largest of her four children pulled her from the man's body.

"Come on, Mama. We need to prepare the house for his wake. They'll bring him home later. Won't you?" The boy looked at John, who only nodded.

It turned out that Kaly was wrong about the man. He was no transplant. He had come to Butte as a kid and had grown up here.

"I need to take a break," Kaly finally said. The sky was so dark. It had to be past midnight.

"Go ahead, get some food, take a nap. There are some cots over by the ambulances. You might find an empty tent by the train cars. I'll see you when you feel rested." John wiped the soot from under his eyes with a red handkerchief.

"I'll be back. I just need to get my bearings."

"We'll get through this," he assured her. "Don't lose heart."

Kaly ate a sandwich and took a blanket over to the train cars. She slept a deep sleep. She woke to the sound of humming and instantly slipped from the peaceful sleep back into the dread of the mine yard.

Tommy sat nearby. "Hey," he said.

"What are you doing here?"

"Thinking about us."

"That's nice. Not to be trusted, but nice." She wiped the sleep out of her eyes and rose to leave. There was so much work to do she couldn't be distracted by Tommy right now. This conversation, the one she thought he wanted, would hold for another time.

"Wait," he said. "The child is mine. Ours."

She sat back down, feeling the burn of his stare. Her cheeks flushed hot and she dropped her chin, looking at her knees. "Our child," she said with a smile. "You know I don't like to share."

"I've done a lot of things wrong, but a man can change. I laid off the booze and took a good look at my life. I was really scared when you got hurt, scared you wouldn't recover. Then I found out you're pregnant and I'm the father." He took a deep, ragged breath. "I want to do something good. We both know what it's like to grow up without parents. I could be a good dad."

"Tommy, what are you up to?"

"Our child has parents."

"You don't know the first thing about kids. Neither do I. We got no business raising a kid. Besides, you're likely going to war."

"If I go, I'll be back."

"Promises are hard to believe."

"The child could have a good life with us."

The day stretched out before Kaly, endless, shapeless. Her life after today was hidden in a cloud of smoke, impossible to imagine. She couldn't give Tommy anything. She couldn't say yes, maybe, or no. She just couldn't. She stood up, brushed the soot off her dress, and dropped her head in a barely perceptible nod. "For now," she said, "there's work to do."

When she got back to the morgue, Tara McClane was there, talking to John Hurt. So far there'd been no sign of Dan and Kaly felt a surge of compassion for the woman.

"Hello, Mrs. McClane," she said.

"For God's sake, girl, I'm your mother. Call me by my first name, if only for today. This is no time for formalities or distance. We've had enough of them. It's Tara."

Kaly was so stunned, the empathy drained out of her as if through a sieve. She knew all about loss. She didn't need a sudden 'mother' scolding her on the topic. She stormed across the morgue to resume her work.

Mrs. McClane, Tara, surprised her by following her and pitching in. The woman took over Kaly's job of wrapping the men in canvas and helping John pack them into the dead wagon. Kaly directed the helmet men as they put victims on the benches.

Things were moving rapidly now, to stop the spread of disease. The corpses were decomposing much more quickly than normal, due to the extreme heat and gases they'd been exposed to. Serious concerns about public health spurred them on. Now they were fast and efficient.

John was called to the medical area to pronounce a miner who had just died. He'd come out of the fire unscathed, and turned immediately and went back in, as if he'd forgotten something. Or maybe the gas had twisted his thinking and he'd confused the way out. Rescuers went after him, but he'd gone too deep, and by the time they got to him he'd already succumbed to the deadly fumes.

Kaly and Tara followed the undertaker, to help identify the man. His long red hair fell away from his shoulders. Kaly spotted the thick blue scar snaking down his collarbone. She stepped back.

"Do you know this man?" John asked.

Kaly froze. Bert Brown was dead on the bench in front of her. But Kaly was hearing his last heartbeat. She was hearing the howling snowstorm on that long ago day. Bert had Anne Marie pinned to the ground. "No!" Annie was yelling with all her might, tearing at his coat and shirt. He'd put his large hands around her neck and squeezed. Kaly had attacked Bert's back with her fists, screaming for him to get off her sister. She pulled at his collar with all the strength she had, his coat tearing off in her hands. She tossed it into the snow and dug her nails into his face. Annie turned quiet and weak in the snow. Bert turned on Kaly, lifting her with what seemed like superhuman strength and carrying her deep into the woods. The blue scar was on her then and it hurt. By the time it was done hurting, Anne Marie had stopped breathing.

"Do you know this man?" John asked again.

"Yes," Kaly said, her own voice sounding a million miles away. "Bert Brown. He killed my sister." The world around her blurred and warped, turning small and surreal. Even the smoke stopped in midair. Kaly had a sudden urge to step into the pure white flame of the mineshaft. But it was too late for that. The flame had come and done its damage and been contained. "Lord have mercy," she whispered, mimicking the prayer she'd heard at Stojan Lailich's funeral.

Tara stared at her.

Out of the corner of her eye, Kaly thought she saw Bert Brown get up and walk away from himself.

After a moment of silence, Tara retrieved a large piece of canvas from the morgue.

Kaly spotted Nickel Annie at the edge of the yard and motioned her over. "Please," she said. "Go get Miss Anderson. And Beth."

"No," the woman answered and left.

But soon Miss Anderson came and identified her son.

Beth stood beside the matron, one arm wrapped around her shoulder. Long ago Beth had held Kaly's shoulder like that.

"You knew he killed Annie," Kaly said to the matron.

Coral Anderson nodded. "I wasn't certain, but I thought it possible."

"He killed Annie and you protected him."

"He was my son."

"He murdered my sister!"

Coral just stared at Bert, tears streaming down her face, shaking, her hands coiled in front of her. "Whatever he did he's paid for it now."

"After living his life. Annie never got that chance."

"I did the best I could."

Kaly flew at her. Beth stepped between them. "Kaly. Not now."

She turned on Beth. "When then Beth? You tell me."

Beth gathered her in her arms. "Shhh. Not now. We're all hurt. I didn't know. But I loved him. She was his mother. She loved him."

Kaly leaned into Beth and wept. The world had gone so crazy. When did it start? Twenty-seven years ago when she was born.

And before.

She remembered that Coral Anderson was not allowed to hold her son when he was young. She looked over at her and the woman was sobbing and holding him now. Suddenly Kaly's heart broke for all of them, herself, Beth, Miss Anderson, the families, the town. Beth was right. They were all hurt.

When Beth let her go, Tara McClane reached out and took Kaly's hand. Exhausted and numb, the tears drying on her cheek, Kaly went with her mother. The outburst followed her like a ghost. It wasn't over, but it would never be over.

Coral Anderson had guessed that her son had killed Annie and done nothing. But Kaly had guessed exactly the same thing. And done nothing.

She shook her head and tried to let things settle, tried to get her bearings so that the world wouldn't fall down around her. She focused on the good she could do right now, right here, and returned to the makeshift morgue.

Hours later, Kaly and Tara were still hard at work with the undertaker. It seemed as if the stream of corpses was infinite. They would be there forever. John sent them outside for a much-needed break.

"With Danny gone," Tara said as they sat near the ambulances, "I'll need help with the bakery. There's a small apartment upstairs. You and the baby could live there as part of your salary."

Kaly looked at her, surprised and instantly fuming mad. "You don't even atone for your own mistakes, but you want to make an honest woman out of me," she said, her voice falling over the edge again.

"I want to get to know you. From the very first day, I regretted giving you and your sister up for adoption."

"It wasn't adoption! We didn't get adopted." Kaly tugged at the hem of her dress. Why did this woman have to talk about this right now, of all times? Kaly was so tired, so emotionally drained.

"With your father gone I had no way to feed you. I was so afraid you'd end up like them." Mrs. McClane pointed toward the dead wagon.

Kaly stretched her aching neck, holding onto some invisible thread, hoping for a tiny bit of control over something, anything. She held her breath. And let it go.

Tara McClane kept talking. "I hoped you'd be adopted, or that I could return for you. When I married Daniel, I meant to tell him about you and Annie. I just couldn't figure out how. I was so afraid that he'd leave if he knew I'd had children by another man. A man that I'd married in secret. I needed his help to raise Danny so that I didn't lose Danny too. I wanted so badly to tell him but I felt trapped. The more time passed, the more difficult it was to tell him that I had two daughters at the Polly May.

"Then Daniel died in the Leonard Mine accident. I was left alone to raise Danny. I kept thinking that soon the bakery would bring in good money and I'd be able to bring you and Annie home to live with me. But the money never came. Then Annie died. And you were alone.

"My life had gotten away from me. It spiraled out of control. I had to accept it. Now Danny's gone, too. I've lost two children. I refuse to accept any more loss. You're my daughter. Neither you nor God can change that."

Kaly shook her head. The death she'd seen here on the hill was enough to wipe the last sour scrap of anger from her heart. But somehow her bitterness plumed up like the smoke from the mineshaft. The ashes of her life seemed to float in the air. They settled in her hair and on her skin.

They got into her eyes. Life as she'd known it was gone. It had burned up and disintegrated.

How many times had she yearned for a mother? When Anne Marie died. When she lost her job at the cafe and moved in with Beth. When she first learned she was pregnant. For years Kaly had searched the town for faces that resembled hers. Now, here it was, right in front of her. She had a mother. But it was not as sweet or as sad as she'd imagined.

She just couldn't let this woman who'd abandoned them so many years ago take her in. Yet something inside of her was cracking. Kaly tried to ward it off, stuff mud into the bulkhead of it, but the crevice deepened with each word from Tara.

It was too much. Too fast. "I'm going to check on George," she said. "You say he's on the other side of the fence?"

"Yes," Tara replied, a dazed expression on her face.

Kaly found the boy with his back to the fence, hugging his knees to his face, rocking. The wolf dog lay next to him, his long nose pushed under George's knees. "Hey, Georgie, you should go home," Kaly said.

He shook his head. "Is my daddy in there?"

Kaly said nothing.

"That girl said her daddy is in there." He pointed to a girl about his own age who was sitting on the other side of the dog, braiding the animal's tail. "She says a lot of daddies are in there. My daddy could be inside, too."

Kaly knew the girl. Leesy, one of the "L" sisters. Kaly'd visited with her and the other "L" sister over a game of jacks last winter. She nodded to the girl. "Hi, sweetheart."

The girl waved at her.

"I don't know if your dad is in there or not," Kaly told George. "I don't know your father."

"Your mommy's in there," George said.

Kaly nodded.

"She might know Daddy. He's tall with a big belly and a

furry face. He's been gone a long time."

The wolf dog whined under George's knees. He lifted his head and put his long snout in the boy's lap.

George rubbed the dog's ears together.

Kaly didn't know what to say to the boy.

"If we can't find him, will you share your mommy with me?"

Kaly slid her back down the fence and sat beside him. She put her arm around his shoulder and pulled him close. "Sure I will."

"Promise?"

Kaly started to speak and stopped. She didn't know if she'd share the ghostly mother she thought might be out there somewhere waiting for her, or the actual flesh and blood mother who waited for her on the other side of the fence. "I promise I'll share my mom with you. Now you promise me you'll go home and get some sleep. We'll talk about it when you wake up."

"Cause you said if I told the bad dream to go away, it would go away. But it didn't. Now it's dark and people are crying all around me, just like in my dream." George rubbed his eyes. "So, you promise you'll share your mommy with me?"

Kaly remembered George's dream. A man had chased him into a black room and lots of people were lying very still on the ground. "I promise," she told him.

Back in the pine morgue, families combed through the dead, trying to identify what bodies were left.

Tara comforted one distraught woman.

The others comforted each other.

A few hugged tightly to themselves.

John labeled each named man.

Kaly continued identifying the men no one claimed. It was surprising how many she recognized, but didn't know their names. She felt truly sorry for them, being marked "unknown" in large letters across their canvas.

Out on the flats, men were already digging their graves.

Tommy brought in another body so badly bloated identification was impossible.

Tara helped him lay the man on a recently vacated bench.

Kaly watched the two of them as they held the man. The connection leaned toward her like a falling timber. Her baby's father and grandmother working together. After so many years and so much loss, here in this temporary morgue where over a hundred men had already been prepared for the grave, Kaly softened like flame-lashed skin. It hurt, but there was nothing for it. The fire had already reached the bone.

Tommy returned to the shaft.

She helped Tara wrap and pack the bloated body. "The child is his," she said, pointing her chin toward the door where Tommy had just exited.

She said it casually, as if they were not holding a dead man in their arms, and she hoped she hadn't jinxed the baby by talking about her in the presence of the dead. She knew how long a jinx could last.

Tara looked at her, the ghost of another time showing through. "Does he know?" She asked.

Kaly nodded.

"His child. My grandchild."

They helped move the man to the wagon.

Kaly remembered the day the dead wagon came for Anne Marie. The undertaker had wrapped her sister in canvas and placed her on a bench attached to the wagon sidewall and drove off with her, just like that. She remembered the woman veiled in gray, standing at the edge of the crowd at Annie's funeral. Now she knew that woman was her mother.

So much had gone so wrong.

"We've got some live ones!" The shout came from the head frame.

Kaly and Tara rushed from the building to see.

Michael Jovich carried a man in his arms and laid him as gently as a caught bird on the canvas tarp.

Dr. Fletcher immediately began resuscitating him.

Someone moaned from another rescuer's arms.

Several survivors managed to walk, only to collapse onto a cot or tarp or the ground.

"The nipper. He did it. It's because of him we survived. Get the nipper!" One man kept mumbling over and over again, they had to find the nipper. "He led us to a draft, helped us build a bulk head. We stuffed our shirts in the cracks. He kept saying we'd be fine."

Tommy disappeared with Michael and Marko.

Michael and Marko returned, Michael holding a man's arms and Marko holding his feet. The man was out cold.

Marika talked to him. She placed the resuscitator over his mouth.

Kaly was sure they'd lose him.

The girl who looked like her sister, who was her cousin, became very quiet, as though summoning the dead.

Suddenly the man shook, gasped, and heaved a huge breath.

Kaly helped Marika by handing her tools, fetching water, or getting burn salve.

Together they watched for Dan.

The sun was shining, its glare so bright it hurt Kaly's eyes. She couldn't stand any more disappointment. When she was a kid at the Polly May, a couple of times a year parents would come to claim their children. The good luck had never once passed to her. Her eyes adjusted to the sun. There was Tommy, with a man in his arms. The rescued man wore Tommy's oxygen mask. Being in the tunnels without a helmet was taunting death. She knew Tommy had risked his life for the man.

The victim hung limply as Tommy struggled to put him on a cot.

Marika pulled the helmet off, faltered, and put a resuscitator to his mouth. The brief moment between the helmet and the resuscitator had revealed the man's face.

Kaly saw it. Dan. Her Dan! Their Dan! Her brother was alive.

Tara, who had been watching, crumpled at the edge of the medical station.

Kaly went over, pulled the woman up, and walked her to her son.

He was blue and swollen, his cheeks bulging under his eyes. His limp arms flopped over the medical cot.

Marika worked the resuscitator, pumping hard, her muscles flux and smooth. She called to Dr. Fletcher. Together they pumped his heart, cleared his throat, and pumped the precious air for him.

"Keep pressing," the doctor said. "He's got a heartbeat."

"He'll breathe," Marika said.

Several helmet men stared wide-eyed and motionless, waiting.

Even the sun stood still.

"Get a blanket," Dr. Fletcher said to Kaly.

She ran and brought one from an ambulance. Nearby, relatives loaded their loved ones into the ambulances. Kaly put the blanket over Dan's feet and legs.

Marika continued pumping air to him.

Kaly thought of John Hurt's words. "Don't lose heart," he'd said. But she was losing heart. They were losing Dan. They'd found him and they were losing him.

Marika took a deep breath, closed her eyes, and let it go. The wind blew her hair across her face.

Dan shuddered twice, but still didn't breathe.

She glided the resuscitator sides, gentle, smooth angel wings.

Again and again.

Finally the breath caught in Dan's lungs. He coughed. He breathed, once, twice, three times, until he breathed in a sporadic, unnatural rhythm. Then his breath steadied and hummed.

Marika smiled at Kaly. "We've got him back," she said.

Kaly nodded, so grateful that she couldn't speak. She stuffed her words of thanks to this astounding cousin, stuffed them like the miners' shirts in the bulkhead. They would be there, happy and sure. One day Kaly would pull them out and say them.

Dr. Fletcher tugged the blanket up over Dan's chest and prepared him for the ambulance. Once again, they'd done the impossible. They'd pulled a ghost from the tunnels and breathed life into him.

Dan's chest moved up and down. He had a ways to go to a full recovery, but he'd make it.

Marika and Dr. Fletcher transferred him to a gurney. As they lifted him, Dan opened his eyes, turned his head, and closed them again. They put him in the ambulance. Tara McClane climbed into the back with her son.

With Kaly's brother. Brother. She had a brother.

The driver waited while the other ambulances cleared the ground.

Before he hit the siren and headed down the hill, Tara McClane leaned out the back door. "I still need that help at the bakery," she said.

Kaly looked her in the eye. "No secrets," she said.

"No secrets," Tara agreed.

Kaly nodded. She watched the ambulance wail out of sight.

People rejoiced with the news of their recovered loved ones. A slight hope stirred the crowd, lifting their hearts. There might still be others. For the moment at least, some of the grief had stopped.

Tommy sat, winded, near the change building. He held his stomach.

Kaly sat next to him.

He wheezed. He smelled like smoke and gas. Water dripped from his clothes. His boots and pant legs were covered with mud.

"You risked your life for him," she said. "He wouldn't

have had a chance if you hadn't put your oxygen on him."

Tommy shrugged. He rubbed his legs as if they were cramping. "The fire conditions are better," he said. "Now the danger is the flames getting beyond the bulkheads and deep into the mines. The fire at the Minnie Healy has burned underground for eleven years."

"You saved Dan's life."

Tommy only nodded.

"Well, his family is grateful," she said. "Thank you."

A light wind blew through the town, taking the smoke out across the flats to the beautiful mountains. It was peaceful here with Tommy. Feeling tenderness like she'd never known, she caressed his dirty cheek, leaned closer and softly kissed him.

Twenty-five men rose from their graves that day.

Marko Lailich carried a young man, the nipper who'd insisted Dan and the twenty-four other survivors build a bulkhead and stuff it with their shirts. They had survived as he had promised. But he had perished.

John helped Kaly wrap and wagon the young hero. The dead wagon took him home for his wake—one that was sure to be well attended.

Twenty more bodies came in and Marko helped Kaly with them.

The secret of their family scratched at her chest. How would he and Marika react when they learned that her father was their Uncle Vuko?

Later that evening seven more bodies came in.

Kaly and John cleaned them, wrapped them, and put them into the wagon. The undertakers drove them home for their wakes. Finally the building had emptied out.

It was well past midnight when she curled up on her side on a bench, and fell sound asleep. She woke up aching, the new life kicking inside of her. A foot stretched the skin of her belly toward the world. She put her hand over it and it lashed back. "Already a fighter, aren't you?"

she murmured, sitting up straight on the hard wood bench. Her sweater lay crumpled where she'd used it as a pillow. Outside, the sun rose over the East Ridge, its shattered rays beaming through the smoky clouds like broken glass.

Marika sat on a cot near the medical station.

Michael slept on the ground next to her.

Tommy's long body stretched out on the ground on the other side of Michael. Tommy had refused a cot last night, but Marika had insisted he stay nearby in case he suffered ill effects from the gas.

Kaly walked over and sat on the cot next to Marika. She reached out and took her hand. "Thank you," she said.

Marika nodded. "Kaly?"

"Yes?"

"I heard you tell Mrs. McClane no more secrets."

"True," Kaly said. "I'm tired of the hidden world."

"Well, I have a secret that I want to tell you," she paused and took in a breath. "Before Papa died he told my mother that Uncle Vuko was your father." Marika stared at Kaly with soft, questioning eyes. "Making you my cousin. I would have helped you in any case, but I want you to know that we are here. We are family. You and me, Michael, Mama and Marko, we are all here together, for each other."

Shocked, Kaly didn't know what to say. The secret had been held for so long and suddenly everyone knew. More importantly, she'd been alone for so long and suddenly family that claimed her was everywhere. She had wondered how she'd tell Marika and Marko and how they'd react. Well, now she knew. They welcomed her. Or at least Marika did.

"Thank you." She said. And that felt right.

Tommy woke up and rubbed his eyes. Marika nodded to her to go to him.

Kaly sat on a bench next to Tommy. "How do you feel?" She asked.

"Like I'm living in a bucket of tar. Moving is painful."

He wiped the sleep from his eyes. "You're up early. John set you free?"

"A few bodies came in during the night, but it's finally slowed down."

"Have you thought about what I said? I want to marry you."

"I did think about it, but I'm scared Tommy. You'll be going to war."

"If I go, I'll be so careful over there. I'll think of you and the baby every minute I'm gone."

"I want you to feel something." She took his hand and put it on her stomach. She placed her palm over the back of his hand, held her breath and waited. Within a minute she felt the tiny hiccup.

He smiled. "I'll be back," he said. "A kid needs a dad. I'll send money. We can be good for each other."

"Name one time."

"The future."

She laughed at that, a good laugh.

"You did kiss me."

"More than that, evidently," she said patting her very large belly. "The future looks good to me."

"Together, you and me, and that little guy?"

She nodded, smiling. "Only one thing."

He looked at her quizzically.

"This little guy? Is a girl."

Kaly walked back toward the morgue. Helmet men slept next to a lone ambulance. The small tents had turned black from the sooty smoke. Black grime also covered the southern storage shed, the change house, and the changed ground of the North Butte Mine Workings of the Speculator and Granite Mountain mine shafts.

Many of the men who were on shift that night had been found. Smoke was still pluming out of the mineshaft. Kaly watched it lift and settle. It seemed as natural as changing weather, as if fire itself belonged to the town.

During the past few months, Kaly had lost a lot—but she had also gained. She wasn't sure which was more dangerous.

Near the fence she took the tansy-and-arsenic mixture out of her pocket. Slowly she removed the lid and poured the potion into the soot. It soaked the ground and disappeared. She breathed in the dark, smoky air of her town.

It was as good as courage.

George would be waiting for her. He'd be sleeping with his head resting on the dog's belly. She'd made him promise to go home. He'd promised. But she knew he'd stay. She peeked through a hole in the fence. Sure enough, there he was lying on the ground, his front pasted to the dog's back.

She'd made the boy a promise too. And she would keep it. She'd share her mother with him.

They'd go back to the Polly May and sleep, but he couldn't stay there. Children would only be safe at that house with another adult supervising both the children and the matron. Lord knew how Coral Anderson would resist some form of supervision. But Kaly promised herself that she'd make sure it happened.

Later in the day, she and George would go see Dan at the hospital. Tara would be there. Tommy would also be there, or somewhere. They'd find him and spend part of the day with him. Later, she'd visit Mrs. Lailich, her aunt, and maybe her cousins.

In the mine yard the morning whistle blew and people stirred. A warm breeze caressed her cheek and she felt, more than heard, Anne Marie's good-bye. She smiled and nodded. "Take care my sister," she said. She walked into the morgue, picked up her sweater and put it on. In the mining town's fractured light, she made her way through the rubble. It was time for her to go home.

1895
AS SPIRITS SOAR

The bitter cold has gone. The snow has melted and the ground has thawed. Down on the Flats, under the morning sun, a gravedigger shovels dirt aside. The old-time miner will at last be laid to rest. The white dog will likely be buried at the edge of the cemetery with the other animals.

Free of his earthly body, the miner watches the dog wander one last time to the big house where the look-alike girls curl up together under a heavy quilt. The new boy, down the hall, has stopped crying. A mine-whistle sounds and the children rise to eat breakfast. The morning's north wind fans the smelting dust out over the Highlands. The sky turns a brilliant blue.

After breakfast, the look-alike girls run through the backyard holding hands, laughing. They roll down the hill to a large tree in a forest that has somehow survived the poisoned air. The new boy stands in the doorway, turned in their direction. The dog walks over to him and nuzzles his hand toward the girls. The boy waves, calls out, and runs to join them. Together they walk up the hill toward the head frames, to the candy shop where they'll spend their saved pennies. The dark-haired girl walks close to the new boy. The light girl lags behind. The boy stops several times and waits for her, watching over the girls as if they are precious stones.

The dog leaves the girls to their protector, and trots up the street to the Goldmine Café. No one puts a steak bone or a muffin out for him. No one runs fingers through his fur, or pets his soft ears. He's immaterial. He's an errant shadow from the warehouse fire. The streets are clean again after the explosion, and the dog wanders freely through the people that crowd them. Off-shift miners stroll toward home. Young mothers, children in tow, shop for new dresses or a game of marbles for the kids.

The youngsters of Butte hop on trolley cars or catch a ride to the Flats. Laughter sounds through the open door of a tavern. The smell of popcorn wafts out from the hardware store. The sun is bright, the money good, and once again the city is alight in wild joy.

On the Flats the gravedigger has eaten his lunch of corned beef and cabbage. He starts the last job—replacing the dirt over the caskets.

The old-time miner and the white dog soar above the Copper Camp now, to the rock outcropping of the East Ridge. Here the miner sits a while, rubbing the dog's ears. He looks down on the packed houses hugging the hill, the dozens of black metal head frames. He looks down on the land where William Clark will one day build a massive amusement park complete with pansy gardens in the shape of huge butterflies. He sees the lake where two ladies of the line will canoe past a trumpeter swan and her tiny cygnets.

It's love he feels, love and gratitude for the Copper Camp. For a life filled with dark blessings.

He says his happy good-bye. The city fades and disappears.

He and the white dog follow a silver thread to a new city of shining streets, where the moon glows bright and the sky waves out a blue welcome. The streets are alive with vibrant colors: trees with leaves that turn crimson red in the fall; grass that grows into a thick green cushion; lilacs that bloom. In the new city, gold flows above ground, out of ruby streams. The place smells like rose water and lavender. It tastes good, like pasties, polenta, spaghetti, and spring rolls. The old-time miner and the white dog settle into the new city like copper angels, free and beautiful, stripped from the rich mountain vein of another world.

AUTHOR'S NOTE

The warehouse fire of 1895 and the Speculator Mine Disaster of 1917 are real Butte tragedies. At least 51 people died in the warehouse fire and 168 men died in the Speculator Mine Disaster. *Copper Sky* is a work of fiction and I have taken great liberties with the events, the town, and Butte's history. Any mistakes in fact or representation are entirely my own. All characters are figments of my imagination and are not meant to portray any actual persons, alive or dead.

ACKNOWLEDGEMENTS

I would like to thank my editors and publishers at Open Books, Kelly Huddleston and David Ross for their support and their belief in *Copper Sky*. They took a chance on me and I'm glad that they did. A huge thank you to Maggie Plummer for her brilliant editing. She helped me find the heart of this story. Thank you to Christine Dodson Kearney for reading an early version of this novel and loving it, and for her absolute faith in my writing from the beginning.

Many, many thanks to Phyllis Walker and the Wild Horse Writer's Group, to the University of Montana creative writing programs, especially Debra Magpie Earling and Phil Condon, and to all of the early readers of *Copper Sky* who offered comments that helped shape this story: Cindy Williams, Judith Bromley, Tom and Jennifer Groneberg, David Bolinger, Mac Swan, Mary O'Brien, Jim Vogele, Jyoti SaeUn, Kathy Shore, Cheryl Agan, Kari Marsenich and James Buchanan. Thank you to Greg Leichner for so many good talks about writing and life over the years.

I am eternally grateful to Mary Gertson for her amazing

support, and to Jyoti SaeUn for teaching me her "cloud-clearing" method. Thank you to Leslie Nyman for offering a flexible work schedule, with time to write. Thank you to Sid Gustafson for his kindness and for taking calls from a stranger, and to Leslie Budewitz and Don Beans for their advice, encouragement, and inspiration. Thank you to Ellen Crain and the Butte Archives.

All my Butte stories begin with my family and early friends. They shaped my life, my language and my stories. They taught me to love. To them I am forever grateful: My parents, Milan and Frances Marsenich; my brothers and their wives, Ed and Roxanne Marsenich, Bob Marsenich and Karen McMullen, Mark Marsenich, Dorie Riordan; my earliest friends, Carol Carreau, Marty Phillips, Cheryl Agan, Shirley Johnson, and Terri Smith.

A giant thank you to the people of Butte for their beautiful and generous hearts. Without them, this story would not have been possible.

Milana Marsenich

Made in the USA
San Bernardino, CA
08 July 2017